"If you are hungry for a great police procedural, look no further. Cannell knows what he's doing…this mystery works on every level."
—*Tulsa World*

"An intriguing, torn-from-today's-headlines premise on his fifth Shane Scully outing."
—*News Press* (Fort Myers, FL)

VERTICAL COFFIN

"Readers will enjoy watching [Scully] puzzle out the twists and turns of the plot and watch breathlessly as he undertakes a climactic high-speed chase."
—*Publishers Weekly*

"Cannell certainly knows how to tell a story…You'll probably read the entire book with a smile on your face."
—*Cleveland Plain Dealer*

HOLLYWOOD TOUGH

"Cannell, creator of such TV shows as *The A-Team*, clearly knows the ins and outs of the entertainment industry, and the detective story, with its wry, subtle humor, doubles as Hollywood satire…the cops-and-robbers sequences hit the mark as well. Well-drawn characters and keen observations on the similarities between Hollywood and the mafia make this a winner."
—*Publishers Weekly*

"Scully has ample opportunity to prove how 'Hollywood tough' he is...veteran writer/TV producer Cannell has concocted his special brand of reader candy."

—*Kirkus Reviews*

RUNAWAY HEART

"A cop thriller with a futuristic, sci-fi twist...Cannell has a genius for creating memorable characters and quirky, gripping plots...this is a fun read."

—*Publishers Weekly*

THE VIKING FUNERAL

"Stephen J. Cannell is an accomplished novelist."

—*New York Daily News*

"Stephen J. Cannell's *The Viking Funeral* is the sort of fast and furious read you might expect from one of television's most successful and inventive writer-producers."

—*Los Angeles Times*

"Solid plotting with nail-biting suspense and multiple surprises keep the reader guessing and sweating right up to the cinematic ending...Cannell has a knack for characterization and a bent for drama that will satisfy even the most jaded thrill lover."

—*Publishers Weekly*

THE TIN COLLECTORS

"I've been a Stephen Cannell fan since his remarkable *King Con*, and he keeps getting better. *The Tin Collectors* is an LAPD story that possesses both heart and soul; a fresh and different look at the men and women who, even more than the NYPD, are the most media-covered police force in the world. Stephen Cannell has the screenwriter's fine ear for dialogue and great sense of timing and pacing as well as the novelist's gift of substance and subtlety. Cannell likes to write, and it shows."   —Nelson DeMille

"Cannell turns out another winding, suspenseful thriller."   —*New York Daily News*

"Readers who enjoy cop novels by Robert Daley or William Caunitz will find Cannell right up their dark, dangerous alley."   —*Booklist*

"Cannell has created a reputation for top-rate suspense in four novels...his latest, *The Tin Collectors*, is his best...Cannell...knows how to tell a good story."
                                     —*Wisconsin State Journal*

"Cannell conjures up images of McBain, Wambaugh, and Heller; only tougher, grittier, more underhanded, with plenty of street-smart savvy, and a frightening and wholly believable plot and characters...crackles with high energy and suspense...Cannell is in top form."   —*Charleston Post & Courier*

St. Martin's Paperbacks Titles by STEPHEN J. CANNELL

Three Shirt Deal

Stephen J. Cannell

St. Martin's Paperbacks

THREE SHIRT DEAL

Copyright © 2008 by Stephen J. Cannell.
Excerpt from *On the Grind* copyright © 2008 by Stephen J. Cannell.

Cover photograph © Amanda Friedman / Getty Images

For information address St. Martin's Press, 175 Fifth Avenue, New York, NY 10010.

Library of Congress Catalog Card Number: 2007039413

ISBN: 0-312-94531-0
EAN: 978-0-312-94531-2

Printed in the United States of America

St. Martin's Press hardcover edition / January 2008
St. Martin's Paperbacks edition / November 2008

St. Martin's Paperbacks are published by St. Martin's Press, 175 Fifth Avenue, New York, NY 10010.

10 9 8 7 6 5 4 3 2 1

This one's for my two girls.

Tawnia, you always see the truth and show me how to succeed with grace. You have enriched my life in so many untold ways.

Chelsea, you put a smile on my face, keep me young, and with your generosity show me how to be a better friend.

No father has ever had two more beautiful daughters. I love you guys.

CHAPTER 1

"How do you feel about that?" Dr. Lusk asked.

"I don't feel much of anything about it," I answered, dodging the question.

"Detective Scully, I won't be able to help you if you keep putting up barriers, shielding me from your feelings and emotions."

"It's her car, okay? What happens to it is kinda her business, not mine. I was just saying it seemed odd."

"So you booked an appointment through the psychiatric support group and drove all the way over here from Parker Center on your lunch hour, but you don't have any feelings about the accident? It just seems odd to you and that's it?"

"I'm concerned, okay?"

"Concern is an intellectual response. Your wife crashes her car, doesn't tell you about it, drains your bank account to get it fixed on the sly instead of putting it through the insurance, then rents a duplicate car to hide it from you. But despite all this, you have no anger, no sense of frustration or betrayal. You have concern."

"Yeah."

I was thirty minutes into the forty-minute "hour." Dr. Eric Lusk leaned back in a beige, leather wing chair, peering over tiny half-glasses, his huge Buddha belly, and ten feet of tan Berber. I was in a matching chair opposite him, trapped in a colorless cocoon, trying to affect nonchalance. My body wouldn't cooperate. Angst smoldered. Telltale emotional exhaust leaked out of me. I crossed my legs, and then uncrossed them while nondescript music oozed from ceiling speakers at subhuman volume.

"Let's talk about the meds you found yesterday."

"I found them in her purse. She'd peeled the label off the bottle so I wouldn't know the doctor or what they were for. I had the police lab identify them. The results came back this morning. Carbamazepine and sodium valproate."

"Do you know what those are commonly prescribed for?"

"According to the lab, they're for seizures."

He nodded. "Has your wife been having seizures?"

"I don't know. I haven't seen one, but if Alexa was taking this stuff, maybe. She stopped driving her car last week. She gets picked up and brought home by a department driver now. I was hoping she'd tell me on her own what's going on. So far she hasn't."

"Your wife was abducted last July and suffered a gunshot wound to the head resulting in a severe traumatic brain injury. That was less than eleven months ago. TBI seizures often crop up months afterward and can continue for years. And you say she's already back at work?"

"She had a lot of stuff pending. It's a big job. She supervises two hundred people."

"Chief of the Detective's Bureau at the LAPD."

"Yes."

"Pretty high stress."

"Yep."

"Who, if I might ask, approved her to return to duty?"

"Alexa went through a battery of physical and psychiatric tests at the Police Academy a month ago. She went to the union. They took up her case and she requalified and was marked fit for duty."

"But you don't think she is."

I wasn't about to answer that one.

We sat back and looked at each other. Dr. Lusk slouched in the heavy chair, his huge gut pushing up on his diaphragm, causing him difficulty breathing. His slick complexion shone white as a fish belly. I wondered why I booked this damn appointment and drove all the way over here.

"I'm not a neurologist, Detective Scully, I'm a psychologist. But I *have* studied the brain. According to what you told me, your wife Alexa's TBI affected the frontal and temporal lobes. We generally associate behavioral disorders with injuries to the frontal lobe. That's the emotional and personality control center. Damage in that area can diminish judgment. It can also cause trouble with concentration and thought organization. Sometimes it leads to an array of more serious behavioral problems such as inappropriate statements, or impulsive or inappropriate actions: social as well as sexual."

"I see."

"Do you?"

"I'm living with her. Kinda hard to miss stuff like that." Now he was pissing me off.

"So what specific kinds of changes have you witnessed?"

"She used to be organized. Careful and specific. Now she's all over the place. It's causing her problems at the department. She's never been wild or unpredictable before. She knows the ropes and plays by the rules. Alexa is brave and has risked her life in the field many times, but as far as department politics, she's always been a team player. Now she doesn't seem to have any early alert warning system. She just does stuff on impulse without regard to consequence. It's getting her into a pile of trouble with Chief Filosiani."

He nodded and then, without warning, asked, "Has your sex life been affected in any way?"

That was a big one. We'd only made love two or three times since she came home from the hospital six months ago. At first I'd thought it was just her headaches and the after-effects of her injury. But now it had become a pattern. We used to make love regularly, but now almost never. I didn't say any of this, afraid to answer. Afraid of what he might tell me. Awkward silence filled the space between us.

"Why did you make this appointment if you won't discuss any of this with me?" he said.

"I think this was a mistake." I looked at my watch and saw him smile slightly, as if my little peek down at the dial was a confirmation of some secret diagnosis he'd already put on me.

"From the little you've said I can't help you much. Maybe your wife shouldn't have gone back on the job so soon. If you could get her to stay home, it might lower her stress level and her symptoms might subside. People with brain injuries are often in a race to get back to normality. They want their old life back. They want it to be the way it was before the injury. By putting everything back the way it was, they think they can accomplish this. They can't."

"I see."

"No, you don't. But that's okay."

"Whatta you mean I don't? Where do you get off saying that?"

"Detective Scully, you don't want to be here. I've

seen guys in the electric chair look more relaxed. The very thought that your wife is having seizures, crashing the car, and whatever else, is abhorrent to you. It threatens your existence. You don't want to focus on it."

"Then why am I here?"

"Because it's become unbearable. Your wife has changed. She's become reckless and unpredictable. That behavior was previously reserved for you. Now you're experiencing a major role-reversal in your marriage. It's suddenly become your job to contain her mistakes instead of vice versa. You don't like it. It's limiting the way you behave, impinging on your own sense of self."

"You got all that in just thirty-five minutes? Not bad." Trying to back him off, because he'd pretty much just nailed it.

"You know that you both need help. She won't come in and talk to me, so you did. You're looking for a quick fix, but I can't possibly treat your wife through you."

"I see."

"You keep saying that. Pardon my bluntness, but you don't see. You don't want to. At least not yet. You're in denial."

We stared at each other, locked in his beige-on-beige, forty-minute time capsule.

"Will she get better?" I finally asked.

"Recovery from traumatic or acquired brain injury can take years. A patient will sometimes experience mood changes, major shifts in behavior parameters, even temper control problems. Sometimes these changes will only be temporary and the patient will return to normal, other times not. I'd have to have many sessions with your wife to determine what, if any, of these things are present and how permanent they might become. The meds you found in her purse indicate she's having seizures. Maybe that's what caused the traffic accident."

"She won't book an appointment with a psychiatrist. She has a neurosurgeon in Westwood, Luther Lexington. He did her surgeries and he recommended a psychiatrist last summer. She only went to that doctor once and never went back."

"A mistake."

"You don't understand. She's running one of the highest-profile bureaus in the city. If it gets out she's going to a shrink or having seizures, crashing her car, or whatever, it's going to destroy her career."

"I'm hesitant to make a diagnosis not having seen the patient. But I will tell you this much. I don't like what I'm hearing. If I were you, I would get her help regardless of the danger to her career."

I looked at my watch again.

"If you have someplace to go, don't let me keep you." Somehow he managed the sentence without sounding snotty.

"I'd have been better off going to McDonald's. At least I would have gotten lunch."

"Then I won't charge you for the hour."

"No. I want to pay. I want . . . I want to come back next week."

"Why?"

"I don't know."

"Same time, same place?"

"Okay."

I stood, accidentally hitting the little table with a Kleenex box next to the chair and tipping it over. Another slight smile. I righted the table and replaced the tissue box.

"Well, I guess that does it then," I said.

"That does it," he replied, wheezing it at me through tiny teeth buried in a fleshy smile. His chubby hands were laced across his belly. He had no intention of standing to see me out.

I turned and walked to the door.

"Detective?" I stopped and looked back at him. "People change. Even people who didn't get shot in the head. Change is an inevitable part of life. Sometimes by embracing change, it becomes less frightening and we open ourselves to the good that may be hiding there."

"I see."

The smile flickered again. Then he said, "Here's something you can do. Keep a diary. Everything that she does that bothers you, write it down. To be valuable, it should be mostly about what *you* feel."

"Okay."

"Next week, then."

It was the first day of summer, but I stepped outside into an unseasonable Alaskan cold front, which had roared out of the north, blasting Los Angeles. A frigid wind whipped down the mountain passes, into the Valley. Even though it was June, it felt like November. The palm trees that lined Van Nuys Boulevard creaked and bent, swaying like gaunt old men in the brisk wind, leaning over to peer down as I wandered in confusion toward my car.

CHAPTER 2

I drove to my assigned parking space on the third underground level of the Police Administration Building at Parker Center. When I arrived, there was a black-and-white "shop" parked in my spot. "Shop" was cop terminology for a patrol car. This one was a slick-back with no light bar, and I could tell from the "00" city tag number that it was a detective car from Internal Affairs. The Professional Standards Bureau is located in the Bradbury Building, five blocks over on Broadway. When I.A. dicks come to the Glass House on business, they tend to poach our parking spaces. After all, who in their right mind is going to have an Internal Affairs car towed? But today, I was in no mood for some iron-ass from the rat squad. I decided to park directly behind this rude bastard and lock my car, forcing him to come looking for me. Then I would set him straight on PAB parking etiquette. I pulled in, blocking the vehicle.

Just as I was getting out of my car, a woman's voice said, "Detective Shane Scully?"

I turned and saw an extremely attractive, raven-haired lady in a tan pantsuit, carrying a briefcase. She looked Hispanic, early thirties, nice shape.

"Is this your slick-back?" I asked, nowhere near as

annoyed now as I was a second before, beauty trumping anger. "Can't you read my name on the sign?"

"I parked it there because I wanted to talk to you and I didn't know what you looked like. I'm Secada Llevar." She smiled and handed me her card. D-III Investigating Officer with Professional Standards.

"Don't tell me I'm in trouble over at PSB again."

"Not that I know of."

"There's a first."

"I need to talk to you. I didn't want to do it upstairs. You mind if we go get a bite? I haven't had lunch."

I studied her for a moment. Her demeanor said she was used to getting her way. I reasoned this was partly because she knew she was hot looking, and partly because she had natural self-confidence. Whatever it was, it was working.

"Get in. I haven't eaten either. We'll leave your shop where it is."

She settled into the front seat of my Acura MDX and I headed up the garage ramp. Her perfume immediately filled the car with a lavender scent. Or maybe it was peach. Whatever it was, she smelled great.

We picked an Italian place called Leonardo's, two blocks from the Glass House. The joint was *Godfather* corny with plastic checkered tablecloths and wine jugs hanging in nets from the rafters. The pungent smell of garlic clung to the walls. We took a booth in the back and ordered. Lasagna for her, pizza for me. After the waiter left, I faced her with my dumb, hard look in place. Whatever Secada Llevar wanted, I was determined to fend her off.

"I'm sorry I took your parking space. Seemed easier than going upstairs and asking around."

"What's on your mind, Detective Llevar?"

"Call me 'Scout'; everybody does."

"What's on your mind?"

"I'm having a little problem and I thought maybe you could help me."

I didn't respond. Experience has taught me that dealing with I.A., at best, is never much fun. If she was having a "little problem" and managed to lay it off on me, then I was going to end up hosting a disaster.

"I got a letter from Corcoran State Prison two days ago," she began. "It was sent to me by an inmate named Truit Hickman who's doing life for Murder One. Tru is twenty-five and a crank addict. He pleaded guilty to killing his mother, Olivia Hickman, a little less than a year ago. The police report states he got into an argument with his mom over two hundred dollars she apparently had in her purse and wouldn't give him. She had just cashed her paycheck from a part-time job as a checker at a Vons Supermarket. The detective report speculates her son wanted the money to do crystal meth."

"I've only got about twenty minutes. Is this going to be a really long story?"

"I'll go fast," she said. "According to neighbors, Tru and his mother hadn't been getting along for years. The police report says when she wouldn't give him the cash in her purse he waited that night for her to come home and stabbed her to death with a kitchen knife. Then he took the money and ran. According to the primary detective's notes and the confession he eventually signed, Tru woke up from a drug haze the next morning in some alley, realized what he'd done, and came up with a revised plan. He knew he'd be the prime suspect in his mom's murder, so he returned home and pretended to find the body. Then he called nine-one-one. His original story was he'd been at a party, got tweaked on meth and can't remember who was there, stumbled out to the alley and passed out. So basically he had no alibi. Later, in the I-room at Van Nuys Station, they threatened him with a premeditated, lying in wait murder for financial gain. A death penalty case. Under the threat of going down for capital murder, he changed his story, copped to a straight first degree homicide, and took a jolt for twenty-five to life. That was last August. Because of prison overcrowding, he was in the inmate classification center for seven months. They should have assigned him to a Level One minimum support unit because he's basically a brain-dead tweaker with no prior violent crimes, but somehow, he got a classification score above fifty-two. The poor schlub ends up being sent to Corcoran and placed in Level Four with a bunch of hardcore assassins. It's a rough car, full of gang killers." A car was what inmates called a housing unit.

"That was over two months ago. He now says the confession was coerced, that he didn't do it."

"Try singing that to 'Over the Rainbow.' It won't change the outcome, but it might sound a little better."

She ignored me and said, "You know Internal Affairs is tasked with checking up on incomplete or inadequate investigations. If we get a complaint alleging any problems with due process, it's our job to check it out. I got this one."

"Sounds like fun." I had no idea where she was going, and certainly didn't want to find out.

"Actually, it hasn't been fun at all." She pulled a stack of photocopied arrest and police reports out of her briefcase and started to push them toward me.

"Don't give that stuff to me. I don't want anything to do with this."

"Just listen then."

I made my face look disinterested and dull, something I'm uncommonly good at.

"The primary investigator on the case is a lieutenant named Brian Devine. As it turns out, Lieutenant Devine has an I.A. record of borderline brutality cases going back fifteen years. It's a thick folder. He's been in all the high testosterone units: SIS; SWAT. Suffice it to say, the lieutenant's a cowboy. Now he heads the Van Nuys Division Homicide Squad. How dirtbags like him make supervisor baffles me."

"If he's the head of Van Nuys Homicide, he should be behind a desk. What's he doing in the field running a murder case?"

"You're right. As a supervisor he normally wouldn't take on a homicide investigation. But his story is he was a block away from the house when Tru Hickman phoned nine-one-one. So he rogers the call and shows up as the primary on Olivia Hickman's one-eighty-seven. After they take this kid in and sweat him, they put him on the Box and, according to Lieutenant Devine, he tanks the polygraph. There's a bloody shoe print at the scene, same size and shape as Tru's boots, and Lieutenant Devine's initial report speculates that Tru made the print. Stepped in his mother's blood while in the act of killing her. Under all this bad news, the kid panics. He's got a laundry list of old drug busts, a deceptive poly, and no alibi. He knows nobody will believe him and he's headed to death row, so in less than forty-eight hours, he accepts a plea."

"This is fascinating, but it's still no excuse for leaving your car in my assigned parking spot."

She smiled. Her teeth were pearl white against almond skin. Secada "Scout" Llevar was a stunner. That smile brought her another few minutes of this nonsense.

"It gets better. Tru Hickman has this Hispanic friend,

Miguel Iglesia. Miguel has anglicized his name. He's Mike Church now. Iglesia means 'church' in Spanish."

"Okay."

"Church is your basic, gang-affiliated, West Valley gorilla. All through high school he ran with the VSLs—the Vanowen Street Locos, a bad Valley gang. He's been banging since he was fifteen and now he's one of their most feared veteranos. Tru Hickman and Mike Church met in tenth grade when both were doing juvie time in the sheriff's Honor Rancho. They're an unlikely pair. Hickman was in for gas-bagging crystal and selling it around school. Church was doing a stretch for agg-assault and attempted murder. They're from opposite ends of the food chain so it's a little strange these guys hang together at all. Church is a shark. Hickman's bait. In his initial police statement, Hickman said Mike Church came over to his house the day of the murder and got into an argument with his mom. They screamed at each other. Mrs. Hickman didn't like Mike Church because she correctly thought he was a bad influence on her son. Tru told the lieutenant about Church being at the house and screaming at his mother. Before he confessed, Tru said he thought maybe Church was the doer. Lieutenant Devine went out and had a talk with Church about this, and guess what?"

"He has an alibi."

"Nope. He's got deep knife cuts all over his palms and fingers. The kind you'd get if you stabbed someone using a kitchen knife with no scabbard and your hands slip down on the blade during the attack. Church explains the cuts by saying that he got into a knife fight in a bar, but doesn't know the guy who cut him."

"That makes Mike Church the new prime suspect. So why is Tru Hickman the one doing Level Four time?"

"Because Lieutenant Devine turned Church loose.

He was so sure Tru killed his mother he never went any further with it. The investigators speculated that Truit laid in wait and killed her for the two hundred dollars to buy meth. The lying in wait and killing for financial gain aspects allowed the D.A. to kick it up to a Special Circumstances death penalty case. It looks to me as if Lieutenant Devine didn't want to muck up his slam-dunk murder with another suspect, even one who'd had a recent argument with the vic and had knife cuts on his hands. Classic target fixation."

Our food came and we started digging in.

"Anyway, I got the letter from Corcoran two days ago, and got permission to work it from Captain Sasso."

"You report directly to Jane Sasso?"

"Yeah. You know her?"

"She's so driven, can anybody really know her?"

Scout didn't answer, but something shifted behind her eyes. I'd struck a nerve. Captain Jane Sasso had been appointed by my wife, Alexa, to head the Internal Affairs unit. She was a notorious department hard-ass. After a moment Scout nodded, went on. "I ran Tru Hickman's yellow sheet. This kid is such a loser, he couldn't find the ceiling if he was on his back looking through binoculars. I called him on the phone up at Corcoran and he says he didn't do it. He doesn't understand how he could have flunked the lie detector test. He says that bad poly was the main reason he pled out, but he says nobody ever showed him the test. He never really had a lawyer. The P.D. who got the case met him once or twice for an hour and cut a deal to drop the special circumstances. The straight Murder One plea was accepted by the D.A. and the whole mess cleared the system by the end of the month."

"This is great pizza," I said. "How's the lasagna?"

She frowned at me. "I've been looking into the case with Captain Sasso's tacit permission for the last two days. She's not too big on these bad due-process things. But the more I checked, the more it seems that what Tru claims in his letter is more or less accurate. They sure didn't look at Mike Church very hard. Lieutenant Devine got a quick confession from a confused guy who'd cooked off too many brain cells doing glass. But now that Tru's had a chance to think about it, he says he was framed."

"Show him the poly."

"Can't."

"Why not?"

"It's missing."

"Happens."

"Also, I can't find any lab work matching the photo of the bloody shoe print to Tru Hickman's boots. I don't think they ever finished that part of the investigation. After Tru confessed, they just never sent it through for a match."

"That can also happen."

She wrinkled her nose. She was getting frustrated with me. "Mike Church has a long and prolific criminal VSL gang history that includes multiple aggravated assaults and multiple attempted homicides. Lame as his story is, I don't think Tru Hickman premeditated his mom's murder, or killed her for two hundred dollars to buy drugs."

"Why not?"

"When I talked to him yesterday, I got the impression that Tru couldn't premeditate a decent bowel movement. He's in a perennial daze. A loser with a capital L."

I finished my pizza, pushed the plate away. "Why are we talking about this? It doesn't concern me."

"Yesterday, I take my doubts to Captain Sasso. I tell her I think there's enough here to put a new homicide number on it and reopen the case."

"Good. Way to go." I took out my wallet. "I gotta get back. Let's dutch the bill."

"Sasso took the case away from me. Told me it was closed."

I shrugged. "She's a captain."

"What does that mean?"

"Captains get to tell detectives what to do," Secada deadpanned me. "Don't take my word on that. If you don't believe me, look it up in your manual."

She gave that a frustrated shake of her head, then plunged on. "I had already filed a request for a duplicate photo of the bloody shoe print to get the lab work done. I went to pick it up, just to add it to the IO file before I sent it down to records. Then, at end of watch last night, I get called into Captain Sasso's office. It's a regular sixth-floor ambush. There's a commander named Summers, in there along with Deputy Chief Frank Townsend, from operations. They found out I'd been down to pick up the photo after Sasso told me to drop the case. All three of them start bitching me out. 'Why didn't I do what I was told to?' 'Don't I know how to take a direct order?' I try and explain that I was just gathering up loose ends, but they won't listen. They start threatening my career. 'Keep this up and you'll be back on traffic detail.' That kinda thing."

"So now, in a gesture of friendship, you want to give this glowing red ball to me, is that it?"

"Shane . . . can I call you Shane?"

"No."

"This is a bad investigation. Shit is missing from the file. The right moves weren't made. When I start looking into this, which is my fucking job, I get hijacked by sixth-floor brass and told to drop it immediately or my career goes in the bag. A slight overreaction if you ask me, which makes me wonder what the hell is really going on here."

"I'm not taking this case!"

"This kid is scared out of his skull. How the hell CDC qualified him for Level Four is a mystery. Somebody's got it in for him. They have him housed with hardened gang killers, for God's sake. I was going to drive up there tomorrow, but after that meeting in Sasso's office I don't think that's a good plan anymore."

"Are you through eating? I really need to get back."

"Listen, Scully. Listen to me."

"What?"

"This is wrong, okay? It's wrong. I've read about you. I've heard the stories, how you make your own way around here. You aren't afraid of these sixth-floor guys. You've got *cojones,* homes."

"Aaawwww, come on. Stop it."

"Look, I'll work it with you. On the sly. Okay? After hours. This has my Latina blood boiling. I'll risk it if you will. You're the only one who can help me."

"Yeah? Why's that? And no bullshit about my *cojones* this time."

She took a moment and then leaned forward and lowered her voice. "Your wife is the head of the Detective Bureau. She's tough and smart. If she can cover us, I know we can find out what's really going on. With Sasso on the warpath, we're gonna need her help if we want to survive."

CHAPTER 3

What kind of dumb-ass reputation did I have around here anyway? Was I just the guy you bring your shit flambé to? The guy everybody knows is willing to run headlong into a threshing machine? I'm supposed to be this dumb-as-dirt kamikaze who'll ignore a direct order from Captain Jane Sasso, the bitch queen of Internal Affairs? Not to mention Keith Summers and Deputy Chief Townsend. I'm supposed to go sailing straight into that trifecta of perfect assholes without any regard for my career or pension? What do these people take me for?

That being the case, what the hell was I doing riding up in the Parker Center elevator with this damn Hickman file under my arm? Why did I agree to take it from Scout Llevar in the PAB garage? What the hell was I thinking?

What I was thinking, I guess, was that Lt. Brian Devine had some serious Scully payback coming. I owed him from fifteen years ago when I was working Valley Patrol, riding in an X-car with Zack Farrell. Back then, Brian Devine was assigned to the Special Investigation Service. SIS had a reputation on the job, and in the press, as being little more than an assassination squad. Their beat was predicate felons—criminals who were unredeemable repeaters.

The unit employed a murderous methodology. They would wait for some hard case to get out of prison and then follow him around while he bought a new gun, or hooked up with his old ex-con buddies. All crimes worthy of a parole violation. But SIS wouldn't P.V. the guy on any of that low-weight stuff. Instead, they'd wait until he and his crew held up a bank or a liquor store. Then they'd swarm in and initiate a shootout, killing everybody. The operative theory being that a dead asshole can't beat the system on a technicality. SIS got a lot of bad press, but also took out a lot of bad guys. Subsequently, the unit was reorganized.

In those days, before Alexa and my son, Chooch, came into my life and gave me a reason to live, I was drunk on the job most of the time, depressed and cynical. My partner, Zack Farrell, had mother-henned me through each watch, keeping me out of the clutches of Internal Affairs.

One Saturday night in November, we happened to stumble into one of those SIS takedowns. It was a mini-mart robbery that turned into the *Gunfight at the OK Corral*. Three innocent civilians were wounded. Fortunately, none of them died. But when it was over, the incident morphed into a big media stink because witnesses stated that SIS could have affected an arrest without killing the three hold-up men and wounding innocent bystanders. I.A. filed charges and Zack and I were called to testify against Brian Devine and his crew of razorbacks at an Internal Affairs hearing.

Two weeks before the Board of Rights, Devine and his squad rolled up on us one night at three A.M. while Zack and I were cooping behind a liquor store. They pinned us in at the curb and threatened both of our lives, as well as Zack's family.

Back then, Brian Devine was a Policeman II, and

there was a definite craziness about him. An unhinged feeling. Uncontrolled violence buzzed dangerously behind his eyes. He was a known gunfighter. The kind of cop we used to say had Wyatt Earp Syndrome. He'd rather shoot a suspect, than hook him up. A killer with a badge.

Zack and I decided to hedge our statements at the B.O.R., rather than risk confrontation with a murderous cowboy like Brian Devine. We reasoned that nobody but three hard-case killers had died. Let somebody else step up and put the hat on him. Zack didn't want his wife and young son at risk. I had no family then, but was barely functioning. I was afraid my alcohol abuse would be brought out at the hearing by Devine's defense rep in an attempt to impeach my testimony and ruin my career. So I went along and kept quiet. It was a bad choice, even cowardly. Devine and his crew got off, and to this day, I've never felt right about it.

Back at my desk in Homicide Special, I opened the Hickman file and read through it to kill time. Secada had included copies of Lt. Devine's initial police reports as well as copies of crime scene photos showing the bloody shoe print and Olivia Hickman's body. All of this stuff was third generation, and the pictures were hard to see clearly. She had probably photocopied them hastily before turning the file over to Captain Sasso. I stared at the material, unsure of what to do. It was a file full of leaking nitro. I knew if I messed with this, it would explode in my face.

I had been thinking of trying to get a couple of days away with Alexa. We needed some private time together. Why had I even agreed to read this damn thing? It was nuts. I left it on my desk, got up, and walked into Captain Jeb Calloway's office.

Cal runs Homicide Special. His family came here

originally from Haiti. He has a shaved bullet head and is short—just at department height minimums—but he's made up for his diminutive stature by building an upper body that looks like it belongs on the pages of a Marvel comic. The Haitian Sensation. You screw with this guy at your own risk. But I liked him. He was a good boss who stood up for his detectives.

I caught him going through a budget analysis, something no supervisor likes to do, so he seemed glad for the interruption.

"How's Sally doing?" he asked as I came through the door.

My partner, Sally Quinn, was in her eighth month of pregnancy. She was out of the office, testifying in an old Valley murder case of hers that had come up on appeal, leaving me with phone calls and paperwork on the few open cases we were handling. After the trial she was going to take maternity leave. In the meantime, I was an assigned floater, picking up odd cases with other detectives whose partners were out sick or on vacation.

"She's still in court," I answered. "That trial is really dragging on. I got a little problem, Cal."

"Let's hear," he said, pushing some spreadsheets aside.

"It's personal. As long as Sally is out, I thought maybe I could take a few vacation days."

"Everything okay?" his expression projecting more than his words.

Everybody knew that Alexa was upstairs tearing the paneling out of her office. Things hadn't been right since she came back on the job three weeks ago. Temper tantrums, unexplained absences, opening unauthorized investigations. Before Chief Filosiani left to go to London for an international police conference, he told her that she was going to have to undergo a performance review upon his return. It was scheduled for next week. She was going crazy getting ready for it. Half the building was rooting for her to pass while the other half wanted her to fail. The last month had cost her a year's worth of goodwill.

I just shrugged, not wanting to get into any of this with Cal.

"I guess you can take a few days," he said.

"Good."

"If something comes up, I may need to pull you in, so keep your cell on."

"Right. Thanks."

It was only three o'clock, but I was in no mood to shuffle paper on old cases, so I left Parker Center and killed some more time by going over to the criminal courts building. I rode the elevator down to the subbasement, to the evidence lockers. The Hickman file was under my arm. I figured this shouldn't take me long. I had already decided to just take a cursory look at the evidence boxes so I could tell Scout I at least gave it a nod before I sent all this back to her with a "no thanks." I found the police graybeard assigned to the court property room. He led me to a storage alcove.

Evidence boxes for current court cases were held down here for a year or until the appeals had cleared the system, then they were moved over to a warehouse facility downtown. The Hickman case wasn't being appealed because it had been pled out. It was close to the year cutoff, but we were running about six months behind on filing this stuff so I was pretty sure the material would still be here. It was.

I collected four cardboard boxes, sat down at a small wooden table, and opened the first one. More crime scene photos. These were originals and now, since I could actually see them, I examined them carefully.

Whoever killed Olivia Hickman had done a damn thorough job of it. She'd been stabbed twenty times. What we call in law enforcement, overkill. When you see that many knife wounds it generally indicates extreme anger and usually the perpetrator is someone with a strong emotional attachment to the victim. Like her son. It was probably one of the reasons that Lt. Devine was initially so fixated on Tru Hickman.

I kept looking. I saw many pictures of the bloody shoe print. All the downstairs windows and doors had been photographed. No forced entry. Whoever murdered Olivia Hickman either had a key, or at least had entered through the door. Again, this fit her son.

There were two boxes of physical evidence. The first contained Tru Hickman's boots and clothing. I picked up the boots and looked at them. I couldn't see any blood, so I put them back. His clothing was carefully packaged in glassine envelopes, and upon examination, appeared to be free of blood spatter. The second box held his mother's bloody nightgown with twenty knife holes in it and a pair of slippers splattered with blood. There were little Baggies with vacuumed hair and fibers all neatly labeled LIVING ROOM, KITCHEN, BATHROOM, BEDROOM, etc.

Her purse.

Taped to the plastic handle was an inventory tag with a list of the contents: lipstick, hairbrush, Kleenex, eyebrow pencil, comb, and wallet. I opened the purse and looked inside. It was all there as listed. I opened the wallet. Vons market employee ID card, union card. No credit cards or paper money, incidental change. I put everything back inside the box. Just before I replaced the purse, I noticed a small zipper concealed in a fold of the lining. I patted it carefully and felt a slight bulge, then unzipped the pocket and pulled out the contents.

It was a wad of bills. I straightened the money and counted it carefully. Two hundred dollars. Exactly the amount that Tru was supposed to have killed his mother for.

Why hadn't Lt. Devine found it? Could he possibly be that careless?

Of course, that led me to a much bigger question. If Tru Hickman hadn't killed his mother for this money, then what the hell was his motive for the murder?

CHAPTER 4

I went back to Parker Center and took the elevator to the sixth floor to check on Alexa. I found her dressing down a new administrative assistant. Detective II Paul Paskerian was a clean-cut guy in a suit who had only been assigned up here since Alexa's return. Because you had to go through Paul to get to Alexa, and because cops love nicknames, everybody quickly took to calling Paskerian, "Pass Key."

"You can't post crime stats for homicide divisions on the COMSTAT board without a cross-reference to division troop strength," she scolded him. "What the hell is wrong with you, Paul? I can't do the percentages without the prime numbers. Do you think, just once, you could do something right?"

Paul turned and left, looking angry but resolute. Then Alexa glanced up at me.

"Not now, Shane."

"Jesus. What did *I* do?" I stood there looking at her, my hands on my hips, trying to decide which way to jump.

"I'm sorry. It's not you." She crossed quickly to the door and shut it with a little too much force. Before it closed, I saw her assistant Ellen frowning.

"I can't seem to get any decent help up here. This damn performance review of Tony's. . . . Why the hell am I wasting time defending my performance when I've got a city full of hitters out there? I should be doing my job instead of wasting a week covering my ass."

"I was wondering if you wanted to catch a bite downtown after work. You pick the joint."

"Can't you see what's going on here?" She motioned toward a stack of papers on her desk. "That stuff alone is just support figures for the city crime reports I did last year. I have to go through all this material and present it again." As she stood there looking at it, without warning, her lower lip started to quiver. "Dammit, don't cry, Alexa," she ordered herself angrily as tears started to flow.

I went to her and took her into my arms. She is so beautiful and strong that sometimes I forget how vulnerable she's become recently. I held her and rubbed her back. She felt stiff. Her muscles jumped under my touch.

"Listen, honey, this performance review isn't the end of the world."

"What if Tony sacks me? What if he sends me down on a medical? I can't deal with this." She pushed away from me and turned back to her desk, looking down at the reports with frustration, gathering her emotions under her, getting set for another run at being tough.

"Alexa, you can only do so much. Ten months ago you were lying in a coma in the UCLA neurology ward. Nobody, including your doctors, thought you were going to survive, much less recover. I was advised to think about unhooking your life support. Now you're back here trying to manage two hundred detectives. You're not ready yet."

"I don't want to hear it, Shane. This is such bullshit. I just . . . I was out so long. I got behind. I'm swamped. It's not TBI or ABI or whatever Luther calls it, okay?

It's just that this damn job never stops. Never slows down. I'm getting plowed under."

"I want you to come home with me. I want you to take a few days off."

"Are you nuts?"

"I got Cal to give me the time. We could go to Shutters in Santa Monica, get our favorite room overlooking the beach, let the RPMs slow a little. Talk, make love, have a laugh or two. Whatta you say?"

"What part of the word 'no' escapes your understanding? No, I don't want to go to Shutters. No, I don't want to fuck or have candlelight dinners. No, okay? I'm getting torched here. I gotta straighten this stuff out, get this right."

"Alexa, you're pushing people too hard. You can't make up for lost ground by going to the whip. You're driving people away from you."

"Is that what's happening with you, Shane?"

"Of course not. I love you."

Then, as if she hadn't even heard me, she started rummaging on her desktop. "Where the hell did Ellen put the Valley crime reports? I swear, that woman is becoming useless." She moved to the door and threw it open. "Ellen, I asked you for the Valley crime reports for August through November. Is that ever going to arrive or were you planning on giving them to me to take home over Labor Day?"

"Alexa, you already looked at them. I saw you put them in your Out box ten minutes ago."

I was standing by her desk and I looked down at the Out box. Sure enough, there they were.

Alexa closed the door, crossed to the desk and picked them up. I saw frustration and anger in her eyes.

"How can I catch up when I can't even remember what I'm doing?" she said

"Come home. Take two days off. It'll do you more good than spinning your wheels down here."

"Shane, get out of here, will you? I can't do this now, okay? Have a shred of understanding. Can't you please just do that one thing for me?"

"Okay. When will you be home?"

"I don't know. By ten, I hope."

At ten-thirty she called me at home and told me she was staying at the office. She would sleep on her couch. She said she needed to reconstruct last year's rape and robbery numbers. Tony especially wanted to see those, and somehow she had misplaced them.

After we hung up, I went into the backyard and sat looking at the Venice Canal, my mind in turmoil. When I sit out here, it usually calms me. I needed the quiet perspective that my canal house always provided.

In the twenties, a dreamer named Abbot Kinney designed Venice, California, to be a scaled-down version of Venice, Italy. The real estate development had been an immediate success. Replica gondola canoes floated on the six square blocks of shallow waterways under arched Disneyesque bridges. Over the next seven decades it had fallen into a state of despair, but now, eighty years later, Venice had been rediscovered. Julia Roberts, Anjelica Huston, and Nicolas Cage had all bought property here. The area had gone from hippie-chic to Hollywood-chic. Now it was a mixture of architectural styles and social clichés.

Dot-com execs had built million-dollar houses on postage-stamp lots next to clapboard houses owned by seventies-style social misfits and a few throwback romantics like me. Still remarkable, the six blocks of replica canals had been folded into today's urban sprawl of Southern California's strip malls and cultural bric-a-brac. I loved it here: living on a canal designed to look like fifteenth-century Italy, living in my own throwback house made of fifties clapboard and shingles. It was my castle, my refuge from doubt.

As I sat on my painted metal lawn chair, I worried about Alexa. My wife was breathtakingly beautiful. High cheekbones, black hair, eyes the pale blue color of reef water. She had world-class beauty, but had chosen the rough-and-tumble dog pile of police work. And it was a good choice, because it suited her courage and heroic sense of right and wrong. That is, until Stacy Maluga fired that bullet into her head a year ago and changed everything. Alexa was so used to being in control of her environment that this new personality, and the reckless behavior that came with it, unsettled her. She was no longer able to see the potholes in the road ahead. These last months, she was constantly forced to confront who she had been and to compare it to who she had become. Frustration and anger always followed.

Franco, our adopted marmalade cat, suddenly jumped up in my lap, startling me. He sensed that I was troubled and stared at me with knowing yellow eyes, wondering what my damn problem was as I slowly stroked his fur.

I heard the door behind me open and Delfina Delgado walked out into the yard. She was my son Chooch's girlfriend and had come to live with us when her family died two years ago. She was going to USC as a freshman in the fall and was getting a head start by enrolling in summer school. She had come home to do her laundry. Chooch was in his sophomore year at SC on a football ride. He had red-shirted last season and was just beginning his second year. Two-a-day football practices had already started and he was at the team dorm by Howard Jones Field. Delfina crossed the lawn and sat in the chair next to me. She was beautiful, just eighteen, and from Mexican heritage.

"Has anybody fed El Gato Grande, here?" she said, reaching over and scratching Franco.

"I think he's still got food. I probably should check though."

"Is Alexa coming home?"

"I guess not. Another night sleeping on her office couch."

Delfina was silent and I looked over at her. She finally said, "This will get better, Shane. You have to give it time."

"I know."

"You think she has changed, but she hasn't. I can see how confused she is. She doesn't want to show this to you."

"I'm not gonna split and run, Del."

"I didn't say that."

"But everybody thinks it. I'm better than that. If I can't see her through a rough time, then what good am I?"

"This will all end up for the best. You'll see."

"Sometimes I wish I had your belief in the future. You always seem to be able to see what's really important."

"So can you, Shane."

"No, I'm a pusher. I try to force results. It's been my way since childhood. To do right by Alexa, I have to fight my natural instincts. But I'll learn. I even went and got some help today."

"Good. It will get better, you'll see."

I wanted to change the subject, so I said, "Heard from Chooch?"

She beamed at that. "Oh, yes. He calls every day, that one. Right after practice. He had a good day today. The coaches gave him twenty first-team repetitions. He says that's good for a second-year quarterback."

I knew it was too late to call him. They had a ten o'clock curfew.

"Listen, when you talk to him tomorrow, tell him I'm going to be out of town and to check in with his mom."

"Where are you going?"

"Prison."

"Oh, Shane. Come on, it's not that bad," she teased.

"No, really. Since I can't go to Shutters, I'm going up to Corcoran State Prison on a case instead. I'll be back by sundown."

"Okay." She picked up Franco from my lap. "Come here, you. I'm gonna give you some fresh food."

She left me alone looking at the still canals. The cold Alaskan air was still blowing along the coast, so I decided to go inside and found a new spiral notebook in my desk. It was one of the ones I used on crime scenes. Over the years I'd filled countless numbers of them, noting gruesome case facts and laying out crime scene sketches and drawings. Now I opened a fresh one and on the first page, wrote:

Alexa's Diary

Then I wrote down everything that had happened when I visited her office. I remembered to include my feelings: how worried I was; how angry I'd become at her. Dr. Lusk was right: she'd invaded my space, become the reckless, impulsive one. It wasn't in my nature to be holding a leash, constantly warning her of potential danger. It cramped my style and when I stopped to analyze it, I realized that it really pissed me off. I still loved her, but as I wrote all of this down, I realized how frightened for us I had become.

CHAPTER 5

I left the house before six o'clock the next morning, picked up some coffee at Starbucks, and by six-thirty was on the interstate, heading north. I knew from having made this trip many times that it was going to take me almost three hours to cover the hundred and seventy-nine miles to Corcoran State Prison, which is located in lower Central California.

I had called ahead and talked to the visitor's custodial sergeant, told him who I was, and that I needed Truit Hickman sent over from general population to the visitor's center. After I gave him my badge number, I informed the sergeant I would be there around ten A.M. and that I was investigating some anomalies that came up during Hickman's appeal. There was no appeal, so I kept it vague, and he seemed satisfied.

I hate the drive through the desert and since I had all day, I decided to take the more scenic, coastal route. By the time I was approaching Santa Barbara, my thoughts had again turned exclusively to Alexa. I didn't want to call her until later hoping that she'd get some needed sleep. She was running on nervous energy, and recently had been losing weight. I could see the strain on her face, the tightness around her eyes and mouth.

North of Santa Barbara I turned inland and after forty minutes drove out of the low hills into Central California. It was mostly farmland up here, but after twenty miles the fields gave way to high desert. Along the roadside, I passed an occasional saguaro cactus standing like a man at gunpoint with his hands in the air.

By nine-thirty I was nearing my destination and turned on Poplar Avenue for the eleven-and-a-half-mile stretch before hitting Central Valley Highway. I called Alexa, but was told by Ellen that she was out of the office.

"Out?" I said, concerned. "Out where?"

"She went across the street for some breakfast."

"Oh, okay. How's she doing this morning?"

"Compared to what?"

"Stick with her, Ellen. She needs our help."

"I'm trying. You too," she said.

I hung up and finally turned on to Otis Avenue.

The huge, foreboding prison loomed in the tan dust up ahead like randomly stacked chunks of gray concrete. Corcoran was ugly, like all prisons. It was built on the site of what was once Tulare Lake, the long-ago home of the Tachi Indians. The dry lake mitigated the prison's relentless, unforgiving architecture because everything out here was relentless and unforgiving. In this hopeless landscape Corcoran State Prison somehow managed to belong. Level One inmates had placed painted, white rocks along the drive and lining the visitor's parking lot. Very festive.

I found a spot, locked up, and walked under a cloudless sky to a large structure with a painted sign that read:

CALIFORNIA DEPARTMENT OF CORRECTIONS VISITING CENTER

If everything went according to plan, Tru Hickman would have already been transferred here from Level Four, saving me a long wait.

The visitor's building, like everything else, was poured concrete with slit windows that resembled gun ports. The buildings were sending a stern message.

The inside of the CDCVC was more of the same. Brown linoleum floors, pale yellow walls, hard metal furniture that looked like it had been intentionally designed to hurt. I talked to a desk officer, showed my creds, and handed over my gun, which was locked in a gun box. He handed me a receipt and I was buzzed through a sally port into the police and attorney's waiting room, a grim little space with faded leather chairs and one window.

Thirty minutes later, a prison sergeant who looked like a college linebacker came through a door and told me to follow him. He led me through another sally port into a large visitor's room full of wood desks and chairs. There were already two prisoners with their families at opposite ends of the room. Both inmates were holding infants. Their wives each carried transparent plastic diaper bags, which were mandated by the prison visiting rules and allowed staff a clear view of the contents inside. The two families were huddled as far away from each other as possible, whispering. Large killjoy signs were posted that read:

YOU MAY HOLD HANDS ABOVE THE TABLE.

**TO AVOID TRANSFER OF DRUGS,
ABSOLUTELY NO KISSING.**

I sat at a wooden table and waited. The two inmate families gave me a quick look, knew what I was at a glance, and further turned their backs on me.

Then, Tru Hickman came into the room, escorted by a yard bull. I'd seen his booking photo, so I certainly wasn't expecting Jay Leno, but in person this guy was sad and pitiful. His walk was puppet gangly and loose-jointed, as if nothing really quite connected. Hips forward, elbows out, head bobbing, trailing a loser vibe. He was implausibly thin like a lot of tweakers, having spent years forgoing food in favor of meth. His jaw was undershot, his complexion pockmarked, with ears that stuck out. He had recently been beaten. There were bruises all over him and his left eye was swollen half-shut. His nose looked as if it had been broken and badly set. This kid was a target for aggression.

He sat down and immediately looked down at his hands, then started to pull at a loose thread on one of his frayed cuffs, his eyes steadfastly refusing to look up at me.

"Tru, I'm Detective Scully. I'm looking into your case. I'm here because of the letter you wrote to LAPD Internal Affairs. I was asked to talk to you by Detective Llevar. You spoke to her on the phone the day before yesterday."

"'Kay." He continued to stare down at his cuffs, showing me the top of his head.

"Tru, you want to look up at me?"

"'Kay." He didn't look up.

"Now. You wanta look up now?"

The eyes slowly came up and found me sitting across from him. We locked gazes for a second and I saw fear and pain swimming in brown pools of confusion before his eyes darted away, then came back, then darted away again. It was as if he was taking me in, one quick little glance at a time.

"I read your letter. You need to tell me *why* you think

you were framed. You need to start at the beginning. Walk me through it."

"Man, this is so . . ." Then he looked over at one of the inmates across the room. "I can't snitch people out with them in here. I'm already wearing a rat jacket. It's why I keep getting stomped on."

"This is the visiting room, Tru. They have a right to be here."

"But . . ."

"I drove all the way up from L.A. I'm interested in what you have to say. Forget about them. Just talk to me, okay?" He didn't speak, so I said, "Let's just start with the day of the murder. Your friend, Mike Church, came over and got into a fight with your mom. Start there."

Now his eyes finally found mine. "Ain't my fucking friend," he said, his voice barely a whisper. "That guy's like a case of the clap I can't get rid of. Been on me since tenth grade."

"You met him at the California Youth Authority, right?"

"Yeah. Pounded my ass every fuckin' mornin'. My crime was I was alive and that seemed to really piss him off."

"If he's not a friend, why was he over at your house the day your mother was killed?"

"To fuck with me. To make my life suck. That's all he ever wanted me for. He'd pop a bunch of Arnies, get all 'roided out and come lookin' for my ass."

"No other reason?"

"That afternoon he said he wanted me to go buy a case of beer for him. Like I'm still his CYA yard bitch."

"That's it? That's all he wanted? Why?"

"Why? How the hell do I know? He wants my life to

be shit. He'll kick my ass just to get the lint in my pocket. He's a fuckin' psycho."

"Why didn't he buy the beer himself?"

"I just told ya. He likes fucking with me. He knows my mom hates his guts. He likes to rile her up. Sometimes I wouldn't see him or his greaser gang friends for months, then all of a sudden, there he is. Back in my life like a boil on my dick. Nothing I can do about it, either."

"So he comes over to your house that Saturday. What time was that?"

"Two, two-thirty in the afternoon. My mom is home Saturdays. He knows that. He makes a point a frontin' her off. She gets all pissed. It's like a dance they did. Finally, she's out on the front lawn screaming at him. Called him a dumb *cholo*. Fucking Church snapped and almost killed her right there. It was all I could do to get him to leave."

Tru looked down at his sleeve again and started picking at loose threads. Then, without looking up, he blurted, "I been raped three times in a month. Had ta have my asshole stitched up twice at the infirmary 'cause they ripped me open back there. I can't . . . I can't stay here anymore. You gotta get me outta this car." Tears started rolling down his cheeks. He rubbed at them savagely with his cuff, fought desperately to rein in his emotions, glanced at the other inmates furtively to see if they were witness to his breakdown.

"I could see if I could get you moved into the Administrative Segregation Unit."

"I asked. They won't move me to ASU."

"Let me see what I can do."

He reached out and grabbed my hand in both of his like he was clutching a lifeline. "I made a lot of mistakes in my life, you know? Stealing shit, slamming drugs . . . but I didn't never hurt anyone and I sure didn't kill my mom. I didn't do it. I loved her."

He was shaking, or shivering, I don't know which. I fought the urge to bolt. This kid was such a victim it was starting to rattle me.

"Go on," I said. "You and Church left the house to get beer. What happened next?"

"'Kay." He sat with his eyes down, said nothing.

"You gotta tell it now. Go on."

"'Kay." He sat there for a long time. Then finally, like an engine taking a long time to wind up RPMs, he started again, slowly at first, then gaining momentum.

"Church makes me go to this strip mall on Sepulveda to buy the case of beer. It's halfway across the Valley. For some reason, he has to buy beer from this exact fucking store. It's the way he was. He was always like that. Everything's a project. Mike Church is insane. He really is."

"What next?"

"It's gotta be Bud Light, you know? Nothing but Bud Light. Here's this guy, weighs over three hundred pounds, and he's gotta have diet beer. He gives me a hundred bucks and says buy all the Bud Light in the market, we'll take it and drink it at this party he knows about where there's all these girls. Putas, he calls 'em. I told him I couldn't drink booze 'cause I was on Antabuse. Antabuse makes you sick if you drink alcohol. Mostly though, I just wanted to get away from him."

"Was the Antabuse court mandated?" I asked him.

"Yeah. I agreed to take Antabuse, so they didn't incarcerate me for my last DUI. Had t'go into a program. Lotta shit like that. It's why I was doin' crystal."

"And Antabuse doesn't hit the crystal meth," I said, knowing it didn't.

"Ain't that a hoot?" He smiled at me. His teeth were

crooked, but there was something innocent and strangely unaffected in his smile. In that instant, I knew he hadn't stabbed his mother to death. Why, I can't exactly say. It was a vibe. An instinct.

I've come to realize that in this world some people are predators, others are prey. Sometimes it's hard to know which is which because you'll find guys who look like they can kick ass, but underneath they're weak. The reverse can also be true. In the animal kingdom, the predators are easy to spot. They all have their eyes in the front of their heads to facilitate an attack. Lions, tigers, and wolves are designed by nature to kill. Antelopes, deer, and rabbit all have their eyes on the side of their heads. These prey animals are designed for flight and their vision allows them to see things coming at them peripherally. In the wild there are no exceptions to this rule. With people, it was a lot harder to tell. You had to read body language and to try to see into a man's soul. When I saw the innocence and simplicity hiding behind Tru's smile, I suspected that there was no set of conditions that could ever bring him to murder. Tru Hickman was not a predator. He was food.

"Go on," I said. "So he wants you to buy beer at a particular strip mall."

"Yeah. I go into this mini-mart and buy this beer while Church waits outside. There's only one six-pack of Bud Light in the fucking cooler and Mike is so adamant about me buying Bud Light at that exact store, I remember thinking, thank God they ain't out, 'cause he'd bust my ass if I walk out empty-handed. I buy it and leave. Church's on his cell phone when I walked out. He owns a garage and towing service in the Valley and after he hangs up he says there's a guy had an accident on the one-oh-one Freeway and he's gotta go back to his garage, get the tow rig, and pull this guy's

car. He tells me to take a cab and to take the beer home
with me. He says he'll be over at my house in an hour
and then we'll go to the bang, shag pussy, get wasted.
Again, I try and beg off, but Church says he can hook
me up with some crank, so that does it. I'm down, you
know?"

"He wants you to take the beer home with you?"

"He says, 'cause CHP cops would be at the freeway
accident. He's got one DUI beef of his own and I guess
he didn't want a six-pack in the truck."

"So you go home."

"I go home. He shows up a few hours later, but my
mom is on the warpath. They get into another huge argument on the lawn. It's so loud the neighbors next
door and across the street come out to watch. This time
it's over the damn six-pack of beer. My mom won't let
him have it because I'm on Antabuse. I tell her it's
Mike's beer, but she's not having any. This time she
throws a rock at him, hits Church in the chest. He would
a killed her right there if I hadn't pointed to the neighbors watching. She pulls out her cell and calls the cops
while we're all shouting at each other. Me and Church
had t'split before they arrived."

"You left without the beer?"

"Mom wouldn't let us have it."

"Then what?"

"I got totally buzzed at this party in the Valley.
Don't even remember where it was. I did a lot of crystal and just aired out. The next morning, I have to walk
home. I get to my house at eleven-thirty and find my
mom dead on the kitchen floor. Man, it's a mess. Blood
everywhere." His eyes started to fill up and the tears
came again. "She was all I had, you know? She used to
scream and bitch, but I'll be honest with you, man, it
was just 'cause she cared. All my life nobody but her

gave a damn what happened to me. I was such a fuck-up, on drugs and everything. I deserved everything she said."

I didn't want him to melt down again. I wanted him to stay on the narrative, so I interrupted this memory and said, "You walked in and found her dead. Then what?"

"I called nine-one-one. This guy, Lieutenant Devine, arrives almost immediately. He takes me down to the Van Nuys station and asks me if I'll take a lie detector test. Since I didn't kill my mom, I say okay, if it will help, sure. He gives me the test, then tells me afterward that I flunked it. He tells me my shoe print matched the one by her body, but I know I didn't step in the blood. I was so scared I didn't go near her. I could tell she was dead from the back porch. She was pale as ivory, gallons of blood on the floor, knife wounds all over."

"He told you he matched the shoe print to your boots?"

"That's what he said, but I don't know how. Like I said, I never stepped in any blood. There wasn't no blood on my shoes, or on the soles. Nowhere. He also tells me I was laying in wait to kill and rob her, which is a lie, but that makes it premeditated murder and a murder for financial gain. Both those things qualify me for special circumstances. The death penalty. I've got a long drug record. I know how the system works. After Devine tells me all this, I know I'm dust, so I signed a confession they wrote."

"And then you pled out?"

"Yeah. The court assigns me a public defender named Yvonne Hope. It's this girl with red hair and braids, looks like she should still be in high school. I couldn't fuckin' believe it when I saw her. They cut a deal, offer me twenty-five to life, and I took it. Shit, I had no idea what it was gonna be like in here. I only done CYA and county time before this. I didn't know my asshole was gonna get torn open and have to get stitched up twice in one month. I didn't know I'd get a yard beat-down almost every day. I can't live like this, Mr. Scully. I'll kill myself if this goes on much longer."

"Okay, Tru. I'll talk to somebody. I'll see if I can get you transferred to ASU. But you'll be lonely in there. No yard privileges."

"Hey, man, for me, the yard ain't no privilege."

"I'll try then."

"'Kay."

I stood and he suddenly reached out and grabbed my hand again. "Don't go yet, man, okay? Please? I don't want to leave the visitor's center. Can't you stay a little longer?"

"I gotta leave now. I'll be in touch." I started to exit, then turned back and looked at him. He was standing there, head down, pulling at his frayed cuffs. There's a place where pathetic becomes heart-wrenching. I knew what Scout meant when she said Tru had been sacrificed. I also thought she was right when she said somebody must have it in for him. This wasn't right.

"Did you tell Lieutenant Devine that the second argument was over that six-pack of Bud Light?" I finally asked.

"Of course. I told him everything."

"So what happened? The six-pack wasn't in the court evidence box. Didn't he find it in the refrigerator?"

"I don't think he ever looked."

CHAPTER 6

"All this railroad needs is tracks and a whistle," Secada said.

We were in a Mexican restaurant on Olvera Street named La Golondrina. The food was always excellent and after six P.M. mariachis strolled between the tables and performed for the dinner guests.

Olvera Street was the first street built in Los Angeles and is just a few blocks from both Parker Center and the Bradbury Building. We had agreed to meet here after work. Scout's black eyes danced in an almond face, framed by shiny, black hair that shimmered in low flickering candlelight. We had already ordered dinner and, while we waited, were on our first margaritas.

"We need to get Hickman moved to ASU," I said. "I filed a request before I left, but it's gonna creep through channels. He could be dead by the time it gets approved."

"I agree. Our best bet is to keep working and see if we can get him a writ of habeas corpus for a new trial."

"I found the two hundred dollars," I told her.

"The murder money? How can that be? Devine said Tru spent it on crystal meth the night of the murder."

"It was in the court evidence room. In the side pocket of Olivia Hickman's purse."

She put down her margarita. "No way." She looked

puzzled, her brow furrowed. "So if Tru or Church didn't take the money, what's the motive for murder?"

"Near as I can tell, it was over a six-pack of Bud Light that Church and Hickman bought that afternoon."

I told her about the trip to the mini-mart, the two arguments with Olivia, and about Tru being on Antabuse. I ended by explaining how Mrs. Hickman threw a rock and hit Church in the chest, and how they left because the cops were called.

"It sure ain't *Leave It to Beaver*," she said as she finished the last of her margarita and looked up. "A six-pack of beer, huh? Not much of a motive."

"Rage was the motive," I said. "The six-pack of Bud Light was just a trigger. I've been worried about the twenty knife wounds. That kind of extreme overkill would seem to indicate a close relationship like with a son, but Tru said Church was on anabolic steroids. If he was popping Arnies and having 'roid rage, then maybe the overkill actually fits him as well. I don't know."

Our combo plate dinners arrived, along with a second round of margaritas. I love margaritas, but two is definitely my limit, especially when I'm with a beautiful woman who isn't my wife.

Secada smiled and took a sip. "*Mamacita, yo amo* Cuervo Gold."

"Aye, Chihuahua," I smiled back.

We both dug into the huge enchilada-taco-burrito-and-bean dinners. She ate like it was serious business, holding her knife and fork like instruments of war—nothing dainty about Secada at mealtime.

"So, what're we gonna do with this buncha *pendejos*?" she asked between bites.

"We got two doors here. Door One is we go check out Mike Church. See what kind of slime trail he's leaving behind him these days. Or we can go talk to the District Attorney who pled the case. Get the state's version of what happened."

She thought about it for a minute. "How much cover is your wife going to give us?" she asked.

"I haven't talked to her."

"Don't you think you should? I mean, Captain Sasso took this off the board. If you and I ask the wrong questions of the wrong guy, this could snap up on us and we'll both be facing an internal review. If that happens we'll need Lieutenant Scully to shut it down."

"I'll tell her when or if I feel we need to."

"Look, Shane, I don't mean to tell you how to deal with your wife, but that's a mistake."

"Drop it, okay?" Our eyes locked for a moment. I wasn't about to get into Alexa's problems with her.

"The only real reason I came to you was because of her."

"I thought it was because of my huge *cojones.*"

"I've been ordered off this case. If we go to Tito Morales and he makes a call to check on why, we'll be in deep grease."

"Tito who?"

"Morales. He's the D.A. who pled the case out for the State."

"*The* Tito Morales?"

"Yeah. But don't let it panic you. He's my *carnal.*" She grinned and pointed to my plate with her knife. "The guy eats burritos just like us."

"We're talking about the lead prosecutor for the whole damn Valley? Tito Morales? The guy who runs the Van Nuys D.A.'s office?"

"It's why I think it's a good idea to have your wife riding shotgun."

"Why didn't you tell me that up front? According to the *L.A. Times,* he's planning a run at the mayor's job in two months and has a great chance of winning."

"Mexicans are eventually gonna run everything around here." She grinned at me. "Look out, Scully; you might have to get a Green Card yourself one day soon."

I sat looking at her for a long time, trying to digest this.

"Don't worry. *Yo hablo español.* Better still, I understand the culture." She was still smiling.

"I'm glad you find this funny," I said. "It kinda explains a lot of this other stuff though. It explains why Jane Sasso pulled Townsend and Summers into that meeting to convince you to drop the case. Since Tito Morales cut the plea deal, and since he's the front-runner for the mayor's office, he undoubtedly won't want it to come out two months before the election that he sent a guy up on an incomplete investigation. He probably called Sasso when he heard you were looking into it."

"Shane, I don't think the pressure is coming from him. He's a Democrat. Cops are mostly all Republicans. It's Plain Jane's doing. She's from the Dark Side. That woman is Darth Vader in sensible shoes. For all we know, Townsend and Summers were in her office on something else and for sport, she just let 'em sit in on my beat-down."

"Get some rearview mirrors, lady, or you're gonna get run over by an I.A. dump truck."

"This Hickman one-eighty-seven is a nothing case. Even if Church was the doer, it's still just some gang-affiliated tow truck driver who killed a supermarket checker. Despite Morales, this isn't the kind of case that gets the sixth floor's attention."

"But even still, you think my wife needs to be involved to protect us? You're not being honest with me."

She shrugged. I continued. "Brian Devine's head of Van Nuys Homicide. Tito Morales is head of the Van Nuys prosecutor's office. This is starting to sound like a lot more than some tweaker murder over a six-pack of beer."

"I thought you were supposed to be a White Knight—a walk-alone who wants to get it right and doesn't sweat the fallout."

"That's the Disney movie," I said. "In the Miramax version I shit my pants and run like a rabbit."

"Okay, look. You don't want to alert Morales. I think you're wrong, but let's say I buy into that for the moment. So let's finish dinner and then go check door number one. Mike Church is a criminal dirtbag, so he won't call the police to complain."

"How did you last in PSB for three years being this naive?"

She looked angry, almost fierce. "My parents came from a country where the government is basically corrupt. My uncle disappeared into prison and never came out. My papa calls the Mexican government a criminal organization posing as a government. There's graft and corruption everywhere. My parents came across the border as *braceros*. They got their citizenship status under the Reagan eight-one amnesty. This country is a much, much better place than anywhere else. Better because Americans don't look the other way when there's injustice. Remember what Edmund Burke said. 'All that is necessary for the triumph of evil is for good men to do nothing.'"

"Let me write that down. It might work on my IRS review."

"Make fun if you want, but I love this country. I love what it stands for. I love police work because I believe in the principles of the law. I know that sounds corny, but my family came from a place where evil reigns and good people did nothing. I don't want that to happen here. If you want to preserve what we've got, you gotta take on the shitty ones, Shane. You gotta fight evil one case at a time."

We sat looking at each other. I wasn't sure whether to laugh, cry, or just give her a raspberry.

"Mike Church," I finally said. "That's what you wanta do?"

"Let's go brace the motherfucker."

CHAPTER 7

On the way out to Church's house in North Van Nuys, Secada and I reviewed his five-page rap sheet, which she'd just handed me. He'd been raised in the north end of the Valley, but a lot of his early crimes took place at "Tragic Magic," which was LAPD speak for Six Flags Magic Mountain, a notorious gang hangout. At the tender age of eleven, this guy was already getting busted for aggravated assault, throwing down on line-cutters out there.

The Gang Squad had him getting jumped into the Vanowen Street Locos at fifteen. The VSLs were a particularly violent, Hispanic gang that worked the corners around Vanowen Street and Gloria in Van Nuys. That neighborhood was a drug corridor and the Locos sold more bags of rock than McDonald's sold bags of fries. According to his rap sheet, Mike Church had been doing more than just making Tru Hickman's life suck. He made everybody's life hell.

Most gang members are in it for the relatively easy money or to clique up for protection. The membership quickly separates into several criminal levels. At the low end are the 7-Eleven beer run bandits who clout refreshments for weekend partying and chase girls. Next come the purse snatchers and carjackers, then the narcotics dealers with their crew of lookouts and runners.

The very top of the criminal pyramid was where you found the designated hitters—guys who were called in to make blood flow—retribution killers and assassination shooters.

By the age of seventeen, Miguel Iglesia, aka Mike Church, had been busted three times on aggravated assault and twice for suspicion of murder, but the Van Nuys D.A. had been unable to put either murder beef on him. All of this court and street action had only resulted in a short stretch at the California Youth Authority.

In his file under "Unusual Hobbies" the gang squad had noted that he liked to ride Colossus, the big wooden roller coaster out at Magic Mountain.

His booking photo showed a glowering, thick-necked, twenty-five-year-old with pockmarked skin and a black Brillo pad–textured moustache and beard.

We pulled up in front of Church's house on Califa Street in Van Nuys, a mostly Hispanic neighborhood. The houses were old and half the residents had elected to park the family cars on their front lawn.

Scout and I sat across the street in my Acura, which was beginning to feel like a pearl button on a work shirt. Young men in lowered vintage Fords and Chevys drove by and hungrily scoped my ride.

"Whatta we do?" Secada asked, looking at Church's rundown house, which was old and large, with weed-choked flower beds.

"Let's run some of these plates," I replied. "I always like to get the player roster before getting in a game."

We started picking out tag numbers from the five or six cars parked in front of Church's house and on his lawn. I fed them to Scout who had the dash mike from my Rover in her hand.

"Wants, warrants, and DMV on Adam-Sierra-Ida-

six-six-five." Seconds later the records division spit
back a name.

"Jose Diego," the RTO said. "Six-sixty-four Woodman Avenue, Van Nuys. Jose Diego has outstanding
warrants for failure to appear, unlawful detention, and
assault."

The RTO went on to report that Diego's gang name
was "Torch." His gang affiliation, the Vanowen Street
Locos. It went on like that. Most of the cars that we ran
showed owners with paper pending. One belonged to a
guy named Tyler Cisneros who our records department
said was a VSL shot caller with the street name "Little Loco." It seemed Mike Church's crib was a gang
hookup. I didn't want to just call for more cops and arrest these people, even though some had outstanding
warrants, because that would put both of us in big trouble with Jane Sasso. It would also close down this thread
in our investigation. So it seemed this teepee full of *veteranos* was going to get a temporary pass.

Some kind of sports car was parked in the drive under a car cover. It looked low and expensive. The cover
couldn't quite hide the vehicle's wide stance and elegant design.

"Wonder what the hell that is?" I pointed at the car.
"Looks expensive. Whatta ya bet it's stolen. Can you
make out the plate?"

"Nope. Want me to go ever there and check it out?"

"Better let me do it."

"This is a Mexican block. Your Wonder Bread ass
won't last ten seconds. I'll do my homegirl thing."

"In a designer pantsuit. Good luck with that."

She started to roll up the legs on her expensive tan
pants and took off her scarf. Then she stripped off her
tan jacket, showing a white silk shirt with a pointed collar. "You got a raincoat or anything in the back?"

"Yeah, but its EPA rating is beyond biohazard."

"The grimier, the better."

I went around back and got it while she folded her scarf into a bandana then tied it over her head. She put on the rumpled raincoat I gave her, then leaned over the seat and started digging around in the back. I had a paper shopping bag back there that we'd used when we bought Chooch's school books from USC last week. She took it and stuffed her suit jacket inside.

Then she turned and looked at me. *"Te gustan mis ropas, señor?"*

It was an amazing transformation. In seconds, she had turned herself from Jennifer Lopez into a Mission Street *chola*.

"See ya in a minute. Stay in the car," she cautioned, then crossed the street and limped down the block. I watched her sneak onto Church's property, and slip across his brown lawn toward the low car in the driveway. She knelt down behind the vehicle and pulled up the car cover, exposing the plate. As she was writing down the tag number, the front door to the house was suddenly thrown open, and four tattooed guys wearing wife-beater tees and head-wraps ran out, screaming at her.

The lead guy had to be Mike Church. He was a hulking six-foot-three steroid case who weighed over three hundred pounds. His basketball-size head sat low on water buffalo shoulders.

"The fuck you think you're doin'?" Church screamed and grabbed Secada by the collar of my grimy raincoat, yanking her to her feet.

"LAPD. Back off, asshole!" I heard her scream, but in the next second they had thrown her to the ground. Her prop bag with her wadded-up suit jacket fell open as they proned her out facedown in the dirt.

I was out of the Acura the second I saw them. I

started by circling around the rear of my car, staying out of sight. I was going to need the element of surprise. Church was now holding Scout's gun, kneeling heavily on her back. They were all staring down and didn't see me coming from across the street. I couldn't figure out how they had been alerted so easily to her presence unless they had motion sensors covering the front of the house. I'd seen drug houses with sensors like that in the past.

In order to get to an effective firing position I had to cross the lawn. I pulled my short barrel .38 and ran lightly, trying to muffle the sound of my approaching footsteps by staying on the dead grass. The short-barreled Air Light magnum felt small and insignificant in my right hand. As I neared the five of them, Church yanked Scout up off the grass and pulled her violently toward him.

"Why you fuckin' with my ride, bitch?" Then before she could answer Church yanked the scarf off her head, freeing a pound of lustrous black hair.

"Back off. I'm police," she shouted at him.

"Slow down, homie," one of the *vatos* exclaimed. "She's po-po. This *chica's muy guapa, también?*"

I saw a vein throbbing on Mike Church's forehead as he reached out and grabbed a handful of Scout's hair, yanking her painfully closer. Then he pointed her gun at her. "That's nothing to me. I killed plenty a cops." He pulled back the hammer on the gun.

I didn't trust him not to do it. I wasn't quite where I wanted to be yet, but I was out of time.

"Hey, Miguel," I said softly. "Fire that and you're in the obits."

I was close enough, so I didn't have to shout. I wanted it to be a whisper, to sound a little crazy.

"The fuck?" He turned slightly so he could see me.

I was behind him on his left, my gun pointed directly at the back of his huge head.

"I ain't bagged me no fat, outta-shape whales in a while. Do exactly what I say or you're a fucking grease stain on the pavement here. Now put the gun down, step away. Get going. You're on the clock, asshole."

He stood there, not sure of what to do. I had him dead to rights. He looked spooked. "What is this?" he finally said as he stood there trying to calculate his odds.

They were all packing but, except for Mike, nobody had a gun out yet. If I wanted to control this, I had to act crazy enough to convince them to back off. Everyone's afraid of crazies, even VSL killers.

"Let go of her. Drop the gun." Then I giggled to add a little insanity to the moment.

After almost ten agonizing seconds, Church let go of Scout's hair and slowly lowered the gun, letting it fall at his side.

"Good. Now give her the gun back."

"Fuck you," Church snarled.

"You're on my wish list. I'm two seconds from pulling your drapes."

He looked at Scout, then tossed the Smith and Wesson at her. It landed at her feet. She scooped it up and immediately aimed it at the other three guys.

"This is private property," he said. "If you're cops, where's your fuckin' warrant?"

Scout waved her gun at him. "This is my warrant," she hissed. Then we both backed across the street to the Acura and got in. I started the car.

"Shit!" she said, once we were inside. "I left the bag with my suit jacket on the lawn."

"Leave it."

"That outfit cost me six hundred bucks," she complained as I put the car in gear and squealed up the street.

Still pissed at herself, Scout grabbed the dashboard mike and called in the plate number from the sports car. "This is L-fifty-six. Warrants and DMV for Adam-Boy-Victor-one-nine-three."

"Roger, L-fifty-six. Stand by."

She turned to me. "It's some kind of Mercedes. I saw the emblem. A big, new, expensive one."

The mike crackled. "L-fifty-six, on your tag number. That plate comes back as a two-thousand-eight Mercedes McLaren registered to Wade A. Wyatt at three-eighty-seven Bel Air Road in Bel Air. No wants or warrants."

"You sure it's clean?" Scout asked. "Check recent stolens."

There was a pause, then, "No wants," the RTO confirmed.

Secada hung up the mike and looked over at me. "A McLaren. Isn't that worth a pile of money?"

"Like about half a mil."

"Not to be racial profiling or anything, but what the hell is a half-a-million-dollar race car doing on that dickhead's front lawn?

"Good question." I looked over at her and saw a faint smile play on her face in the passing streetlights.

"Something funny?"

"You were amazing. I actually thought you'd gone bug house myself."

"It was a bad situation. We needed to turn a corner. It was all I could come up with."

"We're onto something here, Scully. Can't you feel it? This case has a heartbeat."

"Yeah. Let's just hope they don't find out who we are before we can put it down."

"Don't worry. They won't," she said, as she put her gun back into her holster, then started fumbling around on her belt. I saw a look of alarm pass across her face.

"What's wrong?"

"Put a hold on that," she said, then slammed her palm on the dash in frustration.

"What?"

"When I was proned out, eating dirt, Church musta stole my badge."

CHAPTER 8

"This is gonna cause a pile of trouble," Scout said. We were parked in the lot behind La Golondrina, two spots over from her slick-back detective car. It was nine-thirty P.M. "One of the investigating officers in our unit had her purse stolen a while back—lost her badge. It's a whole rigamarole. First, I gotta notify my supervisor, Captain Sasso, how I lost my ID, and you know that's gonna turn into a mud fight. Next, she's gotta send a teletype through the whole damn department with my badge number. Then an area headquarters team has to maintain the list of lost badge numbers indefinitely and send 'em each month to all divisions and station houses. Looks like I just blew our covert investigation."

"Just tell Sasso the purse was stolen, same as your IOs. Don't tell her we were over giving Mike Church a chest bump. If you tell her that, we're screwed."

"Except I don't like lying."

"That's ridiculous. Lying is the first great art of police science."

"Yeah, right. For you, maybe." She got out of the car, then turned and looked back in at me. "Anyway, thanks for the rescue."

We looked at each other. We had bonded over the dustup in Church's yard, and we both knew it.

Finally, I said, "Secada's such a pretty name, why don't you use it? What's with the Scout thing?"

"There're two theories on that," she smiled. "One is because I'm always out in front."

"I saw that."

"The other reason is my last name. Llevar. In Spanish, Llevar means 'to carry.'"

Secada left and I called Alexa. She was still at the office but said she'd be home in an hour or so.

"You're not gonna have a change of heart, like last night, are you?" I said.

"No, not tonight. I gotta get outta here. My brain is broken. I need a drink. I'll see you at the house."

I hung up and took the freeway heading for Bel Air. On the way I radioed Records and Identification and asked them for a deep check on Wade A. Wyatt, giving the 387 Bel Air Road address.

While I waited for them to come back to me, I transferred to the 101 Freeway heading toward the 405. Then the radio crackled.

"L-fifty-six. On your background check for Wade A. Wyatt. Subject is a white male. Twenty-six years. Six-two, one hundred eighty-two pounds. Brown hair, brown eyes. He has two arrests for possession of narcotics. One in two thousand, the other in two-thousand-four. Both busts were expunged. He is the only son of Aubrey and Beverly Wyatt, same address. His father's a well-known L.A. attorney."

"Yeah, I know who Aubrey Wyatt is. Thanks."

I hung up but almost missed the interchange to the 405 because I was wondering how Aubrey Wyatt fit into this. He was one of L.A.'s biggest movers and shakers. A letterhead founding partner of the law firm Wyatt, Clark, and Cummings. Aubrey Wyatt was definitely somebody who could throw around some weight in this town, which his son's two expunged drug busts certainly proved.

I took the 405 to Sunset and headed east. After fifteen minutes I pulled up in front of Aubrey Wyatt's mansion on Bel Air Road.

The house was a gorgeous, oversize French Normandy with a slate roof and lots of blond stonework. It sat on over an acre of property with a beautifully manicured lawn that sloped from the front porch to the street where an eight-foot-high wrought-iron fence protected the estate. There was an electric gate with gold-tipped spears. I wondered if French horns would blare theatrically when it opened.

I parked across the street and looked at the beautifully landscaped property wondering what to do next. One thing was obvious. This was a much more appropriate address for the McLaren.

Just as I was pondering my next move, the solenoids on the gate started clicking and the heavy wrought iron swung slowly open. Seconds later, a red sports car flew down the drive and bounced hard as it hit the street. The front undercarriage left a little trail of sparks as it powered out of a right-hand turn, almost clipping my car before it sped away up the street going well over the speed limit. I'm not an expert on exotic cars, but I thought this one was a Ferrari Enzo, which if I remembered correctly, is a limited edition model worth close to a million dollars. The car was going fifty by the time it hit the end of the block.

A lot of law enforcement is just playing hunches. If I'd stopped to think about it, I probably would have let him go, but I didn't stop. On an impulse, I put the Acura in gear, spun a smoking U-turn and headed after the million-dollar sports car.

It was hard to catch. Whoever was behind the wheel was way over the speed limit and paying little attention to traffic laws.

Finally, I got close enough and gave the siren hidden under the hood a growl. I also flashed the red lights the police garage had installed in the Acura's chrome grill. The Enzo didn't slow, so I pulled up on his bumper and hit the wailer again, this time letting it go for twenty seconds. My red lights flashed manically, strobe-lighting the big trunk of the midengine Ferrari. The car finally pulled to the curb. Before I even got out of my MDX I had already worked up a healthy dislike for the driver. As I crossed to the car I pulled out my badge.

When the window of the Ferrari came down, I was looking down at a handsome young man in an expensive black leather jacket. His left hand was up on the wheel and I could see a ten-thousand-dollar Presidential Rolex on his wrist.

At that exact moment, the silver and black Black-Berry on the passenger seat rang. He picked it up.

"Shut that off. You're not available," I told him.

"Gotta go," he said into the phone and then shut it down.

"License and registration," I said.

"Come on, a traffic bust? Give me a fucking break."

"Hey, you almost hit me coming out of that driveway."

"It's my street," he said defiantly. "I've got someplace I've got to go."

"Your street? You really gonna stick with that?" I was smiling at him. It was my wide, humorless smile that contained no warmth. It hung on my face like a vacant warning. "Gimme your license and registration or you're going to the Men's Central Jail," I told him.

"Jesus." He leaned over, grabbed the registration out of the glove box and thrust it angrily through the window at me along with his license. I took my time looking them over.

"You're Wade Wyatt?"

"That's what it says, doesn't it?"

"You better rein in some of that attitude, Wade. It's not getting you where you want to be."

He glanced impatiently at his expensive Rolex, then looked at me with disdain as I continued to check his registration.

"This car is registered to Aubrey Wyatt," I said.

"My father. It's his car. I have his permission to use it, of course."

I leaned in. "Listen, Wade, I was just coming over to see you when you spun out of that driveway and almost clipped me."

"See me? What for?"

I played out a little line. "Some Hispanic guy in the Valley is driving around in your Mercedes McLaren. The oh-eight. I couldn't catch him, but he didn't look like his name should be Wade Wyatt. I was wondering if the car was stolen."

"Look, there's no problem. It's okay for him to use it. I'm really late. I've got an important appointment. Do we have to do this at ten o'clock at night?"

"Where are you going?"

"None of your business."

"So tell me, what's your connection to Mike Church?"

"Mike who?"

"Mike Church. The guy you're letting drive the McLaren."

"Oh, him."

"Yeah, him."

"I hardly know the guy."

"You hardly know him, but you let him tool around in your half-million-dollar car?"

"He's a good mechanic, okay? The McLaren was having trouble with the suspension and Mike what's-his-face was taking a look at it for us. I guess he's gotta test-drive it to fix it, okay?"

I stood looking at him, smiling my big empty smile, trying to look like any minute I might snap and turn him into pavement paste.

"Can I go?" He seemed less sure now.

"Whatta you do when you're not almost killing people with your dad's car?" I asked.

"Whatta I do?"

"That was the question."

"I've got a summer job at Cartco. My uncle owns it. It's a big factory operation in Burbank. They make cartons to ship stuff in. I'm working part-time in their Legal Affairs Department while I'm studying for the California Bar. I just graduated from Harvard Law. Ever heard of it?"

"Yeah, I've heard of Harvard. Smart kids with bad manners. In Boston, right?"

"Boy, listen to the man. Really got it dialed in, don't ya?"

"With your attitude, I think you're gonna make a great lawyer." Still smiling. Still holding his license and registration.

"Can I go now?"

"You keep it down, Mr. Wyatt. The speed limit on these streets is twenty-five. I could write you for reckless driving, but since we hit it off so well, I'm gonna let you go with just a warning."

He took his license and registration and started the engine. The Ferrari sounded tight and he revved it up to high RPMs, goosing it twice for effect before squealing away from the curb. The million-dollar sports car was so overpowered it left an inch of rubber beside my right foot. I watched the taillights swing left at the end of the street. I heard that distinct Ferrari whine as it roared up Sunset Boulevard, taking Wade A. Wyatt to wherever it was he needed to be in such a hurry.

CHAPTER 9

When I got home Alexa was on the phone to Chooch. She had tears in her eyes and was wiping at them with her hand as I walked into our bedroom.

"Gotta go, honey," she said into the receiver. "I'll tell your dad." She hung up.

"Couldn't you let me talk to him?" I said, disappointed.

"He was supposed to be in his room by ten. I kept him on the phone for almost an hour. The coaches were starting to circle." She walked into the bathroom and closed the door. "Make me a drink. Scotch. I'll meet you out back," she called.

I knew she was in there doing a repair job on her face. She didn't like to have anybody see her crying.

I poured her a scotch and water and made one for myself and walked out to the backyard. Franco was sitting at the foot of the garden, dividing his attention between me and a family of ducks who had piqued his predatory interest by swimming perilously close to his position. Finally, Alexa came out, gave me a perfunctory kiss, and sat in her chair beside me facing the canal. She was barefoot, wearing jeans and a heavy peacoat.

"For June, this is really nippy," she observed.

"Yep. But a high pressure front is moving in. It'll be back to normal soon."

It seemed we were down to discussing the weather on our short list of safe subjects. Alexa sipped her drink.

"How's Chooch?" I asked.

"He's good. Practice is going great. He thinks he's third on the depth chart."

"Hey, that's pretty good for a sophomore."

"Red shirt freshman," she reminded me. Then she sighed. "I'm afraid I spilled over a little on him." She sipped her scotch again. The ice cubes rattled pleasantly in her glass as she returned it to her lap.

"Maybe it's not such a good idea, putting our problems on him," I said. "Besides, holding your hand is supposed to be *my* job."

"I know . . . I know," she said wistfully. "I started talking and before I knew it, I was just letting it rip. Telling him how I can't remember a damn thing, and how I don't feel right inside my body—like everything got connected back up wrong."

I reached over and took her hand. She smiled at me wanly. "Thank God I have you."

"And always will," I told her. My response sounded forced.

We sat in silence for a while, watching Franco watch the ducks.

Then Alexa mused, "Must be nice to have a life where people put your basic needs in a bowl for you each morning, and all you have to do is chase after things you don't need."

I was only half-listening, trying to figure out a way to bring up the subject of the meds I'd found and had analyzed at the police lab. Any way I tried to get into it would sound like I was spying on her, going through her things. The thought that she was having seizures and that one of them might have caused the car crash, which she still hadn't told me about, frightened me. I'd worked out a way to approach the subject, but sitting here I lost my nerve because I knew it would get ugly, so I settled for chitchat.

We talked about Chooch and about Delfina starting summer school classes at USC. I'm not very good at hiding things from my wife and because I didn't want to deal with her seizures yet, I found myself telling her about the Hickman case. About Secada Llevar bringing the I.A. file to me after Captain Sasso had shut the investigation down. I ran through the problems with Brian Devine's original investigation. I recounted my day, telling her about my trip to Corcoran State Prison and how I thought Tru Hickman had somehow been misclassified and how he was being raped and beaten on a daily basis in prison.

One of Alexa's many talents is that she is a great listener. She sat quietly, asking me a few pertinent questions, until I finished by telling her about the strange arrival of Wade and Aubrey Wyatt to the case after finding the McLaren in the Valley and pulling Wade over in his father's million-dollar Enzo Ferrari. When I was done she sat there thinking. Even though she was the victim of a traumatic brain injury or an acquired one, depending on who you talked to, she still knew how to see into the heart of a situation, and this was no exception.

"Jane Sasso is your main problem," she observed. "She's gonna go after you."

"Yeah, I agree. That's why we're sorta working it off the books."

"There's no such thing as off the books," she said. "There's authorized and unauthorized."

"Well, you know . . ."

"No, I don't. Jane wants the case closed, but you and Secada Llevar are working it behind her and Deputy

Chief Townsend's backs. That's a career wrecker, Shane. You both need to drop it."

"You didn't see this guy," I said. "Tru Hickman's walking wounded, scared out of his skull with stitches in his asshole. Devine blew the investigation. Morales pled it out for the state and this Vanowen Street Loco, Mike Church, was never even looked at. Everything tells me he's the doer and now Wade and Aubrey Wyatt pop up out of nowhere. There's something going on here. This case is a lot bigger than it looks."

She silently considered this for a minute, then got up and said, "Be right back."

She went inside the house. I turned and saw her through the plate glass, fixing a second drink. She looked beautiful, illuminated in the window. Like a photograph in *Sunset* magazine. *The striking young wife makes a drink in her classic canal house.* If I didn't know what she was going through, I would have never guessed the stress raging inside her. She finally turned away from the window, came back outside, and walked across the lawn, then settled into her chair.

"Okay, so drop the other shoe," she said.

"What other shoe?"

"Shane. Please. You've already got a course of action planned. What is it?"

"I want to go talk to the D.A., Tito Morales. But the minute I do, this thing is going to become a shit sandwich. I need your help."

"To protect you from Jane Sasso."

"Yeah."

"She's a captain. I'm a lieutenant."

"You're acting head of the Detective Bureau. You picked her for that job and organizationally, you're on the same level."

"I'm still just a lieutenant. I report to Deputy Chief Townsend in Operations. Sasso's a captain. She reports directly to the Chief of Police, who I might remind you, is the very same guy who is evaluating my whole damn career right now."

"I know. The timing on this sucks."

"I can't duke it out with Jane Sasso. When you're involved, my motive is always suspect." She was looking tight around the eyes again. Her movements became jerky and abrupt.

"I'm just saying, throw a block for us. Buy us a week. In a week I think we can unravel this."

"Shane, you're in Homicide Special. This is an I.A. case. Detective Llevar only came to you because of me. You can't be this gullible."

"She admits that. It's just, we both feel this isn't right."

"I can't take much more of this. I'm shaking apart."

"I'm sorry."

"For once, stop being Robin Hood, or Zorro, or Don Quixote—whatever mythic figure you are this week. You can't right all the wrongs in the world, babe. Some bad stuff is just gonna get past you."

"I'm only trying to right this one bad case. Just this one."

She sat watching Franco for a long moment. He had gone into killer mode, hunkering low on his paws, creeping on his belly toward the edge of the canal, lying in wait. A hunter stalking prey.

"You know how much trouble I'm in with Chief Townsend already," Alexa said. "If he was in the meeting where Detective Llevar was told to drop this, then my boss has already spoken. Don't do this to me. I'm trying to save what's left of this mess I still call my career."

"But—"

"I can't protect you, Shane. I wish I could, but I can't. I can't even protect myself anymore."

She stood and walked into the house. I was watching her through the windows as she crossed the living room. Suddenly, she slipped and fell. I was on my feet and running in one motion. I thought she had tripped on the rug, but when I reached her side I saw that she was rigid—convulsing. I dropped to my knees and grabbed hold of her.

"No, no, no!" I pried her mouth open, then pulled her tongue forward and wedged my wallet between her teeth so she wouldn't bite her tongue. I'd dealt with epileptic seizures when I was in Patrol and knew they generally didn't last long, but seeing Alexa spasm on our living room rug was more than I could bear.

I don't know how long it lasted, but shortly the convulsions began to diminish and then she lay exhausted in my arms.

"I'm calling Luther," I said. Luther was her neurosurgeon.

"No. Please no," she pleaded. "Just take me into the bedroom."

I picked her up and carried her down the hall into our bedroom, then laid her on the bed and put a cover over her to keep her warm.

"I've been having convulsions," she finally admitted, her voice a weak whisper. "This is the fifth one."

"I know. I found your pills."

"You can't . . . you can't tell anyone."

"Honey, you need help."

"This will go away. It's part of the TBI. I've been researching it on the Internet. Convulsions usually pass after a year or so. I'm not running it through the department or using insurance because if I have seizures on my record, I could get retired on a medical disability. I got a doctor friend to treat it. She gave me some medicine."

"But, Alexa?"

"You can't tell. I'm begging you, Shane. All I ever wanted to be was a cop. They'll take it from me. Promise me. You've got to promise."

"I promise," I finally said.

I held her hand until she fell asleep. Then I lay down beside her and cradled her. She felt frail and small, her bones closer to the surface. As I held her I was so sad, I almost cried.

CHAPTER 10

Alexa was out of bed by six, out of the house by six-thirty. I tried to stop her, but she was on a mission. She timed it so I was still in my boxers in the bathroom when her police department driver showed up. I heard the car door slam and heard the car pull away. I couldn't very well chase her down the street in my underwear.

After she was gone I sat at the kitchen table and wondered what my next move was. As I thought about it, a wave of desolation flooded over me. I had problems everywhere, both personal and professional. I had not been lonely like this since before I met Alexa and Chooch. For the last five years we'd been such a team, all the darkness had been pushed out of my life. As a family, we were always there for each other. But that had changed. Chooch and Delfina were now in college and busy with their own lives. That left just the two of us. But with Alexa's TBI causing such a loss of intimacy, we had experienced a shift in our marital dynamics. We had become two people sharing a space; two friends who didn't talk, and when we did, we often said the wrong things. As I sat at the kitchen table trying to down a bowl of dry cereal, I felt more isolated than I had since I was an orphan in the Huntington House Group Home as a boy.

I shook it off and walked into the bathroom to get

ready for my day. I soon found myself staring into the mirror. The guy who was looking back at me was the same angular, rugged thug who greeted me each morning. He had the same lean body, unruly hair, and scar tissue over his eyes, but now he seemed like a stranger. I didn't know what he wanted anymore. I wasn't even sure if I trusted him. Last year I had a magical life with a magical woman and a great son, but that reality was drifting further and further away; close enough to see, but not to touch.

I dressed in a black shirt, a black tie, a black jacket, and pants. It wasn't until I was getting set to leave and caught a glimpse of my Johnny Cash getup in the door mirror, that I realized what a deep funk I was really in. I looked like a mortuary plot salesman. I could have changed clothes, but what the hell. They always say, "Dress the way you feel," and I felt angry and black. Let today's victims be the ones to worry about it. I got into the Acura and by nine I was coming off the freeway, heading toward the PAB downtown.

I rode the elevator up to five and tried to smile, but my humorless grin was stretched tight.

"Who are you supposed to be, Black Bart?" Loni Paul, our media affairs assistant said, as she passed me coming off the elevator.

"I'm The Shadow and The Shadow knows," I said theatrically, going for retro humor, but not scoring.

I got to my desk and hadn't even put my ass in the chair before the phone rang.

"Scully, Homicide Special," I said into the receiver.

"Shane, it's Sally."

It was good to hear my partner's voice. "How's the murder trial coming?"

"Like trying to push shit through a tube with a Q-Tip," she said. "Delays, sidebars . . . these lawyers are making a meal of it. I won't be done until at least Friday."

"Okay," I said glumly.

"Listen, Shane. I overheard some people from the D.A.'s office talking about you in the lunchroom. Couldn't tell what it was about so I cornered one of the guys a few minutes ago and he tells me you've got some trouble heading your way."

"What kind of trouble?"

"The D.A.'s office gets a charge sheet memo from PSB every morning. It's a list of all pending I.A. beefs, sort of a heads-up document so the D.A. can decide if he's interested in monitoring any of our police misconduct boards. Apparently, there's a big complaint on you coming out of Jane Sasso's office. That's all they'd tell me. What's that all about? You wait till I'm out of the building and then go over and tie a knot in that cat's tail? What're you doing, partner?"

"I hesitate to go into it over the phone, but thanks for the warning."

"Okay. Just thought you'd like to know. Whatever it is, it's probably got some weight on it or it wouldn't be in the rumor mill."

I thanked her again and hung up, then I sat for a minute contemplating the Ugly Wall, which is the far wall of our offices where pictures of our felony wants are hung. It was a gallery of unrepentant killers who looked down at me with cold mug-shot stares. I ran Sally's warning through my survival meter. My guess was that Scout had leveled with Captain Sasso about how she lost her creds and that confession had put us on a fast track to the La Brea Tar Pits.

Jeb Calloway came out of his office and crooked a finger at me. I got up and followed him into his office. He closed the door. Always a bad sign.

He got right to it. "You wanted time off for a personal problem. Now I find out you and some I.A. detective named Llevar are working a closed case against the specific orders of the head of PSB, Deputy Chief Townsend, and his adjutant, Commander Summers."

"Sasso shouldn't have closed it. It's a good case, Cal."

"I don't give a shit if you're about to solve the Princess Di mess. You've been told to file the son-of-a-bitch." He was almost screaming.

"Are you gonna listen to me, or are you gonna scream at me?"

"So it's true?" he said, shaking his head in disgust. "Man, sometimes I don't get you at all."

"Captain, if I leave a copy of this file with you, along with my notes, will you at least just read it? At worst the wrong guy is in prison. At best it's an extremely sloppy investigation that needs to be revisited. I.A. is supposed to look at bad due-process cases, not shove them under the rug."

"Captain Sasso called me this morning. She notified me that she's put a charge sheet on you into the system. I should be getting it this afternoon."

"She's charging me? With what?"

"Insubordination, malfeasance, refusing a direct order."

"I never even talked to her. How could I refuse her direct order?"

"Hey, smart guy, did Detective Llevar tell you this case was off the boards? That Sasso closed it?"

"Yeah, but—"

"So you refused her direct order. This is administrative. Prior knowledge is sufficient here. You're probably gonna get put on suspension."

"I can't be suspended like that. I get a supervisor's

review with you and a Skelly hearing first. You guys aren't just gonna throw away the Police Bill of Rights, are you?"

"I'm in your corner, Shane, okay? Why I am sometimes baffles me, but good God, man, if you're gonna set fire to Jane Sasso's hair, at least wear gloves and a mask. Why can't you have a little finesse once in a while?"

"What's my status, Captain?"

"Your status is fucked beyond all belief, but technically still on duty. I'll try and figure out a way to fix this. But, Shane, stay away from the Hickman case. You got that? Are you reading me? This is an order from your immediate supervisor. Do you want me to write it on your arm in Magic Marker so you won't forget?"

"Not necessary. I can remember."

"Then get out of here. Go do something you're supposed to be doing for a change."

I walked out of his office and back to my cubicle. Phones were ringing, teletypes rattling. There was a low din of squad room noise. I looked around at all of this—my chosen profession. I was a blue knight. My job was the application of justice in a world gone mad. I was good at it. The job suited me. So why did I always seem to be on the outside looking in?

I grabbed my black jacket off the back of my chair and left. I'd already decided what I wanted to do next.

On my way out, I left the Hickman file in Captain Calloway's box.

CHAPTER 11

The Los Angeles Superior Court Northwest Division is on Erwin Street in the Valley. The prosecutor's office building is one block over on Van Nuys. I parked in the lot behind the large modern structure and got out of the car. Everything told me this was a terrible idea. Maybe because of frustration with Alexa I was striking out, throwing a temper tantrum, breaking my own toys. Maybe I should go to see Dr. Lusk and get some more beige-on-beige insight.

What I did was walk into the lobby and ask to see Tito Morales. I figured he'd be in because most area supervisors were desk jockeys. Except, that is, for Brian Devine, who it seemed could always make time to roll on a call and ruin a case.

I showed my badge to the lobby security officer. As I signed in I happened to notice that the name on the line right above mine was Detective Secada Llevar. Time of arrival, five minutes ago. Apparently there was more than one kamikaze in the building.

I went up to the attorney's floor on four and walked down the hall to Morales's office. The waiting room was large enough to accommodate two seating areas, both with leather sofas and club chairs. Sitting in the one across from the reception desk was Scout Llevar. She was also in black today. Another six-hundred-dollar pantsuit, but unlike me, she had jazzed it up with a red silk scarf. Her long dark hair curled seductively around her neck and shoulders. The woman was breathtaking. I entered the room and took the chair opposite her.

"Come here often?" she said, smiling.

"You got a bullet I can chew before this guy beats us to death?"

"Don't worry," she said. "Won't happen. This is my best outfit."

"You told Captain Sasso what we were doing," I said. "Not smart. I understand that you hate to lie, but now I've got a charge sheet heading my way for insubordination and a lot of other nonsense."

"Yeah, me too." She uncrossed her legs and leaned forward. "But I didn't tell her. Apparently somebody from I.A. saw us having lunch at Leonardo's and mentioned it to her. Then when you went up to Corcoran, somebody up there made a call to our office to check out your story. Jane Sasso may be a five-foot-eight-inch hemorrhoid with ears, but she's no dummy. She knows how to add up facts."

"Great."

"She called me in last night and confronted me. What choice did I have? So I leveled with her. Sorry. I'm facing a suspension, too, so I figured what the hell, maybe my *carnal* here might be willing to admit his mistake and to drag us out of the ditch."

"That's either good thinking, or the worst idea since pet alligators."

"What're you doing here?"

"I got pissed off. I get impulsive and self-destructive when I'm pissed."

"Immature," she said. "But at least I understand it."

"This guy, if he's not on the up-and-up, is gonna pound us into the sand."

"Look, I know a little about Tito," Scout said. "His parents are from some little Mexican hill town. He's an ex-cop, LAPD. Used to be one of us. Went to Southwestern Law School at night, worked his butt off to get his degree. Now he's got a shot at the mayor's office. He may have cut this bad deal to plead the Hickman case, but trying to get rid of cases to clear the court calendar is part of a prosecutor's job. He was supplied bad info by Lieutenant Devine and he acted on it. Now we're just gonna put some better case facts on the table and ask him to do the right thing."

A female assistant appeared in the doorway. "Mr. Morales will see you now."

"I hope you're right," I muttered.

Scout was fumbling with something in her purse as she stood. "You'll see," she said. "He'll give us a straight hearing."

As we crossed the room to Morales's office, she pulled her backup clip out of her purse. She thumbed a 9mm bullet out and handed it to me before she stepped through the door. "In case I'm wrong." *What a kidder*.

Tito Morales was compact and handsome, with smooth skin and a boatload of Latin charisma. His dark hair and strong jaw gave him an air of prominence. He had one of those smiles that light up a room. His eyes flitted across me, barely registering before they missile-locked on Scout.

"Come in, come in. Sit down. Did Elena get you something to drink?" All of this to her. I'd suddenly become invisible.

"We're fine, thank you, sir," Secada said.

"How can I help?" He sat opposite us and smiled warmly at her.

"Do you remember the Hickman case?" I asked.

"Hickman . . . Hickman . . ." He was looking up reflectively, showing Scout his heroic profile. "Hickman. Jeez, that's familiar." He seemed lost.

"You pled the case," I reminded him. "Probably didn't have it in the system for more than two or three weeks. The story was he killed his mother for two hundred dollars."

"Oh, yeah. Right. I remember now. The kid was a crystal meth freak. That one?"

"That's the one."

"Detective Llevar is an IO at PSB and she received a letter from Hickman alleging that his case was mishandled," I continued. "As you know, it's a function of her job at I.A. to investigate these kinds of complaints and three days ago she started looking into it."

"I have the file right here," Secada said, and handed her copy to him.

He didn't open it, never took his eyes off of her. "As I recall, Truit Hickman confessed."

"Yes, but he's not all there," Secada answered. "He's done way too much meth, Mr. Morales."

"Tito, please. I'm not much on formalities."

He was very easy to like. With our huge Hispanic population in Los Angeles, I could see why he could go far in Southern California politics.

"Thank you, Tito." Secada widened her smile. When she turned the wattage up, I heard him exhale slightly. The hook was set.

"Anyway," she continued, "during Tru's interrogation, he says he got confused and signed a confession that Lieutenant Devine wrote for him."

"I see." Morales opened the Hickman file in his hands and frowned down at it. "Just hit the high points then," he said. "I assume you're here because you feel there's a due-process problem."

"Yes, sir, we do," Scout said.

We ran Tito through the basics. Once we were finished he continued to frown.

"This sounds horrible," he finally said.

"Yes sir," Secada said. "That's why it seems wrong that the case was closed by Captain Sasso just as we started to get into it."

Morales stood and walked to his window and looked out. "This is exactly the kind of thing that really gets me," he said softly. "I have to take the investigator's statements and reports at face value. Same with a confession. I have to assume a suspect was informed correctly of his rights and wasn't lied to about his polygraph results or case facts in order to secure a confession. If this murder was inadequately investigated, or if the suspect was lied to, then it should be reopened. For the primary investigator to fail to follow through on that footprint, or fully interview this Mike Church person, is absolutely untenable. What the hell was Van Nuys Robbery-Homicide thinking?"

"Exactly," Secada said.

"And despite this, Captain Sasso closed the case?"

"Worse than that, she filed a PSB charge of insubordination against us for working it after we were told not to," she said.

He turned back from the window. "Sounds like you've got a little bit of a reckless streak, Detective Llevar." Then he smiled, showing beautiful teeth. "Don't get me wrong, I like reckless when it comes to upholding the tenets of the law. It shows a commitment to principle."

All of this directed exclusively to Secada. If I wanted this guy's attention, I was going to have to drop trou and expose myself.

"If the department ever knew we were over here, we'd both get in major trouble, so we're counting on your discretion," Scout said.

"I'm glad you came." He turned his heroic gaze out the window again. "I was part of that plea bargain. If what you're telling me checks out, then we've made a terrible mistake."

"And you're willing to admit it?" Secada asked. She leaned forward, showing him a nice swell of breasts.

"As you undoubtedly know, I'm running for mayor in a few months." More great Latino porcelain came on display. "There are those in my campaign who would say that to admit such an error would cause me problems politically, but I see it differently. A man has to have a code, a standard he lives up to. My job is to stand up for what's right. If I make a mistake, then I'm honor-bound to admit it. If I sent this boy away on bad facts, then I damn sure should be the one to fix it." Somewhere up in heaven angels were singing.

"Thank you, sir," Secada said, smiling. Then she glanced at me and raised an impatient eyebrow, prompting me to say something.

"Thanks," I muttered.

He crossed to his desk and handed us each his card.

"My private line is on here. I suggest maybe you two should drop your investigation now and let me run with it. If you stay involved, you're gonna have more trouble with Jane. I'll try and help out there, but there's only so much I can do. She can be difficult sometimes."

We thanked him again and prepared to leave.

"So how do I reach you?" Tito said, addressing Secada again.

We both gave him our cards. Mine was going into some bottom desk drawer. Hers would undoubtedly end up in the glassine section of his wallet.

"I hope you can reopen this so Shane and I don't cook in the gravy," Scout said.

"I'll think of something. How 'bout if I tell PSB that

we picked up some investigative discrepancies on this situation during a standard case review."

"That should work," Scout said, smiling widely at him.

"I'll be in touch," Tito promised and led us to the door. "Listen, Detectives, I want to tell you something. Even though the insubordination charge is a problem, I salute your dedication to the truth in this case. After the parade has passed and everything's been adjudicated, it's much easier to just look the other way. You did the hard thing, which is the right thing."

"We really appreciate your time, sir," Secada beamed. I felt a twinge of annoyance, or was it jealousy?

"Tito," he reminded her.

"Tito," she said.

And then, we were out of his office and standing in the hall.

"What a doll," Scout enthused. "And he's still single."

"Still got your wallet?"

"Come on, he's charming. This is just what we needed, Shane."

"Yeah."

"Look at you. Why don't you smile? And what's with this black-on-black ensemble? You look like Steven Seagal. Who picked that outfit, for God's sake?"

"This just feels way too easy," I said.

CHAPTER 12

I left Secada in the parking lot. She seemed as if a great weight had just been lifted from her as she got into her slick-back and tooled off toward the Bradbury Building.

I guess I'm just such a natural skeptic that I couldn't accept a good break even when I got one. Or maybe it was that my luck had been running so cold, I couldn't quite believe in a crusader D.A. willing to flag a prosecutorial mistake on the eve of his own mayoral election, no matter how great his teeth or warm his smile.

Since I was already in Van Nuys, standing in the parking lot of the prosecutor's office, and had the name of Tru Hickman's court-appointed public defender in my file, I decided to look her up and see what light she could shed on this mess.

The Public Defenders Division is part of the prosecutor's office, so I found myself on the second floor of the same building I'd just exited. The P.D.'s office was a cluttered cube farm full of fresh-faced recent law school graduates. Tru had told me that his P.D. had red hair, braids, and freckles and looked like she just graduated from high school.

That pretty much fit my take when I located Yvonne Hope seated behind a battered metal desk that looked like it had been used to block a year's worth of slap shots from an NHL hockey team. She seemed implausibly young. Pippi Longstocking with a law degree. But that was only until you bothered to look deep into her blue-green eyes. They were tired, angry eyes that had seen enough misery to fill a prison.

"Truit Joseph Hickman confessed to killing his mother," she said after I told her why I was there.

"Miscarriage of justice," I said.

"Yep. We get a lot of that around here. John Dillinger, John Gotti, and Al Capone. They all got fucked by the system, too." A cynic. So young and her soul was already poisoned by her experiences.

"Take a look at some of this," I said, and pushed the folder I'd compiled across the desk at her.

Yvonne Hope didn't open it. "Lemme guess, rubber hoses in the I-room, right?"

"You shorten your last name from 'Hopeless'?"

"Don't be a smart-ass. I've been on this job for almost two years now. The average for P.D.'s in this meat house is eighteen months. The burnout rate is through the roof. You wanta know why?"

"Not really."

"I'll tell you anyway. Because just about everybody I represent is a scumbag liar. Including this guy." She tapped her short, chewed-nail ring finger on my folder. "I have baby-rapists and child molesters as clients. I have to try and get deals for people you wouldn't waste a bullet on. My job is to ignore the crime and save the criminal. It can warp you. Tru Hickman killed his mother. He copped to it. Now he's up in Corcoran and it's worse than he thought so he's had a change of heart. Next case. You got any idea how often I see that?"

"Listen, Yvonne. Can I call you that?"

"Vonnie."

"I'm not some bleeding-heart, hand-wringing, social activist, Vonnie. I'm a homicide cop. I scrape dead people off the pavement for a living. If you want to compare battle scars, I bet, with my years on the job, I'll beat yours. I'm telling you, Lieutenant Devine and Tito Morales flushed this kid on bad evidence. Pardon me for saying it, but you were supposed to defend him and you let it happen."

She sat there, all hundred and six pounds of her, and looked at me with eyes that had been hardened to the approximate texture of pale, green marbles.

"Okay, I'm listening. But I'm a stone cold bitch so make it convincing."

I gave her the rest of it, stopping when I got to the bloody shoe prints.

"Did you ever finish the match on those prints? I can't find a record of it anywhere."

"Probably never happened," she said matter-of-factly. "After we dropped the special circumstances and he copped to the murder, the plea went to my division supervisor, got signed off on, and shipped to the prosecutor's floor upstairs to get executed."

"How about the lie detector test? Were you there when he took the poly?"

"No. He did that before he asked for an attorney, before I got the case."

"It's also nowhere to be found," I said. "You ever see it?"

"He confessed to the crime. What part of that sentence is confusing to you? The confession makes the damn poly irrelevant."

"Brian Devine told him he flunked the poly. He panicked. That's why he confessed. Don't tell me you've never seen that before. A ten-year veteran of Homicide is now standing here telling you the wrong guy is probably in jail. I think this VSL gangster, Mike Church, is the doer."

She sat behind her scarred metal desk, still clocking me with machine gunner's eyes. "Whatta you want?" she finally asked.

"You handled his case a year ago. I think it was a miscarriage of justice. I guess I'm over here attorney shopping. If I can get enough evidence to refile, how'd you like to have another swing at this? Go for a writ of habeas corpus and a new trial?"

"My division chief is going to love that," she sneered. "My job is to see how many of these things I can kick down and plead out. How fast I do it counts. It's all about plumbing around here. My boss doesn't like the cleared cases to bubble back up in the bowl. What goes down must stay down."

"In Homicide, I've got the same problem. That doesn't mean either of us wants to see innocent people convicted of crimes they didn't commit. At least I hope not."

She watched me for a moment, then sighed. "Okay, Detective Scully, you get me something I can use, and I'm not talking about hearsay air balls from Tru's old meth buddies or an alibi statement from his Aunt Bea. I need something watertight as a frog's ass. If it looks good, I'll take a shot. But don't waste your time coming back here with bullshit."

Hardly Pippi Longstocking, I thought as I stood to go.

"Thanks. Gimme your card." She did and I saw that her two years' seniority in the P.D.'s office had allowed her to rise to the position of Deputy Assistant. I started to go, but she cleared her throat, so I turned to look back.

"You know, Tru Hickman won me that month's loser pool," she said.

"I'm sorry?"

"We've got a pool around here. Everybody puts in fifty bucks and picks a number. Then we ask every client who gets convicted how much he or she weighs. We add it all up and at the end of the month, the P.D. who comes closest wins the pool. I remember Hickman's case was finally settled and he was sentenced on the thirtieth of August. My number was twenty-five hundred pounds. Tru weighed one-sixteen. Put me a hundred pounds off the number. I won nine hundred and fifty dollars. Went to Vegas with two girlfriends, got drunk, screwed a guy whose name I can't remember. Don something. I always wondered if part of me accepted that plea so I could win the pool. Never been one hundred percent sure. After twenty-four months of shoveling human garbage, I still wonder about it."

I stood there and looked at her, not sure what to say to that.

"Know what we called the pool?"

"Haven't a clue."

"Justice by the pound." She frowned. "Some pretty cold shit, huh?"

CHAPTER 13

In the elevator on my way to the lobby, I reflected on the damage that working in the criminal justice system could do to the people who pulled the ropes and turned the wheels. Yvonne Hope had undoubtedly started out as a caring person. She probably went into the P.D.'s office with hopes of defending the downtrodden. But the endless supply of craven liars she got as clients killed the dream. Calluses had quickly formed to protect her from the ugly reality of her job. It had cost her a large measure of her humanity.

Nobody is immune. Cops also develop dark humor to protect themselves. After the probationer period and a rookie year in squad cars, a lot of it spent prying corpses off their steering columns or rolling in on the worst that mankind has to offer, it's hard to see things the way you used to. It says "Protect and Serve" on the door of your patrol car, but after a short time, it's hard to know why you'd want to. After finally making it to detective you're then given the pleasure of walking into a crime scene where some dope-crazed lunatic has stabbed his wife in a fit of jealous rage and spread the remains of his three grade-school children all over the walls of the apartment. The humanity you once felt toward your fellow man slowly starts leaking out of you. Nothing seems outside the bounds of normal behavior.

After I left Vonnie, the memory of her was still with me. Those eyes were still glaring defiantly in the back of my mind. I got into my car and headed farther west. There was one other thing I wanted to check on while I was out here.

I'd looked up Valley towing services in the Yellow Pages earlier and had the name of one in Van Nuys that sounded like it might belong to Mike Church. The quarter-page ad pictured two tow trucks backed up to each other so that the towing arms formed a steeple in the center of the ad. The caption under the picture read:

CHURCH OF DESTRUCTION
TOWING AND AUTO BODY WORK

This was followed by a lot of repair jargon: "Bondo Specialists"; "Qualified in Sparkle Paint Jobs"; "We'll Pimp Your Ride"; "Se Habla Espanol."

The address at 6358 Midline Drive was less than two miles from Church's house. I wasn't that far away, so I headed over to take a look.

Ten minutes later I parked across the street from a very shabby-looking auto body shop with CHURCH OF DESTRUCTION painted in faded red lettering under the eaves of a tin-roofed concrete block building. There was one paint bay and two body and fender garages, both busy. Hispanic men wielding hammers and metal sanders were creating a symphony of screaming metal. The yard out front was a clutter of automotive junk and rusting Detroit carcasses. There were trashed motorcycles, dirty oil drums, and old lumber scattered in amongst the twisted wrecks. It looked like a backyard in Tijuana. Two heavy tow rigs, big, muscular eight-wheel monsters with rear-end dualies, stout suspension, and long towing arms were parked inside the gate.

I didn't stick around long. I just wanted to get a look. I put the car in gear and pulled away. After seeing the place, one thing troubled me. Why would Wade Wyatt have any work done on his five-hundred-thousand-dollar collector Mercedes in that automotive graveyard? It was a brain stopper.

When I got back to Parker Center there was a note from Captain Calloway on my desk.

> *6 o'clock—O'Herlihy's?*
> *Cal*

O'Herlihy's is an Irish green-beer joint two blocks from the PAB. Cal wasn't in his office, but the rumor about me getting beefed by Internal Affairs had spread to the fifth floor, and people were avoiding me like I had a flesh eating virus, so I left and walked two blocks east to the bar/restaurant.

Cal was in a back booth with his feet up on the bench and his back against the side wall. His shaved black head glistened while his Mighty Mouse muscles bulged the short sleeves on his shirt. The Hickman file was open on the table in front of him.

"Sit down," he said.

I slid in. There was a half-empty pitcher of green beer already on the table with a spare glass, so I helped myself.

"This is fucking amazing," Cal said, still looking down at the pages in the file.

"Isn't it?" I agreed, sipping some beer.

For the life of me, I can't get into green beer. It always looked like lizard piss to me. Beyond that, O'Herlihy's was an Irish cliché. Green walls, wood booths, sawdust on the floor, and "Danny Boy" coming out of the speakers at least five times an hour.

"Why did Sasso close this?" Cal asked, as he read. "If ever a case needed to be looked at, this is it."

"Somebody told her to."

"You think?"

"Whatta you think?"

"I think there's so much wrong here it's hard to know where to start," Cal said.

"And you didn't even have the pleasure of hearing Tru Hickman whine about getting his asshole ripped."

Cal turned to me and pitched the file onto the table between us. "Your charge sheet came over from PSB today."

"I didn't see it."

"It was missing a signature on the write-up page, so I sent it back. Buys a few hours, maybe a day."

"To do what?"

"I don't know. You tell Alexa about this?"

"She's got her hands full with her performance review," I lied. I didn't want to tell him that even my wife wouldn't help me.

"These due-process things are all I.A. cases," he mused. "I've just been sitting here trying to come up with a way to get it over to us, but I can't think of one. Jane is territorial as all hell. We try to hijack and work one of her cases, especially one she just trash-canned, we're gonna learn the full and complete meaning of the words, 'extreme departmental reprimand.'"

"Detective Llevar and I gave a copy of the file to Tito Morales this afternoon."

"And you did this after I told you in no uncertain terms to drop the case? Man, I love being your supervisor."

"Whatta you want from me, Cal? I can't control myself. It's in my DNA."

He waved this away with a muscled hand.

"What the hell did you go to him for? He pled it. He's not gonna help you."

"That's not what he says. He listened. Thought the case sounded bad. Promised to get into it. He was doing his Hispanic Crusader thing. All that was missing was a camera crew and a maroon tie."

"You believe him?"

"Secada does. She thinks he's neat."

"What's your take? I'd rather trust that."

"I think it can't get much worse than it is, so I'm hoping he's exactly what he says he is."

Cal sat there for a long moment. Then he said, "You should tell Alexa. I know she doesn't outrank Sasso, but she was the one who appointed Jane to head the rat squad, and at least they're on the same level of the department flow chart."

"Alexa reports to an A-Chief. Jane reports to the Super Chief. She'll lose in a shootout."

"Yeah, maybe, but still . . ."

"Let's lay low and see what Tito Morales comes up with," I said.

After a moment, Cal sighed. "Want me to get us another pitcher of beer?"

"Sure. I'll drink another beer with you, but it's got to be the right color this time."

It was after eight and I'd had one or two beers too many when I finally left O'Herlihy's, so, to burn it off, I jogged back to the PAB garage. I got into the Acura and headed home. I didn't know where Alexa was. She wasn't in her office and she wasn't picking up at home. I was tired of worrying about her and me. Us. Tired of the Hickman case, tired of this stupid black outfit I was wearing.

Twenty minutes later, I was driving down Abbot Kinney Boulevard a few blocks from my house when I heard a siren wail behind me. I looked in the rearview mirror and saw a black and white with its red lights flashing. How did the saying go? *I only had two beers, Officer.*

I pulled over and was getting my badge ready when my door was yanked open. Without warning, I was pulled forcibly from the car by my suit coat and slammed up against the fender. When I got my bearings I was looking into the meaty face and glinting eyes of Lieutenant Brian Devine. He'd gained some weight since I saw him last, but that crazy, out-of-control look was still there, buzzing maniacally.

"How you been, Scully?" he asked, not at all interested in the answer.

"Lieutenant." A nonconfrontational reply. Waiting him out. Trying to judge his intensity.

"Understand you've taken an interest in one of my old homicide investigations," he growled.

"Wasn't an investigation, Loo, it was a piñata party. You broke that kid on bad facts."

"Really?"

"You wanta back off? You're in my space here."

"Fuck you, asshole."

We stood glaring at each other. Then he said, "Here's the message, cowboy. You leave that case alone. If I find out you're even thinking about it, I'm gonna roll up on you like I did fifteen years ago. Only this time, I won't be threatening. This time, *your* family pays the full and complete price. I can put some serious hurt on your people, Scully."

I felt my adrenaline surge. I was on the balls of my feet. The beer had burned off. I was up and ready for this. Actually, I'd been thinking about it on and off since '93.

"Hey, Brian," I said coldly. "First off, I'm not the same fucked-up guy I was back then. You may want to bear that in mind. Second, you blew the Hickman case beyond all reason. You're an asshole, but you're not stupid, so I figure something else had to be going on there. Whatever it was, I'm gonna find out. Third, I'm not afraid of your bullshit. I've faced worse than you and I'm still breathing. Matter of fact, you're the one needs to be careful. I'm not always a stable person. Read my file. I'm a rage-filled lunatic who could snap at any moment and turn you into wall-splatter."

He was still more or less leaning on me, but as I spoke this craziness the words managed to distract him just enough so I could raise my arms up without his noticing. I suddenly gave him a hard, two-handed chuck, catching him under the nipples on both sides, and knocking him backwards, onto his ass in the street. He scrambled back to his feet and pulled his weapon. Mine was already out.

"You were always pretty good at blowing guys up when they didn't see it coming. How do you like it this way?"

We stood there, right on Abbot Kinney Boulevard, with traffic streaming past. Two assholes in suits, guns pointed at each other. Drivers were slowing down, scoping us out, registering shock, then powering on.

"You got a family, too," I said. "Don't fuck with me, Lieutenant. If I see you anywhere near my wife or my son, I'm coming after you and yours. You'll never see it coming."

The hatred flared on Devine's face, but he wasn't ready for me in this form or location. I saw all this compute in his eyes before he slowly put his gun away.

"Watch out behind you," he finally growled.

"You, too," I said.

Then, he turned and got into his borrowed squad car. It had a pipe front bumper with vertical bars for pushing stalled cars. After he put the unit in gear, he floored it and slammed into the back of my MDX, bouncing the Acura ten feet up the road. Then he hit reverse, Y-turned out, and powered away.

He'd mashed my back bumper and rear door, and shattered a taillight. It was at least a few thousand dollars worth of damage, maybe more. Even so, I was smiling. I had confronted an old ghost. For fifteen years I'd waited to set that bad decision aside. For fifteen years I'd regretted not testifying against him. His hitting my car like that told me something. Lt. Devine was feeling exposed. Whatever this corruption was, he was definitely involved and it was much closer to the surface than I'd originally imagined.

As I got in my car and drove away, one thing was very clear in my mind.

In the end, one of us was going down.

CHAPTER 14

It was eight-thirty when I pulled into my driveway and parked my busted Acura in the carport next to Alexa's rented BMW. I knew her car was still at the Venice Auto Body Shop for repair because the fender guy called the house about a parts problem and I happened to pick up the phone.

Alexa still hadn't mentioned that she crashed her car and that really bothered me, but if I brought it up, I knew it would trigger another argument.

Inside I found Alexa at the desk in the alcove closet we'd converted into her home office. She had papers strewn everywhere. I'd never seen her work space in such disarray. The old Alexa was organized. This new one could never seem to find anything.

"Hi," I said as I entered.

"I wish you wouldn't move things on my desk, Shane. I had all this stuff exactly where I needed it. Now I can't find anything."

"Alright," I said. "I'm sorry."

I hadn't touched her desk, but I didn't want to fight about that, either. I went into the bedroom and changed from my black gunfighter's outfit into jeans and an old LAPD sweatshirt. Then I got a beer and headed outside to the backyard for some perspective.

I was sitting out there trying to sort through everything, when Alexa came out and put a hesitant hand on my shoulder.

"I'm sorry."

"It's okay."

"You didn't move anything on my desk, did you?"

"No, ma'am."

She rubbed my neck for a minute, then came and sat beside me. "I can't organize my thoughts like I used to. I do things, and half an hour later I find myself doing them again."

"Honey, it will get better."

"When? When is it gonna get better? Part of me wants so badly to hold on to this job because I love it, and part of me knows I'm screwing up so badly I don't deserve to be there."

This was the opening I'd been waiting for, but I wanted to come at it another way. For the moment, I changed the subject and said, "I got rear-ended on my way home. Gonna have to get the Acura fixed. I was thinking I should take the MDX to Venice Auto Body on Ninth, then go to that rental car place on the corner of Ocean, and get something to drive until it's fixed."

I saw her stiffen. I already knew the place on Ocean was where she'd rented the replacement BMW. Venice Auto Body was where her car was being repaired. If I went to either of those places, she knew she'd be busted. I held my breath while we sat in silence.

She inhaled deeply. "Shane, I need to tell you something. That car out there in the garage. It's not mine. It's a rental. I crashed my car, too. The first convulsion happened when I was driving home last week. Nobody got hurt. I hit a tree two blocks from here. That's why I've been using a department driver to chauffeur me."

I reached out and took her hand. "I was worried

about you driving when you first told me about the convulsions."

"And you're not mad?"

"Why should I be mad? You couldn't help it."

She thought about that, and then turned to face me. "You knew already, didn't you?"

Her blue eyes were so beautiful, I was always amazed at the many ways she could look at me—sometimes with childlike innocence, other times with sexual mischief and sometimes, like now, with razor-sharp understanding.

"You knew. I can't believe you knew," she repeated.

We sat holding hands silently, for a moment.

"And you didn't say anything?"

"No."

"Why?"

"Because I understood. It wasn't about me, it was about you."

"I sure hit the jackpot when I found you," she said, and laid her head on my shoulder. I put my arm around her.

We sat like that, feeling a closeness we hadn't felt in a long time.

Then, from out of nowhere, she said, "I'm sorry I haven't wanted to make love in a while. I know that bothers you."

"It's okay," I said, still holding her.

"We could go inside. We could do it now," she offered tentatively.

"Is that what you want?" I said.

"Not really." She smiled sadly. "I'm never quite in the mood anymore."

"Then we should wait," I said. "It's more important that we talk."

"I used to be so sexual," she said sadly. "Nothing feels the same anymore. It's not you."

"I know."

"I'll find my way back, Shane."

"I'll be right here."

We continued to sit like that for almost an hour, feeling close, feeling sad, feeling strangely different.

CHAPTER 15

"There were two years, I think it was the fifth grade and half of the sixth, where I stopped being Secada Llevar and became Sally Levitt. I put blond streaks in my hair and tried to become a Valley Girl." Scout wrinkled her nose and her voice shot up an octave. "I'm like totally amped for those bodacious dudes. They're the bomb." She smiled. "My parents put up with Sally Levitt because they understood how lost I was. I felt so *brown*. So not part of it. Nobody looked like me. Not my dolls, nobody on my favorite TV shows. I was a *bracero*'s daughter trying to make it in this mostly white, press-on-nail middle school, so I understand Miguel Iglesia wanting to be Mike Church. A lot of Hispanic kids go through that. I certainly did."

"Only with him, it's not a stage," I said.

"That's because he's big and mean enough to force a result. I couldn't hold it. I wasn't Sally Levitt. I didn't understand her. My blonde streaks all turned orange in the YWCA pool. It was a cheesy disguise, and I knew it. Worse still, I saw the disappointment in my parents' eyes, so I moved on. I had to discover who I was and eventually I came to love that person. A happy ending."

I sat there listening to Secada, thinking about how fragile identities really were. I was forged by loneliness and anger as a boy and then transformed as an adult by a family who loved me. In a millisecond, a bullet had altered Alexa's core, changed who she was and how she thought. It sliced through her mood center, setting in play new thoughts and emotions.

Secada looked over at me and seemed to sense my dark mood. "What about you? Didn't you ever have an identity crisis as a kid?"

We were parked across the street from Aubrey Wyatt's Bel Air estate, sitting in the front seat of a new maroon Cadillac I'd borrowed from the drug enforcement motor pool. The leather smelled sweet. The gelled paint and polished chrome fit this ritzy neighborhood. It was ten-thirty the same evening. I had left Alexa working at her desk, and Scout and I were half an hour into an unauthorized stakeout.

"My whole upbringing was an identity crisis," I told her.

"Come on. It couldn't have been that bad."

"It was what it was. It doesn't help to talk about it."

We sat in silence. I felt her gaze fix on me.

"I don't blackmail or bite," she said.

I don't know why I was hesitant to take this next step with her; why I was reluctant to share my personal backstory and feelings. Maybe it was because I knew there was a strong attraction between us. Talking about my childhood, my early fears, was like letting down a fence, and allowing her to come closer. Close enough to see my shortcomings. That act of trust would put her in another category, and it was one I wasn't sure I knew how to deal with. It felt dangerous, yet at the same time, exciting.

"Do you think I'm coming on to you?" she suddenly asked.

"Are you?"

"I don't mess with my partners, especially married partners."

"Good."

"No, listen. I like you, Shane. I like that you went to bat on this, despite the heat coming from Sasso and PSB. I know why you don't want to tell your wife what we're doing. I've heard the scuttlebutt. I know she's been different since she got back. I knew that before I ever came to see you about this. I just hoped she might be strong enough to lend a hand. But I understand why she can't."

"She's not different. She's just fallen a little behind," I snapped, rushing to her defense.

"I'm not being critical. My God, she was shot in the head. You don't think I understand what you're going through? Listen, Shane . . . listen—"

I was staring angrily at the Wyatts' driveway.

"Look at me," she demanded.

I turned and looked into her dark eyes.

"I find you very attractive. I guess I can't hide that, but I'm not a slut. I was raised with values. I've got a way I intend to live my life. I'm not a home wrecker and I'm sure not going to take advantage of you and your wife, especially not now, when she's going through such a tough adjustment. You have my word on that."

"Thank you."

After a moment a smile started to play across her face, and in Sally Levitt's voice, she said, "You may be cute, dude, but you're a long way from bodacious ta-ta."

I smiled at her, but there must have been sadness and pain in my smile because she saw it, and said, "If you ever want to talk, I'm a good listener."

"I'll get back to you on that."

Half an hour later, the solenoid on the gate started clicking and the wrought-iron monster swung open. We both ducked down in the front seat as the red Ferrari Enzo flew down the drive and out the gate again. I figured it must have been Wade Wyatt driving because he left his trademark trail of sparks from the leading edge of his left front bumper, and nobody who actually paid a million dollars for a car would treat it that way.

"What the fuck?" Scout said as she sat back up and watched the car whine away up the street.

"That's the way he drives. He's a cute kid. Wait till you meet him."

I hung a U as Scout grabbed a portable Kojak light out of the glove compartment and put it on the seat between us, ready to slam it up on the dash in case we needed it. We began a white-knuckle ride trying to stay up with the Ferrari as it blew through stop signs, heading west down Sunset toward the ocean and a low gray mist of coastal fog. On Sepulveda the Ferrari turned right and headed into the hills. Around eleven-fifteen it pulled to the shoulder up on the top of Mulholland and parked.

Scout and I were driving without headlights to avoid detection. When the Enzo stopped at the crest of the hill we backed down on Sepulveda and ditched the Caddie a few hundred yards away. Then we covered the last stretch on foot, moving back up the road, and climbed into the hills above Mulholland. I was carrying my Bushnell binoculars. We found a place where we could watch undetected. The foggy coastal marine layer had not crested the mountain and from here we could see across Mulholland, to the million-dollar red sports car and past that to the million-dollar view of the twinkling lights in the Valley below.

There were now two people standing beside the Ferrari, leaning on the front fender. I put the binoculars to my eyes and focused them. Wade Wyatt was dressed like Field Marshal Rommel in an expensive three-quarter-length, belted black leather trench coat.

With him was an expensively dressed girl who looked like she'd just stepped out of a Victoria's Secret catalog. Long blonde hair, high cheekbones, willowy body.

"You know who she is?" Secada asked.

"Bodacious ta-ta," I said, and handed her the binoculars.

"Looks like they're waiting for someone," she said.

We got comfortable, sitting with our backs against a pine tree. Slowly, over the next half hour, one by one, other expensive sports cars arrived at this spot at the top of Mulholland. Ferraris, Lamborghinis, and Maseratis were joined by souped-up Corvettes and some muscle cars with racked suspensions. Finally, I saw a silver Mercedes McLaren arrive. License plate ABV-193. It was Wade Wyatt's car but this time a slender, dark-haired guy I'd never seen before was driving. By now, there were over twenty men and women, mostly young and attractive, standing on the shoulder smoking dope or drinking booze from silver flasks.

"What are they waiting for?" Scout said.

"I've heard about this, but I thought it was just an urban myth," I told her. "The story is, every now and then, a bunch of these rich assholes bring their expensive sports cars up here and have road races at midnight for high stakes and pink slips. Tens of thousands of dollars and car registrations change hands."

"You kidding? On Mulholland?"

"Yeah. The way I heard it, they block off the road. Look. They're doing that now."

As we watched, two guys in a pickup with yellow construction sawhorses in the back arrived and drove around the corner and down the hill. Scout and I scrambled to the top of the mountain where we could see the streets converging into Bel Air. I looked through the binoculars and sure enough, several miles down Mulholland, barely visible in the coastal fog, the pickup stopped, and the two guys jumped out and blocked off the road with a couple of sawhorses, both of which had flashing amber lights. One of the men triggered a walkie-talkie and spoke into it. Scout and I scrambled back down to our earlier position just as two cars at the top of Mulholland pulled to a makeshift starting line. One was a white Corvette with red racing stripes and an exposed engine. The hood was off to make room for a four-barrel blower. The other car was a blue Lamborghini. Wyatt's beautiful blonde girlfriend stepped out into the center of the road between the two vehicles holding a checkered flag. Wade was booking bets on his computer, his face illuminated by the glow from the laptop.

"What do you wanta do?" Secada asked.

"Beats the hell outta me. I wasn't exactly expecting this."

A minute later, the engines revved high and the girl swung the flag. Both cars squealed away from the starting line toward the sawhorses two miles down the twisting, two-lane road. In less than half a mile, they were going over ninety, engines wrapped tight and whining, the tortured sounds of squealing rubber destroying the quiet Bel Air night.

"*Mamacita!*" Scout gasped as the Vette almost lost it, missing a deadly plunge into the Valley below, by inches, then righted itself and continued. "We need to get some A-Units up here now," she said.

Just then, the silver McLaren, with the dark-haired guy I didn't know behind the wheel, pulled to the starting line beside a yellow Maserati. As the drivers strapped in, money began changing hands. Wade Wyatt was punching keys, making book on the laptop.

"We can't wait for patrol. We gotta shut this down before somebody dies," Scout said.

We ran back to the Caddie and jumped in. While Scout called for backup, I put the car in gear, and we shot up the road onto Mulholland, and made a left turn. Scout slammed the bubble light up onto the dash and turned it on. I hit the switch on the wailer disguised under the hood and we boiled in, braying the siren.

The crowd at the top of the hill saw us coming and scattered like tenement house roaches. As this was happening, the McLaren and the Maserati took off from the line and veered away from us, powering down the hill toward the sawhorses two miles away.

"We gotta stop them before they kill somebody," Scout yelled. I floored it, but the Cad was no match for these two race cars and they quickly left us behind, taking corners neatly while I slewed recklessly around the curves. Soon they were out of sight.

"Faster," Scout yelled.

I had my foot buried to the floor, and the Caddie was leaning dangerously on every turn, threatening to break loose and pinwheel over the side. It didn't seem to bother Secada, who was yelling for more speed. We flashed past the sawhorses, which had already been run through, and now lay broken and in ruins all over the road.

We drove into the coastal fog at Sunset Boulevard and I had to make a decision. The two cars were way out of sight but it would do no good to go back up to the top of Mulholland. That party would be long over. I knew the McLaren had come from Church's house in Van Nuys, so I made a right and headed toward the Palisades and the 405, still hoping to catch up. After several minutes of reckless driving on Sunset, I spotted the Mercedes idling at a light, blocked in by a line of traffic coming out of a concert at UCLA.

"The good guys catch a break," Scout announced as

I wailed the siren and squealed to a stop behind the silver sports car.

I piled out of the Caddie and ran toward the McLaren with my gun drawn. Scout pulled her weapon and took a cover position at the right rear quarter panel of the silver race car just like we'd all been taught to do it at the Academy.

"Hands in the air. Put 'em out the window!" I yelled at the driver, adrenaline pumping up the volume. He was alone in the car.

"Okay, okay. Hold your water, dude," the man said. He poked his hands out the window holding the car keys, then dropped the keys to the pavement. He'd done this drill before.

"Okay, out of the car," I instructed.

He opened the gull wing door on the expensive Mercedes and stepped out. He was a tall, handsome, Latino-looking guy with a tennis sweater tied around his neck. Señor Suave Bola.

"What is this, Officer?" He was the very picture of innocence.

"What's your name?" I barked.

"Enrico Palomino." No accent; no attitude. He could easily have joined the group of UCLA students driving by, staring at us.

"Let's see some ID."

He reached into his pocket, pulled out his driver's license, and handed it to me. Enrico Jorge Palomino. He was twenty-six and lived in Van Nuys on Woodman. I knew from two years working patrol in the Valley that Woodman was in a blue-collar neighborhood.

"Whose car is this?"

"It belongs to a friend, Wade Wyatt, okay? You can call him. I've got his cell. He lets me borrow it. I had a hot date, UCLA girl. Just dropped her off."

"Of course, that's total bullshit because I just saw you racing this thing at close to a hundred miles an hour up on Mulholland."

"I don't think so. Must've been another car that looks like this one."

"It's a half-million-dollar McLaren," Secada said, still standing in a cover-fire position with her gun drawn. "There aren't ten of those in the entire United States. Come up with something else."

He held out his hands and smiled.

"Okay, okay. Look, can you guys put the guns away? It's a little frightening."

I reholstered my weapon. Secada lowered hers but kept it at the ready.

"Keep talking," I said. "I wanta hear the real story."

"Maybe you could cut me some slack, Officer." He smiled again. "Would that be too much to ask?"

"Why would I do that, Mr. Palomino?"

"Professional courtesy," he said.

"Professional what?"

"Can I reach into my pocket? I want to show you something."

I glanced at Scout. She looked puzzled, too, but finally nodded.

"Okay," I said. "Go slow."

He reached into his back pocket and pulled out another wallet. This was thick and black, like the ones detectives carry. Then he opened it and showed me a beautiful gold and porcelain engraved police badge and ID card.

"What's this?" Scout asked.

"My credentials. I'm with the North Van Nuys Transit Authority Police," he said. "I work closely with Homeland Security."

"Transit Authority Police," I said, and looked over again at Scout.

"Is that anything like the Disneyland Police?" she deadpanned.

"It's an actual police department," Rico said. "I'm sure, as brother officers, we can work something out."

"Just a minute. Stand right there," I said.

I led Scout back to the Caddie and handed her the badge. "Look at this."

She examined the gold shield. It was expensive and well made. Across the top was inscribed, NORTH VAN NUYS TRANSIT AUTHORITY P.D. The credentials in the glassine pocket read, ENRICO JORGE PALOMINO, COMMISSIONER OF POLICE.

"What's with this?" Secada said. "This weasel's only twenty-six and he's already a P.C.? I wasn't figuring to make commissioner until I was at least fifty."

"You ever hear of these guys?"

She shook her head. "Lemme check." She got in the car and picked up the rover mike.

I watched Rico Palomino standing next to Wyatt's car, looking cool and confident. I was trying to understand why Wade Wyatt would let this guy drive his super-rare, half-million-dollar car at breakneck speed down Mulholland, risking its destruction. Then it hit me. Actually, it was pretty obvious. The car was undoubtedly insured and they were betting high stakes on the outcome of the road races. That meant Enrico Palomino was probably the best street racer Wade knew.

Scout got out of the car and handed the badge back to me. "It's legit. A small, transit police department, located in North Van Nuys, chartered and registered." She bit her lip. "What do you wanta do?"

"I don't care about citing this guy for reckless driving,

but something isn't right. Let's turn him loose and check this out."

"Okay with me," she said.

I walked over and handed Rico back his expensive badge. "Okay, Commissioner," I said, almost choking on the words. "Sorry for the inconvenience. You have a nice night."

He smiled, unable to hide a tinge of entitlement. He took the credentials and got back behind the wheel of the McLaren. Then he pulled out and drove slowly up Sunset, disappearing like a silver ghost in the dense coastal fog.

CHAPTER 16

It was well after midnight by the time we drove back to Bel Air. I dropped Scout at her car, which was parked on Madrono, two blocks from the Wyatt estate. We agreed to meet for breakfast in the morning. In the meantime I intended to find out more about the North Van Nuys Transit Authority. If I could get an address I would run over there in the morning and check it out.

She got out of the Caddie, but hesitated before saying good-bye. "Listen, I agreed to do this stakeout with you because we weren't gonna touch anything, just watch. But we ended up pulling another guy over and drawing our guns. A police commissioner, yet."

"We must be good," I said. "We're peeling an onion here. I want these guys."

"My grandmother used to tell me an old Mexican story about that," she said. "It's about wanting too much."

"Oh, boy."

"The way the story goes, this little boy is on a beach and finds an oyster with a huge pearl the size of a robin's egg inside. He shows it to the village elders, and they know it will feed and clothe the town for years. But there is a tiny, dark spot on the side. They call the pearl doctor, who comes from another village and examines the treasure. He says he can sand the pearl and maybe the spot goes away, but maybe it gets bigger, making the pearl less valuable. The townspeople tell the pearl doctor to sand the pearl. But as he sands, the spot gets bigger. Now the pearl doctor explains that with more sanding the spot might get smaller again and the value of the pearl will be restored. They decide to keep sanding until it's worth only a few pesos as pearl dust. They ended up with nothing."

"What's your point?"

"That's what this case feels like. It started with a murder over a six-pack of beer, but things didn't seem right. A tiny dark spot. We've been sanding and it just keeps getting bigger and bigger. And now we're in major trouble and if we're not careful, we're both gonna end up getting sacked with nothing to show for it."

"Except we aren't after money, we're after truth," I reminded her. "Didn't you tell me just yesterday that you gotta take on the shitty ones a case at a time?"

She just grinned.

When I woke the next morning, Alexa was already gone. She left me a note.

Shane, got up at three A.M. Went to work.
Tony gets home in two days. Gotta be ready. Love, A.

I went into the kitchen and sat at the table drinking burnt coffee, then called the Fiscal Crimes Division at Parker Center. One of their jobs is checking out business ownerships and incorporation papers. I asked the civilian assistant to run a check on the North Van Nuys Transit Authority.

She quickly came up with the NVNTA's operations charter and read it to me. The little Valley bus company was a nonprofit that was created to shuttle the elderly and people with disabilities to their jobs in the morning and pick them up at night. The bus service had its own transit police department that had been certified by Homeland Security. The transit line currently operated five buses. I asked for a list of the police commissioners and the officers of the company.

I was put on hold while she went on Nexis-Lexis to locate the information. A few minutes later she came back on the line.

"Okay, here it is," she said. "The address is six-three-five-eight Midline Drive in North Van Nuys."

I leaned over and grabbed the phone book, which still lay open on the counter displaying the ad for the Church of Destruction.

"You sure? That's a towing service and body shop," I told her.

"According to their corporation filings, it's also the legal address for NVNTA."

"Okay, give me the names of the officers and commissioners."

"There're five. In no order of importance: Tyler Cisneros, Enrico Palomino, and Jose Diego are all police commissioners. Wade Wyatt and Michael Church are commissioners and transit authority officers."

Most of the people I'd been messing with for the past three days turned out to be part of this little transit authority police department in North Van Nuys.

The more I sanded this pearl, the larger the black spot grew.

CHAPTER 17

Secada and I were seated at one of the upholstered train booths inside the Pacific Dining Car restaurant in downtown Los Angeles. It was almost nine A.M. I was having Swiss eggs, Engineer Style. Secada was slaughtering a Trainman's Breakfast, pushing the avocado, onions, and eggs into a pile in the center of her plate, knife and fork at the ready.

"You're telling me that every one of these people are P.C.s for that little bus company police department?" she asked, glancing sideways at the list of names the Fiscal Crimes Division had given me. "What the hell is that all about?" She wrinkled her nose and stabbed an egg yolk for emphasis. Yellow oozed.

"Maybe, like us, they just like the feel of a badge in their pockets."

"Come on, Shane. These guys are running some kinda scam."

The information seemed to have cost Secada her appetite and she began poking at the mashed-up contents on the platter in front of her, rearranging it with her fork, peering into the mess as if she was searching for bugs.

Our waiter came up and smiled at her hesitantly.

"Everything all right? Is your meal acceptable?"

He was looking at Secada with concern, holding

her eyes for a bit longer than necessary. The Pacific Dining Car is one of L.A.'s gastronomic landmarks, and is housed in an authentic Union Pacific rail car on Sixth Street. Because it's open twenty-four hours, it's a haunt for night owls who often collided with the incoming five A.M. brokerage crowd. The restaurant's also a favorite spot for cops, being just a short drive from Parker Center.

"It's fine," she told the waiter. "Just doing some food art." Then she lanced the poor guy with one of her high-voltage smiles. I heard him exhale before he moaned softly and turned away.

After the waiter left, I said, "A better question is what's the key that connects this little Valley bus line to them?"

"Are we getting sidetracked here?" she said. "Does any of this get us any closer to a writ of habeas corpus for Tru Hickman?"

"I think so . . . I don't know why yet, but there's gotta be a reason Brian Devine and Tito Morales buried that kid on bad evidence. What I want to know is why a cop and a Deputy D.A. were protecting a gangster like Mike Church. We need to come up with that answer, and we need it before our transmittal letters and charge sheets come through from I.A."

"But there's still a big disconnect here," she persisted. "Okay, let's say this miscarriage of justice wasn't just sloppy police work. But does it have anything to do with Wade Wyatt or all of these guys being transit police commissioners?"

"I think it does."

"But what if it doesn't? What if that's just a random fact? What if it doesn't connect up to the motive for the killing, which as you recall, was over a six-pack of Bud Light."

"Okay, we don't have it yet. I admit that. But something is definitely not right and it's bigger than just some bad due-process on Tru Hickman's case."

"I agree. But which of these inconsistencies should we look at first? In a day, we're both gonna be on suspension."

"Let's split up. You go over to the Van Nuys high school where Mike Church spent his early years conking classmates for their lunch money. Check his senior class yearbook for these names." I picked up the list I'd made and handed it to her. "Find out if any of these other characters went there. Also, take that list of license plate names we got from Church's house."

She was skeptical. "You think it goes all the way back to high school?"

"Maybe. I saw Van Nuys High Wolves stickers on a few of those cars we ran. Something connects these people. Maybe it's as easy as they all went to Van Nuys High."

"What're you gonna do?"

"I read in the paper a few weeks ago that Tito Morales had a campaign headquarters in the Valley and was looking for volunteers. I thought I'd go down and join his campaign."

I saw an envious look cross her beautiful face. "Oh, that's a *very* cool idea. But I definitely think I should be the one to do that."

"The old Wonder Bread thing again?"

"Well, yeah," she nodded. "I mean, I'll blend in better, don't you think?"

"Blend in? Are you crazy? I hate to break this to you, Scout, but you blend in about like Eva Longoria at a tractor pull. I'm a better choice. I'll get some glasses and a Woody Allen sweater. I'll fall by and sign up. Don't worry, I'll be so boring, nobody will notice me."

"Shit, good idea." She pouted. "I should've come up with that." Then she looked down at her plate and started forking food into her mouth. "When you get to his campaign headquarters, see if you can get your hands on his contributors list," she said between bites.

"I can't just walk in there and start rifling his files. This is going to require a little finesse."

She wrinkled her nose and shot me the super-megawatt. A second later, I heard my breath wheeze out. But I didn't moan. At least not until I was safely back inside my car.

CHAPTER 18

The campaign headquarters was located in a small storefront on Magnolia Avenue in Van Nuys. There was a large, half-block-size Rite-Aid on one of the corners. I pulled into the drugstore's parking lot, then walked inside and bought myself an ugly pair of tortoise-shell horn rims with a magnifying power of one, which didn't blur my vision too badly. There was a section that had inexpensive shoes, sweaters, running pants, and jeans. I selected a tan cardigan, a Sluggo newsboy cap, and, just because I'd spent all day yesterday looking like the Angel of Death, I went for a less threatening look, adding a plastic pocket protector and a few pens and pencils.

I exited with my bag of goodies, ditched my jacket in the trunk, and put on this magnificent getup. Then I checked myself out in the drugstore's window. As a disguise, it was cresting on ridiculous, but I reminded myself that I was on a limited budget and walked down the street to the Morales for Mayor Campaign headquarters.

From the outside, it looked to be about two thousand square feet. Inside, through the plate glass, I could see cubicles and low partitions. There were perhaps ten people working phone banks and doing paperwork at scuffed metal desks. The windows were loaded with campaign stick-ons. TITO ALONZO MORALES FOR LOS ANGELES MAYOR was festooned in red, white, and blue letters across the top. Then there were a bunch of slogans: "Morales Means Moral Government." "Don't Be Fooled by Shiny Packages—Morales for Mayor." "For Moral-A-T—Vote T. A. Morales."

I was convinced. Where do I sign up?

I walked inside and approached a young, overweight Hispanic girl with a bad complexion and a rat's nest hairdo with about five pencils jammed in at odd angles.

"Hi," I said, smiling at her, trying to project a harmless duffer quality, which, if you're observant and happen to spot all the scar tissue over my eyes, never quite works.

"Hi." She was cutting apart printed one-sheets that depicted a handsome picture of Tito Morales. She glanced up at me and went back to what she was doing.

"I was wondering if you guys could use any help," I said. "I really like what I hear about this guy."

"Are you kidding? We need all the help we can get." She shot me a huge smile, wide and welcoming. "We need these up all over the Valley. We're trying to post at least a hundred a day, but we now have to go back and replace the ones on Magnolia, past Woodman, because the kids over by San Joaquin Elementary School are tearing them down, or worse still, drawing moustaches."

"I gotta fix for that," I grinned. "Just have Mr. Morales grow a moustache to match the artwork. Problem solved." It was a dumb joke, but I was trying to come off dumb and nonthreatening. To put the point across, I gave her my Don Knotts smile.

"At last, a comedian arrives," she said without humor. Then she motioned to a stack of cut posters. "You wanta put these up, it'd be a big help."

"Sure."

"So what's your name?" she asked.

"I'm Shane."

"Carmelita."

"Listen, does Mr. Morales ever come around? It'd be totally bitchin' to meet him."

"Every afternoon during his lunch recess from court. Usually around one o'clock. When he gets here, I'll introduce you." That meant I had to be well out of sight by the time he showed up at one. "He's a great man," she smiled. "Someone who really cares. He's got morals and convictions."

One of the things I've learned as a cop is the minute the word "moral" enters a sentence, look out, because morals are never going to be involved.

I looked around at the others in the room. Most of the volunteers were girls in their mid to late twenties. Tito's heroic profile and Latino charm were probably big pluses in this office.

"So, Carmelita, how many people on the campaign staff citywide?"

"'Bout two hundred now," she smiled. "With you, two-oh-one. But with the election two months away, we're just really going into high gear. We're opening four bigger offices—downtown, Century City, West L.A., and another one here in the Valley. We start the first big swarm of TV ads in a week."

"A swarm of TV ads? Wow, good going."

She motioned at the office. "Next week, we're switching this space over to clerical staff mostly. We set up here originally to be close to the courthouse so Mr. Morales could get over at lunch and help organize things. But the campaign has picked up so much steam we had to get bigger spaces. Once the new offices open, all the administrative and fund-raising stuff will be over at Century City."

"Cool." I reoffered a geeky smile. "New offices, TV. . . . I was going to suggest I could help you guys solicit funds. I'm in a lot of clubs: Rotary, Kiwanis. But it sounds like you're all set in the money department."

"We can always use more money. This campaign is gonna be a street fight." She grabbed a sheet of paper from a file and handed it to me. "Fill this out. It'll help us place you where you can do the most good."

She pointed out an empty cubicle with her chewed-to-the-nub pencil. I sat down at the desk and filled out the form: "Shane O'Herlihy," and the address of the bar downtown. I put down my cell number and lots of nonsense and gobbledygook for job history, including junior high school science teacher. Under reason for wanting to be a part of the Morales campaign I wrote, "Tito Morales is awesome," and underlined it three times. Then I checked "fund-raising" and "helping to register voters" as my two main campaign interests. It took about five minutes. I got up and handed it back to Carmelita.

"This is great," she said, and put it in a file. Then she pushed the stack of one-sheet posters across the desk to me.

"Here you go. You can start by putting those up on Magnolia." I bundled the stack under my arm. "Listen, Shane. Not on every lamppost, okay? Spread 'em out. No more than six to a mile."

"Right."

I left the campaign headquarters, walked back to my car, and put the one-sheets in my trunk. I ditched the disguise, put on my jacket, and walked about four blocks down the street to get some coffee at a Denny's. I brought the coffee back, and parked my MDX where I could see the storefront campaign headquarters and the parking lot on the west side. Then I took out a telephoto lens and screwed it onto my Canon digital camera, slouched down in the seat, and went into surveillance mode.

The first surprise came at a little after twelve-thirty, when the McLaren pulled into the parking lot. I guess Wade had finally become worried about leaving it in Mike Church's weed-choked yard, because he was back behind the wheel of the silver race car. I gunned off some shots as he got out and sauntered casually into the building, hands in his pockets, like he was back at Harvard, going for an early drink at the Hasty Pudding Club. Today he was wearing shiny leather jeans and a thousand-dollar sports coat. Since I now had it on good authority that morality didn't come in shiny packages, I wasn't expecting too much from Wade in this outfit.

At exactly one-ten, in came Tito Morales. I got shots as he exited his tan Mazda—car of the common man—and lugged a fat, worn briefcase into the campaign headquarters. I wondered what was in that case. As I'd told Scout, I couldn't just go in there and rifle the files. No warrant, no probable cause, and within twenty-four hours, probably no badge. Should it become necessary to access anything in this campaign headquarters, it was going to have to be a black-bag job done at midnight. For now, I'd just have to rely on guile.

Nothing happened for a while, so I pulled out the spiral notebook and started to make entries in my Alexa log, bringing it up to date. I added the fact that she had finally admitted to her car accident and noted that she had also told me about having convulsions. When I got around to my feelings about all of this, I realized that I was mostly sad, disenfranchised, and lonely. I had also started to project a dismal future for us. Was my relationship with Alexa finally coming to an end? If her dark, destructive moods were just something that had happened a few times, I wouldn't have been having such dire thoughts. But this behavior had been going on for almost a year and I was finding it harder and harder to hold on.

Then I remembered a patrolman named Bart Cook who'd gone through the academy with me. A few years after we graduated, he married a patrol car officer named Brenda. One night, while his wife was on patrol, she'd tried to arrest a guy who got belligerent after a traffic stop. He suddenly pulled a gun, fired, and severed her spinal column, paralyzing her. My academy friend had left the department and gotten a job in phone sales so he could stay home and care for her. He'd been doing that for almost ten years. The memory made me feel small and cheap. In the face of that, even writing all this junk down seemed like an act of betrayal. I made a promise to myself to see this through, no matter what. Dr. Lusk had cautioned me that my feelings were what they were, and that it did no good to deny them. But didn't I have a deeper obligation than just to myself? I closed the journal and stashed it out of sight under the seat, hating myself for my selfishness.

Just before two o'clock I got another surprise. Lt. Brian Devine pulled in. He parked his department is-sue Crown Victoria next to the silver McLaren and glared at it as if he was considering having it booted. *Click, click, click*—the auto drive on my camera fired off half a dozen shots. Then Devine went for a boot of a whole different kind. He kicked the half-million-dollar silver sports car in the rear-quarter panel with the sole of his Brogan. *Click, click, click*. I could see the brownish divot he left from all the way across the street. He leaned down and looked carefully at the rear panel, seemed satisfied with his scuff mark, and walked brusquely through the rear door of Tito Morales's cam-paign headquarters.

I didn't know what I was witnessing, but anytime there's friction inside a criminal conspiracy, it's always a law enforcement plus.

At three-fifteen, the side door to the headquarters opened. Brian Devine and Tito Morales spilled angrily out into the parking lot. I started snapping shots. Lt. Devine was waving his fist at Tito in rage. Hardly a smart way for a Valley police lieutenant to treat L.A.'s leading mayoral candidate. Right now, Tito Morales didn't look much like a heroic crusader. He didn't look overly concerned with moral-A-T. He looked like he wanted to tear Brian Devine a new asshole. They stood in the shade at the side of the campaign headquarters, faces purple with rage, screaming at each other. Both men were totally out of control.

Then Brian turned, got into his gray Crown Victoria, and powered out of the parking lot, heading east on Magnolia. I ducked down as he roared past.

"Fuck you, *codelincuente*!" I heard Tito scream after him, before heading back inside.

CHAPTER 19

Tito Morales and Wade Wyatt both came out of the headquarters together about fifteen minutes later. I shot some more film as they talked. After a minute in the parking lot, Tito got into his Mazda, Wade into the McLaren, and they took off in separate directions. I stuck with Wade Wyatt and the half-million-dollar McLaren because Morales was probably just heading back to the courthouse.

The Mercedes left Van Nuys and took the 101 Freeway heading east. As I drove through a warm summer afternoon, I was glad that the Alaskan cold front had finally passed through. Angelenos are spoiled by our weather, and this magnificent day was one of the reasons. The usually brown San Gabriel Mountains were cloaked with emerald green from recent rains. They framed the north side of the Basin, rising majestically into a cloudless, smog-free sky. Tonight, people all over the Valley would be snatching the canvas covers off their barbeques. Unfortunately, I wouldn't be one of them.

Wade transitioned onto the 5 Freeway and once he neared Sunland, he shot down the off-ramp north of the Glendale-Burbank Airport. We were driving through a manufacturing district. In the forties, this was all World War II factory space where B-25s and other aeronautic weaponry had been designed and built under these same bow-truss roofs, then trucked a few miles to Burbank Field to be test-flown before being shipped overseas. Many of the same old structures remained, but most had been refaced and today looked almost new. The area was now zoned for light manufacturing, but the shoulder-to-shoulder placement of the buildings remained. They were lined up along Bradley Avenue like soldiers at parade rest.

Wade seemed to know where he was going and took all the corners way too fast, turning off Bradley onto Penrose Street. Then he slowed down before flipping the silver McLaren carelessly into a large, gated factory parking lot that fronted a line of new concrete, tilt-up buildings identified by a sign that said:

CARTCO
SERVING AMERICA'S CONTAINER NEEDS
WORLDWIDE

Wade Wyatt had his own parking place in the executive section. He lifted the McLaren's exotic gull-wing door and stepped out. The front gate remained open during business hours, the guard shack, empty. As a result, I pulled in unmolested and parked. The rear end of my Acura still looked like I'd just lost an elimination event at a destruction derby.

I watched as Wade, in his rock star leather pants and sports coat, entered a two-story structure marked BUSINESS CENTER — ADMINISTRATION BUILDING.

This case was touching one of L.A.'s major power brokers, so caution now dominated my impulsive brain chemistry.

Wade had told me that his uncle owned this place. I certainly didn't want to add Aubrey Wyatt's brother to my crowded I.A. case, but I was running out of time. If

I wanted answers, I was going to need to take a few chances.

I looked at the huge container factory, which had to be at least ten acres under roof. I wasn't sure what I was after. Maybe this would turn out to be an elaborate dead end, but I learned long ago that when working a case, you should never force a result. The best things happen when you just follow your leads. I searched my memory for an old case that I could plausibly sling at these people to gain access without tipping them to my real motives.

Then I remembered the Four-thirty Bandits from five years ago. Three idiots were robbing mini-markets in one section of town at a few minutes after four-thirty every afternoon. I finally guessed that the reason for the four-thirty timeframe might be because they all got off work at four-thirty and went directly to the closest liquor store and stuck it up. It turned out I was right. By showing police artist sketches compiled from descriptions by the mini-market managers to people who worked at companies in the vicinity of the robberies, I quickly located the automotive center that employed the gang and got the collar.

To make my ruse work, I needed a few props. I took a photo six-pack from a just-cleared murder case out of my briefcase, along with its incumbent folder. Then I walked around to the side of a loading dock where three skip-loaders were hefting pallets of raw cardboard sheets and stacking them next to a door.

"Help you?" somebody called out. I looked up and saw a man in a hardhat standing up on the dock off to my right. I went for my badge and flashed it quickly, not giving him any chance to read the ID card.

"Hi. Van Nuys Robbery Division. Talk to you?"

"Sure. Use the steps over there."

I climbed up and faced a stout, muscular guy who didn't shave. Before I even started talking, he was impatiently tapping his clipboard on his leg in frustration.

"I need to ask you about some robberies that are happening at local mini-marts in the area. I wondered if you would look at this identi-kit and tell me if . . ."

He immediately held up a protesting hand, interrupting me. "Don't show me. You gotta talk to Miss Pascoe in Operations."

"She around?"

"Hang on." He crossed the loading dock to an inter-office wall phone, dialed an extension, and spoke softly to somebody. Then he hung up and said, "Wait here. There'll be somebody by in a golf cart in a minute. Miss Pascoe's over at the D-Center."

I had no clue what a D-Center was. Demonstration? Development? Defecation? I waited to be surprised while he went off to supervise some guys stacking cardboard. Why couldn't I get a nice low-stress job like that?

While I waited for my ride, I watched several people enter the factory area. It had security worthy of the Pentagon's E-Ring. First, the employee would hold his or her ID pass up next to their face and stand in front of a camera lens. Then they placed a full palm and five fingers on a glass photo plate for a scan. Next the employee punched in a security code and spoke their name loudly into a mike before the lock buzzed and the door opened. All of this to protect a bunch of cardboard cartons? Go figure.

The golf cart finally arrived with a young girl in jeans and a sweatshirt driving. She motioned to me.

"You the cop?"

"Just the facts, ma'am," I said to prove it. She frowned at me like I'd just thrown up in the pool. I guess *Dragnet* wasn't one of her iPod downloads. I got in the cart and off we zipped.

"Miss Pascoe is in with Mr. Dahl right now, so you may have to wait," she told me tartly.

"Who's Mr. Dahl?"

"*Who's Mr. Dahl?*" Like I'd just asked who Brad Pitt was.

"Yeah. Who is he?"

"He's the owner. Duh. *Roger Dahl*. He started this place in seventy-three when he was only twenty. Roger Dahl like designed and manufactured the first FedEx package."

"I thought Aubrey Wyatt's brother ran this place," I said.

"Mr. Dahl is Aubrey Wyatt's brother-in-law," she replied, clearing up Wade's genetic connection to all this.

"Yeah," I said. "Guess that's what I meant." Then, to get on her good side, I added, "I've certainly heard of Aubrey Wyatt though. He's pretty famous in L.A." Didn't work. Her frown only deepened.

"Everybody should know about Mr. Dahl, too," she snapped after a few seconds, sounding almost like she had a crush on him. "He's like famous in packaging."

"I must have missed that issue of *People*."

She sighed and pulled up in front of a very attractive, greenish-beige office building. It was architecturally pleasing, if a little avant-garde. But the effective land-scaping softened its modern look. Shrubbery in all the right places, a nice strip of lawn that was well-watered. A sign said: DESIGN CENTER. So now I knew.

I followed my escort into the building and was told to wait. I chose a hard, chrome-frame red leather chair. Like a lot of places that sold design concepts, this lobby showcased minimalist design with cold, uncomfortable furniture. It was a triumph of form over function. The floor was shiny terrazzo and there were at least twenty windowed alcoves cut into three lava rock walls. A plate-glass fourth wall looked out onto a Japanese garden.

Each of the lighted alcoves featured some cardboard container that Cartco had manufactured. There were McDonald's cartons and the original FedEx box. Video cassette boxes and DVD packages were on display. The alcoves also featured all kinds of food and consumer containers. Everything from 7-Up to Pampers.

I was looking at the displays when the side door opened and a willowy, attractive, blonde woman entered. She wore an expensive, cream-white, tailored dress that hung perfectly on her athletic frame. She was followed into the lobby by one of those tall, executive, squash-player-type guys dressed in gray slacks and a dark blue blazer. He was in his early fifties, with a great head of silver-gray hair, and a robust health-club tan. His sculpted jaw parted the air like the prow of a Viking ship and framed a square, handsome face.

"We can't afford to put too many of those manufacturing bays in one design mode," he was saying as they entered the lobby.

"I'll have graphics draw up new estimates and get us a fresh set of D costs," she responded.

"Make sure everything is run past the entire development committee. I don't want a design kickback because of some needless boardroom squabble."

She turned and spotted me while he pulled out a new BlackBerry, just like Wade Wyatt's. Then he squinted and started poking manically at the keys.

I was hoping the goddess in the cream outfit would turn out to be Miss Pascoe and my luck held. She crossed to me.

"Are you the policeman?" she asked pleasantly.

"Yes, ma'am." I flashed my tin. Fast, but effective. If I was lucky, I'd get out of here without anybody knowing who the hell I was.

"I'm Dorothy Pascoe, Head of Operations. How can we help?"

I unwrapped the egg foo yung and let 'er fly. "What time does Cartco end its workday?" I began.

"We let the day shift off at four-thirty. There's an hour of maintenance and cleanup, then the night shift starts at six."

I nodded gravely, as if I'd just received her terminal biopsy report.

"Is that a problem?" she asked.

"Markets are being robbed all around this area and these robberies are happening at about four-thirty in the afternoon," I said solemnly. "Now we find out that your company lets out at four-thirty."

"Yes?" She seemed puzzled as to how her factory shift times had anything to do with my robberies.

"Maybe the reason all these holdups happen at four-thirty is because one of the robbers is an employee of this company and doesn't punch out until then." She just stood there, so I said, "We wondered if you could identify any of these people as employees?" I handed her my photo six-pack from the old murder case.

"We have almost five hundred people on our day shift. Of course, unless they're very new, being in operations, I'd probably recognize most of them." She took her time studying the six faces. "Sorry, I don't think so," she finally said and handed them back.

The squash player broke away from his text messages and came over. He'd obviously been eavesdropping because he said, "Let me see."

I showed him the six-pack and waited while he studied them. When interviewing people, you always get more with praise than punishment. We all have a pass key that opens us up. For instance, A-type corporate guys who build and run things for the most part dearly love to talk about them. If this was the esteemed, but rarely recognized, Roger Dahl, maybe I could lure him into a broader conversation.

"Sorry," he said, and handed the six-pack back. "Don't think so." He turned to leave, so I took my shot.

"Excuse me, but aren't you Roger Dahl?" I asked, letting a little gee-whiz seep into the question. He spun back, smiling like I was holding a plate of Russian caviar.

"Why, yes. Do I know you?"

"No, but my goodness, I've certainly read all about you. Didn't you start this place in seventy-three when you were in your early twenties, and then build it up from nothing after you designed the first FedEx package?" Using up the extent of my knowledge in one compound, complex sentence. I looked around at all the products shining under an array of alcove tinsel lights, gawking like a six-year-old girl at a Barbie exhibit.

"Just goes to show you what a good idea, carefully pursued, can accomplish," he said proudly.

"Man, what is this place, like ten acres under roof?"

"Eleven point six." Then, because most people like to work their fan base, he said, "Wanta see something? Since you're interested, come here, follow me." He led me through a back door, leaving the striking Miss Pascoe tapping an expensive Prada sandal in cream-white exasperation. We walked down a narrow hallway into a small design office where several architectural concepts were pinned up on a cork wall.

"This is what we're planning next year. It's going to be built down in Louisiana. I call it our two-fer because it helps create new badly needed jobs for people in

New Orleans since Katrina, and we get to put our buildings on fifty acres of cheap land. Acreage down there is still in the crapper because of the hurricane. We're gonna do all our manufacturing for the East Coast from this new south Louisiana site. Alleviates a manufacturing crunch here and cuts our clients' shipping costs in half."

"Nice," I said, admiring the pastel renderings of a modern-looking factory complex, embellished with colorfully sketched trees and slender, pencil-thin executives walking in and out of clean-lined buildings or strolling on manicured walkways, carrying wafer briefcases. "So you just make the packages, stuff like that?" Throwing up a jump ball. No clue where I was going.

"Yeah. Client companies hire us to make their packages, containers, shipping crates. Anything that holds their products."

"So that's like almost everything, then."

"Well, not cars or heavy equipment. We're cardboard manufacturers. That determines what we can do."

"I saw the incredible security system you have outside. Pretty damn impressive." More bread on the water.

"That's just on the E-Building because that's where we make the rares."

"Right. The rares." No idea what he was talking about. He picked up on my confusion.

"Prize-winning containers." I was still lost. "In a promotion, a rare is what we call a prize package," he explained. "As opposed to, for instance, a common, which is just a regular carton." I must have still looked confused, because he added, "It's a prize. A scrape-off. Some of the companies we make containers for put on big, national promotions, which they advertise in magazines and on TV. In these promotions, they often give away big prizes. If somebody buys the rare and scrapes off the winning number, they could win a car or even, in some contests, up to a million dollars in cash. Since some of the containers we make have million-dollar scrape-offs on them, we had to put in all that top-shelf security to protect the integrity of the contests."

"Got it."

"Employees working in areas making or distributing rares have to be logged in during contest weeks. We even give lie-detector tests."

"Makes sense."

He looked at his gold watch and appeared startled by what he saw there. He'd already wasted too much valuable time on me. "Well look, good luck catching your robbers. Sorry we couldn't help. Gotta go."

As soon as he was gone, I hurried out of the room and back down the hall into the lobby. It was empty. Miss Pascoe had left. Only a faint wisp of her perfume remained behind to tease me. I started looking in the glass windows of the alcoves containing the Cartco products.

I was halfway around the room, when I stopped. Looking very frosty and inviting, sitting under its own pin light, there it was:

A million-dollar, prize-winning, six-pack of Bud Light beer.

CHAPTER 20

Alexa was waiting in the entry when I got home. It was nine o'clock that night and she was holding a charge sheet and transmittal letter from the Professional Standards Bureau.

"We've gotta talk." Her voice was hard, even threatening. The one she uses when she questions suspects.

"Calm down," I cautioned.

She didn't answer, but thrust the charge sheet at me. I saw the PSB seal and the three typed yellow sheets that every cop dreaded receiving. In my distinguished career I've already received three.

"Yeah, I've been expecting this," I said.

"The IO served it here, an hour ago. Since you're the charged officer, the detective didn't want to leave it with me, but I insisted. Pulled rank."

"It's good being king." I pushed past her, feeling busted, and went into the kitchen where I snatched a beer from the fridge. Alexa followed close on my heels.

"Shane, we've got to discuss this."

"Not with your voice like that, we don't."

I pushed past her again and walked out to the backyard.

"Stop doing that. Stop just walking away from me," she called, then followed me outside.

I plopped in one of the lawn chairs, put my feet on

an ottoman, and popped open the beer. It chirped loudly in the still night and I could tell it pissed her off that, under these circumstances, I would be sitting out here with my feet up, drinking beer. She came around and stood in front of me, blocking my view of the canal.

"You don't have any idea what I'm going through right now, do you?" she asked angrily. "You have this bullshit idea that your career and my career are separate, but they're not. I'm your fucking boss, guy."

"Is that a job description or a marital condition?" The minute I said it, I regretted the comment. I was tired and upset, but I knew I needed to handle this carefully. It was a critical moment for us, both personally and professionally. I looked up at Alexa. There was an awful look on her face. I don't know exactly what it was—anger and disappointment, of course, but it seemed there were other, even more destructive things in the mix. Contempt or even disdain. I'd never seen that look before. Or at least, it had never been directed at me. I forced myself to take a step back emotionally, to not fully engage.

I reminded myself that I was the one out of line. I'd been breaking more crockery than a karate master, ignoring supervisors, working without portfolio. I also knew this angry person in front of me wasn't Alexa. This was TBI. This was a brain anomaly. This was caused by changing neurological functions. She must have read all that on my face because she shook her head sadly.

"I'm not crazy. You can't blame this one on Stacey Maluga. I'm not the one ignoring the specific orders of a division commander and a deputy chief. You are."

"Whatta you want, Alexa? I'm sorry. I admit that I've been reckless here. But no matter what I do, I can't make that charge sheet go away."

"I want . . . I want you to . . ." She turned and faced

the Grand Canal. Her mood was dark, a stark contrast
to the canal water that sparkled brilliantly in the orange
twilight. She turned back to me and finished her sentence. "I want *you* to help *me*, but you won't."

"I'm trying to, honey. I know this is a stressful time
for you, but now I really do need your help."

"With this Hickman thing? Jesus! Can you please
put that away for a minute?"

"Alexa, you're stressed. You're frightened, okay? I
get that. I also know you feel horrible about this review
Tony is putting you through tomorrow, horrible about
what's been happening to you. I sympathize, because I
know how unfair it is. It's just . . . I stumbled into this
thing and now I don't know what to do about it."

"What does that mean?"

"This kid—this boy is only a few years older than
Chooch. He's stuck up in Corcoran doing Level Four
time. His prison car is full of net-heads who beat him
up and rape him. They're putting him through hell. If I
don't get him out of there, he's gonna commit suicide.
I saw it in his eyes. And the worst part is we did it to
him. *We* did. *We* put him there on a manufactured case.
The more I look into it the surer I am."

"You don't have anything, Shane. Not one solid
fact." Her voice had softened.

"I'm getting closer. I've turned up some important
pieces." I took a breath and, because we'd always worked
through tough cases together and because I wanted the
old Alexa back, I tried my theory on her. "I think Wade
Wyatt and Mike Church ripped off a beer contest to
win a million dollars." Working it in my mind as I went.
"That's why Church made Tru go to that exact market in
a strip mall halfway across the Valley. The motive for the
murder wasn't an argument over a six-pack of beer. It
was over a rare worth a million dollars in prize money."

"I have not the faintest idea what you're talking about," she said.

"Alexa, I want you to listen to me. You and I could always work stuff out together better than any partner I ever had. Let me just run it down for you. We'll get a theory. Select a course of action."

"No. I'm ordering you to drop this, Shane. Your behavior is bound to come up in my review tomorrow. This Hickman case, Deputy Chief Townsend, Jane Sasso. It's all gonna come out. They're going to wonder what kind of division chief I am if I let my own husband break all the rules. I already look impotent and out of it. Nothing I do lately seems to come out right." She snatched up the charge sheet from the table beside me and shook it under my nose. "And now this. Now I've got to try and explain *this* insanity."

"I've got to get him out."

"Why? *You* didn't put him there."

"Hey, Alexa, we *all* put him there. You did when your Valley Bureau commander missed the sloppy case work on review. I did when I didn't testify against Brian Devine when I was in Patrol. Internal Affairs did when they let a hitter like Devine slide for twenty years. We're all guilty. We made the corruption that spawned this mess. How do we just say it's inconvenient to deal with now, because we both have more important career considerations? This kid is being beaten and raped."

We stood in silence for a moment. Then she laid the charge sheet down on the table and started ticking off the charges from memory.

"Refusal of a direct order from A-Chief Townsend. Malfeasance of duty. Making false or misleading statements during an inquiry. Failure to cooperate with an ongoing investigation inside proper department channels, and ignoring the direct order of the Head of the Internal Affairs Division."

"Because she was wrong."

"So now *I'm* giving you a direct order."

We looked at each other over a chasm growing wider and deeper by the minute.

"You get your supervisor's review and your Skelly hearing. Both are being scheduled by Cal and Jane Sasso. In the meantime, you're suspended. Relieved of all your cases and responsibilities. See Callaway about transferring your workload in the morning. And this order is coming straight from the Head of the Detective Division. Ignore it, and you're out on your ass, Shane. Understand?"

"Seems pretty clear."

"Good."

She turned and went back into the house.

I stood, went inside, grabbed my jacket, then went to the garage, got into my busted MDX, and headed out, not sure where I was going, just needing some space. Needing to be away.

I got on the freeway and drove toward town. Of course, one way to fix my problem was to just drop the Hickman case and start kissing rings on the sixth floor, begging for forgiveness. I had Alexa to worry about. She needed my help and understanding. This Hickman case had become a huge career mistake for me. What if I just cut and ran? I considered that option carefully as I drove. How much would that act of self-preservation cost me in self-esteem? Could I swallow more career cowardice like my refusal to testify against Brian Devine fifteen years ago? Could I just drop this mess and move on? I tried to come to terms with the idea. But I kept seeing Tru Hickman standing there in the visitor's center, skinny and pale, pulling at his frayed sleeve, begging me to save him. I was his only chance and I knew I had to keep trying.

I dialed Chooch. I promised myself that the call wouldn't be about Alexa. I didn't want to put him in the middle. I just wanted to hear his voice. But his cell went directly to voice mail. He was probably in an evening film session or some place where he couldn't talk.

I kept driving and wondering what I should do. I knew Alexa was right about my behavior being an issue in her review. The brass would hammer her for my misconduct. But weren't some things bigger than this job? Didn't dedication to a principle count for something?

I wasn't sure anymore. I didn't know what to do. I needed help.

I dialed another number.

"Hello?" Secada said.

CHAPTER 21

"You sure that's what he yelled?" she asked me, scrolling through the pictures on my digital camera.

"Yeah. 'Fuck you, *codelincuente.*' Morales yelled it just as Lieutenant Devine was pulling away from the campaign headquarters. This was after almost five minutes of screaming at each other in the parking lot."

"*Codelincuente* means 'partner.' But more negative than that. More like 'partner in crime.'" She set my camera down.

We were in the living room of Secada's beautiful, candlelit, loft apartment. She lived in one of those renovated factories downtown on Fifth. Developers had come in and gutted the old buildings, turning Skid Row junk into expensive yuppie housing. I estimated this one was up over half a million dollars. I wondered how the hell she could afford it or, for that matter, the six-hundred-dollar suits she wore.

We were sitting by an expansive window, drinking red wine. If I wasn't in such a horrible mood, I would have thought the atmosphere inviting. The top of the Bonaventure and Nob Hill were visible from her windows. I watched as half a mile away, an old, rebuilt, and freshly painted Angels Flight tram car crawled slowly up the small cliff face on dark cables. At midnight the last car would descend to the terminal, bringing visitors and tourists to the bottom of the hill.

"I keep wondering what ties Tito Morales and Brian Devine together," I said. "A kick-ass head breaker and a politically engaged Latino prosecutor. These guys don't seem like they should be drinking from the same fountain."

I looked over at Secada. She was dressed in a white running suit, her dark hair and brown skin made lush by its contrast.

"I'll check that out," she said. "See what I can find." She took a sip of her wine. "You were right about all of those guys we ran at Church's house being in the Van Nuys school system. Jose Diego, Mike Church, Enrico Palomino, Wade Wyatt, and Tyler Cisneros. But they weren't at Van Nuys High. Only Church and Diego went there. I checked back and the whole bunch were at Van Nuys Junior High. Wade Wyatt transferred to private school in the eighth grade when his dad left the Universal Studios Legal Affairs department in the Valley and set up his own law firm in Century City. A few years later the family moved to the estate in Bel Air. I talked to a vice-principal who remembered them. Apparently Mike Church stole Wade's new ten-speed bike in the seventh grade. It was a big incident because Wade got his father's gun, brought it to school, and threatened to kill Church. Aubrey Wyatt gave the school money for some new science classroom equipment and the problem went away. After that, Church and Wyatt became friends under the social principle that states, 'Assholes are inevitably drawn to other assholes.'"

"Okay, so junior high is the nexus," I said.

"And you think these *codelincuentes* all got together last year to rip off that million-dollar beer prize?"

"Yeah. Wade Wyatt works in the legal department at

Cartco. He'd have access to the market locations of the rares. But he can't win the prize himself because he's a member of the carton manufacturer's family, so he gets together with Mike Church."

"Church can't be tied in directly either, because he's only one generation removed on the friendship chart. I did a lottery rip-off investigation once and it's customary to run intense background searches on winners to make sure there's no cheating. Church, Wyatt, and these other guys are all involved with that bus company police department. That's too close a connection. It would pop up on a computer run. The prize committee would find out they were all friends."

"So they recruit poor, half-out-of-it, Tru Hickman to buy the beer. He's a certified tweaker and Mike's old yard bitch from CYA. He can't be tied directly to Wade Wyatt or Cartco."

"I like it." She got up and poured some more wine for herself, then freshened my glass and sat back down by the window.

"Yeah, I like it, too," I said. "Olivia Hickman wouldn't let them take the beer when Church came over to pick up Tru. Big argument. They leave without the million-dollar six-pack. Church, and maybe Wyatt, come back to the Hickman house later that night after Tru gas bags on meth at that party. Things get out of control and they kill Olivia, then take the prize-winning package."

"Okay, so who's got the million dollars?" she asked. "After he was charged with murder, Tru couldn't collect it."

"Obviously, Wade Wyatt got it somehow," I said. "I think maybe that's what paid for the half-million-dollar McLaren. I think he split it with Mike Church. What we don't know is who actually collected the prize. We know it wasn't Tru and we know neither Wyatt or Church could do it. It had to be somebody they trusted, or someone who was afraid enough of them to just turn it over and not complain afterward."

"Then that's where we start tomorrow," she said.

We sat silently, looking out the window, sipping red wine from crystal glasses, neither of us mentioning that tomorrow we'd probably both be off the job and facing I.A. boards. Then, without warning, the moment turned awkward with sexual tension.

"This place is nice," I said, trying to alter the vibe. I started looking around the apartment, then brought my gaze back to her. Low light from flickering candles danced in the hollows of her neck and glinted seductively off her hair. "How does a D-Three afford a place like this?"

"My ex-husband was a very successful stockbroker. I got this in the divorce."

"Good going," I said, unaware before this moment that she'd once been married.

"There was anger, I'm not certain it was worth it. We still don't talk."

"I got my charge sheet today," I told her, changing the subject again because I could tell from her body language she was uncomfortable talking about her broken marriage.

"Me, too," she said.

"I'm suspended until my Skelly hearing, whenever it's scheduled."

"I thought they couldn't suspend you 'til *after* the Skelly. Who did that?"

"Head of the Detective Bureau."

"Your wife suspended you?"

"Yep."

A long moment passed before Secada leaned forward. "I knew something bad had happened. I saw the pain in your eyes."

We sat in silence as disapproval for Alexa spread across Secada's face. I again felt a need to protect my wife, to rehabilitate her in Secada's eyes.

"I was nothing until she came along," I said softly, the sense of loss and regret seeping out of me. "She gave meaning to my life. Because of her, I opened myself up, became a better person."

"I understand."

"And now I feel empty. I'm lost without her. We're fighting all the time. That bullet in the head changed her. She's worried about this internal performance review that Tony is putting her through. It's all she thinks about."

Then I was talking about my marital problems, blurting it all out. All the stuff I hadn't told Dr. Lusk. I was talking about Alexa, my fears, and anger. It was all rushing out of me, fouling the candlelit atmosphere.

"I can't give up on her. I can't let it all go. But I also can't go on like this. Just being in the house with this person, who isn't the woman I married and love, is killing me."

"What do you want from me?"

"I don't know."

Silence.

"I can be your friend," she said slowly. "Or later, if you and Alexa don't figure this out . . . maybe even your lover. But I won't be your sister, Shane."

More silence.

"I need help," I finally told her. "I need a friend."

She thought about that for a long moment before she said, "Okay, as your friend, I have one idea that might help." I leaned forward. "I know Jane Sasso and she's pissed about us staying involved with this. She's gonna

take this all the way to a full Board. But according to
Paragraph Six of the Police Bill of Rights, an accused
officer can pick anyone in the department below the
rank of captain to represent him at a board. Alexa is
still just a lieutenant. Why don't you pick her to be
your defense rep? I understand when she was in I.A.
she was the best advocate in the division. She knows
how to argue a legal case. You pick your wife to defend
you, then you two can work on the problems surrounding this together. She'll see that you are right. She will
see what I see. Alexa will fall in love with you all over
again."

She fell silent, regarding me with undisguised sym-
pathy. Then she looked me directly in the eyes and said,
"It's good advice, Shane. You know it is."

"I hadn't thought of that," I admitted. "But what if
she says no?"

"Department rules forbid it. If she is picked by an
accused officer, she has to agree to serve unless there
are extreme reasons why she can't. You'll make her see
the wisdom in this idea," Secada said. "Now get out of
here and go home, Shane. If you stay any longer, you
will be forced to watch me cry."

CHAPTER 22

It was eleven-thirty when I pulled out of the underground garage next to Secada's loft apartment. Technically I knew she was correct about my protections under Rule Six of the Police Bill of Rights. Anybody in the department below the rank of captain could be compelled to serve as my defense rep unless unusual circumstances were present. I knew that Alexa could invoke the Unusual Circumstances clause because, as a division commander, she had greater responsibilities. On the other hand, maybe she would hang in there with me. I wondered if it would be possible, or even fair of me to ask her to take on my Board of Rights with everything else she was facing. However, the more I thought about it, the more I realized that the idea of Alexa defending me had a lot going for it. Getting it to happen was going to be another thing altogether.

Tomorrow my gun and badge would probably go into a holding locker, and as far as the job was concerned, I would be up on blocks. If I wanted to have any further effect on Tru's predicament, I had to get busy and bust a pretty good move in a hurry.

I got on the freeway and twenty minutes later was back on Penrose Street parked across from Cartco. The up-lights illuminated the building's poured concrete facade and the large, ornate company sign.

Here goes nothing, I thought, and drove the MDX into the parking lot and up to the guard gate. There had been no guard on duty in the afternoon, but the night shift was protected by a rickety old white-haired guy with a sagging gun belt and a light blue uniform. I showed him my badge. I even let him hold it for a second. Tomorrow, it wouldn't be mine anyway.

"LAPD Homicide," I announced.

"What's this about?"

"Murder," I said, theatrically. "I need to talk to the head of security."

The old man picked up the phone and called a number. "Kit? It's Leo at the front gate. LAPD Homicide dick is out here askin' for you." He listened for a moment, then hung up.

"Park over there." He pointed at a guest spot.

I parked the Acura as instructed. All of the spaces in front of the Administration Building were empty. After a minute, I heard the electric hum of a golf cart and looked over as a four-seater with a fringed roof and security seal on the hood rounded the corner and came to a stop next to the driver's side of my car. Behind the wheel was a middle-aged man with a buzz cut wearing a lightweight suit. His sloping, weightlifter's shoulders and muscular neck told me that he took his job seriously.

"Hi. Help you?"

I showed him my badge and he looked it over carefully before handing it back.

"Okay, Detective Scully. I'm Doug Carson. Ex-L.A. Sheriff. Back when I was on the job everybody called me Kit. I run night security. So what's up? Who died?"

I didn't know if I should lay all this out. Especially to somebody who wanted to be called Kit Carson. But I was out of time.

"Alright, Kit. I'm working on a murder out of Homicide Special. On the surface it looks like a nothing killing over a six-pack of beer, but the deeper I dig, the more I think the real motive was the theft of one of your high-dollar contest packages."

"A rare."

"Exactly. I was here this afternoon and talked to Roger Dahl." I saw him relax a little at the mention of a familiar name.

"So what do you need?"

"I need to know how it works. The contests, who knows about them. All about the security. Anything you know about those promotions would help."

"Guess there's no harm in telling that. It's all been written up in the press."

"Good. I wouldn't ask you late at night like this, but I have a major case review in the morning. My supervisor's a real asshole about having every single detail down in the murder book."

"Man, do I know that type. I had a Loo on my old bank squad who would take your head off if you didn't have every damn case fact on your daily I-report."

"Then you know my problem."

"Okay. We print the rares over in E-Building." He pointed at the big warehouse structure with the loading dock and all the topflight security I'd witnessed earlier.

"Mr. Dahl showed me that security system this afternoon," I said to further loosen him up. "Pretty impressive."

"Right. Security to get in there is bulletproof. Can't get inside unless you're on the approved list."

"Okay, what else?"

"Each prize package is hand-delivered to randomly selected distribution points. A distribution point is like a market or a store where the rare is put on a shelf by a bonded member of Promo Safe."

"Who?"

"Promo Safe. They're an independent company we hire that guarantees the integrity of the contest. Cartco employs them to watch the rares."

I grabbed my notebook and started to write. I would have used a tape recorder, but this was off the record, and it always spooks people when you shove a mic under their nose, so I stuck with the spiral pad. "Promo Safe. Okay, what do you need them for?" I asked as I wrote. "Why not just watch the rares yourself?"

"On these big national promotions the company putting up the prize always does a lot of advance advertising on radio and TV to alert the public they're giving away millions in prize money, or whatever. The idea is to get everybody to think they're gonna win so they'll buy more product. In your case, beer."

"Makes sense."

"But lots of times, the rares will get bought by somebody who has no idea the beer company, or whatever, is having a contest. They bought the prize package, but because they didn't know, they just throw the package away when they're done with it and they don't claim the prize. If nobody wins, then inevitably there's people out there who'll say, 'You guys never had any prize packages in the marketplace to begin with. The whole contest was just a lot of promotional B.S.'"

"I see. So the Promo Safe guys protect you against that kind of claim."

"Exactly. They hand-carry the prize packages to the stores, then stand in the aisle and watch for as long as it takes until the rare is purchased. They follow the buyer home and log the address. Then they fill out an affidavit. That way, if the purchaser of the prize package doesn't know to scrape off the number and there's a complaint that no prize was won, there is somebody from Promo

Safe, a totally independent company, to certify that he witnessed the purchase of the prize-winning package, who purchased it, and where he or she lives. That way everybody knows the contest was on the up-and up. Promo Safe employs security agents who are ex-FBI or Treasury guys. They're all bonded."

"There's no way somebody else could turn in that prize package?"

"No, sir," Kit said. "In most of these contests, the rules mandate that the actual buyer has to claim the prize. The rare can't be passed to someone else. If we don't get the signed affidavit back here from Promo Safe attesting to those facts, then the rare is judged invalid, or if a prize claim comes in that doesn't match with the name and address of the person who the affidavit says actually bought the package, it's also invalid."

"I see." I didn't like where this was going at all. It bitched up my beautiful theory. If Tru Hickman bought the six-pack, and he already told me he did, and if Wade knew an agent from Promo Safe would be in the store to watch him do it, then what good was Hickman to Wade Wyatt and Mike Church? Tru would have to be the one to collect the money. Tru never said anything about a rare, so my guess was they hadn't told him, which meant he wasn't in on the scam. But how did that work? According to Kit, if he didn't turn in the rare himself, the prize would be disqualified. Something was definitely out of whack. I stood next to the security golf cart and thought for a minute. "Listen, Kit. I assume you have computer clearance. Do you think you could take a peek at that recent Bud Light contest from last August and tell me who won?"

"Man, you should really talk to Mr. Dahl about that in the morning."

"Except in the morning, after my supervisor is through with me, my badge is gonna be pinned to the inside of my colon."

"Yeah, I remember how that went." He looked at me for another half a minute, still trying to decide if he was going to take a chance. Then he glanced at his watch. I could read his frown. *Too late to call Mr. Dahl and ask.*

"Come on. Favor for a Brother Officer," I pleaded.

Still nothing.

"Can't you just go into the office, pull up the computer file, and sneak a peak?"

"Jeez. Go through files in the office?"

"This isn't exactly confidential material, is it? The winner was undoubtedly announced in the paper. Just look it up for me. I'd get Mr. Dahl to do it in the morning, except my review is at eight o'clock."

He heaved a deep sigh and shook his head. I thought I'd lost him, but then unexpectedly, he said, "Okay. Get in the cart. But you better not give me up on this."

"I'm cool," I assured him as I got in. We zoomed off in the direction of something called the Administration Annex. He pulled up, then used his keys and let us both inside.

The annex was next to the business center and was a less impressive, neon-lit, two-story shoe-box-shaped building, laid out in long corridors with doors on both sides. He walked down a carpeted first-floor hallway to an office door marked PROMOTIONS, took out his key, and opened it.

"Come on in. Close the door."

"Thanks. This is really a huge help," I told him.

I took a seat across the room while he sat behind the desk and booted up the computer, then typed in his password.

"What was the contest again? What beer company?"

"Bud Light."

He searched for a minute, and then said, "Okay, here it is. We did that one nine months ago. Ten rares were in the market, all worth different amounts. Five came up as winners." He started scrolling down the page on the screen. "One in Newark. Third-tier winner. Guy won a Hummer. One in Tulsa, second tier, half a mil in prize money. One in Odessa, Texas, a grand-slam million-dollar winner; Ashland, Oregon, a Hummer; and the one here in Los Angeles."

"In the Valley? Little mini-mart in a strip mall on Sepulveda Boulevard, right?"

"Yep. That's the one. Guy won a million in cash."

"And the six-pack was bought by Truit Hickman, right?" I was getting a little ahead of myself.

Kit Carson shook his head. "Nope," he said, then leaned in and squinted at the screen. "The winner lives in Valley Village. Somebody named Tito Alonzo Morales."

CHAPTER 23

When I got home, it was after one A.M. Alexa was in bed, but her eyes were wide open. She sat up as I came through the bedroom door.

"How come you're still awake?" I asked.

"Can't sleep. Gonna get sunk at this review tomorrow. I've got everything set up, ready to go, but I can't remember anything. I can't just be reading facts off a page, I'll look like I don't know anything." She hugged her knees. "Maybe I should just cut to the chase and resign."

"Don't say that. That's not what you should do." Then I added, "You want a beer?"

"Everything in life can't be fixed by a beer, Shane."

"Come on, get up." I handed her the heavy robe and walked out of the bedroom to get the two beers. I met her in the backyard and handed her the can.

The canal was dead still. Like glass. As we watched, a lone mallard duck paddled by, breaking the flat mirrored surface and sending a tangle of messy water to both sides of the canal behind him.

"You're gonna do fine tomorrow," I told her, but deep down I knew she was headed for a disaster. She had lost her command presence and Tony would pick up on it.

"I can't hold it together, Shane. This isn't me, but it is me. It's who I've become. I fired Ellen today."

"Oops."

"Over nothing. Over not bringing me my lunch on time, which of course she did. It was sitting inside my briefcase with the top closed. Worse still, I kind of remember putting it in there. Jesus. Who puts their just-delivered lunch inside a briefcase? Talk about gimpy behavior."

"Did you apologize?"

"Yeah. After taking her head off and accepting her resignation, I begged her to stay. She's thinking about it."

"After tomorrow, the stress will be off. You'll be better."

"By the way, you're not suspended. That's out of policy. I forgot I can't do that until after the Skelly hearing."

"I know."

"I'll call Cal and unravel that tomorrow." She looked over at me and smiled sadly. "Thank God I still have you."

We sat for a minute in awkward silence. Then I asked, "What do you know about Tito Morales?"

"Please, not this Hickman thing again."

"Did you know he won a million dollars nine months ago in a beer contest?" I held up my can and saluted her. "One of the many benefits of drinking the bubbly. I think he's using the money, or part of it, to fund his current campaign for Mayor. He's renting offices, hiring staff, placing TV ads."

"So what?" she said, her voice cold.

"Nothing. Just information." I decided to let it drop. "Listen, Alexa. I know Jane is gonna take me all the way to a full B.O.R. Since I have a thick package at PSB, I'll need a great defense." I took a deep breath. "I'd like you to be my defense rep."

"What?"

"I know the timing sucks, but you'll be out of your

review tomorrow and my Skelly hearing is in ten days. I need someone to be there for my supervisor's review. You were the best they ever had down at Internal Affairs. I was wondering if you'd agree to defend me."

"I can't defend you, Shane. We're married. I'm your division commander."

"Anybody under the rank of captain is eligible."

"I'm the head of the Detective Bureau. That makes it an unusual circumstance. I'm invoking that clause."

"I just thought . . ."

"Forget it. No way. Not gonna happen." She stood up and looked down at me angrily. "Honestly, Shane, sometimes I wonder what goes through your head. It's inappropriate for a division commander to be a defense rep. Even though I'm only a lieutenant, I'm still the acting head of the Bureau. It would be completely wrong for me to do it. It would skew the entire hearing."

"Okay. Sorry I brought it up."

"The fact that you even asked with all I'm going through says so much more than any words could ever say."

"You know what it says? It says I still want you on my side. We used to be a great team and I want the team back. I love you, and even though the rest of the department wants to throw you away, I still believe in you enough to put my future in your hands. That's what it says."

She stood quietly with her back to me. When she turned, I saw tears running down her face.

Then she went quickly inside.

CHAPTER 24

Alexa was out of the house early. Her review with Chief Filosiani was scheduled for ten A.M. I ate breakfast alone and then looked up the number for the Police Officer's Association on my phone caddy.

At ten o'clock I walked into Jeb Calloway's office at Parker Center. He closed the door and eyed me with concern. "I talked to Jane Sasso this morning. Your Skelly is scheduled for next Tuesday—nine A.M. That's right on the ten-day timeline guaranteed you by Paragraph Six. She's really pushing to get this done. I need to do the supervisor's interview this afternoon so her IOs have time to go through it. How's three-thirty? You're allowed to bring your defense rep and a union steward from the POA."

"I guess that's okay," I said. "But I don't have a defense rep yet."

"If I were you, I'd get one now. Either way, be back here at three-thirty. We'll go over the charge sheet first, then I'll take your statement." He looked like a man walking on quicksand as he added, "Alexa's office called down yesterday and said you were suspended. I think that's out of policy, but I guess we can transfer your case load anyway."

"She rescinded that last night. She was going to call you about it."

Jeb was still frowning as I left his office. He didn't like procedural messes. I returned to my desk and pulled out the slip of paper with the number for the POA. The amount of trouble I keep getting into, I should have it on permanent speed dial. After I got through to the union, I was transferred to the steward section. I asked for Bill Utley, who had sat in for the union on my last I.A. performance beef. I was told he was out of the office, so I left my name and the time of my supervisor's review in Jeb's office. Then I scanned the charge sheet into my computer and e-mailed it to him.

Since I was technically still on the job and it was only ten-thirty, I decided to use up my remaining time by heading back out to Cartco. On the way, I called Secada.

"What d'you have going on this morning?" I asked.

"I'm meeting with my defense rep and POA steward, trying to get prepped for my supervisor meeting."

"Can you meet me out at Cartco in an hour?"

"This is a bad morning, Shane."

"You need to hear what I've got to say, and I don't trust my cell. I'll have you back in the office by one."

"Roger that," she said and hung up.

I had a plan in mind, which was legally sort of out there. But if I didn't get some traction soon, we were both going down in flames.

I drove to a Best Buy in Glendale and purchased a new BlackBerry that was identical to Roger Dahl's and the one Wade Wyatt had used when I pulled him over in his dad's Ferrari. I got back in my car and plugged it into the car cigarette lighter to charge as I drove. When I arrived at Penrose Avenue, I parked across the street from the container factory and waited. At eleven-fifteen Secada pulled in. She was driving her personally owned vehicle, known in the profession as a POV. Thankfully, she had left the conspicuous black-and-white slick-back at the motor pool.

She got out of her green SUV Suburban and crossed to my MDX. "Your car looks like shit. When're you gonna get some of this body work done?" she asked as she got in.

"That's way down on my to-do list right now," I snapped.

"Don't bite my head off. What's up?"

I told her about Tito Morales winning the million-dollar contest prize.

After I finished I saw a look of disappointment on her beautiful face.

"I can't believe he is in on this." She considered the information and then added sadly, "Man, I thought he was going to be a true *carnal*. Another one bites the dust."

I couldn't tell her what I had on my mind, because it was a little shady and she had already informed me that she didn't like to lie. Instead, I told her I thought it was time to have a little talk with Wade Wyatt. I wanted to give him a push and I needed her help. After I finished telling her what I wanted her to do, she was frowning—and I hadn't even told her the best part. She glanced at her watch but reluctantly agreed to stick around and help, providing she could get back downtown by two.

Wade Wyatt kept very gentlemanly work hours. He tooled the silver McLaren into the lot at eleven-forty, opened the gull wing door, and stepped out wearing tennis whites and carrying a beautiful, black alligator briefcase. He started toward the administration build-ing. I had reparked and was now sitting alone in my car, only two spaces away. Before he could get to his build-ing, I was out of the Acura and intercepted him halfway up the path.

"Am I supposed to know you?" he asked. The same look of entitlement I'd seen three nights ago, firmly in place.

"I see you got your car back from the Church of Destruction. Is the suspension all fixed the way you wanted it?" Not reaching for my badge, watching to see if he figured it out. It took him a minute, but he got there.

"Oh yeah." He shook his head and grinned. It was a very endearing smile. "Dude, between us, I was totally surprised you didn't pop me for speeding. I was boned . . . going way too fast. But it's too late now. You missed your window."

"We've got more important things we need to discuss," I said.

"Look, Mister whatever your name is . . ."

"Detective Shane Scully."

"Here's a sad but pertinent fact. You and I don't even live on the same planet, okay? We don't eat the same kind of food or drink the same kind of booze. We don't lay the same kind of women. We got nothing—absolutely nothing—in common. It closely follows, therefore, that we have nothing to discuss."

"Wanta bet?" I grinned at him, trying for my own endearing little smile, although it probably came off more like Jack the Ripper in mid-kill-chop.

"How 'bout a hundred?" he said, arrogantly. "Or is that too big a bet for a guy only making forty grand a year?" He tried to move past me as if with that insult, the discussion was definitely over.

"A hundred sounds good," I told him.

Wyatt turned back, surprised. "You kidding?"

"I think I can keep you conversationally entertained for a while, so you're on."

We stood there in the hot morning sun, me in my two-hundred-dollar blazer, him in his thousand-dollar tennis whites. We both tried to see how this was going to get started.

In an interview, I usually let the other guy go first just to see what he thinks we should be talking about. But Wade Wyatt was perfectly content to just stand there and wait. So I said, "How 'bout we begin by discussing the Bud Light contest that you and Mike Church ripped off ten months ago?"

No reaction.

"Is that the big wow?" he finally said. "Let's see, how's this supposed to track? My dad's worth hundreds of millions of dollars. I have unlimited credit and a Black AMEX card. But despite all this, you're suggesting I was so desperate for cash that I ripped off my own family's business with some brain-dead, West Valley car mechanic as my accomplice. Perhaps you could tell me why on earth I would ever do such a stupid thing."

"Maybe it's just because you just couldn't help yourself," I said pleasantly.

Wyatt stood looking at me, not taking any of this very seriously. It was almost as if he was deciding if I was going to be enough of an intellectual challenge to even waste ten minutes on. Then he turned and walked back to the McLaren, opened the trunk, and pulled out his tennis racket. He held it firmly in his right hand and began taking vicious practice swings.

"If you try to hit me with that I'll delaminate it over your fuzzy head."

"Don't be ridiculous. I just remembered it was in the car. Didn't want the gut strings to cook in the heat." He carried it back to where I was standing.

"Once we finish talking about the prize contest, I also have a few questions I want to ask you about Tru Hickman," I continued.

"Tru Hickman? That name's supposed to mean something to me?"

"Yeah, he was a tweaker friend of Mike Church's that you guys recruited to buy the Bud Light prize package that you knew was being sold out of a Valley mini-mart on Sepulveda."

Wade Wyatt stood looking at me, the smile still locked firmly in place. But I had his interest now. I could see some rapid eye movement.

"I never heard of Tru Hickman. Don't know him."

"Sure you do."

Then he got his confidence back. His smile widened like somebody who knew he was having his leg pulled and was still trying to figure out why. He wasn't used to being baited and his sense of entitlement convinced him he was far above my feeble grasp.

"You're a very funny man," he remarked.

"I get that a lot."

"Okay, Mister Policeman. Since I can't help you with any of that, we're concluded. I've got a busy afternoon."

"We're not concluded. I intend to get the answers to all of my questions before I leave."

"I can make one or two calls and Chief Filosiani, who I believe signs your paychecks, will make you go away."

"The Chief doesn't sign my checks. The city payroll clerk does."

His eyes narrowed. "Don't try matching wits with me," he said softly.

Now it was my turn to stand my ground and smile at him.

"Okay, if you have something so important on your mind. Let's hear it," he said.

"Olivia Hickman. We need to talk about her, too."

For the first time, I hit a soft spot. I saw it mostly in his body language—a slight dimming of the smile, a slumping of his shoulders. But he recovered nicely.

"Olivia Hickman. And let me guess. She's somehow related or married to this Tru Hickman person."

"His mom. Past tense. She was murdered."

"And I know something about it?"

I just let his question simmer.

Wade stood with his expensive briefcase in one hand and the titanium racket in the other, dressed in snappy white shorts, ready to serve America's container needs worldwide. Then he said, "If I could prove to you I don't know about any of this, about this Tru Hickman person buying that beer, or his mother's murder, what then?"

"That would certainly be a huge help," I responded, pleasantly.

"Then follow me."

He led me inside the large, expensively designed Business Center and Administration building.

This building was obviously where the bigwigs worked. All the really expensive art was in the lobby. The carpet was seventy-ounce plush pile and stretched wall to wall. I followed Wade down a hallway to a private office where he had his own private secretary. She was a good ornament. A nine or ten on the office fantasy scale. If she could type, God knows who she'd be working for—maybe even the great Roger Dahl.

"Cindy, bring me the Promo Safe folder on the August Bud Light contest," Wade snapped as he passed by her desk into his office.

She jumped up and exited.

The office was medium-size, but furnished with expensive antiques. There were law books everywhere. I picked up a thick one entitled *Torts, Pleadings and Judicial Reviews* that was marked with what looked like fifty or more yellow Post-it Notes.

"You want to leave my stuff alone?"

"Right." I put it down.

Half a minute later Cindy returned and handed Wade the file. He opened it and went through it like he knew exactly what he was looking for. Then he pulled out a single sheet of paper.

"This is an affidavit attesting to the winner of the West Valley Rare you were talking about." He handed it to me. "As you can see, it wasn't won by anybody named Tru."

The Promo Safe form was signed by one of their senior investigators named Ron Torgason. The affidavit plainly stated that Tito Alonzo Morales, of 4955 Bellingham Avenue in Valley Village had bought the Bud Light at four-fifteen on August 10 at a 7-Eleven in the 6000 block of Sepulveda. Two days later he had claimed the million-dollar prize.

"As you can see, Mister Morales was the winner. The agents from Promo Safe go out and stand in the store and—"

"Yeah, I know how it works," I interrupted.

"Then you can see this is exactly what I said. It's proof positive that Tito Morales bought and cashed in the rare, not this other guy, this Tru what's-his-face."

I stared down at the affidavit.

"Are we done now?" he asked, arrogance again framing every word. "I have to get through three chapters before my bar review class at six."

"Afraid we're not quite done yet, Wade."

"We're not?" Now he seemed frustrated, the smile long gone. "Why the hell not?"

"Because your buddy since the seventh grade, Mike

Church, is a longtime associate of Tru Hickman, and because Tito Morales happens to be the D.A. who filed the murder charge against Tru for killing his mom and then did the plea bargain sending the kid away for life." I did my endearing little smile again. "This is the same Tito Morales who bought a contest rare and won a million dollars from a company that you're involved with, and whose campaign office you visited yesterday, completing a nice little circle of facts. In some crowds, this might be viewed as a scam. But any way you cut it, it's way too cozy, contest-wise."

Wade's smile suddenly reappeared. I was beginning to suspect that it was just camouflage, that he used it when he was in trouble. Either that, or this kid had more chutzpah than the ten best murderers I'd ever worked.

"That is all just a coincidence," he offered. "I was at his office because *after* he won our prize I got to know him, and I'm now working on his campaign. Besides, why would I give a damn one way or the other if Tito Morales won a million dollars? How does that affect my life?"

"Maybe Mike Church is still stealing your toys. Or maybe we just haven't located the reason, yet."

"I see."

"Do you?"

For a moment it seemed he was regarding me almost with affection. He was so sure of himself that he was actually beginning to enjoy this. I decided right then that his giant ego was his biggest weakness. He thought he was simply brilliant. A good technique when you've got a suspect in play is to be exactly what the guy wants you to be. He thought I was a moron and no match for his rapid repartee. The dumber he thought I was, the more careless he would become and the more mistakes he was bound to make. I let fifty IQ points I couldn't spare drop out of my head and hit the floor, then fixed him with a smile as dull as my razor.

"Since you obviously are not going to leave me alone until I figure this out for you, let me see if I can help," he said.

"That would be excellent."

He looked at his watch. "You had lunch yet?"

"No, sir."

"I know a spot near here. Let's go get something and we'll see what I can come up with."

As we crossed toward the office door, I couldn't resist taking one last shot. "Guess this means you owe me the hundred dollars."

CHAPTER 25

We went to a steakhouse ten blocks from Cartco. The decor was plush. Dark green carpets, dark wood paneling, hunting prints everywhere.

He ordered a beer and a rib eye. I had coffee and a Chinese chicken salad. When the waiter left, Wade's BlackBerry rang. He pulled it out and looked at a text message. I pulled out mine, showed it to him proudly.

"Hey, look at this. We got the same damn phone," I said, grinning stupidly, as if I thought we could bond over owning identical BlackBerries.

"Phone rocks," he said distractedly, and started instant messaging.

" 'Cept I can never get the hang of all the new features on this thing," I complained.

"Read the manual." Still working on his IM.

"Well, I would, but even then I get kinda lost. I'm from the old rotary dial age of communications."

He looked up over the BlackBerry with a shit-eating grin. "What are you, about ten years older than me?"

"Little more."

He held up his BlackBerry. "This shit's Y-Gen weaponry. Computers, digital information, it's all moving at warp speed. Unless you were born with a PC on your nursery table, you're bound to fall behind. Don't let it haunt you, dude."

"That's comforting."

His cell rang again and he answered it. Another text message, but this time I reached over and covered his phone with my hand. "I think we need to turn that off," I said gently.

"I'm not used to being told what to do." He scowled.

"Then I'll try and keep these moments to a minimum."

He heaved a sigh, turned off the phone, then looked up and said, "Better?"

"Much."

What came next was so utterly ridiculous it was hard for me to believe this guy was actually trying to sell it to me.

He leaned forward in his seat and fixed me with a professorial stare. "Okay, so as long as we're waiting for our food, why don't I put the time to good use and just go ahead and solve your little problem. Explain how people, who have no real connection to one another, could appear in the same numerical sample."

"Okay." I smiled. "But remember, winning this contest in Los Angeles is, by my estimate, about a ten-million-to-one shot."

"Then this will be a good lesson for you in statistical analysis. In order for you to understand, I'm going to have to start by giving you a short course in probability curves."

"Hang on a minute. I don't want to miss anything." I figured this was going to be rich, so I played it for all it was worth. I reached for my notebook, took out my pen, and held it at the ready, looking stupidly down at a blank page. The only thing I didn't do was lick the ink tip.

"A Y-Gen would carry a little DAT recorder for moments like these," Wade sneered.

"Got one. Can't work it."

"Okay, so where does Tito Morales live?" he asked.

"Valley Village."

"The East Valley. But where does he work?"

"Van Nuys Courthouse."

"West Valley, good. That courthouse, if I recall, is within blocks of where this prize-winning rare was placed out on Sepulveda. Correct?"

"Yeah."

"Okay, now follow me here. In that West Valley section of town there are what, maybe ten thousand people?"

"Ten, probably less."

"Exactly. Probably less. But let's keep it to round numbers and say ten so you won't get lost in the math."

"Good, 'cause I'm horrible with fractions."

"I kinda knew that." He smiled condesendingly. "Okay, ten thousand people. And how many of those ten thousand people in the West Valley would even shop for beer at a 7-Eleven instead of, say, a supermarket or liquor store?"

"Boy, Wade, I just don't know. Don't have a clue."

"Let's estimate on the high side to keep our sample safe. Let's say half. Say five thousand. You think half the West Valley might shop at a 7-Eleven–type mini-market? Sound fair?"

"Okay."

"And how many of those five thousand people do you think buy Bud Light beer instead of some other brand?"

"How many? I have no idea." I tried to sound confused and hopelessly lost.

"It so happens, I can help us there, because as part of my job, I know the company's local market share. It's twenty-two point six. But let's shit-can the two point six and round it off to twenty so it doesn't get too complicated."

"Good," I dutifully wrote it down.

"So twenty percent of five thousand is one thousand people who *conceivably* might buy Bud Light at that particular market in a month. So now we're down from your original, but incorrect, ten million to one figure to a more realistic and vastly more manageable figure of one thousand to one. Still with me?"

"Right." I was scribbling, and furrowing my brow in tortured thought, giving this arrogant asshole a ride.

"Okay. So we're now saying there are a thousand people who would buy Bud Light in a mini-market in the West Valley," he said. "Of that one thousand people, how many do you think would choose to buy a six-pack of beer in that exact store on that exact day?"

"Not very many."

"Ten?"

"Uh . . . I don't see how . . ."

"Stick with me," he interrupted. "You think ten people might conceivably buy a six-pack of Bud Light in that market on that day?"

"Maybe."

"So now we're at ten to one." He smiled at me. "Or the real odds on Tito Morales, who worked just up the street, buying that prize package of beer. Not such a big stretch anymore, is it?"

It was complete gobbledy-gook. He must have thought I learned my math from primates.

"Except, how do we know he'd buy beer in that market on that day?" I asked stupidly. "I don't think you can do it that way."

"Sure you can, because that's empirical evidence."

"It is?"

"Absolutely, Detective Scully. It's empirical evidence because we know that Tito Morales did, in fact, buy beer in that market on that day, witnessed and signed-off on

by Promo Safe. Therefore, that fact stands as incontro-
vertible."

I looked up at him and let a slow smile break. The
dull child finally gets it.

"See?" He smiled back.

"Okay, okay. Now I think I may see what you're
driving at."

"Good."

"Except we still have the other end of it," I argued.
"The coincidence that Tito Morales was also handling
the murder case against Tru Hickman, who's a longtime
associate of Mike Church who, it turns out, you've
known since junior high."

"Same deal. In a statistical sample, it's called the
Rule of Parallel Correlations. So stick with me here,
we'll take those one at a time."

"Okay."

"Tito Morales is the head D.A. in Van Nuys, right?"

"Yes."

"How many murders does the Van Nuys D.A.'s office get, say, in a week?"

"Four, maybe five."

"And isn't the head D.A. the guy who, in the end,
signs off on all plea bargains?"

"Yes."

"Right, so he handles one hundred percent of them
when they occur, so it follows he had a one-hundred-
percent chance of doing Hickman's plea bargain. So now
let's put those two percentages together. We got a one-in-
ten chance Morales would buy the contest six-pack of
beer, and a one-hundred-percent chance he'd handle the
Hickman plea bargain. Same odds. As far as my knowing
Church who knows this Hickman dude, that's just the
six-degrees-of-separation thing. See what I'm saying?"

I was writing all of this down. Of course, the odds against all of this were so high they were off the charts. Incomputable. But to keep Wade in play, I nodded studiously. Then I closed the notebook and tapped the pen on the cover as if a great truth had just been revealed.

"That's fucking amazing," I said, letting my mouth gape open in wonder.

"They probably don't teach statistics at City College." He grinned, trying to sound like he was commiserating, but instead, just coming off like an elitist dick.

"How'd you know I went to City College?"

"Lucky guess," he smiled.

"As a matter of fact, they did teach it, but I only went there three semesters."

"You should've stayed in school, dude. Education is life's greatest tool."

"And here, all this time, I always thought it was a good erection." I gave him my front sixteen. He didn't return the smile. "So you think then that all this isn't too big a coincidence?" I said.

"We're just talking hypothetically here. But no, Detective, I don't."

I snuck a look at my watch. I had to suffer through this B.S. for at least thirty more seconds.

"Man, I probably should've taken that stat course," I told him. "You're a pretty smart guy."

"I've got some intellectual gifts," he allowed modestly. "My mind parses problems well. I graduated top of my class at Harvard Law. It's why I was selected to clerk for a U.S. Supreme Court justice last summer. She said my briefs were the most thoroughly annotated she'd ever seen."

"My briefs are usually thoroughly defecated," I said, grinning stupidly. I was probably overdoing the bit, and decided maybe I should dial it back a notch.

"Don't do the brief joke thing, okay? That's first-year law school stuff."

"Sorry." I was just stalling now, fooling around with him while I waited.

Then I saw Secada making her way hurriedly across the restaurant.

"Shane," she said urgently as she approached our table. "We need to go now! We just got a fresh one-eighty-seven in the Heights."

Now Wade's smile became a dazzler as he took in the beautiful Ms. Llevar.

"Sorry. Gotta go," I said. "You can buy my lunch and send the balance of our hundred dollar bet to me later." I stood and picked up a BlackBerry off the table. His, not mine. He didn't notice the switch because his eyes were busy undressing Secada.

"Shane, you simply must introduce me to this enchanting creature.

"Secada Llevar, meet Wade Wyatt."

"Nice to meet you," she said. Then, before he could respond, turned abruptly and almost dragged me out of the restaurant.

Once outside I got into her SUV, turned on Wade's BlackBerry, and scrolled through his archived text messages. I quickly went back to August 10, the night of Olivia Hickman's murder. There were three IMs back and forth between WW and MC—all of them shortly after midnight.

"What're you doing?" Secada said.

"Checking my IMs," I lied.

I had just finished scanning Wade's messages from that date when I saw him explode into the lot in his tennis whites, holding my BlackBerry in front of him like shit in a black sock. He looked around frantically.

"Over here," I called.

He turned and spotted us in the front seat of the SUV, then ran to the passenger window. He was out of breath by the time he got there. "I think we accidentally switched BlackBerries," he said.

"Yeah, I just realized it, too." I handed his back while he returned mine. A relieved look passed across his face.

"You got nothing on yours," he told me. "You should set up your features."

"Yeah. Maybe you could help me do that sometime," I said.

"Not too fucking likely, Detective. I'm not your personal electronics geek. I got a bar exam to study for." Then he smiled at Secada. "You, I intend to see again," he said, and started to walk away.

All the evidence I'd just gotten off Wyatt's BlackBerry was inadmissable because it was an illegal search. But if he complained, I could still claim it was just an accident and hope the rest of the case would survive a fruit-of-the-poisonous-tree defense. After all, it was his word against mine. As a police maneuver, it was definitely borderline. But I had to take the shot if I wanted to shake up Wade. I needed him to make a bad move that I could capitalize on. He was still heading back to his car when I called out to him, "Hey, Wade?"

He turned.

"Just one question."

"Sure." He still had a smile on his face. He was back in control, but I was about to change that.

"What the hell is a three shirt deal?" I asked innocently.

"A what?" His face went blank.

"I accidentally hit your archived messages." His face fell. "One of Mike Church's messages to you was on August tenth, which coincidentally is the night Olivia

Hickman was murdered. Wonder if that's part of the Law of Parallel Correlations." He looked a little sick, so I went on, "MC text-messaged: 'This just turned into a three shirt deal.' " I gave him my best stupid cop look. "I been sitting here wondering what on earth that could mean. I just remembered, when the mob shot a guy they used to call it buying him a suit because the bullets ruined the clothing. When you stab someone, plunge a knife into them twenty times like in Olivia Hickman's homicide, it would certainly ruin their shirt."

He stood there, frozen.

"I sure hope we aren't talking about murders here. I hope there aren't two more dead bodies in this case that I don't know anything about."

His face paled, his complexion got shiny.

"It's nothing," he said. "It's just bullshit."

"So what's it mean?"

More rapid eye work, some jerky body movements. Then he said, "Vomit. Mike Church used to get drunk and throw up on my Harvard sweatshirts. He used to borrow them all the time. It was the third one he did it to . . . a three shirt deal."

I furrowed my brow in confusion. "That doesn't sound quite right to me, Wade. He threw up three times on three of your shirts? God, what d'ya suppose the odds of that are? Of course, you're the man when it comes to probability curves." I looked over at Secada. "Let's go."

She put the Suburban in gear and we powered away, leaving him in sheer panic.

"You know you can't use any of that. You didn't have P.C. or a search warrant for that BlackBerry."

"It was a mistake, an accident. I couldn't help what I saw."

"You're really full of it," she said. But when I looked over, she was smiling.

CHAPTER 26

I had written down the text messages from memory in a spiral notebook and was reading from my notes. " 'Where R U? R U at Hickman's yet?' " I looked up at Secada. "That was from WW at twelve-oh-three A.M. Then MC said: 'Parked out front. Dark. Ready to roll.' Then at twelve-seventeen, WW's IM: 'Get in there. Get it.' No answer from Church. Then at twelve thirty-five, Church wrote: 'It went bad. Meet you at my place. This just turned into a three shirt deal.' End of transmissions."

"You shouldn't have given the damn thing back to him," she said. "You know he's gonna destroy it, dump it in the river."

"It doesn't matter. We're better off if he ditches it. That way it won't contaminate the case. Without a warrant, as evidence it was dust anyway."

She sat for a moment frowning at that. Then she said, "Here's something else. While you were in the restaurant, the deep check I ran on Devine and Morales came back. There's a big connection between those guys." She looked at me to make sure she had my full attention. "Back in ninety-one, Brian Devine and Tito Morales were cops together. Partners. It was just before Brian Devine went to SIS. For almost a year, these two *jamokes* shared the front seat of an X-car."

We rode in silence, both thinking about it.

"Pull over for a minute. Let's see if we can at least get the timeline surrounding Olivia's murder to lay out right."

"Okay," she said, and pulled her SUV up to the curb. We were only two blocks from Cartco. She set the brake and looked over.

"Let's start with the givens," I began. "We know Tito Morales ended up as the winner of the million-dollar Bud Light rare. We also know Mike Church had knife cuts on his hand the day after Olivia was murdered, and that Brian Devine got to the crime scene six minutes after the nine-one-one call and became the primary investigator, even though he was a supervisor and shouldn't have personally worked the case. Then he and Deputy D.A. Morales, his old LAPD patrol partner, tag-teamed Tru Hickman in the Van Nuys Division I-room, telling him he flunked a lie test and walked in his mom's blood leaving a footprint. The kid panics and cops a plea. Anything else?"

"This isn't exactly a given, but I agree with you that Tru probably wasn't in on it," she said. "He was such a meth head I can't see them taking a chance on letting him in on the scam. It's more likely their original plan was to get him to buy the beer, make sure he found the scrape-off, let him win the money, then just roll up and take it away from him later."

"I agree. That was undoubtedly the plan 'til Church lost it and killed Olivia Hickman. Then Tru became more valuable to them as the murderer."

She thought about it, then nodded.

"Okay, so let's see how much of this we can arrange into some kind of reasonable order," I suggested. "Then when we're done we'll deal with what's left over."

"Sounds good," she said. "Keep going, you're on a roll here."

"Let's say the sequence of events begins that Saturday afternoon with Tru buying the beer and taking it home. Mike Church showed up an hour later to pick up the rare, but Olivia wouldn't give them the six-pack because Tru was on Antibuse. Big fight in the front yard witnessed by neighbors. Olivia calls the cops. Remind me to get Communication to time date that call." She nodded, scribbling in her own notebook. "Tru and Mike Church split from the Hickman house so they won't get arrested. Next Mike and Wade take Tru out and get him so tweaked on crystal he passes out. Church comes back to the Hickman house at Wade's instruction and, according to Wade's BlackBerry, at twelve-oh-three he tells Church to break in. Church breaks into the house at around twelve-thirty to get the beer."

"Only their plan goes bad," Secada continued. "Olivia catches Church in the act of stealing the six-pack. He's roided to the gills, goes tropical, and kills her. Twenty stab wounds with a kitchen knife."

"Exactly," I said. "Church ended up getting a bunch of knife cuts on his hands in the process. Strong physical evidence that was studiously ignored by Devine and Morales. But now they've got a problem because they can't use Tru to collect the prize. He's much more valuable to them as a murder suspect to take the heat off Mike Church." I paused and looked over to see if she had anything to add.

"Up to there, I think it's pretty solid," Secada said. "They panic. They need help. So who do they call, Tito Morales or Brian Devine?"

"Could've been either, but since we still can't tie Lieutenant Devine directly to the beer rip and since Morales ended up with the prize, let's say they called Tito. I can't for the life of me figure out how either Lieutenant Devine or Tito Morales end up as coconspirators with these two twenty-six-year-old sociopaths, but there must be a reason so let's put a hold on that."

"We can put a hold on it but if we try and go after Morales we better not miss. He's probably going to be the mayor in three months. So we need the reason he's involved pretty soon."

"I agree, but I don't have it yet. I don't believe it's because Morales needed campaign financing. There are too many players. Once the million gets split four ways there's hardly enough to get the job done." We pondered that for a minute. Finally, Scout shrugged.

"Okay, so they call Tito," she said. "They tell him Mike went back for the six-pack and fucked it up, killed Olivia, and that the neighbors witnessed the Church-Olivia dustup earlier in the day, making it premeditated. Olivia's dead and Church is gonna be a prime suspect for the murder. Once that happens, the whole Bud Light rip is gonna be unearthed."

"This is kinda working," I said. "We can't prove a shred of it, but as theory, it's great."

We were both getting excited.

"So now we need to bring Brian Devine onstage somehow. How did he end up getting there six minutes after the nine-one-one call? That's too lucky to just be a coincidence." Secada said.

We sat quietly for several moments, both chewing on that, before Secada came up with the answer.

"Let's say, after he gets the call from Church and Wyatt telling him Olivia's dead, Tito Morales calls his old cop friend, Brian Devine, who's still working in Valley Homicide. He gets Devine out of bed and tells him to go park a block from the murder scene and wait until Tru Hickman recovers from his meth blackout and wanders home. Once he finds his mother, they figure he'll probably call nine-one-one, and Lieutenant

Devine is perfectly positioned a block away to jump the call."

"That's probably exactly what happened," I said. "With the primary homicide investigator and the D.A. both in on it, Hickman didn't stand a chance." We both thought about it, looking for holes, but the structure hung together. "So how do we prove all of this?" I asked.

"Haven't a clue."

"The pieces that are still left over are the North Van Nuys bus company and this Transit P.D. full of tattooed police commissioners, most of whom are Vanowen Street Locos."

"We also don't have the way they got around Promo Safe and the ex-Federal agent who witnessed Tru buy the beer," she said. "But I'm starting to like this a lot."

"If a 'shirt' is a murder, and Wade's reaction tells me it is, then who are the other two corpses?" I said. "I think we need to start looking into Wade Wyatt and Mike Church's recent history of personal grief, see how many trips to Forest Lawn these two have made lately."

"Shane, we're gonna both be suspended," she said. "We've got too many power players lined up against us. This isn't going to get finished, at least not by us. We're gonna get shut down."

"Hey, Scout, no backing out. Don't forget it was you who got me into this. Besides . . ."

"If you say, we don't need no stinking badges, I'll shoot you right here in the front seat of my own damn car," she said.

"I was gonna say, the only good thing about these people is they're extremely powerful and they have too many face cards. They already know they're the winners."

"How does that help?"

"They won't be expecting us to attack."

CHAPTER 27

My union steward, Bob Utley, was seated in Sally Quinn's chair across from my desk when I got back to the fifth floor of Parker Center. Utley was one of those overweight guys with a Santa Claus face who looked so friendly I always felt like telling him my life story and what I wanted for Christmas. He was only a reserve officer now, but back when he was still on the job full time, he'd once walked into a bank in Glendale and foiled a holdup in progress. Guns flashed, and before it was over, he'd shot four guys and killed two. According to the security cameras, it all happened in less than forty seconds. Still the department fast-gun record. But the incident finished him as a street cop. He lost his edge after that, became a Protestant lay minister, and went into administrative affairs. Now he was spending a lot of his time as a Police Officer's Association steward. I liked him as my union rep because he was polite in internal reviews and didn't further exacerbate the messes I'd already made. Also, Bob knew his cop law. He could pick the inaccuracies out of a supervisor's report like raisins from a bran muffin.

"Not much backup material here," he said, thumbing through the charge sheet I'd e-mailed him as I dropped my butt in the chair across from him.

"It's an insubordination case where I never had any

face time with the supervisor I supposedly dissed. That's bound to cut down on the affidavits and source material."

"Who's your defense rep?"

"Don't have one yet."

"Mistake."

"Yeah, well I think you and I can stumble through this review. Jeb Calloway's a good boss. He isn't gonna peel me. He knows this complaint is bullshit."

"Listen, Shane, it's a big mistake to count on a supervisor's loyalty. This guy works for the command structure. His job here today is to kick your ass for Jane Sasso. If he fails to do that he's gonna end up getting his own sixth-floor enema. You need a defense rep."

"Well, I don't have one, okay? I'm gonna get one later. If you think it's such a mistake, let's just postpone."

"We can't postpone. You had three days' notice. You should've lined up somebody to represent you. I'm a lowly POA steward. I'm just here to protect your union rights. My job isn't to defend you against the actual charges."

"We'll get through it okay."

He looked unhappy. "You hope." He leaned back in the chair and said, "Let's just go through the essentials here, before we go in." He cleared his throat. "You got the transmittal letter and charge sheet by certified mail?"

"No, it was hand delivered."

"You got a signature receipt on that?"

"My wife took the stuff. I wasn't home."

Bob leaned forward in his chair. His head came up. "Good, good. That's a violation of your rights. You're supposed to be personally served and there needs to be a signature receipt with your name on it attesting to that fact. Your wife can't sign for you. That's one for our side."

I smiled. He didn't. "The Skelly is scheduled for next Tuesday, ten working days from receipt of notice, so I'm putting a checkmark on that."

"Right."

"All copies of written material to be used in your case were supplied to you in a timely fashion?"

"Got nothing but the charge sheet."

"Okay." He pulled a fax out of the file. "What's this then? It was delivered to me an hour ago but isn't in the charge sheet." He read it aloud. "Failure of good behavior outside of duty hours, which is of such a nature as to cause discredit to the appointing authority. What's that?"

"I don't know." I thought about it. "Okay. Maybe it was the thing on Abbot Kinney Boulevard."

"The *thing* on Abbot Kinney? Be specific, man. What're you talking about?"

"The head of the Valley Homicide unit, Lieutenant Brian Devine, pulled me over after work, then yanked me out of my car and after that it got a little physical. We both unholstered."

"I'm sorry, what?! You drew down on each other?"

"It was just for a minute."

He groaned. "That's what it is then, but where's the affidavit from Lieutenant Devine?" He started shuffling through his folder. "It's not in here. You got it?"

"No."

"These fucking people. They're adding more charges after the transmittal letter. They can't do that."

"Guess not."

Then Jeb Calloway came out of his office and motioned to us. Bob and I stood, but he stopped me before we headed across the room to Cal's office.

"Okay. He's gonna have some Legal Affairs talent in there. Maybe somebody from Operations or the Chief Adjunct's office. Keep your tone civil, Shane."

"I'm always civil in these things."

"You're *what*?" He looked appalled. "Don't make me go through the long list of shouted insults and threats of bodily harm I've witnessed." He shook his head and said, "Shake everybody's hands. Write their names down if we don't know them. We both have to keep track of everything that's said in there and by who. It could be extremely important later. Take your notebook. And, for God's sake, be polite. If the situation warrants, you can express frustration, but remain professional."

"Yes, Mommy."

We walked into Cal's office. The meeting consisted of a lieutenant named Arnold Shepard from Legal Affairs; a captain from Operations named David Detorsky; Jeb Callaway, my immediate supervisor; Bob Utley; and me. Bob looked relaxed and Santa-friendly as he eased his wide body into one of Cal's worn chairs.

"Okay," Cal said. "This is your supervisor hearing, Shane. The purpose is for me to lay out the charges against you and to listen to anything you might want to say in clarification prior to the Skelly next Tuesday. At your Skelly you will get to tell your side of things in detail. What we're doing here is trying to determine if there's anything that has been left out, or needs to be deleted from this case for reasons not previously disclosed." He looked up from the cheat sheet he'd been reading and said, "Fair enough?"

"Yep."

"Okay. I see you don't have a defense rep. Are you arguing your own case?"

"For now. Yes, sir."

The captain from Operations shifted in his seat. He knew I might have grounds for a complaint over this later, regardless of the fact that it was my own doing.

City law is full of weird legal conundrums. They had to be careful.

"The charges against you are, one: refusal of a direct order from a deputy chief; two: malfeasance of duty . . ."

"Excuse me," I interrupted. "But where did that malfeasance crap come from?" Anger in my voice. "What malfeasance?"

"Let me just read the charges. Then you can talk," Cal said.

"Yeah, but . . ."

Bob Utley put his hand on my arm. Then he smiled calmly at Cal and said, "That'll be fine, Captain. Go ahead."

"Three: making false and misleading statements during an inquiry," Cal continued, "and failure to cooperate with an ongoing investigation inside proper department channels."

"That's the whole point," I jumped in. "The investigation wasn't ongoing. I.A. closed it despite a plethora of facts supporting a bad due-process complaint."

Again I felt Bob Utley's hand on my arm. I looked at him and he turned his big, sad, hound-dog eyes on me. Eyes that said, *Please don't do this*. I nodded, shut my mouth, and turned back to Cal.

"Lastly, there's this failure of good behavior charge stemming from actions taken outside the line of duty on another police officer in full view of the general public, causing discredit to the appointing authority—i.e., this department." Cal looked up. He was finished and glad to be through it.

"We're challenging that failure of good behavior thing on the grounds that it wasn't part of the original charge sheet and was recently added," Utley said pleasantly. "Our position here is that as a result, it can't be part of this case. And due to lack of correct administrative procedure, should probably never be filed at all."

"I, uh . . ." Cal looked at the Legal Affairs lieutenant.

"We added that charge as an addendum," Lt. Sheppard said. "It saves going through a separate I.A. process all over again at a huge waste of tax dollars. You'll get the charge sheet and affidavit today."

"Can't do it that way, Lieutenant," Utley said.

"Wanta bet?"

"Yeah."

Just as everyone started trading stink-eye, the door flew open, and Alexa came into the room holding a single sheet of paper.

"Sorry I'm late," she announced.

"Lieutenant," Cal said. "What are you doing here?"

"I'm Detective Scully's defense rep," she said evenly. "He asked me yesterday and, as of a few hours ago, I've decided to accept. I was detained upstairs at a hearing that just let out." She sat in the remaining empty chair and nodded at the command staff gathered in Cal's office. She obviously knew them all.

"I don't believe that as a division commander, you can represent him, Lieutenant," Sheppard said softly.

"Yes, I can." She fixed hard eyes on him. "You don't have all the facts, so don't push this, Arnie. I'll drop-kick you out that window."

Man, I love Alexa when she gets like this. I fought to keep my expression stern.

"Anyway, it really doesn't matter whether I can or can't because I'm filing a writ of mandamus on Shane's behalf to strike this whole proceeding," Alexa said.

She handed the lone piece of paper to Cal, who looked down, holding the sheet like it just came off the bottom of a birdcage. Then he handed it to Captain Detorsky, who handed it to Sheppard. Each of them in turn stared at it in disbelief.

"We're filing that pursuant to the Code of Civil Procedure one-oh-eight-five," she said. "The writ requests an inquiry into whether the department proceeded without, or in an excess of, its jurisdiction, and whether there was any prejudicial abuse of discretion. It is the contention of the accused that he was suspended without pay a full day before his supervisor's review and eleven days before his Skelly hearing, and that said action denied him his protections under Paragraph Six of the Police Bill of Rights."

"He was suspended?" Sheppard sputtered. "By who?"

"By me," Alexa said. "In my role as head of the Detective Division, I suspended him without cause, and in so doing, violated his rights of discovery and due process."

She stood and motioned to me and Bob. "Come on, guys. We're out of here."

I followed my wife and my union rep into the hall. There was mass confusion in the office behind us as they started passing her writ of mandamus around, all talking at once.

I looked at Utley. "Can we do that?"

"She's your division commander. If she suspended you before the Skelly, then this case is over on a technicality."

I turned to give Alexa a hug, but when I did, I saw that she had already disappeared. I scanned the fifth floor to the elevators, but she was nowhere in sight.

CHAPTER 28

In less than a minute, I made it up to Alexa's office using the stairs. I found Ellen standing in the outer office talking to the Detective Bureau Deputy Assistant Commander, Chuck Ward, who was holding a thick case folder. Both of them turned as I bolted through the door.

"Where's Alexa?" I blurted.

"Gone. I think she went down to the fifth floor to see you," Ellen said. "She left her review almost twenty minutes ago. Haven't seen her since then."

"I'll come back at a more convenient time." Chuck Ward turned and left quickly.

"What's going on?"

"Alexa's been replaced. Chuck's the new interim head of division now."

"Tony relieved her?"

Ellen looked sad, but tried to put a good face on it. "Listen, Shane. Maybe it's for the best. It's been a nightmare around here. I think she needs to work on getting better, first."

"You don't know where she went?"

"Home, I guess."

I left, got in my car, and blew out of the police garage. I tried her cell. Nothing. It went straight to voice mail. I tried our house—same thing. I made it home in forty minutes, which is excellent time, even for me.

Alexa wasn't there. I went outside and looked up the canal path, thinking that maybe she was walking around the neighborhood breathing in the ocean air and trying to calm herself down. I didn't see her.

I called her cell again, left a second urgent message, then got in the MDX and took off for USC. She might have gone there to see Chooch.

I arrived in record time, mostly by cheating and using my flashers and siren.

It was a little past five by the time I arrived at Howard Jones Field. I found Chooch in a receiver and quarterback meeting of fifteen guys in the east end zone. All of them had taken a knee and were gathered around a position coach at the center of the circle. I spoke to an assistant and had Chooch pulled out of the group. We found a spot on the sidelines where we could talk.

"Has Alexa tried to reach you?" I asked.

"I don't know. I don't think so."

"Where's your cell?"

"It's . . . it's in. . . . What's going on?"

I told him that Alexa had failed her administration review and was being replaced as the head of the Detective Bureau. I told him how she came down and saved my ass in Cal's office by burying herself even deeper and admitting that she illegally suspended me before my Skelly hearing.

"Maybe that was her plan all along," Chooch suggested. "Maybe that's why she did it, so she could use that to help you later."

It didn't sound like Alexa to me. She was too much of a Girl Scout for that kind of blatant manipulation. Then I realized that I couldn't swear to that right now because I really didn't know her anymore. I had no idea what she would now regard as acceptable behavior.

"Chooch, if she calls I need to talk to her. I'm worried."

Chooch reached out and took my arm. "Dad, don't leave her."

"Where did that come from?"

"I know you're thinking about it. I know you."

"I'm not thinking about it." But of course, that wasn't true.

"I know who she is," Chooch said. "We both do. I don't believe God makes us one way, then changes who we are. I think a person's soul is given at birth. It's specific and unchangeable. Character isn't just about brain chemistry and neurotransmitters. That's not what determines who we are."

"Sometimes I don't even recognize her anymore," I admitted.

"I know it's hard, Dad. But you've got to give this some time—years even. If you can't do it for her, then hang on for me. Will you promise?"

I stood looking at my son and wondering how he'd gotten so strong and so spiritual. Did that come from Alexa, or did it get passed down it genetically from his birth mother?

"Okay," I finally said, softly. "I promise."

"Let's go check and see if she's called my cell," Chooch said.

He told the assistant coach that we had a personal emergency and that he'd be right back. We walked to the locker room where he pulled out his cell phone and checked it for messages.

"Three calls from her in the last hour," he said.

"Call her back."

Chooch dialed Alexa back but her phone went to voice mail.

"She's smart, Dad. She knows you'd come here. She obviously doesn't want to discuss this yet."

"Next time she calls, try and get her to talk with me."

"Okay."

I left Howard Jones Field and returned home. It was after seven when I got there. The first thing I did was check our home phone for messages again. There were three. One was from Secada asking me to call her. One was from Jeb Callaway—same message. The last one was from Alexa.

"Shane, it's me." Her voice sounded guarded. "Listen, I know you want to talk, but I need some time to myself right now. Don't chase after me. Don't make any demands. I'm in a place where I can think. I need to find out who I am and who I'm going to be. I love you, darling. Hang on and say a prayer for us."

CHAPTER 29

I sat in the living room making more entries into my journal. I remembered Alexa striding into Cal's office, laying that writ of mandamus on Lieutenant Sheppard, telling him she'd dropkick him out a window if he gave her any trouble. It was magnificent, just like the old days. But just when I thought she was back, she ran off, refusing to talk to me. Preferring to be alone.

I finally finished writing and closed the journal, then turned off the lights and lay on the sofa listening to the distant surf thunder two blocks away. The marine layer must have been rolling in because I heard the long, mournful wail of a foghorn. My thoughts turned inward.

I've never taken good fortune for granted. From an early age, my life as an orphan was a series of fistfights, manipulations, and lies. Like a wolf hovering at the edge of a campfire, I was always waiting for any sign of weakness so I could sweep in and take advantage. Cynicism was my armor, violence a reaction to loneliness, sex a physical release performed mostly with strangers. In all of this, I was only trying to survive.

After I met Alexa and Chooch, I let my guard down. I soon learned that I needed different things to survive. Respect, redemption, and love. I found myself on a new eye-opening path where good deeds were performed for no selfish reason. And finally, in the end, I developed the ability to become vulnerable to others. The next thing that happened was I began to accept love, and then even take it for granted. I never expected to experience the old emptiness, or deal again with the dark creatures that once crawled on the floor of my mind.

But now I was back where I started. All of it courtesy of one sixteen-gram hollow point round that scrambled Alexa's brain, causing a chain reaction that ended up changing everything.

I closed my eyes and wished that I could escape from all of this. Then, mercifully, I fell asleep.

The ringing of the telephone jolted me awake. I scrambled up off the sofa and snatched the receiver out of its cradle.

"Yes?" I was hoping for Alexa, but got Secada instead.

"Sorry it's so late," she said.

"What time is it?"

"Midnight."

"What's up?"

"Somebody got to Tru Hickman right after chow tonight. It happened in the cafeteria. Shanked. I just got a call from the prison hospital because my name's in his letter file. He's in ICU. It's critical."

"Who did him?"

"Gang-bangers from his car."

"Fuck!" I shouted at the walls. We'd been too slow, too predictable.

"I'm going up there now," Scout said.

"Okay. Me, too."

"Want me to pick you up?"

"Where are you?"

"Just leaving downtown. No traffic at this hour. I can be at your place in twenty."

She made it in eighteen. I was waiting out front and jumped into her green Suburban, and we roared out.

It was past one by the time we hit California I-99 to Bakersfield. Big, empty, sixteen-wheel produce trucks churned relentlessly up the Grapevine, grinding through their gears heading over the San Gabriel Mountains into the Central Valley. As Secada drove she filled me in on a few things she'd learned while I'd been in my supervisor review and chasing after Alexa.

"I ran through Mike Church's background this afternoon looking for recent deaths. His father, Juan Iglesia, died in his shower eighteen months ago. There'd been bad blood between them since Mike got jumped into the Vanowen Street Locos at age fifteen. It got worse when he changed his name to Church. After Juan's death, Mike inherited the old man's auto body shop and tow service."

I looked over at her. "You sure Church didn't kill him?"

"I'm having the investigators' report and the M.E.'s statement faxed over to us. According to the coroner's assistant I talked to over at North Mission Road, it was a pinpoint injury. A heavy blow, but only a few centimeters in diameter. His skull was hit with such force it exploded some blood vessels inside his head. A single, massive stroke ensued."

"Do they know what caused the head trauma?"

"They think he just slipped in his shower and went down, hitting the faucet handle. At least, that's what the primary and the M.E. wrote. Death by accidental causes."

"But as a result, Church inherits his father's tow service and bus company," I mused. "I'm not going for it."

"Apparently, Juan Iglesia was 'El Corazón Oro,' " she said. "A friend with a heart of gold. I checked around. People loved this old man. He was the exact opposite of his deadbeat son. He started that little bus company and ran it as a nonprofit because he wanted to help the elderly and disabled. Kind of his way of giving back to America."

We rode in silence for a minute and then I said, "Okay, so what's the story on the Transit Authority Police Department then? Whose idea was that?"

"Probably Mike's. He inherited this little bus company with only one van that his father originally obtained by trading three broken motorcycles. Mike also inherited Iglesia Auto Body, which he promptly renamed the Church of Destruction. Then in September of last year the bus company bought four new Metro Coach fifty-seven passenger buses—big ones. A month later they form a transit police department and buy all kinds of topflight security to go inside the buses—elaborate, infrared cameras and state-of-the-art satellite GPS units to locate a bus if it's hijacked. Except, who's gonna hijack a bunch of disabled senior citizens?"

I looked over at her. "You've been busy. That's a lot of good info."

"Yeah, looks like a lot. But if you want the real truth, I was relieved of duty. I'm still getting paid, but Sasso put me on the rack. Apparently my undercarriage is getting checked for wet spots. Her words, not mine. That left me with an afternoon to kill. Most of this stuff I got off the NVNTA Web site."

I nodded.

"How 'bout you? How'd your supervisor's review go?" she asked.

"Pretty good. I'm off the hook."

"Get outta here." She turned and looked over at me, then almost hit a slow-moving truck before swerving at the last minute and powering on.

"That was good thinking, getting Alexa to be my defense rep."

Then I told her what had happened and how Alexa had saved my ass. After I was finished, Secada nodded her head in approval.

"Awesome."

"Alexa was removed from command by Chief Filosiani, so technically, after that happened she became eligible to represent me," I concluded.

Secada drove in silence for almost ten minutes and then we transitioned onto California 137 heading toward Corcoran. Another ten minutes passed before she spoke again.

"Want to hear something strange?"

"Sure."

"Ever since Doug and I got divorced, I've been looking to fill a huge hole in my life. I thought I would do it with work. I didn't want to start a new relationship. But sometimes we can't control our emotions or the events that produce them." She looked over at me. "You happened to be exactly the right guy at exactly the wrong time and now I feel very lost and lonely."

"Let's wait and see what happens."

"No, I won't do that," her voice firm, almost angry. "I told you already, I won't take what's not mine."

When we got to the hospital ward at Corcoran, we were greeted by an old warhorse, assistant warden who led us into the ICU. The unit was half prison, half hospital. Bars and electric doors with white painted walls. The orderlies wore green medical scrubs with matching prison ink tattoos.

We looked through a glass window at an unconscious Tru Hickman. Fluids dripped into his arm from hanging IV bags. Two pounds of surgical tape and gauze encased his skinny chest.

"Got him twenty-three times in six seconds," the assistant warden told us. He was a big, gray, overweight guy with hair growing out of his ears.

"This is my fault," I whispered, as I looked at Tru's inert form. "This one's on me."

CHAPTER 30

The prison surveillance tape showed Tru Hickman shuffling across the cafeteria, carrying an empty metal tray, moving like a man on Thorazine. Two muscled Hispanics with gang tatts trailed him innocently. Once Tru put his tray on the conveyor they made their move. One grabbed his arms while the other started shanking him. The blade flashed over twenty times, in and out, underhanded and quick, prison style. In seconds, Tru slumped to the floor. The two inmates turned and, as if they'd had nothing to do with it, walked calmly away. The assistant warden, who I had just learned was named Jack Slater, shut off the tape.

"They're both predicate felons up here on third strikes, so killing Hickman doesn't add anything to their sentences. Those two are here for the duration. They'll get charged with murder one, cop to second degree, and when it's all done, the sentences will run concurrently."

"Van Owen Street Locos?" I asked.

"The baddest of the bad," he answered with a put-upon sigh.

"These guys are in Mike Church's crew," I said softly, looking at Secada, who had remained silent throughout the video. Her only reaction had been a sharp intake of breath when the stabbing started.

"I want to talk to them," I said.

"They've already lawyered up," Assistant Warden Slater said. "I've been warned that they're not to be interviewed without counsel present. They're hard targets. Nobody's gonna get nada outta either one of these shitbirds."

"Let *me* try," Secada said.

"Besides the obvious, you don't have anything to trade." The sentence allowed an unattractive leer to stain his already fleshy features.

Hickman was in critical condition and being kept under heavy sedation so we couldn't talk to him, either. With nothing else to do, an hour later we were back in Secada's SUV heading to Los Angeles. The sun was just coming up over the low hills and there was no traffic on the highway.

"All we can do is pray he comes out of this," Secada said. "But even if he makes it, he'll be in ICU for at least a week. I don't think he's safe, even in that hospital. There's a number that buys almost anything on the inside."

I agreed with her. But unless the California Department of Corrections threw in with us, we didn't have the juice it would take to get Tru a transfer to a secure prison hospital like USC in Los Angeles. The situation seemed hopeless.

"This is my fault," I muttered again.

"It's not your fault," she answered sharply. "Why do you keep saying that?"

"This happened because of my dumb-ass move with that BlackBerry. I was so target locked on Wade Wyatt, I ignored everything else. I pushed so hard those guys figured their only move was to kill Tru."

"How does killing him change any of this?" she asked.

"Because as long as he's alive and yelling foul, we

might have eventually gathered enough pieces to pressure the D.A.'s office downtown to go over Morales's head and give us a writ for a new trial. A new trial puts Mike Church back in the grease because no legitimate investigation would ever look past him the way Lieutenant Devine did. But if Hickman's dead, it's kinda over. The city's not gonna run this mess back through the system and eat a ton of bad press just to salvage some dead tweaker's reputation. I didn't think it through. I should have realized they could end this by simply eliminating the problem."

We drove on in silence while my spirits plunged. Tru's fate pressed down hard on my conscious. We were heading south on I-99, on a short stretch of road that had narrowed to a divided three-lane highway, when about a mile ahead, we came upon half a dozen squad cars and a tow rig parked in a disorganized cluster with their flashers on. We saw that beyond the flashing vehicles, an ancient six-wheel farm truck was tipped over, blocking all three lanes.

Secada slowed to a stop. The old stake-bed rested on its left side with its load of artichokes spread across all three lanes. An elderly Mexican man with a young boy at his side was talking to the officers, gesturing with both hands. Secada waited until a highway patrolman came over.

"Sorry, road's closed," the cop said.

She showed him her badge. "Can't we get around?"

"How do you think you're gonna do that?" He had a point. The truck was across all three lanes and the heavy concrete abutment didn't allow us any room to slide past on either side.

"We need to get back to L.A.," Secada said.

"Make a U, go back about half a mile, and take Mountain Crest Road. It's a little narrow and winding but it will take you up in the hills around all this. Hooks back up to I-Ninety-nine near East Bridge."

Secada thanked him and glanced over at me. "There's a California map book in the glove compartment."

I pulled the book out as she made a U and headed back the way we'd just come. After about six-tenths of a mile we spotted the Mountain Crest exit and turned off. While I was studying the map she negotiated the washed-out, badly potholed two-lane. As we climbed up into the low hills, the road quickly became a series of blind switchbacks. It was treacherous, but the countryside was beautiful with big, sprawling oaks throwing uneven shadows on rolling green meadows.

"We should've brought a picnic," she said, trying to lighten my mood.

I was still looking down at the map when I felt the first bullet ricochet off the back of her car.

Secada said nothing, but slammed the throttle down.

I spun around and saw a new, blue Ford pickup truck, no front plate, behind us. Two black-haired Hispanic guys were standing behind the cab, harnessed to a roll bar in the back of the truck, both pointing thirty-ought-sixes over the roof of the cab. As I turned, they started firing again and almost immediately, the back window of the SUV exploded inward, raining glass on us.

"Faster!" I yelled as Secada took the narrow, rutted curves at breakneck speed.

Two more rifle shots cracked. I managed to unfasten the seat belt and started firing back at them through her blown-out rear window. My Airlight Smith and Wesson snubie weighed less than a pound and was a good, easy carry piece, but it was so light it kicked like a mule, and its two-inch barrel had no accuracy at this distance. I wasn't hitting anything.

"What are you packing?" I yelled at Scout.

"Glock Nine. Fifteen in the clip! My purse!" she screamed back.

I grabbed for the bag, pulled out the gun, chambered it, and started unloading 9 mm rounds at the pursuing truck. The Glock had a five-inch barrel and was much more accurate. Immediately, the slugs began to slam into the truck grill. The driver swerved to avoid being hit, then took his foot off the gas and fell back, trailing us now by about a hundred yards, reducing my effectiveness. Every time the road straightened out, there were more shots from their long rifles. Pieces of Secada's car flew off, accompanied by whining ricochets. Then, without warning, a stake-bed farm truck full of produce appeared around a blind turn, coming right at us. Secada swerved to miss it.

Several more shots sounded. Secada yelled out as blood mist flew from her right shoulder and she lost control of the SUV. Suddenly we catapulted off the narrow, winding road into the rutted fields beyond. The left front tire went into a pothole and, in an instant, we flipped over and were rolling.

The next thing I knew I was being thrown around inside the Suburban unable to get my bearings until the SUV finally came to a shuddering, bone-jarring stop, tipped over on the driver's side.

"Gotta get out! We're easy targets in here!" I shouted, struggling to get up.

Secada was pinned underneath me between the steering wheel and the door. Her bloody arm hung uselessly at her side.

"*Vengan! Andele!*" someone yelled, and I heard both truck doors slam.

I finally pushed myself up by standing on the steering column. When I had enough leverage, I heaved the passenger side door up and open, then peeked up over the running board at the field behind us.

The two riflemen had untied themselves from the roll bar and were scrambling out of the truck. The driver was also out and aiming his gun around the front fender. I'd somehow managed to hold on to Scout's Glock during the crash and started cranking off rounds.

"*Chingada!*" one of them yelled and then immediately dove back behind the blue Ford pickup.

"Come out! Come out now and you no get hurt!" a man with a thick Mexican accent yelled.

I fired for effect, hitting nothing, until I was dry.

Secada must have been counting shots, because as soon as the slide locked open, she shouted, "Here!" and handed me up a fresh clip with her good hand. I hit the eject button, dropped the empty, and slammed the new clip home. I tromboned the slide and readied myself to start firing.

"Go out the back window, Scout. Head for the trees. I'll keep them pinned down."

Holding her bleeding shoulder, Secada struggled painfully over the seats, and finally wiggled through the broken back window. Once she was outside, I laid down a barrage of cover fire as she sprinted across the open field. As my slugs smashed into the truck, the driver jumped into the cab and plowed backwards away from me. My bullets bounced off the hood and grill, shattering the left side of the windshield until the driver careened recklessly to a stop behind a huge oak.

I scrambled out the back of the SUV and followed Scout across the short, open field, and up a low rise, toward a stand of poplar trees. She was noticeably losing speed and coordination, moving slower and slower. As

I hurried to catch up to her, I heard the bark of both ought sixes. Then Secada fell.

"No!" I shouted. I finally reached her, scooped her up in my arms, and stumbled on.

The flat crack of more shots sounded and I felt a sharp pain in my back, then another slug tugged at my elbow. I knew I was taking rounds, but a sudden surge of adrenaline numbed the pain. The shots hadn't knocked me down yet, so I kept going, struggling up the slope with Secada cradled in my arms. I crested the hill and started down the other side. Secada's eyes were closed. Blood poured out of two deep wounds in her left side.

Then I felt a wave of numbness so overpowering that I could no longer control my body. Suddenly my legs gave out and Secada slipped from my grasp as the ground rushed up at me. Then I was tumbling downhill. I heard the distant sound of rushing water, which grew louder as I fell, until it became a deafening roar. Ice cold water flooded into my mouth and hammered my eardrums. I had come to rest in a cold mountain stream. I struggled to rise up, to locate Secada, but my arms would no longer lift my weight. I couldn't breathe. I couldn't even get my face out of the bubbling tributary. I panicked as I suddenly realized I was about to drown in less than two feet of water.

CHAPTER 31

Slowly, gray images started coming out of the mist. Silvery silhouettes that shimmered like freshly-minted buffalo head nickels. A white-haired fatherly presence I couldn't quite remember peered down at me, his craggy face etched with curiosity.

Chooch and Alexa floated up like gray-white ghosts. I felt nothing. I was a spectator in a dark theater, watching this parade of colorless tintype people that kept changing into new forms from old memories. I saw the old Huntington House group home where I first knew loneliness and despair. Some of my foster parents came and looked down at me—welfare thieves who took money, then threw me back when I became too much bother. The people in these pictures would appear, sometimes move or even speak, coming to life for a minute, before being pulled back into the mist, getting smaller and weaker until they were gone. Then another image would arrive. Snapshots from my past. I watched, but was strangely detached, as if this had all happened to someone else.

Then Secada was holding me, looking down, her dark eyes filled with love. Her lustrous hair hung in sheaves, framing both of us. She reached out and caressed me, pulling me near. Unlike the others, she was rich and colorful, close and warm. Her naked breast and strong arms caressed me. I felt safe. When she leaned down and kissed me, I suddenly began responding.

"*Querido,* listen to me," Secada whispered.

"I'm listening."

"I tried to keep my promise. But this attraction is too strong. I cannot be *tu otra*—your other woman," she whispered.

"I know."

I found her mouth and smothered it with kisses.

First, I felt a warmth, and then, without warning, a sudden searing pain. It started in my heart, then spread quickly across my chest, crippling my entire body. Far away I heard alarms and buzzers.

"Don't hate me, *querido,*" Secada said.

"We're losing him. Get the crash cart!" a distant voice shouted.

And then the fog was back, swirling around me. This time I could taste it, burning in my throat like acid bile.

"I tried to keep my promise," Secada said, disappearing behind a new gray mist. As she faded, she whispered softly, "I tried. I really tried."

CHAPTER 32

Night.

I had no idea where I was. But far away, I thought I could hear the ocean crashing. I saw the shadowy contours of a sterile, boxy room, and tried to move my head to speak.

"Wheeerree . . . ," I slurred, unable to form even a single word.

Then Alexa suddenly appeared, hovering above me.

"Shhh," she said, putting her finger to my lips.

"Wheerrrree I ammsssshhh." Gibberish.

"Don't try to talk."

I looked up at her. I felt frightened and alone. Then another figure appeared behind her. Round, moon-faced, cherubic. I knew him from someplace. I couldn't remember where.

"Lay still," he told me firmly.

As I felt myself slipping away, I almost had his name. Tony something.

CHAPTER 33

The next thing I remembered, I was looking at a ceiling, studying the cracks in the white paint, again hearing the distant roar of the ocean. Or was it just the air conditioner? Light streamed through the window. I heard whispering, tried to look, but couldn't move.

"Aye . . . Aye . . . ," I croaked. Chooch and Alexa leaned over me.

"Dad," Chooch said, his face drawn into a frown.

"Aye . . . Aye . . ." I couldn't talk.

"Get the doctor," Alexa said. Chooch disappeared.

"You were shot two times. Almost drowned. A farm truck saw you go off the road. They came back and pulled you out."

As she spoke I vaguely remembered some of it. Secada rolling the SUV. Getting shot. Scooping her up in my arms as I ran.

Then a doctor was leaning over me.

"Mr. Scully?"

"Huh?"

"Can you hear me?" He reached out and touched my right hand. "Can you feel this?" he asked.

"Huh?"

"If you feel it, nod." I nodded. "And this?" He reached across to my left side, but I felt nothing over there. My left side seemed numb.

I closed my eyes and in a few seconds I was gone again.

When I next came to, it was dark. I could still hear the distant crash of the surf. I looked in the direction of the sound. The windows were arched, Spanish style. I had no idea where I was. I made a noise, then heard a chair scrape. In a moment, Alexa hovered over me again.

"Shane, I'm here," she said softly.

"Where?" I finally managed.

"Casa Dorinda."

No idea where that was.

She pulled her chair close and sat beside the bed, reached out, and held my right hand.

"I'm here. I'm with you, babe," she whispered. "Don't try to talk. Conserve your energy."

"Se-ca-da?" I finally managed.

"We'll talk about it in the morning. Go back to sleep." I closed my eyes and tried to remember what had happened. As I slipped away, disturbing images replayed in my head.

In and out, in and out. A knife flashed relentlessly. Underhanded and fast, prison style.

CHAPTER 34

Over the next two days, I was reintroduced to my life one little piece at a time.

Alexa was there, and sometimes Chooch and Delfina. A couple of times I woke up for a few seconds and saw the same old, white-haired, fatherly looking gentleman. What I'd thought was curiosity now looked more like disapproval. Somewhere around his second or third visit, I placed him. He was the retired head of the LAPD Internal Affairs Division who had twice tried to get me thrown off the job. I still couldn't remember his name. *What the hell is that guy doing here?* I wondered.

Once or twice, when I was between heavy doses of medication, my mind would actually start working again and through a hazy landscape of missing facts, I would remember the same string of events: The Black-Berry. Switching it with a young, arrogant man inside a restaurant. The shanking in the prison cafeteria. A necklace of ugly mistakes.

Sometimes during my lucid moments, Alexa would be there and translate my slurred questions, answering them for me. She told me Casa Dorinda was a private hospital up the coast in Santa Barbara.

I was slowly coming out of the fog, feeling stupid and exposed, loaded up on painkillers and sedatives.

As my memory of the last two weeks slowly returned, it brought with it deep self-anger.

When I slept, my dreams were tortured accusations. Occasionally, Dr. Lusk was in the mix, Buddha-like and unemotional. *"I can't help you if you won't share your feelings."*

Then one night I woke up at midnight, coming out of the drug-induced confusion like a swimmer from a muddy lake. I suddenly felt a new sense of clarity and control. Chooch was sitting beside the bed.

"Hi," I said, softly.

He leaned over. "Don't talk, Dad." He held my hand tighter. "Dad," he whispered softly. "You and Mom are all I have. You've got to get through this. You've got to do it for me. Okay?"

I loved him so much I suddenly had tears in my eyes.

"Try," I said, forcing the word out.

The next morning I was more or less back. Chooch and Delfina had returned to the hotel to get some sleep. People were tiptoeing in and out of my hospital room.

I looked over and saw Alexa reading a brown file folder in the corner. When we spoke, we settled for small talk and some personal housekeeping. How I got here, how close a call it had been. Apparently, I had actually drowned in that mountain stream. I'd flatlined in the ambulance, been revived by the EMTs on the way to the Corcoran State Prison Hospital, which was the closest medical facility. Our police badges had made it possible for us to be taken there. But I'd had a mild heart attack and then a mini-stroke two hours later. When I asked about Secada, Alexa told me she was in critical care. Her prognosis was guarded. Something in the way she spoke these words told me that was all I was going to get. Whether she was protecting me or what was left of us, I couldn't toll.

Over the next twenty-four hours I discovered the rest of it, picking up pieces, and fitting them carefully back into a broken mosaic of facts that, once formed, made a weird, unhappy picture. Alexa had cut through a mile of red tape to have Secada and me transferred here from the prison hospital at Corcoran. She knew that inmates at the prison changed the bedpans and hospital drips. As Secada had correctly surmised, if left there long enough, somebody would eventually hit the right number and we'd go End of Watch.

"How did you find this place?" I asked her.

"Captain Terravicious," she said.

The silver-haired, disdaining ex-head of Internal Affairs. His name was Victor Terravicious, and he'd been known far and wide inside the department as Vic Vicious, which tells you something about him right there. He ran I.A. back when Alexa was the star advocate in the division. Vic was her first department rabbi and I always thought he had the hots for her.

The Terravicious family was one of those Southern Californian legends, like the Chandlers or the Hearsts. Vic's grandfather had been a successful gold prospector in the 1890s. The family mined its gold on Wall Street now. Victor had elected not to go into their huge investment banking firm, opting instead for police work. He finally pulled the pin in the late nineties due to a diseased kidney, and moved into an expensive senior citizen community in Santa Barbara. A quarter of a million got you a casita and full medical care for life. It turned out that was where I was.

Casa Dorinda, or "The Casa" as everyone here seemed to prefer calling it, was forty Spanish-style casitas and a four-story medical center complete with ICU, operating theaters, and a physical therapy wing, all of it nestled in amongst twenty rolling acres of tennis and shuffleboard courts with a nine-hole pitch and putt golf course.

Over the next two days, Alexa and I skated cautiously across the thin ice of our faltering marriage. Even though I had done nothing with Secada that I wouldn't have been willing for her to observe, the potential had been there. The desire. I knew that in this, I had failed us.

To her credit, I could see she accepted her share of responsibility. Alexa knew her lack of physical interest in me had strained our bond. There was plenty of fault on both sides. So we sat across from each other in this sterile environment, choosing our words with extreme care.

Alexa had also arranged to have Tru Hickman moved to a more secure wing of the Corcoran prison hospital, which was a bit like saying a chicken had been moved to the secure wing of the coyote compound. But she hadn't given up on trying to get Tru transferred to USC County and several times when I woke up, she was on her cell phone trying to get the CDC to approve the move. She didn't seem to be having much luck.

There are some unwritten rules in police work. One of them is you always go to your wounded partner. When I learned that Secada was breathing on a ventilator only a few yards down the hall I knew that I had to see her.

I owed Scout the visit no matter the stress it might put on my relationship with my wife.

"I need to see Secada," I told Alexa one morning after a particularly long and weighty silence. "I want to go now."

"Okay," she said abruptly, and without comment walked out of the hospital room to arrange it.

Secada's parents were expected shortly. It had taken time to reach them because they'd gone to Midland, Texas, to visit relatives.

Alexa told me all this as she helped me into a

wheelchair. Then she watched from the door of my
room as a nurse pushed me down the hall. I was told I
could not enter the critical care ward, but was parked
where I could look through the glass into Secada's
room. Scout's once beautiful body was now pillaged by
drains and tubes. Her eyes were open and she looked
across the room through the observation window at me.
I saw bravery and resolve. She smiled and waved one
hand feebly. We looked at each other through that glass
until the nurse said I had to return to my room.

Later that afternoon, while Chooch, Alexa, and Delfina waited outside, I endured a scrupulous physical
exam by one of the Casa's chief physicians whose name
tag identified him as Thomas Briggs, M.D. After it was
completed, Chooch and Alexa hovered at my bedside as
the doctor gave me the results of the exam.

"You're a lucky man," he started out by saying.
"The gunshot wounds didn't hit anything vital, so bar-
ring infection, those will heal up nicely. You were underwater for quite a while. Your brain was deprived of
oxygen. The mild heart attack and mini-stroke came as
a delayed result of that."

"When can I get out of here?" I asked.

"When there is heart muscle damage during a coro-
nary attack, a specific protein is released into the blood,"
Briggs continued. "If we see that protein, we know a
serious event has occurred, one that will require extensive rehabilitation. If we don't see it, and in your case,
we didn't, then a full and quick recovery is usually expected." I liked the sound of that. "From the neurological tests I've done, we can tell the feeling is already
coming back to your left side. If that tingling keeps up
it means the nerves are reviving. You should be ready
to leave here in a week. I'm going to have our physical
therapist get started with you immediately."

After the doctor left, Alexa, Chooch, and Delfina pushed my wheelchair outside and parked me on the patio. Several other infirm, elderly people were parked out here as well. Most of them had paper-thin, blue-white skin and wispy tufts of spun silver hair. We all sat blinking and squinting like zombies caught in sunlight.

"This is too much for me," Chooch finally blurted. "First Mom, now you." He stood between us. "Why do you two have to be cops? Can't you do something less scary?"

"It's what we do, honey," Alexa said simply.

"It's too dangerous," Chooch persisted.

"So is football," Delfina said, her voice gentle but firm. "Everyone has to do what's right for them, *querido*." Chooch didn't react, but Alexa and I both nodded.

Later, we had dinner in my room. McDonald's catered the event. When visiting hours ended at ten, Chooch and Delfina said goodbye before driving back to USC. He had football, Del had summer school.

"You sure you're okay, Dad? I won't go if you need me." He held my hand.

"Yeff," I told him.

"Yeff? What kind of answer is yeff?" He was grinning.

"Yes," I said carefully, and smiled for him.

After they left, Alexa and I again sat in silence.

The silence was becoming painful. It was more painful than the gunshot wounds, more annoying than my tingling left side.

"Do you love her?" she finally asked, interrupting this thought.

"Huh?"

"When you were unconscious you kept saying Secada's name."

CHAPTER 35

"I was never unfaithful," I dodged.

"That wasn't my question."

"I needed something. Somebody."

She sat in silence, looking at me pensively.

"I was always right here," she finally said.

"I know."

"But I've changed. I'm not me anymore. That's your point, isn't it?"

"I don't know." I looked over at her and tried to find the right way to say all this. I was working with a brain full of mashed potatoes and was afraid I was going to screw this up, but the time to discuss it was now. We'd been putting it off for almost a year.

"Go on. Whatever the truth is, you can say it," she prompted.

Speaking slowly, I began. "Before you came into my life I had nothing. I was barely functioning. On the street I was turning into a thug. Then you and Chooch changed everything. The problem is, I can't go back and live my life the way it was before. These last months, I've been trying to understand what's been happening with us, trying to be supportive of you. But slowly all the darkness has been leaking back—all the angry thoughts that made me so negative to begin with. I can't return to that place.

But I also can't leave you behind. I'm stuck somewhere in between."

"Do you love her?" Alexa pressed. "It's okay to be honest, Shane. If we're ever going to fix this, I need to find out."

"I love *you*, Alexa. Do you still love me?" I asked her. "Do you still want and need me? If the answer is yes, then you have nothing to worry about with Secada."

She got up and came across the room, knelt down beside the chair I was in, and put her arms around me.

"I'm sorry," she said. "This is my fault."

"How can it be anybody's fault? It's just something that happened."

"We'll find our way back to that other place," she said softly.

I fell asleep again, but later that night I woke up and found Alexa in the chair under the floor lamp, reading the same brown folder she'd been reading all day. I triggered the lift on the bed, raising it up so I could see better. She smiled at me over the top of the file.

"Want me to get you anything?"

"What's that?" I asked.

"The Hickman file. I had Ellen get a copy from Jeb and e-mail it up here."

I sat very still, wondering what would happen next.

"For whatever it's worth, you and Secada are right," she finally said. "This thing was horribly mishandled. If there was ever a bad due-process case, this is it. I can't understand why Jane closed it."

"Pressure from Morales," I said. "He's probably going to be the next mayor. Sasso's ambitious. She doesn't want any political grief."

She thought about that for a second then continued. "You need to tell me again everything you found out.

All about Lieutenant Devine and Morales, and this North Van Nuys Transit Bus Company."

"For what purpose?" I said, still not sure where she was heading.

"I'm gonna have a look at this myself," she said. "Off the record, on my own time." Holding my eyes over the top of the folder.

"It's a red ball," I told her.

"Shane, this is going to sound funny, but after Tony relieved me, took the pressure of command away, something changed inside me. I feel liberated like never before."

"Liberated?" I said, cocking an eyebrow. What the hell was this about?

"More than that even. All the rules I used to be so anal about just seem like nonsense to me now. I can see what you kept saying, how stupid some of that shit is."

"You're kidding," I said, not liking this at all.

"No, it's like I woke up reborn or something. Now it all feels like tiresome bullshit. Soon as we can, we should get you up on your feet and signed outta here. Then we'll go work this together like old times."

"This case is a career wrecker," I cautioned.

"My career is pretty much wrecked already. So let's forget the rule book and stand some people on their heads."

"You can't do it that way," I said, not sure how to deal with this new reckless streak. "I don't think you should be doing this."

"Why not? You were."

"But I'm not the head of the Detective Bureau."

"Neither am I anymore."

"You can't be out there breaking your own police guidelines." Even as I said this, I knew that these words coming out of my mouth sounded ridiculous.

"Isn't that a little off the point? Let's focus on this bad due-process problem without all the departmental B.S."

Oh, brother, I thought, wondering what the hell was going on here.

CHAPTER 36

My next few days went like this: physical therapy at seven A.M., then an hour parked outside in my wheelchair with half a dozen Casa patients, all of us with our faces turned skyward, taking in the sun like lizards on a flat rock. Twelve noon, more therapy, followed by lunch, a nap, therapy again, then dinner. Each day I would take some time off from these rigors to park myself outside Secada's room, sitting in awkward silence next to her father and mother, who had arrived from Texas and set up camp in the critical care ward.

Hector Llevar was a stocky, raw-boned man who spoke broken, heavily accented English. Secada's mother, Maria, was thin, almost bony. She was usually wrapped in a dull-colored shawl, praying in Spanish. She wouldn't engage my eyes. They were proud, rough-hewn people who wore their Aztec heritage like red-gold armor. They blamed me for their daughter's plight. Her parents were allowed to take turns inside Secada's ICU room. I was denied similar access.

Secada was now off the ventilator and her eyes were alert. Whenever she saw me, she smiled. I kept asking the doctors when I would be allowed in her room. "Soon," was all they would tell me. I figured Hector and Maria had blocked me.

The street clothes I'd been wearing were ruined, so

Alexa made a quick trip home to pack a suitcase for me. It felt good to be out of the ass-baring turquoise-and-white hospital gown.

By the end of my first week at The Casa, I ditched the wheelchair. In the afternoons Alexa and I took careful walks on the deserted beach north of Santa Barbara. My gait was uneven, slowed by the mini-stroke. I was trying to retrain my gawky left side and pulled myself through the sand at what I hoped was a swift pace. However, I quickly became winded while Alexa walked easily beside me. Afterward, we would sit on the beach and watch the sun go down. Sometimes we talked about what we wanted, and what we'd lost. Sometimes we worked on the case. Slowly, a new connection began to form between us.

But it wasn't easy. This last week, she often spoke about how trapped she felt working inside of what she called "useless department guidelines." A wilder, reckless Alexa had emerged from a cocoon of disorganized confusion and now sat next to me, drying new wings, trying out dangerous theories, and getting ready to attempt all kinds of nonsense. This new person had no alarms or warning buzzers. I couldn't believe some of her harebrained suggestions. I guess anything was better than the angry woman I'd been living with before. Maybe any change was positive, but I couldn't help but be concerned.

"Alexa, the system is based on the presumption of innocence," I said one afternoon while we sat in still-cooling sand, watching the ocean thunder a few yards away. I couldn't believe I was saying this. But I knew that one of us had to be the voice of reason. The more she talked, the more I desperately wanted my original Alexa back.

She still suffered occasional fits of unreasonable

anger and we still had not touched each other, or kissed. The subject of sex was carefully kept off the table. On my end, when I talked too fast, my words came out jumbled. I had holes in my memory and I was guilt-ridden over my near infidelity and mistakes that had put Tru's and Scout's lives in mortal danger. But we had the Hickman case to focus on, so we worked it when it became too painful to deal with everything else. Alexa informed me that after being suspended, she had gone back to see her neurosurgeon, Luther Lexington, again and he had prescribed new medications that had eliminated her convulsions.

I started taking early evening jogs against the mild warnings of Dr. Briggs. My runs were ugly, loose gaited, and floppy. I was only good for about a quarter-mile before I had to stop, bent over at the waist, my chest heaving as I tried to catch my breath. I stubbornly reasoned it was progress.

One night, a week later, Alexa and I were having dinner at a nice Italian restaurant in town. She looked at me across a flickering candle and said, "You're doing really well. You've finally got your color back."

"Thank you."

"I think it's time for us to get out of this town and go kick some ass," she said.

I have to admit that by then I was in a mild state of panic over what impulsive or even reckless moves she might have in mind.

"I've made up a list of things we need to look at." She reached into her purse, retrieved the ever-present Hickman case file, and glanced down at it.

"In order of importance, first we only have Tru's word that he bought that last six-pack of Bud Light."

"Alexa, when he told me that it was just information.

It didn't seem at all important to him . . . in my opinion he wasn't lying."

"In that case then we need to find out why this ex-U.S. Customs agent, this Promo Safe guy, Ron Torgason, didn't blow the whistle when Tito Morales cashed the Bud Light rare instead of Tru Hickman. That's a big hole in our case structure. I'm trying to back channel some info on Torgason and ran a courtesy check through Homeland Security." The law enforcement practice of getting nonsensitive career information on cops from sister agencies had been set up so team leaders would be able to gather background facts on officers loaned out to them from other departments during joint ops. I slowly let out the breath I'd been holding. It was a good first move.

"Church and Wyatt probably bought Torgason off with part of the Bud Light winnings," I said.

She nodded her agreement. "We also need more intel on this transit company. Mike Church takes over this little nonprofit, one-bus line from his father, Juan Iglesia, and in less than a year goes out and buys four brand-new city buses at a cost of one hundred thousand per. Then he equips them with satellite tracking and hidden infrared cameras—all stuff recommended by Homeland Security for maximum threat assessments. Since this bus company is only chartered to deliver handicapped people and senior citizens to their doctor's appointments or part-time jobs, why do they need all the state-of-the-art security? And why on earth does this little bus line need a transit police department?" All good questions. My panic started to subside.

"Mike Church doesn't come off as much of a social activist, so there's got to be a profit motive hiding somewhere."

She nodded, her eyes still down on her list. "One weird thing. Scout's SUV disappeared," she finally said.

"Disappeared?" I couldn't believe it just disappeared. It was the crime scene in an attempted double murder of two police officers.

"Yeah. For some reason, the Kings County cops who were handling the investigation didn't tag it as part of the crime scene. They just left it in the tow company lot up by Woodville. The insurance company judged it a total. Somebody on that lot must have sold it for cash to pay Scout's six hundred dollar towing and reclamation bill. Only now that the heat's on, nobody's admitting to anything."

"You're kidding. Didn't anybody from the Kings County Sheriff's Department even go through it and try to find those ought-six slugs? They might be good for a ballistics match if we ever recover a rifle."

"Nada," she said. "It shouldn't have been left in that tow lot in the first place. It should have been in police impound."

We traded disparaging looks over the ineptitude of small town P.D.s. "We have to find that car," I said.

"Yeah, but it was a cash transaction and with nobody talking and no paper trail, that's gonna be a long shot. Probably already being stripped for parts, so let's saddle up and get started." She picked up her purse.

"You weren't planning on starting tonight, were you?"

"No. But I've been sitting here thinking that you're looking very hot over there. Maybe we should go check out that little place we passed down the road. The Seaside Motel."

"Damn. Let me get the check," I said, fumbling for my wallet.

After I paid the bill, we made it to the motel in four minutes. I had my coat off before the room was unlocked. Alexa went directly into the bathroom and closed the door while I scurried around, snapping the faded curtains closed, dimming the lights, and finding a good music station on the clock radio, acting like a teenager about to get laid for the first time.

When Alexa didn't come out of the bathroom I walked to the door and knocked. "Everything okay?"

"No." I heard a sob.

I opened the door and found her seated on the edge of the tub, fully dressed, head in her hands, crying.

"Change of heart?"

"I just . . ."

"Come here," I said, holding my arms out for her.

We walked to the bed, sat down. I held her, then rubbed her tight shoulders.

"What's wrong with me?" she asked, her voice a little more than a whisper.

"You got shot in the head. It was bound to make a difference."

Alexa buried her face in my chest, and while I continued to rub her back, I slowly began to feel her relax and respond. Then she kissed me. It was our first real kiss in months.

"Oh, Shane, I do love you so much," she whispered.

During the next half-hour we followed through on her offer, but it wasn't much of an experience. In fact, it was remote and stiff. I didn't seem to know what to do with my hands. The clumsy left side of my body made the whole thing feel awkward. We coupled with difficulty. Alexa was not ready, but seemed strangely resigned. Resignation is my least favorite sexual response, so I stopped. Although I was inside her, neither one of us were enjoying it.

"Please, finish," she said, her voice on the edge of tears.

"Alexa, you have to want me as much as I want you."

"But what if I can't? What if that part of me is gone?"

"Then we'll just find a way to deal with it."

"Another girlfriend?"

"She was never a girlfriend," I said softly. "She was my partner, and now she's in ICU."

We lay on the bed, naked and cold. I cuddled her closer, and slowly she came to life, drawing me deeper inside her. My bad left hand fumbled like it belonged to someone else. I was trying to hold her close, but my energy was spent and my spirit low. Slowly, she started caressing me until I began finding pleasure. I hoped I was giving some back. I finally released inside her and we lay still for a moment engulfed in a sense of sexual failure. Alexa got up and went into the bathroom without speaking.

When she returned, she slipped under the covers, turned, and smiled at me. "Was it as good for you as it was for me?" she said, trying to make light of what had been a pretty dismal performance.

I looked over and saw the mischievous, reckless smile that, in the last week, I had come to fear. "I check to the high hand," I said cautiously.

"We always used to be great lovers, but we had a lot of practice. We're just out of practice, so we'll just have to get after that."

"Sounds good," I said.

"We'll keep trying and we'll get it all back, honey. I promise."

"Deal," I said softly.

We spent the night in the motel. It felt good to be out of the hospital, but as I fell asleep I reflected back on what had just happened. I started to feel disappointment, even shame that my sexual prowess failed to give my wife pleasure. I knew she had only made love to me out of a sense of marital obligation. But then I remembered the sexy gleam in her eye when she first suggested it across the table at our candlelight dinner and knew I was looking at it the wrong way. Whatever had just happened, it had at least been done for the right reasons. I closed my eyes and promised myself from now on, I had to keep my male ego out of the equation.

Sometimes I'm a complete jackass.

CHAPTER 37

The next morning when we returned to the hospital the doctors agreed to let me spend some time in Secada's room. I met with her father and mother for a moment before going inside.

"My daughter, we work for her college education," Hector said in halting English, his dark eyes burrowing holes in my self-esteem while her mother looked down at her Bible. "Many hours in fields, many nights in restaurants. She is the first in our family for degree."

"I know."

"Cal State University in Los Angeles," Hector said, still searching my face for a response. "She study criminology, graduated in top ten percent."

"Yes. She's very smart."

"In the police, she has many partners. Many jobs. This is first time for her to be hurt."

Facts issued as a challenge. What he was really saying was, "After all this, look what you let happen." I didn't have much of an argument because Secada was my partner and she'd gone down. I'd been unable to protect her.

Hector couldn't seem to find anything more he wanted to say to me.

I finally said, "I'm sorry I let this happen."

Hector gave no sign that he accepted my apology.

I was allowed into the room and sat in a chair beside

the bed looking into Secada's eyes. She wore no makeup and her hair was tangled, but she was still beautiful. She had been watching my exchange with her father through the glass.

"I see you had a talk with Popi," she said, trying to smile. "He's a very basic man."

"I can see how much he and your mother care for you."

"Yes," she said, softly. "*Sonrisas de me alma*—the smiles of my soul. But you shouldn't feel bad if they don't understand. Popi sees things with ancient eyes. He has loyalties and values steeped in the traditions of the past." I waited, wondering what she was trying to tell me. "In our old hill town near Cuernavaca, we had a family of close friends who all looked after one another. I had many '*tios*,' 'uncles' who treated me almost as a daughter. These families would give us things they couldn't afford if they thought we were in need. In good times, my father always did the same for them. The people in the mountain towns all had very deep loyalties to one another."

That triggered something in me, some idea. But it was gone before I could grab it.

As we talked, Secada was strangely distant, as if by her attitude, she could send me a message. She seemed determined that we would not repeat the personal mistakes of the last week.

"Alexa came to see me," she said, deliberately bringing my wife into the conversation. "The chief, too. Alexa has been back to talk to me three times. She seems very interested in the Hickman case. She's asking a lot of good questions. She's a little different than I thought. Nothing like I imagined."

I didn't respond to that, but said instead, "Alexa agrees with us that the case against Tru was bad due process," I said. "She and I are going to keep working it together."

"She can take over for me," Secada said. "This is good."

"It was your idea."

A small smile appeared, but was quickly gone. "She's intelligent and very beautiful, your Alexa. But she is impulsive. Don't get yourself in more trouble."

The remark had the flavor of a warning as well as a farewell. We looked at each other and I could see that whatever we had once felt, it would never be discussed again. Somehow that was a huge relief.

"I'm leaving here today," I said. "Alexa and I are going back to L.A to pick up the loose ends."

"I will pray for only good things to happen," she said.

The nurse entered the room and beckoned for me to leave. I leaned down and brushed my lips on Secada's forehead. As I stood up, I saw tears glistening in her eyes.

CHAPTER 38

Alexa was taking Luther's medication for her convulsions, and I was not yet one hundred percent, so she drove as we headed back to Los Angeles. Along the way, I thought again about what Secada told me about the mountain people in the towns of Mexico. Suddenly, the idea that had escaped me in her hospital room fell right in my lap.

We stopped for gas about forty miles out of L.A. and while Alexa was in the bathroom, I called Walter Finn. He was a source I'd been saving inside the Records Division who owed me a favor. I asked him for two deep backgrounders.

"Sure," he said. "Gimme your case number." That started a short discussion and negotiation because, of course, I didn't have one. The LAPD had new strict policies forbidding unauthorized record checks. Before Alexa was shot, she had actually been the one who'd instituted these new rules in the wake of a recent scandal where it was alleged in the *L.A. Times* that cops were selling files from the Records Division to a Hollywood private detective, which he was then using to extort huge divorce settlements for his rich and famous clients.

Finn reminded me of Alexa's involvement in these new policy guidelines. He was trying to shrug me off. I asked him how his sister was doing. I'd taken care of a stalker problem for her. It was a low blow professionally to bring it up, but I needed the favor. He got quiet after that, so I begged. I promised never to ask him for another favor again. In the end, he came through. I was just putting my cell away when Alexa came out of the ladies' room and got behind the wheel. We pulled back onto the 101 Freeway.

Twenty minutes later we crested the hills west of Thousand Oaks and dropped into the Valley. She glanced over and said, "That courtesy check I did on Ron Torgason came back this morning. Treasury faxed his topsheet over. You might want to check it out. It's in the folder."

I picked up our now well-used manila file. The fax bore the seal of Homeland Security. Torgason had retired from the U.S. Customs Service in 2003 as a GS-15 assigned to Special Ops out of D.C. I scanned down through the list of cases he'd worked on and found that he had been part of the very controversial, but effective, Operation Casablanca, back in the nineties.

I knew all about that case because it had been run by Bill Gately, a friend and a now-retired U.S. Customs ASAC. Gately had figured out that several large Mexican banks were laundering Colombian narco-dollars from their U.S. drug operations by using bank-to-bank wire transfers. He proceeded to organize a covert sting inside Mexico, using Spanish-speaking Customs agents who pretended to be Columbian drug dealers. Operation Casablanca had finally netted over thirty corrupt Mexican bankers and set off a screaming match over territorial integrity on the floor of the United Nations between then U.S. President Clinton and President Zedeho of Mexico.

"You see he worked Operation Casablanca?" Alexa

said and I nodded. "He had to have been cool before he went to Promo Safe, or Gately wouldn't have used him."

"Kinda makes you wonder how Church and Wyatt managed to turn him," I said, still reading the report. "Says here his last address in on Valley Spring Drive, Thousand Oaks. That's only a few miles from where we are right now. Want to swing by and ask him?"

"Thought you'd never ask," she said, a mischievous smile playing at the corners of her mouth.

Alexa exited the freeway at Westlake Boulevard, and ten minutes later we were on a street lined on both sides with middle-income homes. A lot of retired cops lived out in the far West Valley because the houses were nice and priced in a range that allowed law enforcement officers on twenty-year pensions to afford them. The houses in this development looked to be no more than ten years old. We turned onto Torgason's block, which was in a white-picket-fence neighborhood, nestled up against the low hills. After a short search, we pulled to the curb in front of his address, and found a neatly cared for, yellow-and-white, two-story faux Georgian house with shutters and a wide front porch. The lawn looked freshly mown and there was a big Century 21 real estate sign hanging from a white post driven into the center of the yard.

"For sale," I said. The house had a vacant look.

We got out of the car and were met by a gust of warm desert air that was blowing across the Valley, bringing a low level of hazy, brown pollution with it. We walked up to the front door and rang the bell. Nobody answered. Alexa stayed on the front porch while I walked around back.

A wrought-iron fence protected a nicely landscaped backyard and kidney shaped pool. As I looked around, something fluttered at the corner of my vision. I turned and spotted a little, two-inch-long piece of faded yellow ribbon snapping in the brisk wind. It was tied to the fence near the garage. I didn't have to look twice to know it was a remnant of police crime scene tape. I'd strung miles of this stuff over the years.

"Alexa, around back!" I called out.

A few seconds later Alexa rounded the corner. She immediately saw the tape and stopped. "What the hell happened back here?" she said, crossing to the fluttering yellow ribbon and pulling it off the fence.

We needed answers, so Alexa took the neighbor's house on the left, while I took the one on the right.

After showing my identification to a fish-eye peephole, the front door of my house was opened by a pale, middle-aged woman in a brown-beige Polo shirt dress. She studied my badge carefully before telling me her name was Judy Parker. I said that we were trying to get in touch with her neighbor, Ron Torgason, and asked if she knew where he was.

She stood for a moment, drying her hands on a dish towel, gazing at me through the screen door with a puzzled look on her face, then said, "Well, he drowned in his pool. I'm surprised you don't know. The police investigated it for almost a week. Gosh, that was almost a year ago."

"Drowned?"

"The coroner called it death by misadventure or some term like that."

"How did he drown?" I asked.

She put the dish towel down on an entry table, warming to the gossip. "I don't think they really know exactly. Maybe he slipped and hit his head on the diving board. Apparently, he was knocked unconscious and just sank down to the bottom. One of the neighborhood boys who did yard work for him found the body down by the drain. They said by the time they got him out, he'd been underwater for almost a day."

I looked up and saw Alexa walking up the path to the porch.

"Drowned last August," she said, as she joined me on the front porch. I nodded and turned again to Mrs. Parker. "Was there anything you can remember about that incident that seemed strange or out of the ordinary?"

She thought for a moment, then shook her head. "He was a good guy, Ron. A retired Customs agent. Made us all feel safe to have him as a neighbor."

"If he died in August, how come the house is still not sold?" I asked, struggling with the year-old timeline.

"I heard there was a fight between his heirs. The house got stuck in probate," she replied. "Just went up for sale two weeks ago."

We exchanged numbers. Then Alexa and I returned to Torgason's front lawn and stood looking at the vacant house.

"Those two dirtbags killed him," Alexa said flatly.

"Yep. Last August. Puts it close to the time when Olivia Hickman was killed. So that probably makes him the second shirt. That means there's still one more murder we don't know about."

"Shirt?"

I never told Alexa when I was in procedural quicksand. The old Alexa always got frustrated when I stretched the rules. But who knows how she would feel now, so I decided to run my BlackBerry caper past her. "On Wade Wyatt's BlackBerry there was a text message the night they killed Olivia Hickman. It said, 'This just became a three shirt deal.' I think 'shirt' is shorthand for a murder. Tru's mom was the first, now Ron Torgason is two. If I'm right, somewhere in this case there's another body connected to all this. One that we don't know about yet."

"Wade's BlackBerry?" Alexa asked, arching her eyebrows. "You managed to get paper to go through Wade Wyatt's IMs? What was your probable cause? We need to stay really friendly with any judge who'd write you a warrant without a fucking shred of probable cause." Not much got past her.

"I didn't exactly have a warrant," I admitted, wondering how she would react to that.

"You either had one or you did an illegal search. Which was it?"

"We accidentally switched phones," I said, putting some spin on it. "I accidentally saw some of his text messages before I discovered the mistake and traded him back." Curious if my BS had any traction.

"Since when did you get a BlackBerry?" she said, sniffing the lie.

I dug into my pocket and showed her my new phone. She took the unit and held it for a minute. Then she turned it on. Of course, it still wasn't even set up. She flipped it over. Dumb-ass that I am, I hadn't even bothered to remove the Best Buy price sticker.

"You're simply amazing," she said, shaking her head in disbelief. Then the mischievous smile suddenly appeared.

"It was an honest screwup," I said.

"More to the point, you can't *inadvertently* violate constitutional protections," she said. "There has to be prior knowledge and premeditation. Of course, the evidence you found is lost forever. But the information you attained was probably worth it."

My reasoning exactly. So why did it worry me so much to have her say it?

CHAPTER 39

"The way I see it, Ron Torgason became a big problem for these guys after Olivia was murdered. They needed to switch the ownership of the rare. In order to do that they had to either buy Torgason off or bump him off. If Torgason was a Gately-vetted cop then you know he probably wasn't for sale."

"So that leaves murder," Alexa said. We were back on the Freeway heading toward Los Angeles.

"Right. The original plan was to let Hickman cash the rare and just take the million away from him. But after Olivia's killing, that all changed. In order to get the ownership of that six-pack transferred to someone else, they waited until after Torgason filled out his affidavit. Then once the documentation was sent to Cartco, Wade took it out of the file, changed Hickman's name to Morales. Then before Morales collected the prize, Church rolled out and knocked Torgason unconscious, pushing him into his pool, making it look like an accidental drowning. That way Torgason's not around to say that Morales isn't the real winner and his affidavit was altered."

We rode in silence for a moment, both thinking about it. The structure and timeline seemed solid, but we still had no proof.

"That's only two shirts," Alexa finally said. "Who's the third?"

"Don't have a clue." I sat deep in thought, watching her drive.

"I think maybe you have these murders in the wrong order," she said. "What if Torgason isn't the second shirt but the third? On Wyatt's BlackBerry the night they killed Olivia, Mike Church text-messages that this just became a *three* shirt deal, right?" She looked over at me.

"Yeah. That's what it said."

We were coming into the West Valley near the Chatsworth Reservoir. It was almost three o'clock, and the normally light traffic was beginning to pick up.

"Okay, if Olivia was a mistake and after the murder Tru couldn't cash the prize, then they knew at that moment that they'd have to pass the rare to someone else. That meant they had to kill Torgason in order to keep the scam alive. Olivia is probably the second shirt and he's the third. If so, the first shirt had to predate these other two. The first shirt happened some time before August tenth."

This was neither the angry, confused Alexa nor the wild-eyed kamikaze. This was the sharp-thinking, brilliant woman I married.

"We should start hunting around in all of these back stories for a dead body that got murdered before August tenth," she finished.

We rode in silence again, thinking about it. Just as we crossed the transition to the Hollywood Freeway out by the reservoir, I got an idea and said, "Go downtown to North Mission Road."

"The coroner's office? How come?"

"The only death I know about that happened before Olivia's, was Mike Church's father, Juan Iglesia," I said.

Alexa looked over at me with a frown on her face. "Why would they kill him?"

"So Mike Church can get his inheritance, the garage, and everything."

"How does that add up? Wade Wyatt isn't part of that crummy garage. What's in it for him? Or Morales and Devine? These three murders all have to be connected to our main players, and they have to connect up to what we already have. Either that, or our whole structure is wrong."

This was definitely the old Alexa. My heart warmed. "It all comes back to that bus company," I said, enjoying the back and forth. "He needed his father's inheritance and that included the nonprofit bus line. I don't know why, but something tells me this is all about the North Van Nuys Transit Authority."

"But how does it work? What the hell good does it do to be a police commissioner for a nonprofit bus line?"

"I don't know."

"And how does the Bud Light rare that Morales won fit in? Why give the money to him?"

"I don't know. Somehow the money needed to go to Morales. For his campaign, maybe."

"It's not enough money to make a difference. And why would Mike Church and Wade Wyatt want to finance Tito Morales's campaign for mayor? This isn't working, Shane."

"What if they didn't use the money to finance his campaign?" I said, grabbing at a new idea. "What if Morales found a way to get the money back to them so they could use it to buy those four new hundred-thousand-dollar buses, and all that security equipment?"

"Why?" she said, eyeing me as she drove. "It's a nonprofit company, Shane. Nonprofit means it doesn't throw off any earnings. Morales isn't going to lend a million dollars to them for that. And the Fed won't let them pay out any cash to themselves from the operation. These guys would have to file tax returns on the bus line in order to keep its nonprofit status. None of this makes any sense." Of course, she was right.

"It's some kind of scam," I said.

"But what's the scam?"

"Look, I just had a stroke. My head isn't completely functioning yet. Why don't you come up with something?"

"Hey, I was shot in the brain eleven months ago. Don't put this on me."

We were both grinning. This was a flash of the way it had once been between us. Back before Stacy Maluga fired that bullet and changed who Alexa was. In that moment we both felt it and it felt really good.

Alexa transitioned onto the 5 heading toward North Mission Road. "Why do you want to go to the chop shop?" she asked.

"If we can find a way to get somebody down there to give us a look at the death reports, I'd like to compare Juan Iglesia's and Ron Torgason's head injuries. The neighbor said Torgason might have hit the diving board and fallen into his pool. What do you bet that Torgason's injury looks a lot like the one Juan Iglesia got when he slipped and hit his head on that shower faucet?" I waited for this to sink in before adding, "What if there's a lead pipe or a lug wrench lying around? A murder weapon clotted with hair or blood forensics that ties those two killings together."

Alexa drove for a few minutes considering it. Then she looked over. "That's good," she said, smiling. "I like that."

CHAPTER 40

Jane Sasso was vacuuming up what was left of my police career. Both Alexa and I had become high-profile Internal Affairs priorities and the department rumor mill had already made everyone on the job aware of the jackpot we were in. With all this against us, Alexa was now talking about doing a black bag job on the M.E.'s computer in broad daylight. I've made a career of skirting rules and if you intend to survive these kinds of misadventures there's a certain gruesome technique that goes along with it. My new, wild-eyed, adrenaline junkie wife didn't seem to comprehend that at all.

We parked in the lot at the North Mission Road complex. The plain, four-story, shoe box–shaped death house loomed above us. It was going to be extremely difficult to get our hands on those two M.E.'s reports and I had just finished pointing this out to her.

"What's so difficult? We just grab the stuff and split," she said. "I still have the juice. Nobody in there is going to deny me computer access."

"The minute you put in your command ID number, they're gonna know it was us. We gotta use a little finesse, Alexa."

"This isn't some MENSA-powered, cyber-giant like Google; it's the LAPD," she countered. "They run on jelly doughnuts around here. Believe me, nobody's gonna check back on this."

"I'm not scamming this computer," I said bluntly. Boy, talk about your role reversals.

"We're working a triple homicide, Shane. All this caution isn't like you. Where's the old rule-breaker? Where's the old, don't worry, it's-gonna-work-out guy I married? If we hit this piggy bank hard enough, case facts will rain down like quarters."

"A pig metaphor?" I groaned. Then I reminded her, "It was just this kind of thinking that used to keep you up nights worrying about me back when you ran the Detective division."

"I'm just going to walk in there and tell them I want the two files. Don't worry, I'll get them."

"What you'll get is a standing ten count from I.A. At least let me do this," I said, thinking if one of us was going to go down, it would be much better if it was me. Her pension was larger.

She shook her head. "You don't know my computer password and I'm not giving it to you. The computers are on the second floor, huh?"

"Yes. Don't you ever come down here?"

"I'm a supervisor. I hate the smell of chloroform."

"Nobody uses chloroform anymore. It's formaldehyde now, with methanol, ethanol, and a bunch of other smelly shit."

"Thanks for the update." She was already out of the car.

We walked inside and rode the elevator up in silence.

"Since I'm a little new to this and you're such an old hand, tell me, when stealing unauthorized material from our secure computer system, what have you found is the best way to do it?"

"The first rule is never do it yourself. Have someone do it for you. But I guess we're kinda beyond that."

"Time restraints dictate drastic measures," she said. "Stop hedging and give me the four-one-one."

"I'll make a scene while you slip past the sign-in desk. The computer room where they file the records is on the east side of the building. Grab any available workstation, and get after it. You're gonna need to go to the LAPD mainframe to get the death report numbers for both cases. Don't use any password or ID number that ties it directly back to you. Use the general command division password. Then go into the M.E.'s computer records and print a hard copy of both files so we can take them with us. Don't forget, autopsy photos."

"See? That wasn't so hard," she said.

We exited the elevator and I went directly to the desk where a young, female civilian employee was attending the sign-in log. Her name tag identified her as R. Gonzales.

"Hi," I said, flashing the whole front grill. "What's the 'R' stand for? Rebecca? Rose? Ramona?" I was being intentionally chatty and aggressive in order to focus her attention on me, while trying to block her sightline of Alexa, who was moving quickly toward the side door.

But Gonzales spotted her and leaned out for a better look. "I'm sorry, ma'am, you can't—" But Alexa was already disappearing into the corridor. "You've got to sign in, please," she called after her.

"That's Captain Jane Sasso, with BPS," I said, throwing the worst rep in the department at her. "She doesn't need to sign in. And even if she did, all it would be is a bloody paw print." I gave her a charming leer.

"That's Captain Sasso?"

"Didn't you see the black cape?"

That earned me a flat look. I rushed on, trying to get

her off this. "Listen, I need to talk to Ray Tsu." I was asking about the assistant coroner everybody on the job called Fey Ray, because he always whispered and exhibited absolutely no trace of any kind of personality.

"Who can I say is calling?" the girl said, now sounding like the receptionist at a private club.

"Shane Scully."

Her brow furrowed. "*The* Shane Scully?"

"I'm not sure I know how to respond to that," I said, chuckling. "I'm *a* Shane Scully."

"Aren't you like in major trouble around here?"

"I'm the current target of several unfortunate misunderstandings." I was hoping Alexa wouldn't waste much time getting the files. I was quickly running out of road with this girl.

Finally, she picked up the phone and informed Ray that I wanted to see him. She listened for a moment, then looked up at me and put her hand over the receiver.

"He doesn't want to talk to you."

"Nonsense."

"That's what he said."

"Gimme that." I plucked the receiver from her hand before she could object.

At least now I had her full and undivided attention. She seemed to have completely forgotten about her Alexa–Jane Sasso problem.

"Hi Ray, it's me."

"I'm not helping you, Shane." Ray's voice came through the headset in his characteristic, vanilla-toned whisper.

"Ray, I was wondering if you could pull a couple of files for me."

"I'm not pulling any files," Ray said softly. "You've got career leprosy, man. I touch you, I get warts."

We argued about this for about a minute until I sensed Ray was about to hang up.

"Hey, Ray, hang on a minute."

"This conversation is over. Put Ruina back on."

Out of the corner of my eye I saw Alexa slip back out of the side door with some manila folders in her hand. She speed-walked to the elevator. Ruina Gonzales peered around me to catch a look at the fearsome Jane Sasso.

"That's not Captain Sasso," she said. "I saw her picture on the command ID chart. That looks more like Lieutenant Scully to me."

"Nah, come on. You don't think I'd know Lieutenant Scully? I'm married to her."

On the other end of the phone, Ray Tsu was shouting, "What's going on? Are you down here stealing evidence again like last year?"

I hung up without responding and joined Alexa in the elevator just as the doors were closing.

"Got the files," she said happily. "But you were right. We should have had somebody else snag them."

"What happened?"

"Priority lock. I still had enough command clearance to override it, but I had to use my personal bureau ID number. You can bet in an hour there'll be some pissed-off people over in the PAB." Her eyes were shining with excitement. "What a ball it is doing it this way."

"It sucks," I growled, thinking I needed to get my ass back on Dr. Lusk's couch in a hurry.

CHAPTER 41

We stopped for an early dinner at the Bistro Garden in the Valley. We didn't have reservations, but I scored a good table because it was five o'clock and the after-work crowd hadn't arrived. The Bistro was Alexa's favorite Valley eatery. It's a spacious, high-ceilinged restaurant that sits on the corner of Ventura Boulevard and Van Noord Avenue. The interior dining area was showcased by tall wood-framed, garden windows. The walls were faced with white trellises, lush with greenery. A rich oak bar dominated the entire east end of the room. Alexa was still grinning over her Mission Road caper when the bottle of Pouilly Fuisse I ordered arrived at our table.

"All these years I used to criticize your methodology. How boring. I'm surprised you didn't throw a shoe at me. That was a total rush!"

As the waiter uncorked the wine, I said, "We can't just ignore department rules, some of which, I might add, you helped to institute."

"I don't want to argue about this," she said gently. "We're going to have a nice dinner. The chef here is gonna do your special whitefish thing you love with the lemon butter and capers. We're gonna kill this twenty-five-dollar bottle of French grape, and it's all gonna work out."

"We're gonna end up being arrested for obstructing justice," I said grimly, trying to slow her down. "Jane Sasso is going to unload her full quiver at us."

"Okay, not to be argumentative, but you've got to stop thinking like a cop and start thinking a little more outside the lines." Alexa was reciting directly from my playbook but I knew she had no idea what the hell she was getting into.

"Officially, we are no longer on this case," she continued. "So technically, if you stop to analyze it, anything we do is gonna be off limits as far as Jane, or Tony, or the other blocked hats on six are concerned. We're without portfolio, so how are we going to do this thing if we don't bend a few rules and take a few liberties?"

Just then my cell phone rang and while Alexa swirled wine in her goblet, watching it cling to the sides of her glass, I got a report back from Walt Finn in the Records Division. He'd run Tito Morales and Mike Church, aka Miguel Iglesia, through the system and had unsealed some of Church's juvenile records to get what I asked. When he finished giving me the info, I thanked him and looked at Alexa. "You'll never believe who represented Mike Church when he got busted for gang violence as a teenager."

She took a sip of the chardonnay, smiled at me, and waited.

"Tito Morales. It was a simple assault. Morales took the case right after he graduated from Southwestern Law School and passed the bar, just before he joined the prosecutor's office."

"How'd you get that? Church's juvie record is supposed to be sealed."

"I had it unsealed," I said. "According to court records, Church's father is the one who hired Tito Morales to represent his son. Tito pled it down to a misdemeanor assault with no time served. Naturally, that makes you wonder how Juan Iglesia knew Tito Morales in the first place. I just found out it was part of the report Walt just gave me."

She leaned forward, anxious to hear the rest.

"I had my friend in records also check on Tito Morales. He pulled up the Bar Association paperwork Morales filed after law school. His place of birth was Pueblo Viejo, Mexico. His parents immigrated here with him when he was a year old. Tito got his citizenship in eighty-one under the Reagan Amnesty. Juan Iglesia's immigration and naturalization papers say he was also born in Pueblo Viejo. The Iglesia and Morales families go all the way back to that same little hill town in Mexico. That's the connection we've been looking for between Church and Morales. Of course, we can't exactly use it because the information was illegally acquired."

"A fact not directly in evidence," she said, smiling. "Besides, isn't that more or less part of the public record?"

I think technically she was right. But it was a stark glimpse of what it must have been like for her dealing with me for all these years.

"Let's look at the stuff you downloaded from the M.E.'s computer," I said to change the subject.

She opened the folder and handed me the coroner's reports on Juan Iglesia and Ron Torgason. As I read, I saw that several identical phrases appeared in both autopsy files. "Pinpoint fracture" was one, "subdural hematoma," another. Both injuries were to the temporal lobe of the brain, which was behind the ear.

"These both look like the same injury," I told her.

"Yeah," she agreed.

I picked up the autopsy photos she'd downloaded

and squinted at them. The poor quality black-and-white printout was hard to read.

"These are terrible," I said. "Why didn't you use the color printer?"

"Outta color ink. It could have been fun to go upstairs and borrow the actual skulls themselves, but you said only three or four minutes and I was out of time."

I closed the folder and looked across the table at her. She had a sort of deadpan grin playing at the corner of her mouth. "Okay, look, babe. I don't want this to screw us up. I want us to find some coordination here. I know this all feels very liberating to you. I know it doesn't bother you now, but it bothers me."

"Alright, but since we've already been ordered off this, how do you suggest we proceed then?"

"I don't know."

"How 'bout this? Let's take turns," she suggested. "You pick a move, then I will. Like a game of Monopoly. I just bought North Mission Road, a City utility, which turned out pretty good. So now it's your turn. What do *you* want to do?"

"Sit on you 'til you settle down," I said.

"Sorry, that card's not in the deck."

A waiter hovered with his pad, so we ordered dinner. After he left Alexa looked at me, her eyes sparkling in the evening sunlight that was now streaming through the large windows. I felt a surge of sexual energy.

"Your choice. Go ahead," she said again.

"Tomorrow let's go over to UCLA, show all these photographs and autopsy reports to Luther," I said. "See if he thinks both blunt force traumas could have been caused by the same murder weapon."

It was a good move and we certainly needed the info, but Alexa was frowning.

"You're no fun at all," she teased.

CHAPTER 42

It was still early when we pulled into our driveway in Venice. The sun was down, but in June the sky in Los Angeles remains light until after nine. We unlocked the front door and walked inside.

The house was hot and I instantly knew nobody had been there in a while. Delfina and Chooch had obviously returned to school directly from Santa Barbara. I checked outside and refilled Franco's food bowl while Alexa went to the fridge and got us a couple of cold ones. Before heading out to the backyard I went into the living room to put on some music. When I turned on the stereo, 93.9 FM started playing. Country radio. I looked at the dial, puzzled, and then I retuned it to 103.5, a station I knew Alexa preferred.

I wandered outside and sat down as the music drifted through our patio speakers.

Alexa handed me a beer and we clinked bottles.

Almost immediately, Franco appeared from around the corner of the house and jumped up onto Alexa's lap, turning around three times before dropping anchor.

"When did you start listening to ninety-three point nine FM?" I asked, wondering if her taste in music had also changed.

"That's a country station, isn't it?"

"Yeah."

"I never listen to it. Why?"

"The tuner was on that station."

"Maybe Chooch or Delfina?"

"When did those two ever listen to country?"

"Yeah, you're right." She fell silent, thinking about it while she ruffled the fur behind Franco's ears, then she said, "If it's not one of us, who turned it there?"

"Back in the early nineties, when I was on patrol in the Valley, Brian Devine was our urban cowboy. He was always listening to C and W."

"You think he came in here and played our stereo while he went through our things?"

"I think Brian Devine is crazy. I wouldn't put anything past him."

We sat for a moment thinking about that, and then, almost in unison both turned and looked back at the house.

"How do you want to do this?" she asked.

"You take the front rooms, I'll take the back. Meet you in the middle."

We got up and went inside. I started with our bedroom, looking for anything that was out of place, or might have been moved. I knew it wouldn't be an obvious mistake. Brian Devine was a pro and had probably done his share of unauthorized, warrantless shakes. He knew how to toss a room and not leave any obvious telltale signs. But no matter how careful someone is, there's always something.

The closet looked okay. The medicine cabinet and bathroom drawers checked out. I looked in Alexa's alcove at her desk, but decided I'd have to leave that to her. It was so messy these days it was hard for me to tell what, if anything, was out of place.

In the kitchen, the scratch pad I'd used to write down the names of Church's crew was missing. I wondered if, after the attack in the mountain, Brian had removed those names so they wouldn't become part of a future investigation. Then I pushed a button on the phone caddy. It opened to the W's. The last number I had looked up was the Police Officer's Association. If Alexa hadn't moved the dial, and if Chooch and Delfina hadn't been here, then maybe Devine had been checking out my phone numbers. Nothing else seemed out of place. I couldn't shake the strong suspicion that Brian Devine had been in here poking through our lives during the ten days Alexa and I were up in Santa Barbara.

I walked into the front room to ask Alexa if she had changed the phone dial or removed the scratch pad. I found her sitting in a chair at my desk. She had one of my spiral notebooks in her lap. As I got closer I saw that it was my Alexa Journal. I had recorded all my doubts about our relationship on those pages, remembering as Dr. Lusk had instructed to include my innermost feelings.

She heard me behind her and turned to look up at me, a stricken expression on her face. "Oh my God, Shane, is this what you really think?"

CHAPTER 43

I reached out and took the notebook from her.

"I'm sorry you saw that," I said gently. "I was so worried after you crashed the car that I went down to the Support Services Division and they recommended a psychologist named Eric Lusk. He told me he couldn't treat you through me, but suggested I keep a journal. I've been doing that in the hope that it will somehow help us."

Alexa sat in silence for a moment longer, then stood up and walked into the kitchen. I heard her rummaging around and after a couple of minutes she returned with two glasses of champagne in long, stemmed flutes.

"Here," she said, handing one to me.

"I think we need to discuss this."

"You were right to get help, Shane. I should have gone to someone myself. It's time I faced up to the fact that I'm different. I hear things coming out of my mouth and half the time I can't believe it's me saying them. I'm not sure how many men would have put up with what you did this past year. But I don't want to talk about that now." Alexa clinked her glass on mine. We both took a sip. Then she set down her flute, and drew me to her. "Practice time," she said softly.

She kissed me tentatively at first, then deeply. Her tongue slipped into my mouth and her body pressed hard against me. I felt the sudden driving heat of shared passion. We fumbled with buttons and zippers, pulling off our clothes in a desperate attempt to find each other. She was quickly down to her bra and panties and unbuckling my belt, helping me shed the rest of my clothes. Then we were naked, on the floor.

"You are everything to me," she whispered.

She held me tightly and guided me into her. Her breath quickened, warm against my ear as she began to move with me, dictating the passion and the pace of our lovemaking. Tonight was no dutiful performance. She was in control escalating us higher and higher, from one orbit to the next until we both climaxed. She moaned in pleasure as I released inside her. We smothered each other with kisses, inhaling each other, holding tight. Something valuable that once was lost had just been found. We lay like that, out of breath for several minutes.

"Practice, practice, practice," she whispered.

I had a friend who once explained his successful thirty-year marriage to me this way. "It's like team sailing," he'd said. "But you are never in the same boat. You are never one craft, always two. You sail along without problems the first few years after marriage, lust and love at the tiller, your two boats easily staying side by side. But as time passes you inevitably encounter strong winds or bad seas, and your two boats start to drift apart. The careless sailor pays no attention. He kids himself that a little separation doesn't matter. It's healthy. No need to smother one another. But soon you are so far apart no line is long enough to pull you back together. The good sailor senses the danger the first moment the boats separate and throws a line." My friend said that conversation, lovemaking, and vacation time are the ropes that keep a marriage together.

I knew that during the past year, Alexa and I had drifted far apart, but a line had just been thrown and caught. I was determined to pull with all my strength until our boats were again side by side.

CHAPTER 44

Something woke me. I almost went back to sleep, but some instinct, bred from four years of marriage, told me that Alexa was out of bed. I opened my eyes and saw her moving around our darkened bedroom. It was still the middle of the night. I lay quietly and watched while she dressed, putting on black jeans, a dark sweater, and tennis shoes. She clipped her backup gun to her belt, and then slipped into a black windbreaker.

"Better take a mask," I said, and she jumped, letting out a little squeal.

"Shane, I'm sorry, I didn't mean to wake you."

"Right, thanks. So what's all this?" I pointed to her outfit as I glanced at the clock. It was only twelve-fifty A.M. She was obviously heading out somewhere.

"Just taking a little canal walk," she said. "Couldn't sleep."

"You always dress in black and pack a gun when you take canal walks?" I sat up and squinted at her.

"Shane, I . . ." She stopped and then gave me a sheepish smile. "Go back to sleep."

"Come on, babe. We just got our mojo back. Don't run off and ruin it."

"I'm not ruining it."

"I want to know what you're doing." I stood up, put

my own jeans on, and slipped into a T-shirt. "So what's up?" I said.

"Okay, look. I can't get those M.E. reports out of my head. You're right. Wade Wyatt or Mike Church committed all three of these murders. And like you said, the same murder weapon might have been used on both Juan Iglesia and Ron Torgason."

"Exactly."

"Exactly." She stood with hands on her hips, not wanting to say more.

"So what's with the cat burglar duds?"

"I . . . I just picked what was handy."

"I don't think so."

"Look, Shane . . ."

"Alexa, I thought you said you wanted us to work this case together. Together doesn't mean sneaking off and doing something stupid while I'm over here sawing lumber."

I started looking for my tennis shoes and spotted them under her side of the bed. "Please don't tell me you were just about to sneak over to the Church of Destruction and toss that place looking for a murder weapon."

"Okay, I won't tell you that then."

"Why would you do that without me?"

"Because all of a sudden, you've turned into this nagging voice of caution and because these assholes came in here and went through our things, and because I don't know what else to do."

"Sit down."

"I don't want another lecture."

"Sit the fuck down," I commanded, pissed off this time. She finally moved over and sat on the corner of the bed. I sat facing her, our knees almost touching.

"Since Tony relieved you, you've changed again."

"Right. I already told you that. I'm finally seeing what you've been saying all these years. You should be flattered."

"It's just another version of TBI. It's not you."

"What isn't?"

"This Bat Girl thing. This don't-give-a-shit methodology."

She took both my hands in hers. "Shane, you keep telling me about how, before me and Chooch, you used to be this dark person—this negative force—and how after Chooch and I came into your life all that changed and how much better you feel about yourself now. Well, I was just the opposite. I was this boring little Girl Scout. Never broke a rule or caused a problem. I raised my brother, Buddy, after my parents died. I picked up his messes and fixed his screwups. But in the process I became this rigid control freak who was more or less living my life to please other people. Even though I criticized the way you did things, some part of me admired you for being free enough to walk your own path and strong enough to pull it off."

"So now what? In an attempt to be like me, you're just gonna crash and burn for the amusement of our enemies?"

"Who says I'm gonna crash and burn?"

"This isn't you, Alexa, okay? This new person, this gun-toting cat burglar is not you any more than the angry, disorganized person from before. I want the woman I married."

"What if she isn't around anymore? What if she's gone forever?"

"I talked to Luther. He says these kinds of personality changes are just symptoms of the TBI. People often revert back to who they were before. I'm trying to keep you from destroying everything before that happens."

"But what if I don't want to be the old me anymore? What if I now think the old me was a tedious bore?"

"You don't know what you want," I said.

"Don't patronize me," she barked, the intense anger back in a snap.

"Okay. That didn't come out the way I wanted. But, honey, I don't like where this is heading."

"You and Scout were right to work the case. Tony, Jane Sasso, everybody up on six just wants us to go away and let Tru rot in there. But we're stuck with this because, like you said, we let it happen. We're probably both finished in the department anyway, so what do you suggest we do? Just let Tru's car up at Corcoran finish the job? I keep asking, but so far you haven't answered. You just lecture me."

"If we break into that garage and find a murder weapon without paper backing the search, the weapon will no longer be usable evidence."

"But just like you with that BlackBerry, at least we'll know we're on the right track."

"That's a terrible answer," I said.

"I want . . ." Then she stopped.

"Go on."

"I want to make this right. I feel responsible. I never should have put a queen bitch like Sasso in charge of Internal Affairs. Vic Terravicious warned me about her and I didn't listen."

"But an illegal search will just make things worse."

"Bottom line? I don't think we can fix this bad due-process thing or set Olivia Hickman's murder straight," she said. "Too much has gone wrong that we can't change. We've already got a big fruit-of-the-poison-tree problem." She was referring to the legal principle that states all facts stemming from illegally obtained evidence are automatically inadmissible. "All that we can do now is get enough information to keep Church from trying to kill Tru again. He won't risk going to prison for premeditated murder if we can discover what his motive is in advance. We have to forget Olivia Hickman, the miscarriage of justice, and just focus on trying to keep Tru alive."

I'd been slowly moving toward that same conclusion myself. All of the questionable searches I did were on Secada's bad due-process case and they were all part of the Olivia Hickman murder. They had nothing to do with any future crime that might be committed such as a second attempt on Tru's life.

"They won't kill him if we know the motive for the murder. That's your point, right?"

"Exactly," she said. "That's why I was gonna look in that garage. I didn't think you'd understand."

CHAPTER 45

We drove to the Church of Destruction in Van Nuys, arriving at a few minutes after two A.M. The place was deserted. I pulled Alexa's rented BMW to the curb and turned out the lights. My wife already had her hand on the door handle and was opening the passenger side when I reached over and stopped her.

"Hang on a minute," I said, looking at the dark concrete block building.

"Why? What are we waiting for?"

"It's called casing the joint," I said.

"Come on, Shane. What's to case? You're stalling. Let's jump the fence."

"Hey, you sure this junkyard doesn't have killer rots roaming around inside?"

That slowed her down and she settled back into the soft leather seat. Across the street in the tow lot, we could see the four new Transit Authority, fifty-passenger buses parked next to the original 1974 Ford van, which was the first vehicle in the North Van Nuys Transit Company. The new buses, like the van, were all painted a fresh pale blue with NVNTA in fancy script on the sides. The rest of the place looked pretty much the way it had when I'd been here two weeks ago—like a rusting parts farm in a Third World country.

"What now," Alexa said, impatiently.

"Let's take a slow drive around. Go down the alley
in the back and see what we can see."

"Why?"

"Because that's the way I do it," I told her.

I put the car in gear and started slowly around the
block with the headlights off. I turned left into the alley
that ran behind the garage and drove at five miles an
hour before pulling to a stop under a galvanized metal
junction box that was affixed to the eaves of the roof.

"Shine your flash on that," I told her.

Alexa hit the box with the beam of her police Mag-
lite and I grabbed my binoculars off the seat and focused them up at the roof eaves.

"Video security," I said, reading the name "Land
Mark" off the box through my magnified lenses. "We've
got to disable that unless you want infrared pictures of
us at our trial for trespassing and illegal entry."

"Good get," she agreed reluctantly.

"Thank you."

As I continued our slow roll down the alley, what I
was really doing was trying to come up with a way to
do this that wouldn't cost us our careers in the process.
Then I spotted two huge, dark green Dumpsters parked
behind the roll-up door in the back of the garage. I
pulled the BMW to a stop half a block up the alley.

"Gonna check that out," I said.

"What?" Excitement was shining on her face. "You
found a way to scuttle the security?"

"Gonna take a walk through those garbage cans," I
said, pointing at the Dumpsters. "It's discarded trash,
which means it isn't personal property anymore and is
not subject to a search warrant. We can hunt around in
the garbage all we want. Keep a lookout."

I got out of the car and walked to the Dumpsters while
Alexa stood ten yards away with her gun out. I grabbed

the edge of the nearest one, threw open the lid, and looked inside. The first thing I saw was a ripped-out interior door panel in brown leather. I pulled it out and examined it. Something seemed familiar. My heart started racing. I vaulted up on top of the bin and dropped inside, landing on green metal.

SUV green.

"Holy shit," I whispered.

"What?" Alexa's voice came through the dark.

"I think I just found Scout's Suburban."

I checked the parts in the Dumpster and pulled them out one by one, holding them up to my flashlight. I needed to find the manufacturer's Vehicle Identification Number. I really wasn't too concerned about trying to find those .06 slugs because they would probably trace back to some street gun, which wasn't going to get Tru out of jail. What I needed was to use this SUV to get enough probable cause to get a search warrant on Church's garage. I was hoping to find an airbag because I could easily trace a car with that installation number. After searching, I realized they weren't here. Church could get a few hundred for each one on the black market, so he'd probably already sold them. I finally found something in the second Dumpster. It weighed about forty pounds but I managed to lift it out and then dropped it at Alexa's feet.

"Present for m'lady," I grinned over the lip of the Dumpster. "Transmission housing."

"And here I was hoping for pearls," she quipped.

I climbed out and then shined my flash on the small stamped number on the broken housing.

"Write this down." I read the VIN aloud then looked up at Alexa and smiled. "If this came off Scout's car, we can get a warrant on this place."

"What a lucky bastard you are," she said.

I got into the front seat of our car and took a card from my wallet.

"Who are you calling?"

"Yvonne Hope," I said.

"Tru's old P.D.?" She was frowning. "You sure she wasn't part of this to begin with?"

"Yeah."

After ten rings it was picked up. "This better be fucking great," a sleepy voice said.

CHAPTER 46

"I can't wake up a city judge in the middle of the night over a stolen car," Vonnie complained, after I told her what I wanted.

"Then we'll sit on this place until you can get here with a warrant. My crime scene is being chopped up one piece at a time."

"This connects up to the Hickman case?"

"If you get me a broad enough warrant to search this whole garage it could," I said.

She was quiet, pondering her options.

"This is your case," I pushed. "Hickman's your client. Why don't you stop hedging and go to work for your guy? Use this transmission part number to get me a warrant on this place."

"Does anybody actually like you?" she asked.

"Does it matter?"

"I'd like to know where to send your fucking ashes."

She slammed the phone down, but I knew she was on board.

The sun came up at six-fifty-five. Alexa and I had reparked the car and were now sitting half a block from the Church of Destruction, sipping McDonald's coffee out of happy-looking red Styrofoam cups. At nine-oh-six, Church arrived along with a dozen beefy guys who didn't know where to buy clothes that didn't have the

sleeves ripped off. At nine-forty-five, inside the garage
I heard the sound of saws screaming in tortured metallic harmony.

"They're back to ripping up the Suburban," Alexa
noted.

I tried Vonnie's cell phone for about the fiftieth time.
Like all the other attempts, it went straight to voice mail.

I got out of the car and while Alexa watched the front
of the garage, I went to the alley behind the building and
stood behind a phone pole. Then, because everything in
this case had to be a huge problem, at that very moment,
along came a jumbo-sized garbage truck, preceded by
a little shepherding forklift that scooped up the full
Dumpsters parked along the alley and placed them on
the front of the big truck to be tossed over the top into its
giant bin.

As the forklift pulled up to the first of the Dumpsters behind the Church of Destruction, I hustled down
the alley to intervene.

"Hang on," I shouted to the driver.

"Huh?" the operator said, turning a blank stare at me.

I showed him my badge. "LAPD. Please don't do
that."

"Huh?" *What cave did they find this guy in?*

"The contents of this bin are evidence in an ongoing
case. Leave it."

"Huh?"

I was wondering how I was going to get through to
him when he solved our communication problem by
removing his earplugs.

"Come again?" he said.

Before I could go through it once more, the huge
elephant doors at the back of the garage started to open
and Mike Church, along with a rough looking bunch of

characters with grease up to their elbows, stood glaring out at me.

"What the fuck is this?" Church growled. Then recognition dawned. "You again?"

"*Como esta?* How they hangin', bro?"

"Get away from my garage, asshole. First my house, now my business. The fuck you think you're doing?"

I saw Alexa moving down the alley. Her purse was slung over her shoulder, her right hand inside. It was one of her favorite bags, but even so, I knew if this went sideways, she wouldn't hesitate to dust this guy right through the expensive polished leather.

"We have a warrant to search this place. Step aside," I said.

"A warrant?" Church seemed surprised. "What's the charge?"

I looked past him into the garage where I saw what was left of Scout's Suburban. It was down to the axles and half a chassis.

"The charge is destruction of evidence in the attempted murder of two police officers."

"Let's see the paper."

"On the way," I shot back.

"That means you don't got no damn warrant." Church turned to the forklift driver. "Hey, buddy. Get that Dumpster on the truck and outta here. I need it empty. You got a job to do, so do it."

"Don't touch that thing," I said to the driver. "Get out of here before I take you in along with him."

The garbage man bailed. He put his forklift in reverse, motioned to the dump truck, and in a minute they were gone.

"What does she think she's doing?" Church said, as his eyes flicked nervously toward Alexa.

"I'm getting ready to park four ounces where you don't want it," she said.

"Hey, Rodriguez, get this fucking door down," Church barked, and two guys started pulling a chain, dropping the heavy metal.

Just then, two black-and-whites squealed into the alley, followed by an old 1994 tan Geo Metro. To my relief, Yvonne Hope sprang out of the Geo and handed me a warrant.

The garage door was still coming down as I stuffed the warrant into Church's hand.

CHAPTER 47

What happened next was right out of a bad episode of *The Practice*.

Church called some ambulance chaser named Maximilian Morris. He turned out to be two hundred pounds of black marble with a neck like a fire hydrant, and enough attitude to be working home plate at Dodger Stadium. Worse still, his office was only six blocks away so he made it there before we even had time to set up for the search.

"How does this warrant apply to my client?" the lawyer said, leaning into my space and glowering.

"That car was part of an attempted murder scene in central California," I told him.

"My client tells me he bought the vehicle as parts from a towing service up in Kings County. He's scrapping it."

"Got a receipt from that towing service?" I asked. "Got a valid transfer of title?" I shot back.

"Don't need a title transfer. It's not a car anymore. I just told you, it's being sold for parts."

"Let me put it to you another way," Alexa said. "Your client is an accessory before and after the fact in the attempted homicide of two L.A. police officers. This car was the crime scene and it's being illegally destroyed. Before we're done, your guy is gonna be so deep in charges you're gonna need a new meter to keep up with the overtime."

That bought us a call to the Superior Court judge who had signed the warrant. He was a big, gray-haired jurist named William Saxon, who had the reputation of being an easy guy to get a search warrant from, making him a frequent target for attorneys and cops with shaky P.C. But he was also a jittery personality who frequently changed his mind, earning him the courthouse nickname Windsock Willie. When Max Morris got on the phone and started complaining, Judge Saxon told Vonnie to hold on until he could check some case facts with the prosecutor's office. A bad sign. It sounded like the Windsock was about to shift positions.

That brought Tito Morales to the scene. He pulled up in his tan Everyman's two-door twenty minutes later and parked it next to Vonnie's Geo. Tito got out and crossed the street like a man about to stomp somebody to death. His lips were dark purple curtains, exposing only the tiny bottoms of all that beautiful dentistry.

"You insist on always doing things your own way, don't you?" he said to Vonnie, who, despite his power over her career, refused to retreat from this treacherous legal standoff.

"This car was illegally removed from a police impound," she said stubbornly, indicating the axle and what few pieces were left on top of it.

"I'm not some law school dropout," Tito said. "You don't think I know what's going on here? These two"— jerking a thumb at me and Alexa—"don't give a damn about any impound theft, if one even occurred. All they care about is reopening a second-degree homicide that I handled a year ago. And you know why?"

"Because it desperately needs to be reopened?" Vonnie said, still facing him down.

"Because they're seeking to humiliate me in the press on the eve of the mayoral election. This is politically motivated and has nothing to do with Hickman. According to the Kings County sheriffs, what happened up in central California was just a case of road rage. Some drunk farmhands lost it and started shooting. The Kings County sheriffs are working it. This car wasn't even impounded. The cops up there never wrote a hold order on it so there's no grounds for your warrant."

"You seem to know a lot about the case," I said.

"It's my job to know what's going on. There's nothing here. I'm instructing you not to serve that warrant, Yvonne."

"With all due respect, Tito, you can't instruct me on one of my cases. I may technically work for you, but on this case we're still legal adversaries."

"What case? You don't have a case. This damn case isn't even in the system." He was losing it, anger turning his Hispanic features red brown. "You're spending city time and resources on a case that's already been adjudicated. You're working it without portfolio or division approval."

That produced a second flurry of phone calls—Yvonne to her division boss, Lynn Siegel, head of the Valley P.D.'s office; Tito to Judge Saxon.

I could see the Windsock slowly turning against us. We stood in the unsearched garage as Mike Church's smile got wider and wider. Finally Morales shoved his cell phone at Vonnie.

"You need to hear this," he snapped. "Judge Saxon."

She listened on the phone as Saxon filled her ear with indecisive nonsense. While she was listening, I happened to notice that Alexa had moved away from us and was standing over by the garage's office looking through the plate glass window at an array of plaques and Little League photos that hung on the walls inside.

Finally, Vonnie said, "Okay. If that's Your Honor's decision."

She hung up the cell phone and handed it back to Tito. Then she turned toward me, a long frown on her freckled face.

"The judge has rescinded the warrant. No search," she said. "He says the SUV got towed by a local company in Kings County. The insurance company judged it a total loss. The Kings County cops didn't put a hold order on it, so after ten days, the towing company could legally sell it to cover costs. They sold it to Church for two thousand dollars, refunded the difference to Detective Llevar. It was a legal transaction."

Tito turned to the four city cops who had arrived with Vonnie to help us search the place and issued a new order: "Escort these people out of the building, please."

Moments later we were all standing in the alley.

"This isn't over," I told Tito. "You've got a major conflict of interest here. After law school you represented this guy, Church, on a felony, and your families both go back to Pueblo Viejo, Mexico."

That didn't slow Morales down. He turned toward the patroleman. "If these two suspended police officers give Mr. Church or anybody else in this garage any further trouble, I want them arrested for obstructing justice and police harassment." Then he got into his cheap little car and pulled away.

We walked out of earshot of the cops and had a postgame huddle.

"That's it for me," Vonnie said. "My show just got closed. If I know the great Tito Morales, starting tomorrow I'm gonna be down in part six handling DUIs.

I think it's finally time to put my legal skills to more constructive use."

"I'm sorry," I told her.

"Hey, life is all about taking chances. It was getting time for me to move on, anyway."

Then she returned to her tan Geo and drove off. In a minute, the thin trail of white smoke that had spewed from her hanging exhaust pipe was all that was left to remember her.

"Nice gal," Alexa said. "We got hosed, but she brought the wood."

"Except everybody now knows what we're doing," I told her. "Tony, Jane, the entire sixth floor is gonna find out in less than an hour. We're in the sauce."

She didn't answer, remaining strangely quiet for a long moment. Then she asked, "You ever hear of anybody named E. Emmett Riley?"

"Who's E. Emmett Riley?"

"There are plaques and framed certificates of accomplishment to Mike Church and the NVNTA from this Riley guy hanging all over that office in there."

"So?"

"According to the plaques, Emmett Riley's kind of muckity-muck with California Homeland Security."

I must have looked lost.

"I wonder if Mr. Riley knows what's really going on with this little bus company," she said.

CHAPTER 48

E. Emmett Riley was in an oversize tenth-floor office at Homeland Security located on Wilshire Boulevard. He was the Assistant Secretary to the Deputy Director of California Homeland, or some equally confusing title. I've long held the belief that ninety percent of the people who use initials in front of their names are purebred assholes. The evidence of this is overwhelming. F. Lee Bailey, for example, or H. Ross Perot. Watergate was full of them: E. Howard Hunt, H. Robert Haldeman, G. Gordon Liddy. Liddy probably was an exception because, unlike the others, he manned up and went to prison without giving up teammates.

E. Emmett Riley was a little man in a brown suit whose hair looked like it had been drawn on his head by a cartoonist. His rosy complexion shined and he had glossy, manicured fingernails that reflected light like little shiny windows.

"I don't see how this information is any of your concern," he said, busily protecting one of America's great national secrets.

"Mr. Riley, all we're asking is that you tell us what the Department of Homeland Security's interest is in this little bus company. It's not such a big deal," I said.

"Do you have a supervisor I might contact?" he said, looking directly at me, ignoring Alexa because after all, as everyone could plainly see, she was just a great-looking chick.

"Yeah. She's my boss," I said and nodded at Alexa. He flicked a glance over at my beautiful wife.

"Hi there," she said, smiling at him.

"She's your boss?" Incredulous. Struggling to adjust.

"Yes. She's Lieutenant Alexa Scully, and if you can have somebody go to the LAPD Web site, you'll see she's pictured there as the acting head of the Detective Bureau."

He turned abruptly around and for the next minute, those polished fingers flew over his computer keyboard. He quickly accessed the LAPD Web site and, sure enough, right there on the command structure management tree was a smiling press photo of Alexa. Then, with a little flourish, like Liberace finishing a piano run, he removed his polished fingernails from the keyboard and swiveled slowly around in his giant chair until he was again facing us. His expression seemed only slightly more cordial.

"I still don't—"

"Humor us," Alexa said, interrupting him. "Please don't make me take this to Chief Filosiani. I thought we were all supposed to be sharing information these days. Part of the new interagency guidelines."

It was a tough problem for E. Emmett. Like any good midlevel bureaucrat, he knew information was power and he hated sharing power with anyone. But the fact was, in this post–9/11 world, we'd all been tasked by the President of the United States with information sharing. I could see all of this calculating behind hazel eyes. Finally, he leaned forward.

"I'm not sure—"

"I am," Alexa interrupted.

His resolve began to dissolve like Alka Seltzer in a

glass of cold water. He tipped forward and hit an inter-
com. "Liz, bring me the NVNTA file." Then he leaned
back in his chair.

Two minutes of uncomfortable silence followed. Man,
I hate bureaucrats. Give a guy an office with any kind of
government seal on the door, and you instantly have a
testosterone problem.

Finally, Liz arrived. Liz, as you might expect, could
have worked in reception over at *Penthouse* magazine.
She swept into the office on three-inch platforms and
handed Emmett the folder before disappearing back
out the door like a vision sent by God. E. Emmett licked
his fingers carefully before opening the file and exam-
ining the contents.

"Okay, what do you want to know?" he asked, the
words coming out like tooth extractions.

"You sent several letters of merit and congratulations
to this bus line. We were wondering in regard to what?"
Alexa said.

"Which tells me, you obviously don't have enough
P.C. to serve a warrant on this bus line and that's why you
came to me. This is just a fishing trip." Snotty and bitchy,
even in defeat.

"Obviously you haven't worked many investigations," Alexa said pleasantly. "If you had, you wouldn't
make that statement."

"I wouldn't?" he said, smiling at her. I guess he smiled
because she was too pretty to sneer at.

"No, you wouldn't because the minute you serve a
warrant, you alert the suspect that you are investigating
him. We like to save the warrant serving for last."

He tried to look as if he was evaluating this as a tac-
tic. Then he shrugged slightly as if to say, "If that's your
silly way of doing things, okay, but at Homeland we do
it differently."

"So, what were all the letters and commendations about?" Alexa pressed.

She had him on the run. E. Emmett Riley was obviously enamored of beautiful women, but they made him nervous and he wasn't quite sure how to handle them.

"The NVNTA has been upgrading their security," he said reluctantly. "They've been spending a great deal of money to conform to our threat assessment transit guidelines. That's why I wrote the letters."

"You are, of course, aware of the fact that this non-profit bus line only provides transportation for a limited number of senior citizens in a very small community," she said.

"They met the minimum two-hundred-fifty-seat bus-line-size limit, which qualifies them as a full-fledged transit authority," he said. "Beyond that, it's not our concern." He was back on familiar ground, curling a lip at us.

"Why not?" Alexa now gave him a beautiful, sweet smile. You could almost feel him wilt under it. Like Secada, Alexa knew how to use her assets.

"Because we're tasked with trying to get any qualified transportation agency to conform to our top threat level security guidelines. In order to do that, these companies have to undertake a significant capital outlay, which quite frankly, many are unprepared to do. So we provide incentives to encourage them. The more security a bus line, train, or airline has, the harder it is for terrorists to strike. I should think that's pretty obvious."

"So NVNTA was spending a lot of money," Alexa stated.

"NVNTA has been simply incredible," he said, looking at his file. "They are a nonprofit line and transport only about a thousand people per seven day week. But despite that, they've met every single one of our guidelines. They've passed all of the safety checks, as well as meeting this agency's most stringent requirements. Everything, I might add, at great expense."

"And that's it. That's the whole deal," I said.

E. Emmett shot a hard look at me. "Are you being flip?" he snapped.

"No, sir," I answered. "I'm trying to find out what these guys are doing."

"They're growing. They're attempting to expand their services in keeping with the highest threat assessment standards of this agency and we're helping them do it."

"Helping them? How?" Alexa asked.

"They've applied for and received a DHS government grant."

"I'm sorry?" I said.

"A grant. Money from the government."

"Really?" Alexa looked over at me. "How much money?"

"For transit authorities that meet our most stringent guidelines, the federal government is approving nonrecourse grants to continue growth and defray cost. It's part of the incentive program I just mentioned. But in order to qualify, the transit authority must meet every single guideline. They must have a transit police department with at least six members. They must install all of the preferred security materials—GPS and satellite tracking equipment. Only about six or seven percent of the transportation companies in the nation have qualified. I'm proud to say NVNTA is one of our better examples."

"How much money did you give them?" Alexa asked.

E. Emmett Riley looked through the folder and found it on the last page.

"To date, just a little more than fifteen million dollars," he announced proudly.

CHAPTER 49

Alexa and I were sitting in our backyard in Venice, both of us wearing self-satisfied grins. We'd figured it out, cut through all the B.S., and had finally gotten to the bottom of it.

"It locks every piece in place." I tipped back the ice-cold Corona I'd just pulled from the fridge and drained half of it.

"Yep," Alexa agreed. "We be good."

"Mike Church isn't smart enough to figure all this out on his own. This is pure Wade Wyatt. That arrogant asshole engineered it. He sees that one old rusting bus and he knows about the Homeland Security grants. Maybe he got the info from his father, or while he was clerking for the Supreme Court. It's just the kind of get-rich-quick fast-food idea that would appeal to that little putz. He tries it on Church, who is so greedy he decides not to wait, so he kills his father to get the bus line. They end up scamming the government outta fifteen mil."

"You need to call Secada," Alexa said. "After all, it was her case."

I went inside and called the hospital at Casa Dorinda. After I finished reporting everything Alexa and I had learned, Scout said, "This is amazing, Shane. You guys actually fixed it."

"I still don't know how to drop this mess on the department," I told her. "Alexa and I are working on that part now. We have to be careful about procedure here. Some of this evidence is a little compromised."

"You'll find a way. Good work. Tell Alexa thanks for me, but I think you need to move fast. Tru isn't going to last long once he goes back into gen pop."

"Don't worry. This all gets done first thing tomorrow." Then I changed the subject and asked her when she was getting out of the hospital.

"They told me I can go home next week. Popi is getting a nurse and he and Mama are moving into my apartment on the hill."

"I'll call you with our next moves."

I hung up and turned to find Alexa standing in the doorway looking at me.

"They say, life's a journey," she said, a tinge of sadness in her voice. "But for me, it usually feels more like a lesson."

I took her in my arms and kissed her.

We went into our room and made love. It wasn't as wild as the last time, but we had found our rhythm again. The closeness that followed was incredible.

Alexa snuggled against me, burying her face in my neck. "I love the way you smell," she said.

"Gym socks?"

We cuddled and caressed and ended up making love all over again.

Later, as the sun began to set, I dressed for my normal evening jog.

"I'd go with you, but you wore me out," Alexa teased. "I'm gonna hang here and see if I can come up with a way to lay our cards down. We can't go to Jane Sasso. I don't trust her."

"Maybe Jeb," I suggested.

"Maybe," she said, "or Tony. You can bet Tito Morales is already working on a way to shut us down. He doesn't know that we've got the Homeland piece yet, but we've got to move fast."

"Gives me something to think about while I'm on my run."

I left the house at eight-forty-five, just as the sun dipped below the horizon. The Pacific Ocean looked flat and the setting sun had turned it a beautiful shade of red-orange. I jogged along the bike path toward Venice Beach feeling stronger with each stride, my steps landing with more authority. I started to get into it, running evenly, feeling at one with my body.

As I ran, I began looking for the right way to expose all this to the department. I knew people inside the LAPD would want to keep it quiet, so there would be political forces lined up against us. I also couldn't dismiss Wade Wyatt's powerful father, Aubrey. God only knew what kind of trouble he could cause. One option was to go straight to the press. Once it was all out in the open, it would develop a life of its own. Even though that option had merit, I sort of hated it. I still carried a badge. Blindsiding the department in the press was cheesy. Nonetheless, it had some positive elements, so I figured I should probably discuss it with Alexa.

I thought about my wife. I now saw only occasional flashes of the disorganized Alexa who had shared my home, but not my life for the past year. The wild, damn-the-torpedoes woman was fun, but not exactly what I'd bargained for. I desperately wanted the woman I married. Our ships were closer, but not yet side by side.

Then, it felt like my head exploded. It was like a starburst. Flashes of white and a burst of bright orange. One brief thought occurred as I started to fall.

Another stroke?

In that millisecond before I lost consciousness, I knew whatever was happening was major. As I blacked out I knew I was in big trouble.

CHAPTER 50

I regained consciousness.

Rivulets of sweat ran down my back and into my crotch. I was instantly nauseous, on the verge of throwing up. I opened my eyes into blinding light. My shirt was off and silver duct tape pinned my arms and legs securely to the frame of a rolling office chair while my exposed upper body slowly turned bright pink. *Where the hell am I?* I thought.

Then I saw a professional paint sprayer with a long rubber hose attached to a compressor hanging from a rack. Four wall-sized aluminum reflectors fitted with large heat-producing lights shined down on me from two walls. That's when I knew. I was inside the paint bay at the Church of Destruction, being cooked alive.

My head throbbed while my stomach continued to churn. Mike Church and a VSL veterano I remembered as Tyler Cisneros were standing on the far side of the room beside a partially open door trying to escape the oppressive heat.

"Turn 'em off," I croaked, unable to stand even another minute of this.

Mike Church spun around. His overlit pitted complexion was slick with sweat. He walked over, leaned in, and studied me like a bug pinned to a board. In his right hand, he was holding an Arwen 37, which I knew from a week of intense riot training at the Academy was special-issue police department ordnance. The Arwen fires two-inch-long, cylindrical, baton rounds made of hard black rubber. According to the LAPD information office, we use these weapons exclusively to quell "incidents of civil unrest," which is code for riot gun.

Suddenly Church backed away and pointed it at me, saying, "Check it out, homes."

He fired from only fifteen feet away. The two-inch-long, hard rubber cylinder flew out of the tube barrel and hit my shoulder like a Mike Tyson right. I let out an agonized moan. The Arwen is supposed to be a non-lethal alternative weapon, but our Academy instructors had told us if fired at point-blank range to the head, it could be deadly.

"Get ready to have a bad last forty minutes," Church said maliciously.

That's when the lights that were cooking me suddenly went out, taking away the wall of blistering heat and leaving the booth dimly illuminated by two small overhead bulbs.

"Turn those things back on," Church ordered Cisneros, who was standing by the door. "I'm cooking me some roasted pig here."

My stomach suddenly lurched and I projectile-vomited the booze Alexa and I had consumed earlier in premature celebration. Some of it splattered on Mike Church.

"Sorry about that," I muttered weakly.

Church stepped forward and hit me with the butt of the gun, bringing it down sideways across my head. It opened a gash on my cheek and I almost went out, fought for consciousness, managed to hang on.

"We've got to wait for Brian," Cisneros said. "He doesn't want us to mess him up too bad."

"Fuck Brian. Turn the lights back on," Church demanded.

"If we take him out to Six Flags, we don't want the cops to find no body that's all charred and shit. That won't look like no accident," a third man argued. My eyes, slow to adjust in the sudden gloom, could barely identify another VSL banger, Jose Diego, on the far side of the room.

"You two are fucking pussies," Church said, but the lights stayed off.

For the next twenty minutes, Church never let go of the Arwen 37 and, just to amuse himself, he would occasionally turn and say "Hey, Scully, here comes the Goodyear blimp." Then he'd fire another rubber baton at me. The round would strike my body, breaking blood vessels under my skin, leaving big, blue-red marks wherever it hit. Each time he fired, I almost lost consciousness.

During this ugly demonstration of riot gun effectiveness, I had one coherent thought. If the Arwen was what had knocked me out when I was jogging on the Venice bike path, then it was also probably the murder weapon Alexa and I had been looking for. I wondered if Church used it at point-blank range to kill his own father in the shower, and later to incapacitate Ron Torgason before drowning him in the swimming pool. The hard rubber batons, if fired to the head at close range, would probably result in the kind of skull trauma we'd seen in both autopsy photos. But even as I had this thought, I knew it came way too late to do me much good.

I don't know how long I was forced to endure this punishment, but sometime later Brian Devine walked into the paint bay wearing jeans and a police windbreaker. He took the riot gun out of Mike's hand and smiled. "You really love this thing, don't ya, Churchy? If you behave, maybe I'll let you keep it."

He checked the clip, looked over at my bruised body, then smiled. "Man, this may be the new American record. How many did you fire at him?"

"Lieutenant, this is coming apart," I croaked. "The department knows about everything. You can't be dumb enough to partner up with these idiots."

" 'Cept I'm not the idiot taped to a chair," he said.

"They got fifteen million. I hope you got a fair cut of that," hoping to produce some trouble. It didn't work.

"Nice try," he said. "But I'm a very happy citizen. Got my boat all stocked and ready to go in Mexico. Right now, we're just in the loose-end business. Pisses me off I didn't close your account years ago. Would've saved me a lot of trouble." Then he turned and fired the Arwen at me from ten feet away. The hard rubber round hit my forehead and I was out. I never even heard the riot gun's report.

CHAPTER 51

"Colossus is still the largest dual track wooden coaster in the world," Mike Church was saying.

"Yep. That's one sweet ride, homes," somebody on my right agreed.

As I came to, I realized my hands were bound. My shirt was back on, but blisters were starting to form on my chest and, of all places, under my arms. My forehead throbbed where the rubber baton had knocked me out. I sat in agony playing possum.

"They built that monster way back in the seventies." Church was speaking again. "It was already old school by the time I started banging out here. When I was a TG, I sold seeds and stems in the midway. I was just eleven. When I was fifteen, I even got a summer job here and worked the maintenance shed. I learned where the underground service tunnels are, how to sneak on rides. Still got my old park maintenance badge." Through slits in my eyelashes, I saw him hold up a plastic-encased ID card dangling from a cord around his neck. "Ever since that summer I don't never even have to pay to get in this place, 'cause I know where the old drainage culvert opens up that runs under the park."

I opened my eyes a bit wider. I was in the back of somebody's big SUV. A Cadillac Escalade. Gray leather. Lots of video extras. I didn't move, trying to scope out the car without turning my head. The same three were in here with me. Tyler Cisneros and Jose Diego were on either side of me in the back. Church was driving, spinning out happy memories from his banging days at Tragic Magic.

"You won't believe how it was back then," he went on. "Back before these dumb park fucks realized they had a youth violence problem. This place was supposed to be a gang demilitarized zone, but there were *asesinos* out here, so you better believe bad shit went down every weekend."

Church put on his blinker, then turned off the highway into a parking lot. Out of the corner of my eye I glimpsed acres of parked cars. We pulled up to a booth to get a parking ticket. I kept quiet, looking for any chance to alter the odds.

"Busy out here tonight," I heard Church say to the booth operator. I knew they had good radio communications between all park employees and was about to try something when I suddenly felt a knifepoint press between my ribs. I looked right and saw Tyler Cisneros shake his head sadly.

"*No lo hace*," he said softly.

"Lot Four. Follow the yellow line," the ticket taker instructed.

"Thanks," Church answered. The Escalade started moving again. "Fuck Lot Four," he said. "I want to go to the north end of Six, way over by the fence."

"This guy's awake," Cisneros said.

Church turned and looked back at me. "Don't go cowboy on us, Scully. Keep it cool, dude."

We drove in silence for a minute before Church craned his head and looked up at Colossus. "Man, look at that *chingada*!" The giant coaster loomed a hundred and twenty-five feet above us. Occasionally, a trainload of joyriders would streak past, screaming in delight, as the wheels rattling on the hardwood tracks set up a thunderous roar.

Church pulled out a cell and dialed while he drove. "We're here," he said. "We're gonna take him in through my special way. You got your guys ready?" There was a long beat. "I'm just asking. Don't have a fucking aneurism." He closed his cell. "What an asshole." There were a lot of assholes in this equation, but I figured he had to be talking about Lieutenant Devine.

I tried to come up with an alternate plan. It felt like my hands were secured with plastic riot cuffs. I was in such pain that I had to fight not to cry out every time the Escalade lurched or bounced over one of the parking lot's speed bumps.

"The last drop is one *hijo de puta,*" Church enthused. We were cruising the north lot while Church looked for a suitable parking space. "Hundred and fifteen feet, straight down. Hey, Scully, hope you like coasters, man." I didn't answer. Church laughed as he nosed the Escalade into an empty slot. We were at the far end of the new north lot and there were very few cars.

"Get the wheelchair," Church ordered.

Diego got out of the Escalade and started to unload a wheelchair from the back luggage area.

"Hey, Scully. Check it out," Church said happily. "This fucking coaster goes over sixty miles an hour. It's not quite as fast as Goliath or Viper, but those two run on pipe ramps. You gotta appreciate retro when it comes to the great coasters. You feel me, homes?"

I didn't answer.

I felt the back door open and then Diego pulled me out of the SUV. My blisters were killing me, my body bruised and broken. When they yanked me, I let out an agonized scream.

Somebody shoved an old sock into my mouth and the next thing I knew, I was being loaded into the wheelchair. A smelly red blanket was thrown over me and tucked under my chin. I was starting to shiver and hoped I wasn't going into shock.

Church pulled out his cell and hit redial. "We're here," he said. "Get Juan and Ramon to check the refit shed under the ride. It's usually empty after six. We'll be in the park in a few."

He hung up, then took the handles on the wheelchair and began to push me across the parking lot. "Man, I love this place," he rambled. "Put in my first real work here. Shanked two North Hollywood Razas under this bitch. My 'blood in' ritual. After that, I was *bueno por vida*." He tapped the back of my head. "You know *por vida*, Scully? Means 'for life.' Once I shanked those two dirtbags, nobody in my set ever had the balls to fuck with me. From then on, I was a designated hitter."

We stopped in front of a chain-link fence, which had been precut. Diego and Cisneros pried it open and bent it back, then the three of them picked up the chair and handed it roughly through the opening in the fence with me still sitting in the damn thing. Then they lifted the chair over the curb on a concrete drainage sluiceway and set it down again. Church started us rolling and suddenly we were moving way too fast down the sides of the steep drainage ditch.

"Whooooeeee!" Church sang out as the chair picked up speed, rocketing down the forty-five-degree side of the culvert with him riding the back, holding the handles.

I could hear the heels on his cycle boots scraping on the pavement as he skidded along behind, holding on, trying to keep the chair from tipping over. I almost fell out twice, but Church kept me upright as we finally rolled out and came to a stop on the mossy, weed-choked floor of the decommissioned spillway.

"You know, back when I was a TG I used to think if I hadda die, it should be on this fucking coaster. Ride one of those new California-style PTC fiberglass cars right off the track and out into space. Take a hundred and fifteen foot drop to the ground. What a cool way to cross the border, know what I'm sayin'? All these years later and you're gonna get to live my dream, homes."

CHAPTER 52

As they wheeled me through an underground drainage tunnel, Mike's flashlight played along the walls where somebody had painted the names of the various coaster rides in white paint next to metal ladders that led up to the catch drains above. We passed Viper and Superman the Escape, and kept moving along the damp tunnel until we finally stopped under Colossus. Church left us in the tunnel and scrambled up the ladder.

"Okay, it's clear," he called down a moment after he disappeared. "Hand *el pito* up." I was pulled out of the chair and lifted, still handcuffed. Again, I cried out through the sock in my mouth but my screams were muffled. My head bumped on the narrow drain opening as I was pulled up into a large, four-foot-high drainage catch basin. Church had the drain cover off and they pulled me out of the basin, up into the cool night air. I looked around and saw we were underneath Colossus's huge wooden scaffolding. Trains roared by overhead, the screams of the coaster riders creating a deafening wall of noise.

"Get him up there," Church ordered, pointing at a set of wooden stairs. They led to a platform and a large warehouse building.

I felt hands yank me upright. My legs barely worked as they hustled me over pavement littered with trash that had dropped from the coaster above. Then I was carried up three flights of metal stairs, across a concrete stage, through a door, and into a large basketball-court-size building full of broken cars from Colossus. The fiberglass coaches sat on five or six fingers of track, each one with a service order stuck to its front. Some were waiting to be worked on, others were marked to be returned to the ride.

Brian Devine was waiting for us with three gangbangers in white wife-beaters, none of whom I recognized. The *vatos* all had ornate VSL tattoos high on the back of their necks identifying them as *veteranos*.

"Get the sock outta his mouth," Devine said.

Somebody ripped it out and pushed me down onto the floor. The lieutenant grabbed a dirty metal folding chair, planted the legs over my body then straddled the chair, looking down over its back into my upturned face.

"Okay, tough guy, you're about to take the final exam." His manic eyes flashed dangerously. "Don't screw with me here, 'cause I have it in my power to make the end of your life fucking gruesome."

"I know everything, Brian. I know about you guys killing Juan Iglesia to get the bus company, how you dumped Ron Torgason over the beer contest. I got the whole playbook. It's already been turned over to PSB. You can kill me, but it doesn't make this go away."

"Really." He looked at me, a slight smile flickering on his flat, hard face. "These last two days I've been on you and your wife like a coat of blue paint. I hung a wire in your house, put taps on your phone. When you shit, I hear the dookies splash. I been following you and your dingy wife around for almost two days. You ain't told nobody shit. You're both dead people. All I need from you before I croak you is your case notes."

"My wife's already gone to Tony. Killing her does nothing for you. You're done, man."

"Your wife's so fucked up, nobody's gonna believe anything she tells 'em. But just to be safe, after I'm done with you, I always planned to swing by and pay her a visit. She's some damn fine hot-lookin' trim. Maybe she gets some sublime Devine before I dump her. I can make it easy or tough. But you stonewall me and I'll take both of you down in pieces."

"The department knows. There's no place you can hide where they won't find you."

"Tell that to Bin Laden," Devine growled. "Who else besides your wife?"

"Captain Calloway."

He studied me for a long time before he said, "Bull-shit." Then he smiled. "You're bluffin'. I like to clean up loose ends, but you know what, it doesn't really matter. After tonight, I'm gone. Gonna ditch my nagging wife, kill yours, and split this fucked-up country for good."

Devine stood up out of the chair and looked at Mike Church. "I'm done here. He's all yours, *muchacho*. Make it hurt." Then he turned and walked out of the shed without looking back.

Church pulled the metal chair off of me, yanking me to my feet. My body screamed in pain. They muscled me toward one of the repaired coaster cars with a "Return to ride" tag wired to the safety bar. The car sat on a wooden track, which ran through a canvas curtain on the east wall of the shed. Cisneros and Jose Diego were already working to remove the bolts from the safety bar that secured passengers into the seat. After they freed the bar arm, they placed it back into the housing without tightening the bolts.

I could see the plan. Put me on the coaster and let me take a twelve-story drop with no safety bar. I was about to be Magic Mountain's next unfortunate accident victim. Devine would try and kill Alexa before she got our file to Tony. The fact that Captain Calloway knew probably wouldn't matter because by the time the LAPD could mobilize, Lt. Devine would be long gone, cruising the coast of Mexico in his brand-new, million-dollar sport fisher. Alexa, Scout, and I had solved the mystery, but were half a beat too slow.

"Get him in the car," Church ordered.

Two of the VSL *veteranos* picked me up and set me into the coach. They covered my bound hands with a jacket and shoved a ball cap on my head, then pushed the car out of the repair building through the curtain. I looked down and saw that the track I was on was about twenty feet off the ground. I was weak, but decided that once I was a few hundred yards from the repair shed, I would find a way to lunge out of the car and drop down the two flights to the ground below. If I didn't land on my head, the worst I would get is some broken bones. However, my plan was instantly rendered useless as Mike Church ran along the landing beside the track, grabbed the rail of the cart and jumped over the side, easing his huge frame down, filling the space beside me.

"Ready to go coastering, homes?" He grinned.

Diego and Cisneros continued to push the car along the track that led to the staging area. The giant scaffolding loomed above me. As we neared the boarding platform the crowd noise grew, merging with the occasional roar from the streaking Goliath coaster a few yards off to our left. We were buffeted by the slipstream as it passed.

Suddenly, I started to convulse. I couldn't control my lower body. My legs cramped and I spasmed violently.

"*Coño! Que te pasa?*" Church blurted. "Do that again, I'm gonna slit you right here." He flipped open a four-inch serrated blade and stuck it in a spot between my ribs

on the left side right next to my heart. I could feel the
sharp point poking my skin.

Our car was pushed in front of a line of empty carts.
Diego and Cisneros hooked us to the next empty train,
which would soon be filled with waiting passengers. We
were in the first car. Church yanked a knit watch cap
from his pocket and pulled it low above his eyes. Then
he donned a pair of dark glasses and settled back in the
seat, the knife still poking between my ribs. I felt the
hooks under the roller coaster suddenly engage the car
and we began to click forward toward the loading ramp.

When the car reached the white boarding line, the
train stopped. One of the ride captains came up and
frowned down at us. "How'd you get in there, man?
You gotta board through the load line."

"We work the refit shed, dude. Makin' a test run.
Gotta make sure this car don't still have no brake drag."
Church showed the man his old, plastic maintenance
badge. The loader barely glanced at it before he turned
to check the other passengers who were now climbing
into the cars.

I suddenly realized that this might actually work. Then,
before I could come up with any kind of new escape
plan, a loud bell rang and the cars were again engaged
from below and clicked up the wooden scaffold, pulled
up by a chain toward the first drop on the ride.

As we ascended the wall of white scaffolding Church
used the serrated pocketknife to cut off the plastic ties
binding my wrists, then put the knife back between my
ribs. I reached out with white knuckles and gripped the
useless safety bar that rattled uselessly in front of me.
There was nothing I could do now—nowhere I could
go. I was too high to jump. If I yelled out, I knew he
would shove that knife into my side, piercing my heart.
As the cars inched up the near vertical incline, the park

fell away below us. Masses of people swarmed like
ants at the base of the ride. Then we were at the summit
of the first drop.

"Man, I love this fucking coaster!" Church said, his
face an ugly mask of perverse delight.

Another loud bell rang.

Then the car launched forward and locked into place
at the top of the ride. I was suddenly looking over the
edge, straight down the track, at the pavement over ninety
feet below.

CHAPTER 53

The brakes released and the ground rushed up at us. I could barely keep from flying out of the coach and desperately gripped the safety bar clattering in its metal housing. Church sat beside me grinning as the train plummeted straight down toward the ground. I tried to use my knees to wedge myself tighter into the car, but could get very little purchase. We hit the bottom of the first dip and the car lurched dangerously into a right turn going over sixty miles per hour. The jolt almost threw me out of the coach. We were pulling at least two G's as we whipped through the first turn.

Mike Church craned around theatrically and shouted at the people in the car behind us. "Hey! This safety bar is loose!"

The guy riding behind us yelled, "Huh?"

The car began to bank left, gathering speed heading into a looping turn along the wooden track approaching the double bumps.

"This bar is out! It's out!" Church screamed. Then, to prove it, he picked it out of its housing and it flew from his hands, falling to the ground below us.

I looked frantically around the inside the coach for something to hold on to and spotted a place where the metal frame had separated from the fuselage. Just then, the coaster whipped around another curve going at least sixty, rocketing toward the double bumps ahead. I was vibrating so hard in the seat, I was barely able to focus on the track. That's when the airbrakes whooshed loudly and the train suddenly slowed.

"*Adios,* motherfucker," Church said and hit me with a powerful right hand to the rib cage.

I doubled over, gasping for air. The coaster continued to slow as he leapt out of the car and hit the little guardrail on the side of the track. He held on as the car rumbled past, then released and dropped about twelve feet to the pavement below.

I fought to catch my breath as the coaster traveled over the double bumps and began the steep ascent to the top of the next huge scaffolding heading for the final, gut-churning drop.

We were almost forty feet up before I got my head out from between my knees. I'd been so busy gasping for air, I'd missed my chance to bail. I pulled off my belt and managed to loop it through the separation I'd spotted between the fuselage and the metal frame. But by then, Colossus had reached the peak of the scaffold and was cresting toward the big drop. It lurched and stopped at the very top and I was looking down twelve stories.

"Oh, shit," I muttered as I wrapped my belt around my right wrist and gripped it tight.

The airbrakes whooshed off and we catapulted straight down the vertical track toward the ground. My body became weightless and for a few seconds I was floating freely around inside the car tethered only by my belt. We hit the bottom of the drop and banked violently to the right. I was sucked suddenly over the side of the car and was hanging on outside, being pulled at breakneck speed, perilously close to death.

"The fuck?" the guy in the car behind me gasped as he watched me dangling outside the car.

I held on to my belt in a death grip as the train lurched into a tight left-hand turn. Centrifugal force pinned me hard against the outside of the car's fuselage. My feet banged into the face of the guy behind as I struggled desperately to hang on. Then I saw a metal superstructure coming up at seventy miles an hour. In seconds, I was going to be cut in two by the support beam. I lunged for the car, pulling with all my strength, and tumbled inside as the scaffolding flashed by an instant later.

In another forty or fifty seconds the airbrakes hissed and we began to slow until we were back at the staging area where it had all started.

"You all right, man?" the guy behind me shouted.

Fuck no, I thought but didn't answer.

My forehead was split open and fluid was oozing from all of my broken blisters. I had a half-inch-deep knife wound in my left side and it felt as if Church had broken a couple of ribs.

Aside from that, I was peachy, but boy was I pissed.

CHAPTER 54

The next thing I knew, I was up to my ass in park emergency staff.

"LAPD. There's just been an attempt on my life," I said, but nobody responded.

"The bar arm was broken," the guy who'd been in the car behind me contributed. He had been less than three feet away but because of the wild ride had misread the entire murder attempt.

"Get me some park police officers," I ordered.

But then I saw Brian Devine sprinting between Colossus and Goliath, heading toward the main gate. I felt like hell, but anger and adrenaline formed some kind of ungodly cocktail in my brain. I found myself pushing the park medic aside and struggling to my feet.

"You've got to lie down, sir. You're gonna go into shock," he said.

Alarms and sirens were going off all around me while an ambulance was trying to nose toward us through the milling crowd. I began to stumble down the exit stairs, intent on following Lt. Devine, who was almost at the end of the walkway that ran between the two giant coasters. He looked back as he ran, shocked that I was not only still alive, but coming after him like a creature in the last reel of a horror movie. At the bottom of the stairs, I lost him in the crowd, but a golf cart pulled up with a park security cop behind the wheel. I reached for my badge case.

"LAPD!"

"That ambulance needs to take you to the hospital," the security guard said.

"Which way's the front gate? We've got to stop that guy." Devine had already disappeared in the crowd, so the security guard had no idea what I was talking about. He just stared in disbelief.

"Looks worse than it is," I said to break him out of it.

He'd vapor-locked. I pulled him from the cart, slipped behind the wheel, and floored it.

"Hey!" he shouted, and ran after me. But I was moving too fast and soon left him behind.

I didn't know what road hooked up to what. I headed west toward where I thought the front gate was located. But the roads looped and turned, and soon I found myself driving down a path that veered east toward a thick stand of trees under another massive pipe track coaster, which appeared to span half the park. This one was a unique piece of physical torture called Superman the Escape.

The road was a dead end. I was frantically trying to turn the golf cart around in the confined space when a loud electronic voice announced, "Prepare to launch." Seconds later, a car full of screaming joyriders streaked by overhead at almost one hundred miles an hour, powered by huge positive/negative electromagnets that hummed loudly under the track allowing the coaster to ride on a force field of negative polarity, reducing friction while increasing speed.

I was directly beneath the ride, and as the train screamed by overhead, it blew my hair straight up in its powerful slipstream. The startling force was so great, and the screaming passengers so loud, that I lost control of the cart and swerved into the metal housing on the side of one of the huge electromagnets, and knocked the wheels on the golf cart out of alignment. Half a mile away, I saw the Superman cart climb straight up a vertical tower until it slowed to a stop almost at the top and then began to fall backwards down the track, heading straight back toward me. A few seconds later it again streaked by overhead.

I jumped out of the golf cart and started to run from underneath the ride. But something was wrong. I felt weak, dizzy. I couldn't coordinate. Was this the beginning stages of shock? Then just when it seemed things couldn't get much worse, Brian Devine stepped away from the side of one of the nearby electromagnets. Apparently he had doubled back to finish the job that Mike Church had started.

There was a large 9mm automatic in his hand. He fired and, using what strength I had left, I dove inside the golf cart just as the bullet crashed into the metal housing on the coaster magnet right above my head. Using my hand on the golf cart's throttle, I tried to maneuver the damn thing out of the line of fire. But the wheels were jammed. It wasn't going anywhere. Devine was still firing rounds at me. The 9mm slugs were easily punching holes into the flimsy plastic sides of the cart. The only thing that was saving me was the fact that he couldn't see where I was on the floor of the little vehicle.

"You're a resilient motherfucker, I'll give you that much," Devine shouted. He had his gun out in front of him, and began circling closer to the cart to find me.

I was suddenly filled with mind-numbing anger. *Enough was enough. How much of this shit was I supposed to take?*

My body looked so destroyed that Devine probably didn't see me as much of a threat. He hadn't contemplated the suicidal rage that now drove me. When he was ten feet away, I launched myself at him, hitting him high in the chest. His Beretta went off, firing wide. I jumped on top of him, violently pummeling him with both hands. In seconds, two of his teeth were out and a huge gash had opened over his left eye.

He rolled away, then stumbled to his feet still holding the gun. I was seconds from death as he pointed the barrel at me.

"Prepare to launch," the metallic voice announced. Just as Devine was about to fire, the ride flew by overhead, blasting us with its powerful slipstream and forty screaming riders. Devine glanced up, startled. That split-second saved me.

One of us is going down, I thought, remembering my promise as I launched myself directly at his chest. But before I hit him, a strange thing happened. Some unseen force lifted him right out of his shiny black loafers and threw him five feet in the air backwards away from me, landing him on his ass. He sat there staring at me in startled confusion as a bright red stain began to blossom on the front of his shirt. He struggled up to his knees, looking down at his bloody chest, holding both hands over the widening red stain before his expression changed and he finally seemed to get it. He'd been shot. His life was over.

"Son of a bitch," he said in disbelief, then pitched forward, facedown, at my feet.

My beautiful wife was standing in the road next to one of the park security carts. She was still crouched low in her shooting stance, legs wide, her silver-plated Astra nine clutched in front of her with both hands.

Suddenly, all my energy left me as I slumped to the ground.

"This is an emergency. Send an ambulance to Building Six under the Superman ride," I heard her say into a park walkie-talkie.

Then Alexa rushed up and knelt down, cradling my head in her lap. I must have finally gone into shock as she stroked my head and looked down at me, because her beautiful blue eyes were the last thing I remembered seeing.

CHAPTER 55

When I woke, I was in another hospital room. This time I was lying inside a parabolic chamber filled with Freon, which was artificially lowering my body temperature. This was unacceptable. This had been happening way too often. The docs said I had gone into shock but now, several hours later, I was told I was stable.

Alexa hovered nearby and Chooch and Delfina arrived. Shortly after midnight they moved me out of ICU into a regular hospital room. My body was slathered in some kind of foul-smelling ointment. I was told that the burns were mostly first degree with a few second-degree spots on my chest and arms. My survival was assured.

Brian Devine, on the other hand, had gotten his ticket punched. I'd finally put that unreasoning asshole on the ark. They'd scraped his body up from the pavement where Alexa shot him and an ambulance carted off his remains to the coroner's office in Sylmar. Over the next hour, Alexa filled me in on what happened. Mike Church and his posse were apprehended in the Six Flags parking lot but Wade Wyatt was in the wind. Alexa had put out a BOLO, so hopefully he'd be picked up before he could take advantage of his powerful father's connections and get out of the country to some rum-soaked paradise with no extradition treaty, like Cuba.

Alexa told me that when I didn't come back from

my run, she went looking for me. A woman on the Venice bike path told her she'd seen an unconscious runner being loaded into a van by two Hispanic men.

Alexa and Jeb Calloway immediately put the Communications Division to work on the problem. She got Mike Church's cell phone number through AT&T and started a pod track, which was a form of technology that allowed us to key in on a particular cell phone. Transmitters broadcast calls from area pods located all over the city. These pods store all the numbers they transmit. Communications scanned in the numbers from Church's cell and picked up a call from his phone that went through the Venice pod at eight-fifty-five P.M. The next transmission was out near Sunland, then Santa Clarita. The track of calls indicated Church was using his cell while heading northeast on the freeway. Alexa and Jeb mobilized two SWAT teams and headed in the direction of the transmissions.

The last call was traced to the pod right in the parking lot at Six Flags Magic Mountain.

"I can't believe how close we came to not getting there in time," Alexa said.

"Where does it go from here?" I asked, my head still full of mist.

"It's going to take a day or so to sort it all out," she said. "Devine is dead and Church and his homies are all lawyering up. Without Wade Wyatt to turn state's evidence, we still don't have anything that directly links any of this to Tito Morales. You can bet neither Church nor his *vato* posse are going to rat Tito out. Gang ethics. It looks like Morales might actually squeak through this without getting tagged."

"Then he's still in a position to argue against Tru getting a new trial," I said.

"We gotta go over his head, talk to Chase Beal, the

district attorney," she answered. "But first I need to set up a meeting with Tito, the Chief, and Jane Sasso. I need to get Morales on the record before I go to the D.A. Jane needs to set up a new investigation into Olivia Hickman's murder for us to have any chance of getting that writ. That skinny bitch better come through this time."

I had my doubts. It had been a long, torturous journey. If Wade Wyatt got out of the country and Church and the VSLs kept quiet, Tito was in the clear and Tru Hickman was probably going to be stuck doing life in Corcoran. Not a very rewarding outcome to a very stressful three weeks.

As we talked, Alexa's cell phone rang. "Just a minute," she said and looked over at me. "I've got to take this outside. Be right back."

When she was gone I was distressed that there were still things she felt she couldn't say in my presence. But then the door opened, and I knew why she'd left.

Secada stood there looking a little less vivid and a lot thinner. She walked into the room, then sat on the edge of my bed.

"Are you always this reckless?" she asked.

I wasn't sure how to answer, so I said nothing. Finally she broke the silence. "We didn't get enough, did we? All we've got is a kidnapping and attempted murder of a police officer. That could put Church and Wade Wyatt away for thirty years, but it doesn't get Tru out of Corcoran."

"Let's see what happens at Alexa's meeting tomorrow. I'll see you there."

"I've been ordered by Jane not to attend. She wants to represent PSB without my interference." Secada shook her head sadly. "If Morales doesn't accept our new writ, then it looks as if all of this was for nothing."

CHAPTER 56

The meeting took place in Alexa's office at ten the following morning. The room was too small for the crowd we'd drawn. I had checked myself out of the hospital and was feeling queasy and weak. I wore my clothes carefully over two pounds of ointment, burn bandages, and bruises. Jane Sasso showed up looking pretzel thin and severe in one of her trademark Armani suits. She was so brittle, I thought if she moved too quickly she might snap. Her hard, lined face and pixie haircut made her look like a pissed-off Disney character. She sat in the big upholstered chair in the corner. Jeb Calloway was Mighty Mouse in a black suit. I'd never seen him wear a tie, except at police funerals, but today he had on a paisley monster with a big Windsor knot. Also in attendance was Tru Hickman's attorney, Vonnie Hope, who was easy to overlook in this room full of A-type personalities.

The Chief finally breezed into the office, all five foot seven of him bouncing on oxblood loafers, his bald head shiny, his pink face the color of a baked ham. Tito Morales trailed him into the room. The election was only a week away and Morales was still twenty points ahead in the polls and doing daily interviews, so he was wearing a media-friendly red tie.

Tony said, "We're packed like sardines in here."

Without another word, he moved the meeting into the large sixth-floor conference room.

Once we were all settled in swivel chairs with a view of Union Station out the floor-to-ceiling window, Tony put the ball in play.

"I've read the case facts, Alexa," he said. "It appears Lieutenant Devine blew the Hickman investigation and that we may have the wrong guy in the pokey."

"I don't agree," Tito Morales said. He looked cool and in control. He knew we'd been unable to tie him directly to anything, and he knew that with Devine dead and Church and his crew dummied up, his only problem now was Wade Wyatt. From his overconfident attitude, it seemed reasonable to conclude that he'd already cut some kind of a deal with Aubrey. He knew Wade was not going to fall out of the sky and bitch up his victory party at City Hall. Morales had a duplicate case folder in his hand. "There's a lot of what-if speculation in here," he continued. "Unless you can produce Wade Wyatt to testify, everything you've got about Lieutenant Devine's investigation is subject to a good deal of dispute. Since he's dead and can't give his side of the story, the way I read it, you don't have anything but a theory here."

"Hey, Tito, you pled this guy on bad evidence," I challenged. "That bloody shoe print you never ran doesn't match the sole pattern on Tru's boots. Someone else was in that kitchen. I'm saying it was Mike Church."

"Then you'll want to produce Mr. Church's boots and get a pattern match, won't you?"

"It was a year ago. After all this, they're gone."

"So that's nothing, then." He closed the case folder for emphasis.

"Wade Wyatt and Mike Church are much better suspects," I said angrily.

"Except, I have a confession from Tru Hickman saying he did it, and I also have extensive case material supporting that plea bargain. So I'm against a new writ. If the Prosecutor's office keeps going backward, if we keep reopening old cases just to satisfy a few evidentiary nitpicks, we'll never get through even one month's calendar."

"Fuck the calendar," I said.

Alexa took my hand and squeezed it, telling me to get hold of myself. It was a gesture of caution.

"How about you, Jane?" Alexa asked. "It's your bad due-process investigation. What are you gonna do?"

Sasso looked at Alexa, then at Tony Filosiani, whose face showed very little. The Chief liked his division commanders to make their own decisions.

"We're reopening the Olivia Hickman murder investigation," she said. "And we're putting a homicide number on Ron Torgason's death as well."

"Good decision," Vonnie Hope said. "Because if you hadn't, that was going to be an *L.A. Times* front page story tomorrow."

"Don't threaten me, little girl," Sasso said, crisply.

"Not a threat—a promise. I'm still working this murder. After it's adjudicated, and it will be . . ." She glared at Tito before going on. "After that, I'm cutting loose from the P.D.'s office, so it won't do you much good to threaten my job, Tito."

"You can reopen your investigation, but that doesn't mean you're going to get a writ," Morales said. "You still have to convince a judge and I'm gonna be there to make sure that doesn't happen."

As we walked out of the conference room, Jane Sasso, Tony, and Alexa huddled up in the hall. I watched Tito get into the elevator, elegant and self-assured.

Alexa and I left Parker Center and stood outside in

the late morning sunshine. It was a hot day, and I could immediately feel the heat on my sun-sensitive, burned skin.

"I'm gonna go over to the D.A.'s office," Alexa said. "See if I can make a deal with Chase Beal. You set up your appointment with Aubrey Wyatt yet?"

"I'm just gonna drop in on him. I don't want him to have any time to get ready."

"Manslaughter. That's what you want the D.A. to offer?" she asked.

"You get Chase Beal to offer me that kick down and I'll see if I can get Aubrey Wyatt to cough up that little hairball he calls a son."

CHAPTER 57

The law firm of Wyatt, Clark, and Cummings was on the top three floors of a forty-story Century City Office building. The firm did legal work for movie stars and L.A. power brokers, and was heavily involved in political fund-raising, which earned them a lot of expensive lobby art as well as plenty of heft in state politics. I wanted to drop my bomb from altitude. Didn't want Aubrey Wyatt to hear it whistling down until it hit. Surprise is everything in this kind of negotiation.

"LAPD," I told the young Harvard grad in pinstripes working the huge granite desk across from the elevator, showing him my badge. "It's regarding Wade Wyatt and a homicide investigation I'm conducting."

"You don't have an appointment," the man said. "Mr. Wyatt doesn't see people without an appointment." Then he paused and added, "Ever!"

"Tell Mr. Wyatt that I'm here with his son's last chance to avoid life in prison. He sees me right now or he loses it."

"You sure you want that to be the message?"

"That's the message."

The young man leaned forward and started to pick up the phone, but then thought better of it. He got up and disappeared through a door behind the desk. A few minutes after he left, my cell rang. It was Alexa.

"You get Wade back from wherever he is and if he comes through with everything we want, the D.A. will offer Man One, but he's not happy about it. Morales is his deputy D.A. and a mayoral front-runner. Chase told me this is not the way to make friends in California politics."

"I'll do my best to deliver," I said.

I closed my cell phone as the Harvard grad reappeared and said, "Follow me, please."

He led me down a beautifully decorated hallway hung with museum-quality paintings. I was ushered into an expansive, if somewhat sterile, conference room dominated by a long red mahogany table surrounded by twenty oxblood leather chairs, which sat on a sea of cut-pile gray carpeting.

I was drawn by the view to the massive floor-to-ceiling window, which overlooked the city. To the west was Santa Monica Bay and even though the ocean was five miles away, I could make out the white sails on a flock of boats crisscrossing the choppy water. It was a rare, smogless, windswept day. Crisp and clean, full of sharp edges and bright colors. I was still at the window when the door behind me opened.

I turned to see a man over six feet tall standing at the far end of the room regarding me with puzzled exasperation. In person, Aubrey Wyatt was an even more commanding presence than in the pictures I'd seen. He emanated power—from his silver-white hair and aquiline profile, right down to his aura of mild condescending disdain. His foreboding demeanor told me that this wouldn't be easy.

"Interesting message," he said.

"Do you know who I am?"

"Detective Scully," he said, matter-of-factly. "My son told me about you. He says you're a hothead, and not very smart."

I didn't respond. It was a close enough description.

"My son has a superior mind. He's been at the top of every scale society uses to measure aptitude and ability. I've raised him for greatness and I do not intend for a bunch of trumped-up allegations made by semiliterate immigrants and angry cops to change that."

"That may be out of your control." I handed Aubrey Wyatt my carefully annotated case folder.

He took it without comment, then sat in the nearest chair and began to read. After he was halfway through the first page, he got up, grabbed a yellow legal pad from a side table and then sat back down and began making notes with a five-hundred-dollar Mont Blanc pen. After almost thirty minutes he closed the file and looked up.

"Where's your son?"

"I haven't the faintest."

"He can't run from this. The D.A. can file murder charges, try him in absentia."

"You can attempt that. But it doesn't mean you'll get an indictment, let alone a conviction." He tapped the file with his gold pen. "Most, if not all, of this is weak and circumstantial. You don't have one witness to the Olivia Hickman murder who can put my son anywhere in the vicinity of the crime. This Ron Torgason thing is pure speculation. He could have hit his head and drowned in his pool as the coroner's report states. Same with Juan Iglesia. My guess is this Mexican gangster, Church, and his buddies are probably not going to talk. That means you've got very little here save an interesting theory."

"I have one pretty good witness who will change everything."

"Really?" Aubrey Wyatt sat very still and studied me carefully. "The way I read your summary, Lieutenant

Devine is dead. Without Church or this pack of VSL gangsters turning state's evidence, there's nobody else."

"You're wrong. I have one witness who can put Mike Church away."

"And who would that be?"

"Me." I let that sink in for a minute then said, "Church kidnapped and then tried to kill me on Colossus at Magic Mountain last night. I'm the only victim in this whole mess who managed to survive. My testimony will put him away for life. That's probably forty years, or until he dies."

"Fine. Do that then. I don't see how that affects Wade."

"Here's how it affects him. I'm really not all that interested in what happens to Mike Church. Yeah, he's a violent gangster who needs to get stuffed, but I figure once he's gone, another *vato* with a hard-on will just step up to take his place. I'm only interested in one thing."

"What's that?"

"I want to get Tru Hickman out of prison because he's innocent. In order to do that, I need somebody who can help me catch the real killers of Olivia Hickman. Those killers are your son, Wade, and Mike Church."

"You can't prove that."

"I think I can."

"How, pray tell?"

Pray tell? Man, don't you just love it?

"I've just been authorized by the D.A., Chase Beal, to cut the following deal with Mike Church: If Church turns State's evidence against your son on Hickman and Torgason, the D.A. will let him cop to Man One on both killings. He will recommend to the court that the two manslaughter sentences run concurrently. Instead of life, he gets twelve years. In return for his cooperation, I will refuse to testify against Church on my kidnapping and attempted homicide, which is a slam-dunk life without possibility of parole. Without my testimony, that kidnapping/attempted murder case goes away. It represents a net gain of at least twenty-two years for Mr. Church. Whatta you bet he takes it and sells us your ratbag kid?"

I knew I'd drawn blood because he shifted a little in his chair. It was the first sign that he acknowledged any jeopardy for his son.

We stood in that magnificent room trading hard stares until he broke the silence.

"Since you're standing in my office, I assume you have something more you want to impart."

"Right now this is a jump ball. The D.A. will also offer the same kick down to your son. You get Wade to come home from wherever you have him stashed. If he steps up and puts this multiple homicide on Church, who I think did the actual work, then we'll let Wade be the one to cop to manslaughter and take the twelve years. Mike Church can do life without."

"My son is safe where he is."

"I don't think he's safe anywhere. He's an arrogant, self-involved little prick who's bound to make an arrogant, self-involved mistake. If I get him convicted for Murder One in absentia, warrants will go out for his arrest. He's not gonna listen to you when you tell him to stay put. He'll get itchy and end up going to some yacht race in Spain. Once he's out of whatever protected nonextradition zone you've got him stashed in, I'll be there with a warrant. But by then, Church will have already made the plea deal and your son will have to do the whole lifelong stretch."

"I need time to evaluate this."

"You've got until six tonight. If you're as smart as your reputation, you'll get your boy to grab it. If he does, he'll be out in time for his fortieth birthday with half a life still to live. But if you take the deal, there can be no holding back. Wade needs to offer up the whole thing. The rigged beer contest, how they scammed Homeland Security. He has to cop to both Juan Iglesia and Olivia Hickman and, most important, he needs to give me Tito Morales. Only then does he get the reduced charges."

I watched Aubrey Wyatt process all of this, looking for a way out. I could see from his frown that he really appreciated the box I had him in.

I picked up my case folder and left him sitting there.

CHAPTER 58

The blue and white Gulfstream Five with Wade Wyatt aboard touched down from Havana, Cuba, at ten A.M. the following Wednesday. The jet's two Rolls-Royce engines screamed in retro as it came to a stop at the end of Van Nuys Field, turned, and headed back toward us. Alexa, Secada, Jeb Calloway, Yvonne Hope, two uniformed officers, and I stood inside the private Jet Center watching through the window. Aubrey Wyatt, flanked by two stern, briefcase-wielding assistants also waited a short distance from us. Except for initial introductions, nothing was said between our two groups during the twenty-minute wait.

The private business jet taxied up to the terminal and the door descended. Then Wade appeared in the hatch. For the first time since I'd busted him three weeks ago in his father's million-dollar red Ferrari, he looked frightened and small. He walked down the stairs as everyone surged out onto the tarmac to intercept him at the foot of the boarding ladder.

"You take him into custody," I told Secada. "Your case."

She stepped forward and began to read the Miranda in a firm voice. As she continued reading from the card a tight grimace passed over Wade's handsome face. Murderers, I've come to realize, manifest themselves in two basic categories. You have the trigger-pulling, I'll-do-it-myself variety, and then there are the Wade Wyatts of the world, the too-smart-to-get-blood-on-me guys. Planners. On a basic honesty level, I have to admit I prefer the former, but generally, the legal system cuts its deals with the latter. Hitters like Mike Church are hard to sympathize with and are perceived to be more dangerous.

"Come with us," Secada instructed Wade as the two uniforms finished handcuffing him and began to lead him away.

"Dad? Do I have to?" Fear of having to take showers with muscle-bound guys named Jesus and Jamal darkened his prep-school features.

"We'll post bail. You go with them," Aubrey told him.

"There'll be no bail hearing until my client is out of prison," Vonnie Hope said. "You made a deal for manslaughter, but until we take his statement and the D.A. signs off on it and files the lesser charge, your son is still under arrest for Murder One, a nonbondable offense."

"What possible good does it do to lock up Wade?" Aubrey said. "He came back from Cuba on his own. He's not going anywhere."

"Maybe if you hadn't always stepped in to fix his problems he wouldn't be in this mess right now," Secada advised.

Wade was led toward the terminal, but he saw me standing with the others and stopped.

"You did this to me," he said petulantly.

I shook my head. "I think it might just be the Law of Unintended Consequences," I said.

The rest of it took a couple of weeks. Wade Wyatt

copped his plea and made his statements. Tito Morales became an accessory to three murders. They arrested him the day before the mayoral election. He was led, handcuffed, from his office amidst a crush of media.

"No comment," he kept saying, as microphone-toting jackals surged around him shouting questions. I thought, despite the circumstances, he looked very media-friendly in his charcoal suit and maroon tie.

The press flurry died down about a week later and Vonnie's writ of habeas corpus was filed without challenge by the District Attorney's office. It was approved by a judge the following morning. Two weeks later Alexa, Secada, and I made our long, triumphant drive up to Corcoran to bring Tru Hickman home.

The day was overcast. Rain clouds hung over the Grapevine Highway and gently watered the hills of Central California. We arrived at the CDC Visitor's Center a little past one o'clock in the afternoon. Tru was waiting for us in the checkout room wearing the same clothes he wore the day he was arrested over a year ago—a frayed gray sweatshirt, baggy shorts, and tennis shoes held together with silver duct tape. His Dumbo ears glowed pink as he nodded his head during my introduction of Alexa. He looked drug-free, but the old needle scars on his arms promised a difficult future. There was a big grin on his face when he saw me.

"Man, you actually did it," he said to me. "I thought this was all bullshit, but you did it."

"It was Secada Llevar. She's the one who got it all going and refused to let the department shut us down," I told him.

"Thank you," Tru said. He took both of her hands in his. "I was so scared. This has been pure hell. I can't believe I'm going home."

We all smiled. It felt good. A good day.

On the return trip, Alexa drove, with Secada in the front seat. I rode beside Tru in the back. The wipers metronomed endlessly on the windshield as Tru talked on and on about nonsense. The more he talked the less sure of his future I became.

"I'm gonna get this new, first-person shooter Xbox game called Halo Three. I'm all about it, dude," he said. "You build fuckin' avatars and shit, which are your own personal characters. You get to a high enough level, you can actually sell the icon on eBay. I'm death with the Xbox. I could like make a fortune doing that."

"Maybe you ought to think about getting a job," I suggested.

"Not necessary. I'm gonna sell Ma's house. Y'know, take the money to live. Get a bitchin' new ride, throw down for some great new vines. Start doing some serious fuck-around clubbing."

"Sounds like a plan," I said, and traded wary looks with Alexa in the rearview mirror.

When we got to the Valley near Lankersheim, Secada looked over to Alexa and said, "Turn off here. We need to make a stop."

Alexa made the turn and we were soon heading down Forest Lawn Drive.

"Where we going?" Tru asked.

"You'll see," Secada said. By now, all this talk about the Xbox and nightclubbing had pissed off all of us.

Alexa seemed to know what Secada had in mind because without being prompted, she turned in at the main gate to Forest Lawn Memorial Park and pulled up to the security booth.

"We'd like to go to Olivia Hickman's grave," she said. "Can you direct us?"

The guard checked his computer, and then handed

Alexa a map. "East Park Road, plot number E-one-thirty-four. It's behind the Old White Chapel."

Alexa looked at the map and put the car in gear. We wound through the cemetery, and finally parked beside the Old Chapel. Everyone but Tru got out of the car.

"Come on," Secada ordered, snapping his door open, and motioning him outside. "We're going to pay a visit to your mother. Tuck in your sweatshirt and stand up straight."

We walked up the sloping hillside, with Tru lagging behind. Finally we were at Olivia's grave. The rain, which had followed us down from Corcoran, was covering us with a fine drizzle.

"This is it, huh?" Tru ventured. "This is where they put her." He had been arrested before his mother was buried and had never been to her final resting place.

"Tru, I want you to look down at this headstone," Secada said. "I want you to realize that your mother is only here because of you. Because your life was about nothing she ended up being killed by people you brought into her orbit. She loved you, but now she's dead and it's because of you. You need for her to know that she didn't die for nothing. You need to promise her that you're going to find a new way."

"Do we have to do this right now?" he whined. "I just got out of prison."

"Tru, all of us spent a lot of time and even risked our own lives to make that happen," I said flatly. "It would help us to know that what we saved was actually worth saving. That you aren't just going to play videogames and slide back into the same lifestyle you were in before. That you won't waste the rest of your life."

"I'm grateful, okay? How many times do I have to say it?" he defended. "I loved her and stuff, okay?"

"But you want to go home," Alexa said.

"Yeah, kinda . . . It's raining, you guys."

The three of us looked at each other. Nice try, but it wasn't working. Alexa and Secada walked away from the grave marker leaving Tru alone with me. Instead of following them, he hesitated, and stood staring down at the wet marker, wringing his hands.

After a minute, he looked over at me and in a small voice said, "What do you suppose it was that she saw in me?"

"I don't know."

"Always on me to do better. Always nagging. 'Go to school, get a job.' It was nonstop, you know? But I knew she cared. She wanted the best for me but I never came through. I knew I'd never amount to shit, but she never got it. Never gave up. Why, do you suppose?" He looked truly mystified.

"It's never too late, Tru. Why don't you honor her life by writing a better ending to yours?"

He looked at me, and tears welled in his eyes. "Yeah," he said. "That's probably the plan."

CHAPTER 59

We sat in the backyard under the eaves of our roof and watched the light rain dapple the Venice Canal water. It dripped loudly from the roof, splashing on the pavement near our feet.

"We hardly ever get pure victories," Alexa told me. "You shouldn't expect them."

"Is this the new you? First we had confused and angry Alexa, then wild Alexa. Now Alexa the pessimist? Where's that woman I married?"

She smiled over at me. "Tired of my endless permutations? What if I took you inside and practiced some voodoo sex on you?"

"Oh my God, a voodoo priestess, too?" I teased.

"I'm a lot of things," she said proudly. "One of them is the reinstated chief of the LAPD Detective Bureau. Tony called while you were at the market. He's going to give me another shot."

"Way to go!" I grabbed her hand, pulled her over, and kissed her. I could smell her perfume, feel the heat of her. Tonight would be special. The promise was in her kiss.

Just then the phone rang. I got up and went inside to get it.

"Hello?" I said.

"Is this Detective Shane Scully?" a man's voice asked.

"Yeah. Who's this?"

"Sergeant Cooley at the Men's Central Jail. Hold on for a minute, got a guy here wants to talk to you."

Then Tru Hickman came on the line. "You won't believe this, man! This is so fucked! I got popped again."

"Drugs?"

"Fuck no. Come on. I'm clean, you know that. It's just paraphernalia. But with my yellow sheet, these cops are all up in it, you know?"

"I gotta go, Tru."

"Hey, look, man. That wasn't my works. I met some people at this get-down club in Hollywood. The place got raided and this asshole I was with must've put his needle in my jacket pocket. You know what I'm saying? You know me, man. I'm on a new life, like we said. Like I promised my mom. This isn't my artillery. You gotta believe that and come down here and talk to these people."

"Already gave at the office."

"What's that supposed to mean?"

"You're not gonna be some lifelong project for me, Tru. From now on, you're on your own."

"Hey, hey! Hold it . . . Come on, just this once . . ."

But I was already hanging up. I dropped the phone in the cradle and rejoined Alexa on the back porch. The wind had shifted and now the rain was blowing in on our chairs. Alexa was gathering up her things, getting ready to come inside.

"Who was that?"

"Tru. He got popped for drug paraphernalia. He's in MCJ."

"Didn't take him long, did it?"

"Nope." I was bummed out. Something about him ending up in city jail the same night we got him out of Corcoran sort of ruined everything. Alexa reached out and took my hand.

"It is what it is," she told me. "Tru has to live his own life."

"Yeah, that's what I told him." But I couldn't help it. I felt really bad.

"You're such a romantic," she finally said.

"Come on, where'd that come from?"

"You act all tough and hard-boiled, but underneath you want them all to live happily ever after. You want it neat and perfect. Sometimes that just can't happen."

"It doesn't get you that, after all this, that little putz is already back in stir?"

"Honey, this was never about Tru Hickman."

"Then what was it about?"

"This was only about us. About who *we* are and how *we* behave. It was about our values and our principles, fixing our mistakes at great cost when nobody said we had to. It was about doing the right thing no matter the consequences."

Great wisdom from the woman I married.

Our two boats, side by side at last.

ACKNOWLEDGMENTS

Again there are people to thank. It starts with Mark Graham, who happened to mention to me on the beach in St. Barth's that large carton manufacturing companies, like the one he heads, use state-of-the-art security to guard the prize packages for clients who are running million-dollar scratch-and-win promotions. He then helped me with the details of how these contests are run, including great info on the independent security companies that protect the integrity of these contests. Dylan Chaufty did a lot of my Six Flags Magic Mountain research, taking endless photos of the roller coasters and mapping the park layout so I could write about it accurately. Christopher Chaney was my legal expert for this book. He's a great criminal lawyer and a USC fan who always called right back with answers to my uninformed questions and supplied important insight into the vagaries of the law. I'm extremly grateful to all of you. If I got it wrong, don't throw a shoe.

Thanks again to my crack staff of assistants. Kathy Ezso, who fields the daily page count, translates my dyslexic spelling and gets it all back on time. She has also been doing some remarkable editing on these manuscripts, and to her I am very grateful. Jane Whitney is the one who gets bombed with the daily rewrite pages, sometimes as many as six or eight chapters at a time.

Thanks to her good humor under stress and her careful work, I am able to keep up a fast pace. Theresa Peoples is a film-development staffer at our company, but she's also a team player and has helped out by pitiching in to clean up pages on days where I've gone nuts and done too much. Also a big thanks to Joi Wilson for her help in translating my fractured Spanish. I'm not nearly as good with this language as I think I am. Que pasa?

My wife, Marcia, and children, Tawnia, Chelsea, and Cody, continue to give me great personal support. Without them I would be lost. Marcia has been there for me since we went steady in eighth grade. We've had forty-three years of marriage. She'a always kept one hand on the wheel and my ride out of the ditch.

Many thanks to all of you. I'm certainly in your debt.

Read on for an excerpt from
Stephen J. Cannell's upcoming book

ON THE GRIND

Coming soon in hardcover from
St. Martin's Press

Just an hour before my whole life turned upside down, I was making love to my wife, Alexa, in our little house on the Grand Canal in Venice, California. It was the first Tuesday in May and a spring storm was washing across the L.A. basin, filling gutters and runoffs with dirty brown water, pushing a slanting rain against our bedroom window, blurring the view. I knew the police department was about to charge me with a criminal felony, I just didn't know exactly when. I had chosen to make love to my wife partially to ease a sense of impending doom, and partially because I knew it was going to be our last chance.

The Tiffany Roberts mess was already in full bloom, leaking toxic rumors about me through the great blue pipeline down at Parker Center, turning my life and entire twenty-year police career radioactive. Why do I seem to keep volunteering for these things?

So doom and dread hovered as Alexa and I finished our romantic act. Knowledge of what lay ahead had turned our lovemaking bittersweet, changing the tone like a low chord that announces the arrival of a villain.

We were lying in an uncomfortable embrace, listening to the rain on the windows when the doorbell sounded.

"That's probably it," I said.

"Guess so," Alexa replied, her voice as dead as mine.

I got up, found my waiting clothes folded neatly over the bedroom chaise. I skinned into a pair of faded jeans and a USC Trojans sweatshirt that I had grabbed from my son Chooch's room. I padded barefoot to the front hall and unlatched the lock without bothering to look through the peephole. I already knew who was going to be there.

I opened the door into a whipping rain. Standing on my front steps were three uniformed police officers in transparent slickers.

"I'm Lieutenant Clive Matthews, Professional Services Bureau," the cop in the center said. I'd seen him before, mostly in restaurants around Parker Center. He was an IAD Deputy commander. A big guy with a drinker's complexion. He was supposed to be in AA, but the exploded capillaries on his ruddy face were a death clock that told me the cure hadn't taken.

"What's up, Loo?" I said, my voice flat.

"Charge sheet." He thrust three typed, yellow forms at me. A PSB charge sheet lists the crimes being filed against you by Internal Affairs. It's basically an accusation of misconduct which starts a lengthy disciplinary process that usually ends at a career-threatening Board of Rights Trial, which is in effect a police administrative hearing. The fact that a deputy commander in uniform was personally delivering the goods was representative of the gravity of my predicament. Then Matthews handed me a sealed envelope. "Your letter of transmittal." A document that confirmed the delivery of the charge sheet and started the clock on an array of procedural administrative events. "You have to sign the top copy for me. Keep the other," he instructed.

"You guys couldn't wait until tomorrow?" I looked

past him at the two stone-faced IOs standing a foot back, one on each side of the lieutenant. Water droplets had gathered on the plastic shoulders of their see-through raincoats.

"Nope," the lieutenant replied. "Chief and the City Attorney request your presence in his office at Parker Center immediately."

"I get to contact my Police Officer's Association steward before answering these charges at a Skelly hearing," I said. "That right is guaranteed me under rule six of the city charter. The chief knows that, so what's with this midnight meeting?"

"It's not a command performance. The chief is extending you a courtesy. Your POA steward has been notified. If it was up to me, I'd just body-slam you like the piece of shit you are," he said without raising his voice or putting any inflection on it. "You might want to get your shoes and jacket. It's pretty wet out here. You can ride with us."

"What is it, Shane?" Alexa was coming out of the bedroom, walking down the hall. I turned to look at her. Breathtakingly beautiful. Black hair framing a fashion model's cheekbones. Incredible blue eyes that were locked on me. She was belting her robe, her black hair tossed with the memory of sex. I knew these might be the last friendly words we would speak.

"I.A. They have a charge sheet. They want me to come with them."

"It's almost midnight," she said, standing behind me. "Can't it wait until morning?" She should have demanded the circumstances. It was a mistake, but then, I knew she was as upset about all this as I was.

"You might also want to come with us, Lieutenant Scully," Matthews said, glancing at Alexa. "The chief is waiting in his office with several people. I think you both need to hear what he has to say."

So that's what we did. Alexa got dressed. I was in the bedroom with her for a minute to get my nylon windbreaker out of the closet. I looked over and saw that she was putting on her sixth-floor attire—dark pantsuit, blouse, gun, and badge.

"So it begins," she said, her voice lifeless.

"Yep."

I went into the bathroom to run a razor over my chin. A consideration to this late-night meeting with the chief. For a minute I saw my reflection in the mirror staring back. A familiar stranger with battered eyebrows scarred in countless forgotten brawls. The face of an unruly combatant. My brown eyes looked back at me, startled by the sudden confusion I felt.

Five minutes later I was in Lt. Matthews's car with the two IOs. One was named Stan. I didn't catch the other guy's name. Not much talk as we headed to Parker Center with Alexa following us in her silver BMW a few car-lengths back. I had fallen from respected member of society and guardian of the public trust to detestable scum in the eyes of the three men riding in that maroon Crown Vic with me. In their eyes, I was a turncoat. A cop gone bad.

I thought I knew what to expect, but the truth was I had little idea of what lay before me, little understanding of the mess I had so willingly stepped into.

But that's life. I guess if you could see all the dead ends and blind turns, it wouldn't be as interesting. At least that's what I kept telling myself.

The windshield wipers on the detective plain-wrap slapped at the rain as we rushed along the 10 Freeway in the dead of night, the tires singing in the rain cuts. No red light, no siren. Just a maroon Ford with four stone-faced cops. All of us in the diamond lane, heading toward the end of my career at breakneck speed.

Tony Filosiani's office was crowded with pissed-off people. Pissed about being dragged to the chief's office at twenty past midnight, pissed about the reason they were forced to be there. The LAPD sure didn't need another high-profile scandal right now, and that fact was etched on six faces.

I walked in and immediately recognized all of the people standing there. The Chief of Police was dominating the large space. Usually a happy pixiesque, round-faced presence, tonight Tony Filosiani scowled like a Chinese wood carving, his bald head shining in the bright overhead lights. Next to the C.O.P. was an assistant city attorney named Colt Nichols. The ACA didn't want to be there either, but he was filling in for City Attorney Chase Beal, who was up north on some kind of rubber chicken junket. Everybody knew Chase was planning on making a run for governor and was always out at fund-raisers working on his war chest. Next to Nichols was my Police Officer's Association union rep, Bob Utley. He was the only one to hesitantly engage my eyes. Bob was a big, heavy guy with a Santa-friendly face who had twice successfully defended me against bogus charges at Internal Affairs. Next to my union POA was the head LAPD legal affairs officer. The LAO was a tall, black captain named Line Something. Next to him was yours-truly in my stolen Trojan sweatshirt and rain-soaked windbreaker. Behind me was Lt. Matthews, the DC of PSB. But by far the most bitter flavor in this alphabet soup was the Chief of Detectives. The COD was my own wife, Alexa. She stepped through the threshold seconds later and lowered

Lieutenant Matthews closed the large double doors to the chief's office, signaling the start of the meeting.

"Detective Scully, I'm not sure you know FBI Agent Ophelia Love," Chief Filosiani said without a trace of the cordiality that usually marked his demeanor. He indicated a tall, lanky, blonde woman in her mid-thirties whom I'd missed during my first quick scan of the room because she was seated against the far wall by a mahogany console. Agent Love immediately stood at the mention of her name. She wore a cheap off-the-rack tan pantsuit and had a careless beauty that was partially disguised by raw-boned farm girl features, the most startling of which were piercing ice-blue eyes.

"Bob, what's going on?" I asked my POA steward. I already knew the answer, but it's always better to play dumb at these things and let the other guy go first.

"Regarding the Venture investigation, you've been charged with felony case-tampering and blackmail," the chief said, cutting in and answering my question.

"I don't know what you're talking about." My heart rate was inadvertently beginning to rise. *We're into it now,* I thought.

"You can deny it, Detective, but your own partner was the one who brought this to our attention. And her concerns have been independently corroborated by Agent Love and the FBI."

"Detective Quinn turned me in?" I said. Sally Quinn was my partner at Homicide Special. We had only been working together for a year. She'd been out of rotation on maternity leave for the last six months and had just returned to duty. "I only had time to glance at the charge sheet in the car," I said. "It says I intentionally lost evidence. I told Captain Calloway how those tapes were missing."

"Unbeknownst to us, the FBI has been running their

own surveillance on Harry Venture for half a year and they've got you and his wife on tape," Chief Filosiani said. What he was referring to was a Homicide Central case that I had been working for two weeks. Harry Venture's birth name was Harry Weinberg, but he'd legally changed it when he came to America and went into the film business ten years ago, forming Venture Studios. Harry was a fifty-year-old Israeli national who had made his initial fortune as a black market arms dealer in the Middle East. With the hundreds of millions he'd made in the gun trade, he moved to L.A. and went into the movie business, becoming one of Hollywood's most successful action-movie mini-moguls.

Money being the powerful aphrodisiac that it is, Harry soon seduced a budding young actress half his age named Tiffany Roberts, who was starring in low-budget genre movies when he met her. She was beautiful and had a Playmate's body, and, as the showbiz saying goes, was willing to do "nude" if it was shot "tastefully." The gossip on the street was that Tiffany instantly saw what Harry could offer and became Mrs. Venture. Big-budget movies and mega stardom followed. But after doing "tasteful" nude scenes with some of Hollywood's hottest leading men, Harry's bedroom seemed to have lost some of its zeal and Tiffany had been quietly hunting around for a hit man to take her pudgy, foreign-born husband off the count. The word of this was quickly leaked to us by a street informant.

Since a murder solicitation by an A-list Hollywood star was an extremely sensitive situation, the squeal ended up going to Homicide Special, which is the elite homicide squad at the LAPD that only handles high-profile, media-worthy situations.

I'd been working out of that rotation for almost three years and was assigned the Tiffany Roberts case.

I was supposed to have been setting Tiffany up, posing as a hit man while wearing a wire and meeting her behind box stores, working out the terms of the assassination of her husband Harry. I was supposed to have had her solicitation on tape, but told my captain I had carelessly left the tapes in my car one night while I went into a Ruth's Chris to get something to eat. My car was broken into and my briefcase stolen. My boss, Captain Calloway, instructed me to reboot the deal and get her to repeat the offer of murder, but Tiffany became suspicious and broke it off. The case is currently in limbo. Now, apparently, the way they were reading it was I had deliberately lost the tapes in return for some kind of blackmail payoff.

Of course, I'd seen all this coming. As soon as I'd reported the missing briefcase, the shit had started to ooze downhill just as I knew it would. It had ended up as felony case-tampering.

"Why is the FBI involved with this?" I asked, turning to face Case Agent Love. She glanced at the ACA, Cole Nichols, who nodded his okay so she started to tell me. She had a low, husky alto voice which didn't sound like it belonged inside her. The accent was from the south somewhere—the Carolinas or Tennessee maybe. She was a no-nonsense Fed whose demeanor told me she held me in a good deal of professional disdain.

"I'm here because after five years of working Harry Venture for gun smuggling, we finally convinced him to cooperate," she began. "He still has financial dealings with some of his old arms-dealing buddies from the Middle East. New Russian-made Kalashnikov 100 to 106 submachine guns and pp-90 MIs with nine millimeter breeches suitable for NATO rounds are currently flowing into I.A. The AK-100 series ordnance is on Homeland's watch list and we've pinned this smug-

gle to the Hispanic 18th Street gangs in downtown L.A.
They're the new pipeline bringing this stuff into the
county. They're smuggling it up from the Baja desert,
in Mexico. Naturally, we didn't want Harry's wife to
murder him in the middle of a federal op where he'd
just became a cooperative witness. For two weeks we've
been taping you, taping her. Let's say your conduct was
less than professional." I glanced at Alexa, who was
standing by the door, her face a frozen mask. "We can
play our surveillance videos for you, but unless you insist, out of deference to your wife, I think it's better to
say you're in the bag and let it go at that." She hesitated
before continuing, "We accessed your bank statements
and you have a recent ten-thousand-dollar deposit,
which none of your pay stubs or personal finances support. Unless you can tell us exactly where that ten
thousand came from, then we're going to assume that
you got it from Ms. Roberts in return for booting your
undercover sting against her."

"Don't you have to prove that before just accusing
me?" I challenged.

"We think we can," Tony said. "Right now Harry Venture is going through his wife's bank withdrawal slips. If
he finds one that was issued on or about the end of last
month in the amount of ten thousand dollars, then that
act will be established and added to your charge sheet."

"This is all pretty damn circumstantial," I said. But I
knew it wasn't. They would find that withdrawal slip.
I was going down for this.

Cole Nichols said, "I'll take that kind of circumstantial case any day. I can also get the FBI video and, along
with the fact that you reported your UC tapes stolen,
make a very compelling picture for a jury."

"Then why am I here?" I asked, stiffly.

"The City Attorney and the Feds both want to

prosecute you, but I've convinced the mayor and the federal attorney that this department doesn't need any more bad press or police department scandal," Chief Filosian said. "I'm willing to offer you a take-it-or-leave-it deal. You have to decide right now, tonight. It's off the table after this meeting."

"A deal?" I looked at Bob Utley who gave me a hand gesture indicating I should shut up and let them finish. I ignored it.

"I don't want to cop to this flimsy bullshit," I blurted.

"Your IA file is thick enough to choke a goat," Lt. Matthews chimed in from behind me. "Nobody is going to believe anything you say. If I was you, I'd listen to the chief."

"So what are you offering?"

"Resign," the chief said. "Make a statement for the file indicating guilt so we don't have to worry about facing lawsuit over it later. You'll cop to a lesser charge and then we'll dismiss you for cause and seal the case for the benefit of the LAPD. What really happened in this room tonight, the real reason for your dismissal, will remain closely guarded secret."

"What about my pension?"

"You lose it. You confess to the lesser charge, waive your pension, and quit," ACA Nichols said. "This is a great fucking deal, Detective. You don't deserve it. If the department wasn't still in PR trouble from the Rampart scandal, O.J., and the immigration rights melee, they wouldn't be cutting you this much slack. If I try this case I promise a conviction. You'll do three to five, easy. Even if the sentence is halved for good behavior, that still puts you in the dog pile at state prison for at least two years. I'll make sure there's no special housing unit for you. A cop in Gen Pop is a prime target for yard aggression. That five-year stretch will turn into a death sentence."

I stood there looking at Bob Utley. He was supposed to jump up and object, but he said nothing. Every time I glanced at Alexa, her face was cold with fury.

"Could I have a minute with my client?" Utley finally said. We were shown into a little six-chaired conference room that adjoined the chief's office. Bob shut the door. When he turned, his eyes weren't Santa-friendly anymore. He was staring daggers. Like all honest cops, he hated police corruption. He knew I was dirty, and it pissed him off.

"They can't . . ." I started.

"Take it," he interrupted.

"Admit I was on the take? That I took money to boot the case?"

"You tanked a solicitation of murder investigation and got into a sexual relationship with that movie star. I know it, and they all know it. Take the deal. It's a fucking lifesaver."

"And sign away a twenty-year pension?"

"If you're convicted, you'll lose your pension anyway. If you fight this, you'll go down, Shane. They've got a very tight case backed by videotape of you and Tiffany Roberts swapping spit all over town."

"But . . ."

"Take the fucking deal! You're damn lucky the department doesn't want to eat any more bad press." His voice was rising in anger. We'd been friends for years, but I could tell he had nothing but contempt for me now.

"What's the lesser charge they're gonna accuse me of?"

"Obstruction of Justice. A misdemeanor requiring no time served but resulting in your immediate resignation without benefits."

"Can't I at least have a day to think about it?"

"No. The chief said the offer comes off the table the

moment this meeting is over. After tonight, you'll face the full IA charge sheet."

"How come I get the feeling you're on their side?"

"Shane, take the deal." Frustration with me was packed into every word.

"Okay, okay," I said. "Calm down."

"Okay, what?"

"I'll do it. I'll sign the damn confession."